ANGELS BEFORE MAN

RAFAEL NICOLÁS

For my sister, my brother, and Edith.

And for my parents, my grandmothers, and everyone else who can never know I wrote this. I'm sorry. You won't believe it, but I am.

PREFACE

You're reading the second version of *Angels Before Man.* The original, released in 2022, was indie-published after I decided not to pursue traditional presses due to a fear of censorship and personal predicaments, among other things. After *Angels Before Man's* sudden success, however, I was approached about considering to sell my work. I agreed and revised the book for publishers.

Unfortunately, I had to come to terms with money/prestige not being worth putting my safety at risk as a closeted person, especially in this age of book bans and attacks on the queer/trans community. I had to consider the safety of my readers too, many who are in situations like mine. So, I left.

With that, I leave you with some warnings for the content:

Blasphemy, graphic violence, graphic animal death, sexual content, self-harm, use of terms with incestuous connotations, grooming, mental instability, off-page sexual assault, on-page sexual trauma, abuse.

These themes are minor or absent in Part I. It isn't necessary to read Part II.

Your heart became proud
    on account of your beauty,
and you corrupted your wisdom
    because of your splendor.
So I threw you to the earth;
    I made a spectacle of you

— EZEKIEL 28:17 (NIV)

PART I
PARADISE

CHAPTER 1

From fire, there came flesh. It crept out from a red-blazed blister as premature pulp, caught between spindles procuring a body turning unto itself. One eye, then many of them, etched onto four faces — henceforth, a living creature — and locked shut to dribble a gaze down onto cherubic cheeks. And there were wings, thunder, retreated and roaring, in two pairs to mirror the heads before limbs pervaded. The whip of creation, and then its hands — see, there went a titan hand. The Lord's hand — raised and split, conceiving the likeness of a soul and letting it fall. He said, Bring him a fruit from the Tree of Life.

One of two seraphim, six-winged, approached, took the cherub's chin, the most tender of all those he had, and lifted. Struggling, the newborn kept tightening flesh that was unwilling to compose him, until the seraph introduced a softened fruit to gasping lips that softened themselves into suckling. Then — a bite. The seraph coaxed him to swallow; the cherub rose, naked and freezing — even aflame, he was — frightened to obedience. This tempest of an eater, this destroyer.

Listen here — the Lord, our God, spoke once more. Lofted between heaven, another fruit still — seraph-held — found the windswept cherub's loose, wanton mouth, wet still with Life's juice. It opened itself, tongue slithering out, lapping at skin, before teeth pierced. The Fruit of Knowledge — the Lord had commanded His creation to taste the Fruit of Knowledge. Too eager this time, the angel swallowed, nigh whole, nectar sticking to lips, almost taking the seed. And, watch, his eyes opened; it was through rips, gory and great. The end revelation then whispered, it left the watching seraph's mouth — This angel is beautiful, the most magnificent, Father — and the cherub was shrieking, out into wounds. The perfect angel, the Creator ordained, in wisdom and beauty — being dressed now, in shame and in jewelry of every precious stone.

And yet the seraphim rejoiced, Holy, holy, holy is the Lord Almighty.

Lord Almighty and, now, His morning star.

CHAPTER 2

S inging. The sounds of it stirred Lucifer to shift, then stirred the thought that 'I' had shifted a self. An easy grasp, but it burst into the fever of existing in an instant: the sensation that air spread in his body as ink blots, that he was alive, that the rains beating down on the oceans of his mind bloomed into emotion, beating him. A brisk, wooden scent finding his nose and cloth, a thin bedsheet, scratching smooth on skin. He flinched, tried returning to empty slumber, but there was creaking — somewhere. Heavy eyes fluttered open; the mahogany beams holding a ceiling. He drooped his head to one side and met a clothed table holding a candle, but its flame, atop wax body, waved at him, acknowledged him like a sibling.

Not far behind, a figure — visceral horror, the sight of life — reclined half-casually in a cushioned chair. He was comfortable in a sleeveless, dark emerald cotton piece draped over his top half, with just an opening for his neck. And he had a head, too, with long almond hair and eyes that flashed with the fish that swam, infinite, in blue-green irises. Some jewelry adorned him — thinned silver and large sapphire working jointly to hang from ears, throat, wrists.

The stranger was not the one who sang, though he hummed, melodically, as his agile fingers worked at fastening a string around the wood-like stems of a few herb leaves. He didn't look up when Lucifer did his first movement, must have thought the bed's creak was his imagination, but when Lucifer breathed, deep through his mouth — it tasted sulfuric — his gaze flickered upward. Urgently, the figure straightened, face blooming out surprise, eyes widening, lips parting. "Oh." He planted the herbs on the table before a hand reached out and took a post at the end of the bed. Using it to brace himself, he pulled his body up, took just one step, then flopped to sit on the mattress by Lucifer, who stared, blinked once, then continued staring. The stranger smiled at this before presenting a soft palm. "Do not be afraid. I hope you slept well." Lucifer walked his gaze around the room again — the walls were painted, patterned. "But you should sit up now. Take my hand. Can you speak?"

Trembling beneath its weight, Lucifer's arm rose, then his hand felt that of the stranger — the first warm touch of flesh. Lucifer took, held as tight he could, dragged himself up, every muscle beneath his skin seeming to burst. The heftiness of his body feeling like it teetered, rolling downward until a breath fell from his mouth, he said, "I—" The first word.

The stranger waited, hand still cradling Lucifer's.

A cough grazed out. "I can."

"Does your throat hurt?" Tapping free fingers against his neck, as if to indicate where.

The headboard pressed up against Lucifer's back, hard and merciless. "Hurt?" He rummaged for the meaning of the word, couldn't find it. "It's empty. Empty-feeling."

"You need water."

"What is happening?" This voice was small; miserably, Lucifer realized that all of him felt very small. "What is this?" His hand drew away from the other's, finally, as if it had burnt through skin and exposed red muscle. 'Where am I?' he wanted to say next. 'Who am I?'

"That's your hand," was the response, an answer to something Lucifer hadn't asked. He looked downward, still, as the stranger reached out and tapped fingers against his wrist. "It follows onto your arm, then your shoulder, then your neck, and your head. You have a torso, too, that connects down to your legs. This is you, incarnate."

Incarnate; the word was dirt on his tongue. "What am I?"

"An angel." Already anticipating the next question, he added, "You will come to know what that means with time."

"Time," Lucifer repeated, only to allow this other word to sample his lips, then looked to the stranger again. "Thank you. Are you an angel too?"

The smile was pretty and warm as sun. "I am. My name is Raphael. Yours is Lucifer."

"Raphael." Like honey sweetening his mouth. "And I am Lucifer." It had a nice taste as well — sugary as pastry. "It is a very pleasant name; I like it a lot. But where did it come from?"

"You have too many questions," Raphael mused. "I can't spend hours explaining the heavens to you, brother. You'll find learning it all slowly will be easier. If you try to conceptualize it all at once, you'll harm your mind. Though, I have to apologize. I usually rear an angel up in the stars and dip them into the light of an eclipse, and that's where I let them wake. But I couldn't hold you tight, no matter what I did. I didn't want you to fall. So, I tucked you in here and dispossessed you of a spectacular genesis." A delicate exhale. "At the same time, I think there's something quite noble about a modest birth, too."

A door opened, opposite the side of the bed where Raphael had been sitting, and thumped against the wall. "Ahaha," laughed the new stranger, immediate, "I see it's true." He was tall, broad-shouldered, and paler than the tan-skinned Raphael, though not significantly. His hair was obsidian-black, gathered all together in a ribbon, ruby the same as the loosely tied robe drooping from him. "Do forgive me, brother. I know you don't like it when I sneak in without permission, but alas — I heard rumors." His almond eyes were even darker than his hair; his eyebrows were thick. "Oh, I see you can hear the singing from in here." His jewelry was golden, strung all over as if hastily.

Lucifer had forgotten about it, this singing, let the distant words, elongated and rhyming at their ends, join all the background noises of his consciousness thus far — the tiny creaks of the bed, the breathes, the swallows, the faraway footsteps, his heart — he had one — pumping in his chest.

Thump, thump. The stranger's grin was sideways and peeked a sliver of teeth; he was saying, "I see Father really took His time with you." *Thump, thump.*

"Don't make those jokes," Raphael scolded, though relaxed. "He takes His time with us all." He was already shifting, dragging his body away from Lucifer, little by little. "But is that what all the commotion is about, out there?"

"They've been saying that, today, we'll meet our youngest."

"Who said this?"

The stranger waved a hand, dismissing him before settling a knee on the mattress and haphazardly taking one of Lucifer's arms. The young angel made some kind of noise in surprise, something maybe as embarrassing as a yelp. "Come on now." He brought his leg back onto the floor and pulled flailing Lucifer with him. "Get up. Let's see if you can use those feet."

"Asmodeus, don't be so reckless," Raphael breathed but made no visible move to stop him.

The tile was ice-fire on Lucifer's feet, making him hop from one to the other, hissing almost, wishing he could lift both lower limbs off the floor and all of his body, too. He thought, 'No, I don't like the ground. I don't think I belong on the ground—' But his desires were in vain, and soon enough, he was standing, though he had grabbed Asmodeus' other arm at some point — a firm bicep. Lucifer's spine felt pulled, like a string to the point of tear, but it remained intact, and he could feel his weight leeched to it. Gasping, he whispered, "I'm standing," not sure why. One foot slid, and he lifted it, settled again unsteady — a step, his first. "I'm—"

"Good," Asmodeus replied, warmer. "You should try walking, brother." His hands were already drifting away, and Lucifer let himself step back, colliding into the mattress he'd just escaped. "Raphael," he turned his attention to next. "I can take him to his home, if you'd like."

"Yes, I— Oh."

"Oh?"

Lucifer was moving away from them, turning his head all around experimentally, catching the beams of the ceiling again. He stumbled, scampered toward a wall, put a hand on it and felt the dryness of the paint there. But the sensation was piercing against his new fingers, and he staggered away once more.

"I haven't— I was so busy—"

"You didn't find him a place to stay?"

"Maybe—" Raphael sighed, deeper this time. "Maybe if the gossip about Lucifer had reached me sooner, I might've..."

Asmodeus did another one of his laughs. "No, don't make that face, brother. This might work out perfectly. Did I tell you I just moved out of my house? Uriel wanted me to help with building this temple up north, and I wouldn't want to waste half my time traveling there every day, so I'm going to stay with two brothers nearby. But Rosier was upset about living alone."

The youngest angel reached one corner of the room, where there was a sprawl of green, flattened lips — leaves — and white, clustered eyes — petals — climbing up a polished, beige pillar. Lucifer was right by the door Asmodeus had stepped in from, and he looked outside, curious but frightened — more frightened than curious. Would the paints of the room continue out from here? Would these hydrangea flowers follow his steps or abandon Lucifer never to be seen again? He didn't want to leave these things behind; so far, they had been half his world. The comfort of the bed called to him, said return, do not leave and begin a life. Come back.

"Oh," deep relief burrowed into Raphael's voice, "the Lord is so merciful. Would Rosier mind looking after Lucifer, at least for the time being?"

"He'll be excited I'm sure." Asmodeus was still snickering when he came up to Lucifer again and settled a palm on his shoulder. "Come, Lucifer, follow me. I'll introduce you. Do you need help to walk?"

"No," Lucifer whispered; his heart was caving into itself for some reason he didn't know. He was feeling the urge to scratch at his skin; it didn't itch but something deeper seemed to. He was almost shaking. "I can walk." Something felt wrong already, and he didn't know what. All Lucifer could do was watch as Asmodeus moved into a corridor; then, he followed, slow, not knowing to turn back and wish Raphael farewell. He passed the doorway, fluttering his eyes at the suddenness of light pouring in from one side, and braced a hand on the smooth leftward wall. With its support, he walked, but it wasn't so fruitful: various cool windows kept grazing his fingers.

But those windows, crystal, were also tall, enough to be a terror, and hardly more in width than the angel's own body — and yet enough to flood in all of Heaven's brilliance. Lucifer moved past them, taking in an endless expanse of golden streets, cutting between an infinite amount of houses — constructed from all sorts of materials — limestone, wood, plaster, marble — of all different types and styles — most flat-roofed but various also sustaining peaks and domes. A great portion of them were unfinished, behemoths of towers never to be complete, but many also stood sturdy and strong against the yellow-orange current of the sky. The angels below, hundreds, thousands, crowded so that they could have been just one giant creature of an angel. And while the faraway open gates were fashioned from pearl — the walls embracing the city were stone adorned with twelve different magnificent gems: jasper, then sapphire, then chalcedony, emerald, and sardonyx, sardius, chrysolite, beryl, topaz, chrysoprase, jacinth, and, finally, amethyst. Lucifer breathed a little quicker, body acting as if it had been whipped once, twice; he lost his footing, tripped with not a hint of celestial elegance.

Lucifer's gasp turned the head of Asmodeus, but he caught himself with the hand he leaned against the wall. And he apologized, blurting out, "I'm sorry," without thinking about how he knew this phrase, felt it only as the proper name for the tightness in his throat. He looked away, to his right, couldn't think of anything else to do — then stopped. There was an angel there, past the golden doorway into a parallel corridor. He locked eyes with him accidentally, but then he couldn't look away, not at all.

Behind bundles of lavender robes, an extensively embroidered tunic hid, hugging bodily proportions of ethereal plains and steeps. A neck tenderly held a head with plump, cherry pink lips and wide, blameless eyes cradled by long lashes; he held the blaze of all the stars in his face. All his skin was silk smooth and kissed brown as copper, he was clouded by wisps of muted flaxen hair that tumbled past his shoulders, and he was graced with various jewelry of every gem, more than the walls of the city. They were strung along the top of his head, dangling from his ears, holding his throat tight and loose, as well as his arms and legs, even more hidden beneath the drapery. There were sweet dips to his body, soft curves and edges all where they ought to be, and the smoothness with which he moved — it was utterly unbearable. The angel was so beautiful it ached him in the chest.

"Who—?" Lucifer tried, but the moment he spoke, he froze again.

Quick, Asmodeus appeared beside the beautiful angel. A cheeky grin had found its way onto his face, and he opened his mouth to speak, but it was another voice, Raphael's, that called out, "That is you, Lucifer."

Lucifer startled and saw the beautiful angel's cheeks taint faintly with pink, at the same time he felt heat gathered there within himself, and knew it was true. He turned and caught Raphael at the end of the corridor, leaning against the doorway into the room they'd just left. In his smile, there was a little fondness.

Asmodeus spoke: "You're looking into a mirror." Lucifer turned to it again. "It reflects existence back to you."

The youngest angel watched his lips move as he spoke, "No." The itch beneath his skin felt as if it were pouring out now; he shook his head. "How is it that I am so beautiful? It's too much." He turned away, swift, and shielded his face with both hands, blanketing himself with darkness. "If that is what you see, please look away." It was nearly a wail, clawing itself out so rough Lucifer feared it would pull his heart out too, and he would be left there — made empty inside.

"You are shyer than I thought you'd be," Raphael mused. "Take down your hands, brother. You have nothing to be ashamed of."

"But he's young!" Asmodeus argued. "Let him be. If he doesn't want to see himself, then he shouldn't have to. Father does encourage modesty, doesn't He?" As Raphael mumbled a few things, seemingly to himself, Asmodeus addressed him again: "And, you, what are you doing? Have you decided to come with us?"

"No, it's only that I forgot to give you something. Here, come get it."

Lucifer listened to the padding of Asmodeus' sandals against the ground — *thump, thump* — before peeking out from between the separating fingers of one hand. The beauty was, again, like a dagger, twisting in his gut, jerking his body in its place, and he retreated back into shame, shame conceived.

"What is this?"

"A timbrel and pipes."

The small jingle of a noise, and then footsteps making their way back — Asmodeus chuckling. "Alright. You can hide your face after I've brought you to Rosier. I don't want you running into anyone outside." Lucifer lowered his hands, not much but he did, before looking wearily at the towering angel. Asmodeus must've pitied him, then; he softened his gaze and said, "Let me warn you: all the angels will try to speak to you. You can hear them singing." Indeed, he could. "Our Father doesn't create new ones often. Everyone is excited to meet you."

Lucifer's heart cowered — obedience both timid and carnivorous — but he nodded. "I'll try to be good."

Asmodeus grinned. "Good."

And then Lucifer followed him, followed him out into Heaven and toward the singing, though he felt as if his beautiful reflection were walking behind and, at any moment, it would step ahead, and Lucifer would become its shadow. Though, he knew this was ridiculous; he knew hardly anything of life, but he knew this. A little frustration planting a purse to his lips — the angel told himself to keep walking. He couldn't return to the emptiness he'd awoken from; already, it felt as if that time had never existed and, just seconds ago, he had made it up. Yet, Lucifer missed the darkness, longed for what had come before. This was his first wanting.

The stories he'll tell of this time will be about wanting.

CHAPTER 3

The singing faltered when they saw him, in tandem with the drum strikes and wind instrument gusts. Then, a dozen crowds of angels, at once, rushed Lucifer. They awed at the youngest of them all, who looked between them, gawking at their features — gentle between sturdiness, sturdy between softness. Hands refrained from touching him, but a shower nonetheless came of compliment after compliment. They sewed together peculiar phrases, trying to call him the most magnificent thing they'd beheld a thousand times uniquely: "As pleasing to see as a repaired chair, as pretty as a washed grapefruit in a porcelain bowl." The angels shouted after him, "The Lord is good! The Lord is great! He has given us an angel of beauty! Angel of beauty! Angel of beauty!"

And while Asmodeus shooed them away to the best of his abilities, it did little to help: for every two he scared off, three would skip over to replace them.

Many flew, some hovering above and watching from nearby rooftops. It was these that Lucifer was concerned with, even if the sea of angels on the ground seemed intent to stampede him. He watched — couldn't tear a newborn sight away from the wings angels had sprouting from their backs; he remembered the flowers he'd seen, considered angels like flowers. Indeed, their wings fluttered in colors and patterns, sometimes spotted, sometimes one layer of feathers a dark shade and another a lighter one; their beats recalled the percussion instruments.

His hands twitched, hungry to cover his face, as Lucifer drew nearer to Asmodeus. He wondered if he had wings. Were they hidden somewhere beneath all his clothes? Were there feathers pressed so timidly tight to him that Lucifer couldn't feel them? He wanted to know if they were small, like some that he saw, or enormous, like others.

They came upon a fountain — structure complex, smooth marble, climbing high until it towered and you craned your neck. Crystalline water poured down from the peaks, falling in spirals, filigree patterns between them, to a large pool eating the circular plaza in what appeared to be the center of Heaven. Many angels were around, collecting water in cups and bowls, or simply sitting against the edge of the fountain, speaking to one another. From the ripples in the water, pale flowers occasionally bloomed and drifted out petals. Lucifer watched them as they passed, then flinched when his reflection, waving as flames, looked back with a worried curve to his brows. He didn't like that, even with the ends of his lips turned downward, there was beauty still.

An angel hurried to walk at the other side of Asmodeus, who Lucifer noticed held golden tubes, strapped together, and a medium-sized frame drum with hooped jangles around the edges — the timbrel and pipes Raphael had given him.

"It's good this one is finally with us," this stranger, a crown of rose-mary flowers on his head, chirped, before turning to the young Lucifer trying to take advantage of Asmodeus' height to cower. "Those who were there at your creation said they had never seen Father create with such care before. We all thought you were going to be special." Lucifer, slow, slight, perked up at these words, but Asmodeus waved a sluggish hand for the stranger to leave them before doubling the pace of his walk.

Lucifer hesitated, wanting to linger and ask what the stranger meant by all that, but he couldn't risk losing sight of the angel leading him home. Nervous, he hurried after Asmodeus, instead, bombarding him with a soft voice, not used to speaking, "What did he mean? Who is Father? He created me? Why? How?"

Asmodeus snickered smoothly, passing some rowdy, chattering angels, who paused to catch a glimpse of the youngest. "These sort of questions already?" Lucifer, though more insecurely, looked at them too. He noted how much all these beings seemed to differ in heights, widths, hair, faces, as if a creator had paid great attention to make each one unique. "Father is our Almighty Lord, our God, the Creator of everything." Asmodeus turned to him just as Lucifer had lifted his chin to watch the other's face. "Of you and the street we stand on and the fountain and the water that pours out of it — everything you set your gaze on, it was made from Him, by Him."

"Everything?" His body — reacting as if on its own, as if something inside were swelling and about to burst out of him. "But everything is so bright and— and glorious." Nimble hands found each other, interlocked fingers, and a sensation tugged and tingled along his mouth — the first smile. So kind it made him squint. "If all that I see is glorious, then He must be."

"You'd be correct," Asmodeus responded, an odd surprise in his eyes. "More than glorious. He formed us from His hands." Lucifer asked why. "To worship," was the answer. "And serve for all of eternity." Lucifer didn't, couldn't, understand how long that might be. "And obey Him and act out His will." Asmodeus' voice trailed off, then he grinned. "Lucifer, what's wrong with you? You look like you're going to ignite right in front of me."

"Asmodeus, I want to meet Him. Will you take me to meet Him?"

"I'm not the one who can do that." He, abruptly, turned a corner, his voice drifting with him. "You'll see Father whenever He decides it's the fated time to do so." Hurrying to follow, Lucifer staggered on a road that decided to slope down sharp. Here, too, there was a certain sweetness in the air that turned Lucifer's head to catch a group of angels, shouting with the excitement of their talk, exchanging ears of corn, whose kernels were blue, yellow, red. "I hope Rosier is home, but if not, the door should be open." They were leaning against one of the many stucco walls of the buildings lining both sides of the narrow street; these houses — pressed so close together they might as well have been one, differentiated only by their alternating sunny colors.

"Who is Rosier?" Lucifer said, looking away and bowing his head so that nobody noticed that he was the newest angel and thus the culprit of all the bustle. "You told Raphael you lived with him?"

"I finished moving my belongings yesterday, but yes, we lived together."

"Why is that? Are there not enough homes for all the angels here?"

"There are more than enough, but it would be lonely to live alone." He nudged him, a bit too hard, and Lucifer had to regain his balance quickly before he might trip and roll down the road for infinity. "You'll understand once you're older. But yes, Rosier is my dear friend. You'll like him, I promise. There is no kinder angel than him that I know."

Trepidation, bubbling beneath Lucifer's skin, simmered, but where did that fear come from? Why did he feel anything at all? He wanted to ask, but he was beginning to feel like he wasn't supposed to be asking. Lucifer shifted a tongue in his mouth, feeling it refuse to settle properly behind his teeth. Cringing at this, his gaze fell above, to the sky, which was not unlike staring at a sun very close, unable to see its ends — only light, formless. He was feeling his fingers twitch again, like they wanted to grab something — the ends of his robes perhaps. He did; they were soft but not comforting. Then, a snicker, from behind. Lucifer froze, twisted around, and flushed, so badly he thought he'd burst. Asmodeus was many steps back, standing beside a door. "Oh. I-Is this your house?"

"It is, or was, I suppose." Asmodeus knocked a few times — *thud, thud, thud* — then tilted his head at the youngest angel, amusement twirling his lips. "You shouldn't stay in your head so much, brother. Your life is out here." Lucifer rolled his shoulders a bit, not wanting to think about those words, not wanting to think at all. He turned to examining the house instead, thought it not particularly interesting. It had a modest look with inviting red-orange walls around large wooden double-doors, overcrowded with carvings of spirals and twists that made up some kind of abstract, floral pattern. There was a balcony, also, off to the side, on what seemed a second story, with ornate railings made out of a painted-black metal. "Ah," Asmodeus said, as the door opened, "Rosier, did we wake you?"

Rosier was yawning, but it devolved into a serene smile. "That you did, but no worries." He was significantly shorter than Asmodeus and softer — face rounded sweetly, the same as his plumper body. "Who is this you've brought with you?" His melanite hair was straight and long, reaching his mid-back, with bangs fairly neat over his forehead, and his skin was deep brown. Still, Rosier's eyes were exceedingly sunny, like all the gold that made up the streets had been gathered there, and matching the bright clothes he wore — yellows and oranges, not so far removed from the colors of his home. The jewels decorating him carried a similar chipper tone. "I'm Rosier. You're very beautiful."

"Thank you. I could say the same about you." Lucifer swallowed, still unsure of how he was supposed to greet another. "I'm Lucifer." That felt strange to say, wrong almost. "I'm a new angel. I don't know much about anything, but—" Lucifer didn't know what to add to that, and he noticed that something about his language seemed to amuse Rosier, but he tried to ignore it. "Asmodeus said you might be willing to let me share this house with you, at least for the time being." His gaze drifted down to his feet. "But I don't wish to inconvenience you."

"It's not at all an inconvenience, brother. Come in."

While the outside had been simple, the inside was extravagant. Past the entrance was a ceiling-less garden — the scent of wet soil and flowers — composed of mostly ground-level shrubs and gardenias and tulips, not at all neat but laying over each other amicably. This was at either side of a simple stone path toward an open doorway into the inner part of the house. Beyond this, there were painted tile floors — the patterns within them both symmetrical and squirming with life — beneath maroon carpets with overlapping diamond designs; it was a general living area, with three plump couches facing each other, each with their own draped blankets. Like the carpets, they were complicated, the same as the walls, some muraled, most upholding either an art piece or a window. Deeper inside — a kitchen past a wide archway and, here, the tile flooring had crawled up into cabinets and counters. They carried upon them bowls of various goods — breads, beans, fruits, vegetables — the smells intermingling so that one wasn't struck by any particular food but all them.

In short — a house of dizzying, excessive things, a house that was the sum of all wonders.

Lucifer realized he may be acting improperly, caught in a flood of awe, but had trouble stopping. Moving to the couches, he barely quashed the urge to sprint up the steps of a steep staircase, with its own pleasant tiles, up against a wall. He turned away, looked at the two other angels just as Asmodeus fell to sit cross-legged on the floor, twiddling with the timbrel he'd brought. At his side, Rosier watched the instrument as well.

The shorter angel flickered up his gaze, then smiled. "I see you like the house? It's a little over-decorated, but I couldn't help myself."

"It's—" Magnificent? Beautiful? These terms felt hollow. "I don't know how to express how it makes me feel."

The angel didn't seem to mind this and spoke gently, "The words will come to you eventually." Rosier settled onto one of the couches, then looked to Lucifer. "Sit. You walked a lot, didn't you?"

"Yes." Lucifer plopped, almost comically fast, onto a cushion beside Rosier, but then inched as far away as he could, pressed up to the plush armrest, unsure what was appropriate. "Thank you. I'll live in this house then." He nodded, more to himself. "I won't be any trouble." He'd promised to be good.

Rosier laughed airily. "Don't worry so much, Lucifer. You can't possibly be more trouble than Asmodeus."

Asmodeus scoffed, but there was no offense in it. "I wasn't so bad." He shook the timbrel in his hands, the rattle like that of a predator rather than an instrument.

Rosier ignored him: "I'm happy you made it here in one piece. Angels get so carried away with celebrating that they'll forget the reason they're celebrating in the first place. But what about your feelings? How do you feel?"

"Feel?" Lucifer leaned back, the cushions shaping around him. "I feel like an angel." That sounded right, though he noted Rosier quirked an eyebrow. "I have questions. The angel that woke me, his name was Raphael, I want to know more about him. I want to know if

I have wings. And I want to know what happens now, what I should do."

"Raphael is an archangel," Rosier said simply, as if the word were self-explanatory; to Lucifer, it wasn't. "And we all have wings, but it might take some time before you learn to summon and use them."

"I can try and bother Baal," Asmodeus offered, then moved his attention, finally, away from the timbrel to Lucifer. "He's the best flier in Heaven, and he's easy to convince of things, and I remember he said he was excited to meet you. It might take a while for him to get the free time to come, but it'll be worth the wait."

"That's okay," Lucifer replied, quietly, "but what is there to do until then? What is he— What are angels so busy with?"

"That depends on the angel," Rosier answered again. "I'm the angel of fruit, so I tend to all the fruit trees and help them grow." He gestured. "And Asmodeus over there works construction, though he is the angel of friendship." Asmodeus grumbled, like he didn't understand the correlation too much either.

Lucifer blinked, having expected something related to the Father Asmodeus had mentioned before. "Oh." Already, he was linking this to the Lord in his mind; maybe, the Lord liked fruits, maybe the Lord liked the buildings. Did He have a preference for flat roofs over those with peaks? "Are you assigned that work?" Lucifer's questions were never-ending. "Will I do either of those things?"

Rosier's gaze softened. "Assign? That's an interesting word." Lucifer flushed warm. "No, I wouldn't say that. We just do what we're good at, though sometimes the archangels request us to complete a project or two. It was actually the archangel Uriel who ordered Asmodeus to finish some buildings far from here. That's why he's abandoning me, you see!"

A hearty laugh burst from Asmodeus' mouth. "I'll return! It probably won't be long. And when I do, we can figure out the living arrangements in case Lucifer decides to stay."

Lucifer shifted, feeling like nothing was being answered and his concerns were being all ushered out of the house. "Wait— I don't understand." This confusion was beginning to ache, and his eyes were prickling strangely. "I can do whatever I want? Why did you call yourself the angel of fruit? Who gave you that title?"

"Rosier," Asmodeus addressed, cheeky as he rattled the timbrel again, "are you sure you're okay with Lucifer staying here?" The youngest angel blinked, confused; had he asked the wrong things? "I didn't think he was going to be so talkative. It's a bit unfair for someone to be that beautiful and full of curious whimsy, don't you think?"

Rosier scoffed but laughed, twisted his body around some, propped an elbow on the back of the couch, and held his cheek, which had a little of the roundness of a fruit itself. "Don't listen to him. He loves to be irritating. But, see, it's difficult to give a proper answer; you should simply live, Lucifer. It'll all come to you." Raphael had told him the things couldn't be explained, too; Asmodeus had told Lucifer to simply live, too. "You'll find out who you are soon enough." Lucifer remembered how the crowds had cheered after him: angel of beauty, angel of beauty. The Lord has given us an angel of beauty.

"Soon enough?" Asmodeus snorted. "For me, it took more time than you can imagine. And I'm not sure about— Rosier, stop smiling."

Rosier's smile bloomed into a cheeky grin before he leaned closer to Lucifer and explained, "I always knew he was the angel of friendship. I promise you there's no greater friend to make than Asmodeus. Funny, charming, selfless... I could argue he's the angel of hugging, too."

Asmodeus was moving back up onto his feet, huffing — face turned away to hide the stark ruby tint that'd invaded it, and Lucifer couldn't fight his own tiny smile at the sight. "I should be on my way. If there is anything I can do to help you with settling in, Lucifer, don't hesitate to look for me."

Lucifer nodded and stood as well, brushing himself off unnecessarily. "Yes, thank you, thank you—" The taller angel had stepped forward and outstretched the instruments to him. "What's this?"

"Timbrel and pipes, I hear," Asmodeus teased. "Our Father made them for you."

CHAPTER 4

Gifts arrived, hundreds of them. Word spread far throughout the following days that the Lord's newest angel was finally awake, and that he was astonishingly pleasing to look at — so batches of angels landed outside at every other hour. The fruits of their labor came wrapped in ribbons or arranged neat in baskets and sacks; you see, the angels hadn't invented the wheel, or maybe they had but didn't care for it, and opted for carrying whatever they could.

Before long, the kitchen was overflowing with every sort of food, as the garden was with flowers, and the upstairs room — that had been Asmodeus' and found mostly barren on the day of Lucifer's arrival — had grown so mountainous with presents that the youngest angel didn't know where to begin in sorting it all out. He received too many carpets, all of which didn't quite go together in patterns or colors, leading them to be scattered throughout the house then miserably gifted to neighbors. Lucifer began having to deny gifts, though he promised between quivering apologies that he appreciated their hard work and their time.

When one angel frowned as he was told they couldn't accept his bottles of olive oil, Lucifer burst into tears, crying, "Oh, I wish I had an infinite house, just so that all of your presents could hold a place in it! Please, forgive me."

Rosier rushed to comfort Lucifer, then turned his head to the stranger and reaffirmed that Lucifer was still very young. Becoming familiar with every marvelous thing at once was a painful process, after all, and the city of Heaven had far too much history to disrobe, though you might decipher its fortune from its streets, the lines of its palms. "Here, Lucifer, have some water." The riches — when they were so abundant, they could hardly be called riches, but it was true that they were everywhere, and they struck at an angel's heart like they were rare because, even when copious, God's creation was God's creation. "Do you want to rest?" Everything was so, so perfect; what else was there to do but cry?

The first fruit Lucifer picked was a pomegranate. He did it some days later — the subject of angel days won't be discussed now — when he followed after Rosier to one of the orchards. Sometimes, they were contained in acres within the city, sometimes they had the discourtesy of climbing up buildings and taking them over, and there were some that strolled along as angels. Rosier promised Lucifer that they couldn't fly, but he seemed a bit unsure of this himself, and Lucifer had frowned. Then, the two of them had gone around filling cloth sacks with fruits and placing those into larger bags that they tied to their backs. Lucifer asked what they were meant to do next, and Rosier said some angels had kindly asked for fruits from him.

'Oh,' Lucifer thought, 'I was hoping they were for God.' Where was He?

The youngest angel went on to help Rosier, though he felt awkward going about it. He kept his head bowed, usually draped by the hood of a robe or a shawl or a scarf, avoiding gazes and murmuring responses, and if anyone said, "Is that the angel of beauty?" he would turn his head, act as if he wanted to see the angel of beauty too. In some ways, he did. He prayed, had already begun praying so quick after birth, that there was another angel who was so pretty, so young, it was insufferable. He never did.

"Ow, ow— Brother, my legs—"

"They hurt?" Rosier laughed. "Mine too. We've been walking for hours. Usually, I fly."

"Why don't you fly then?"

"Because you're with me!" The words made Lucifer frown.

Luckily — Baal, the angel of flight, arrived just another couple days later. Lucifer was in the kitchen, grinding a rough basalt pestle against cumin seeds, when door knocks called his attention. Bicep throbbing, the angel hopped off a stool and called, "I'll answer that!" before Rosier, who diced vegetables, could say anything.

Opening the door, looking upward. Baal was large, straight-shouldered, but thinner at his hips, so that he had an inverted-triangular build. He had a mane of lighter-brown hair, adorned with tight curls, and the shade of his skin was about Lucifer's, though it was warming at his cheeks. "Oh. Oh, hello." He spoke like he'd forgotten how, and Lucifer wondered if he was young too. "I'm Baal. You're Lucifer, I imagine?" He wore simpler clothes, just a loose tunic and basic sandals made of henequen. "It's nice to meet you." A large nose, deep cocoa eyes. For an angel, there was something quite mundane about him, but like that familiarity of your robes, your blankets — homely.

Though he took a timorous step backward, Lucifer thought, 'Angel of safety,' with a little amusement.

Soon, Baal was in the kitchen with them, helping to eat the heaps of gifted food and telling the story of how Asmodeus broke into his house and threw him off his hammock to ask if he would mind teaching Lucifer to fly. Baal had said he wouldn't mind at all, though now he turned to Lucifer and said he was too busy for a while, so they should plan another date to meet at the Fountain of Life.

Afterward, Lucifer climbed up into his room, covered all the windows with curtains to be shielded from the eternal light of Heaven, and then he curled up in bed to rest.

In between all the fruit deliveries, Lucifer's early days over-brimmed, too, with lessons. How to read and write was the most difficult; Rosier sat with him and flipped through folded bark papers, where the script was logo-syllabic and vertical, which had been the fashion, he said, for the last half-century, but scripts and their languages came and went as trends. To prove this, Rosier showed Lucifer some parchment scrolls with right-to-left cursive, and then he handed him another trend that was catching on — a novel made of folded wooden slips. The youngest angel asked how he was supposed to juggle so much knowledge, as he chiseled a hieroglyph into stone, but Rosier smiled. He said that Lucifer seemed a quick learner — "Though your handwriting is a little atrocious. Oh no, Lucifer, please don't cry!"

Weakly, the youngest angel smiled.

And there was cleaning, which Lucifer revealed to be quite good at, even if he disliked how dust scurried whenever it saw him with a broom. The chase, though, was occasionally fun. Cooking — for this, Rosier invited a friend to come help before the three had to hastily put out the seven great fires Lucifer had managed to set in the kitchen somehow. "Well," the angels comforted Lucifer, afterwards, "at least now we know you're not the angel of cooking!"

Then, finally, one day, Lucifer stepped out of the house and walked alone — his first time doing so — nearly shivering in time with the anxious flutters of his heart. He cradled a tightly-woven basket with both arms and came upon the plaza at Heaven's center with its great, domineering fountain — Fountain of Life, the angels called it. There, Baal was. He was standing by the water, looking to the horizon, before he must've sensed a gaze on him and turned his head. To Lucifer, he gave a cherry smile that the young angel had no choice but to return. "Oh," the great flier said, as Lucifer approached him, "what is the basket for?"

"You ate so much when you visited." Lucifer rummaged through it. "I'm not skilled enough to create a beautiful present to thank you for your time, but I thought you might enjoy some bread."

"Is it a gift or are you still attempting to finish all the food in your house?"

"Can't it be both?" Lucifer smiled at the other's warm chuckle. "I don't have a great appetite and neither does Rosier, but you seem to. Won't you move in for a while?"

"I'll consider it, but I'm not usually so hungry." But, as Lucifer pressed the basket to his side, Baal took it anyway. "Let me eat now, before we begin. I don't want to drop anything while we're in the air and have it hit someone on the head."

"I did mean to ask you a few things." Lucifer sat beside him and caught some pale petals moving over the surface of the water.

"Oh?" Baal uncovered the warm loafs that had been wrapped in a cloth. "What about, brother?"

"How did you find out you're the angel of flight? Was it easy for you? Rosier told me he always knew himself, but Asmodeus said he went centuries and centuries not knowing. I could never handle that. If there is anything I can do..." He trailed off, not sure what he meant, but then decided to keep talking, as Baal was stuffing his mouth. "I asked Father for guidance, but I continue to be lost. It isn't that I don't like helping Rosier. I enjoy my time with him, but... I can tell it isn't what I'm meant to do." Chewing. "I can feel that our Heavenly Father has a different path for me, but I can't decide what it is. He left me with all this jewelry you see on me," he wore it all today, "and some instruments, but I have no clue how to use them! I'm not nearly as good as the angels of music I hear out in the streets. It fills me with shame; I worry our Father looks at me with disappointed eyes."

Baal swallowed. "Hm." A long pause, not unlike the twist of a dagger into Lucifer's side. "I learned my role really early, but I suppose that's because it's obvious. I fly faster, better, than everyone else. But, Lucifer, I thought you already knew. Aren't you the angel of beauty?"

"That's what everyone says," Lucifer replied, quiet, sadness dribbling down from his words. "But in my heart, it doesn't feel right. Even if it were, what is an angel of beauty meant to do? Sit and be stared at?"

"Well, there's no need to be sitting," Baal teased, conjuring a tiny smile out from the other. "One can be pretty and also help collect fruits. But I see what you mean. How about we fly? I think it'll help settle you down." He set the basket on the ground by their feet, then stood. "Take out your wings, just two."

Lucifer moved to stand and swallowed, holding his own hands. He took a moment to glance around them, but they were mostly alone now; it was only Baal, Lucifer, a handful of angels, and the flowers. He admitted, "I've never..."

"Ah. Well, I'll be clear: it'll be difficult the first time. But look at me." And he did. "You're an angel, Lucifer. We're filled up with the glory and greatness of the Lord. Try to feel the fire He made you from, coursing through you." There was definitely a heat that traveled along Lucifer's body, beneath the skin; there had always been. "It's malleable, like clay. Take it in your hands— Not literally, brother." Lucifer apologized and put his hands back down, but now all the flames had rushed to his face at Baal's good-natured laughter. "Try to shape the fire, try to peel it open." With a breath, the young angel concentrated on the shape of his body, but that only brought to prominence a boil in his blood, climbing to the surface. He sidestepped, felt whistles in his throat, and must have looked pained because Baal amended his words. "Or let it peel *you* open."

It certainly felt like that was happening, like his skin, everywhere, was getting pinched and pulled away from him tautly. It made him stumble, grimace, before sharp stings stabbed against his spine, and then he yelped and doubled over as the burns began to trickle down onto his legs. "Ow— Baal, it hurts— It hurts me—" Searing tears of flesh at his back.

"It will hurt," Baal's voice came gently, but his hands were in the air as if he wanted to embrace him but knew he couldn't. "And it'll bleed, but only this once. Don't resist."

"Bleed? Why?" Lucifer wondered if his voice sounded high and panicked to the other, as well. "Why will it hurt?"

"To be incarnate, they say, is to bleed and to hurt." Lucifer's breaths began to stumble from his mouth and crash into the air — throaty, raspy. "Breathe, brother."

Lucifer wanted to scream that he was obviously already doing so, but an inferno ravaged his mouth before it gripped his body tight and crushed. All he could manage was a sharp intake of air before he heard wet ripping, then felt it. It was so much — he couldn't even scream; it was shudders of pain whipping him from the inside, blinding him in white, the vague sensation of dryness in his mouth before a warm, moistness overpowered him from the back. Heaviness followed, tugging him backwards; on his toes one moment, then on his heels, falling, falling.

"Lucifer." Urgent, but not worried. Lucifer felt two hands take his wrists, and the touch made sweetness bloom in the young angel's mouth, sugary, calming. "Look at me." Blinking away the blindness, he saw the face of the other again, and then a radiance, blinding again, but it was only Baal's smile. "I should have guessed — they're beautiful."

Mellow, alluring, deep purple on long, tapered wings, with some minor white outlining feathers; the wings sunset from a slightly warmer hue at the tip to the cooler bottom. They twitched, but not in unison, one wavered and flapped while the other trembled. Lucifer could only yelp as he was propelled to one side, opposite the erratic wing, but Baal caught him again.

"There, there, steady."

Lucifer became violently aware of the wetness still on his back, running down the curve of it, beneath his clothes. "It's— Baal—" Then, he gasped: "Oh, my robes are torn! They're torn! And I'm still bleeding!"

"Your clothes can be fixed."

"They were a gift!"

"Mended clothing is a sign of love and use, brother." But Baal was chuckling, sounding much like the taste of chocolate. "You should worry about the blood loss. If you're too lightheaded, we can end here and continue another time." Lucifer was shaking his head. "Oh, are you sure? You... left a mess on the ground." Following the gaze of the other, Lucifer then breathed out a thank you to the Lord that there was hardly anyone nearby; crimson was left streaked over the edge of the fountain, splattered, formless. And Lucifer surely looked terrified — "Don't make that face. Watch me, instead."

Baal released the younger one and reached for the pool, cupping some of the water with his hands — he avoided the flowers floating there, but Lucifer noticed with horror that some appeared redder than before — letting it cascade onto the marks of pain over the ground. Easily, the water swept the blood away, seeping into the golden street, as if it had never been there.

Lucifer blinked and watched it do so, wonder and confusion crudely swirling in his mind together. He whispered, "That was my first blood."

Baal started. "Really? I'm sorry, I didn't—" All he seemed able to do was shake his head. "Are you sure you want to continue?"

"I'm certain." Rosier had shown Lucifer some slices on his fingers a short time ago, explained with a little voice of frustration that it was due to the thorns of a plant. When Lucifer asked what the red seeping out from beneath his skin was, Rosier had stopped, then laughed. "It's blood!" he'd explained. "When we're hurt, we bleed, but we heal stronger. Bleeding is good."

"You're very determined," Baal mused, before taking both of Lucifer's hands in his own again. "Stretch your wings, then bring them to you. Yes, like that." Lucifer hissed as the new appendages protruding from his back stung and pulled painfully as he bent, then outstretched, them. They moved stiff, like they were meant to creak, but it became smoother each time, despite the stubborn hurting. "Now flap them, both at once."

Lucifer did so and felt the ground escape him for a second, as if he'd jumped. The air ruffling his damp feathers; the embrace of wind beneath them for just a moment. "Am I doing it right?"

"Yes, brother." Baal's own wings sprung out from his back, wide. They were shadow black, spotted with some diluted white accents near the top, a much greater wingspan than Lucifer's. "Try to hover, flap them again, but keep a steady rhythm. It'll take practice."

"I didn't realize this would be so complicated," Lucifer grumbled halfheartedly. He did as told, finding himself squeezing the other angel's palms tight as he focused. It was difficult — forcing his wings to not only move as one but keep consistent strikes against the air. But, Baal was patient — he uttered to use less power, then more, then told him that was perfect, to keep at it, then once again told him that was too much, too little. "These— These wings are heavy."

"You'll become accustomed to it, but yes, they are. With regular flying around, you'll mostly be gliding, though, so don't worry too much." He tugged on Lucifer's hands, bringing him back to the ground, and as the other caught his breath, Baal flapped his own wings, moved into the air. "Come on, follow me."

"Hm?" Lucifer brought a wing around to his front and picked at crisp, dried blood that had stuck a few feathers together. "You want to fly up high? But what if I fall?"

"Have faith in God, and you will always be well, Lucifer."

Lucifer let himself hesitate; he dropped his gaze to the fountain, to the flowers that held some of his blood still. He reached for one, cupped it, raised his hand, and felt cool water seep out from between his fingers. Simply, he placed it in the basket he'd brought. He picked a few of the other crimson-stained petals, knowing that he was making Baal wait and feeling guilty for it, but he wanted to ensure he didn't leave any behind. By the time he was done, the basket was crowded with defiled flowers, and he felt at ease.

"Excuse me for that," he told Baal as he clapped his wings up to meet him, but Lucifer was met with a warm gaze.

"No need. Come. Fly with me." With a powerful beat of his own wings, Baal shot upward into the gulping sea of gold that hung overhead.

Lucifer swayed pitifully as he attempted to hurry behind. His smaller wings meant he had to flap more to compensate, sometimes stuttering a little in place and accidentally pushing himself down rather than up. He kept his eyes on the floor, only occasionally checking to see where Baal was. He watched his dangling feet, took in the top of buildings — scanned them like words on a page, read them to say his every thought, every little desire — and breathed in so great he thought his lungs were expanding endlessly. It all began to look so tiny; he began to feel infinitely tiny himself.

"Lucifer!" Baal's voice, cheery. "Look up!" He spoke the moment Lucifer realized the light all about them flickered. He turned his head upward, as they broke through the firmament, and was instantly enveloped by a cold abyss — could only feel the breath just reeled in drawn out from his mouth again.

In between specs of emptiness, it was anything but dark: the brilliance of hundreds, thousands, millions of burning spheres coming in every color; there were shimmering fogs in spirals, round or flat, and ellipticals. Explosions striking vast against the vacuum, passing streaks of white. Twinkling. The entire universe sprawled before him but peppering his cheeks with enough kisses to make him laugh. Flooded, feeling the cosmos rush his body and consume him, he smiled so much it hurt. And in the embrace of the entirety of everything, he caught Baal, hovering above, watching two faraway moons pass by each other wordlessly.

And then they fell, together, back to Heaven. The two flew up once more and let themselves fall; they did it over and over. They danced along the sky and among the stars.

CHAPTER 5

L ucifer was deeply asleep when Rosier let himself in and woke him by pulling back the curtains.

There were still disorganized mounds of gifts in Lucifer's room — Baal defended him by saying the room looked comfortably lived-in — but better than before. One could now shuffle over the carpets easily to either the narrow bed with its five distinct blankets and heap of pillows, or one could go to the double doors that led out to the small balcony. Two dozen paintings were hanging high and low, nearly every wall fully obscured by them, along with the curtains, the tapestries, and the new furniture pieces, of all different materials and styles, scattered about. His mass of clothing was stuffed into trunks and a wardrobe; and a massive mirror, not far from the door, leaned by a desk where he arranged all his jewelry. Oh — the plants. Like most angels, Lucifer had many of them, and they were everywhere — in pots and on the walls and around his bed, particularly lilacs, peeking out sometimes to nuzzle him awake.

The basket full of flowers stained in blood, ichor, was by a window, one of the three.

Lucifer groaned and pulled the covers over himself, grumbling, "Please, Rosier. I can't handle picking fruits today. If you take me out to do it, I'll throw myself on the ground and let everyone trample me instead."

There was a dip of weight on the bed at his side. "Lucifer, you're so dramatic. I'm not here to make you work."

The youngest angel hoped to crawl back into his dreams; he traveled somewhere, in his sleep — somewhere empty — the gaps in the abyss. "Well, I am not hungry."

"I have not come to feed you." A soft amusement. "Asmodeus is with some of our common friends, and I thought you'd like to go."

Lucifer peeked his eyes out. "You're inviting me? Why?"

"I invite you everywhere. I also think you should make something of your life."

"What you want is for me to have some friends." But Lucifer was smiling, ever so slight. "Alright, as you wish." He stretched his arms, let out a wonderfully sleepy yawn, mumbling, "But I have a question."

"You always do."

Lucifer asked, "Does God dream?" He'd been taught to pray formally, had learned he enjoyed doing it before sleep — on his knees over the floor, elbows on the bed, hands clasped together. He was very good at it, he thought.

Rosier smiled, then flopped to lay comfortably beside Lucifer. "He does. I think He's dreaming now."

"What is He dreaming?"

"This." Reaching over, Rosier pinched Lucifer's cheek. "And me, and this room. Everything you see." Maybe this Heaven was all just a dream, he was saying. A loving God's pretty, pleasant dream.

With that, Lucifer rose from bed and spent a few minutes preparing to be stared at. He donned a sky-blue robe over a tunic and quickly went to wash his face in the tiny room that had nothing but basic grooming supplies and water in a porcelain basin, painted with a sighing moon and sun. Oiling his hair, he watched the city through a thin window, then returned to his room to finish layering on his jewelry — which he found, frankly, a bit tedious and heavy but chose not to complain of because God had gifted most to him. He tied an embroidered scarf over his hair and breathed, before meeting the angel of fruit out in the street.

Though Lucifer had expected to fly — he was hoping to practice — Rosier began walking. Initially, it was through the golden roads, but before long, they were nearing the bank of a lake, where a one-legged angel sat at the edge of a floating wooden dock. He tapped the water with his foot. "Haniel," Rosier called, and the angel raised his head, "do you mind if we borrow your canoe?"

"It's Abaddon's," the angel replied, his smile cheery. "But go ahead and use it, so long as you bring it back one day."

Lucifer didn't look at any of the flat, wooden canoes, busy enamored with the blueness of the lake and, more still, with the small islands of green peppered upon it. Some of these floating gardens were concerned with flowers — pinks and yellows and blues — but others carried wheat and corn and rice. Lucifer kept staring at them, even when Rosier ushered him onto one of the thin boats, and barely noticed the elaborate painting on the wood where he sat. He just about draped himself over the end of the canoe, watching the ripples, craning his neck to see the interweaving reeds beneath the little islands.

Soon enough, Rosier had received a paddle from the other angel, climbed onto the boat — it rocked — and then began moving them through the lake. Lucifer caught little hints of movement beneath the water's surface, then startling whenever the head of a fish broke through. Always, before he could whisper a greeting, the animal would shoot back below with a wet *plop*. Lucifer turned his head around, prepared to ask what that had been, but he saw the standing Rosier grumbling in exertion as he rowed, pushing away any flowers that approached them slowly, perhaps trying to catch a glimpse of the angel of beauty too.

Lucifer immediately frowned. "We could've flown, couldn't we? It's less work."

Rosier chuckled warmly. "You're right it would be easier to fly. But life would be dull if we angels always did everything the easy way."

It was an observatory where they headed. As they reached the dock at the other side of the lake, Lucifer saw it just a couple dozen steps away, with its great dome cutting into the sky and its columns and arches. On tiled walls, there were thousands of eyes painted, all blinking curiously at the two angels drawing nearer.

Meekly, Lucifer greeted them.

The inside was tremendous, but Rosier led him away from the hall at the center — it was bustling with activity, angels and their instruments, these for measurement — to a narrower corridor. There, abruptly, he heard voices, speaking, climbing passionately over one another. And the marble doors were open; stepping, Lucifer saw two debating angels beside a massive slate stone board, chalk scribbled to depict rings turned spirals and elongated arrows. There was a numeral script, as well, running down the height of it, a flying angel was adding lines near the ceiling. He did some small calculations with his other hand, shouting down at the arguing ones to stay in the conversation.

Above, the dome was painted in geometrically complex, bright blue, attenuated patterns on a bed of white. On the ground, there were carpets, made up of reds and shaded browns; there were velvet divans, elaborate and plush. Asmodeus was seated on one himself, beside a friend, before he shot to his feet to hurry over. He embraced Rosier, and Rosier grinned, wrapping his arms around the other and attempting, failing, to spin him around.

"Oh, you're Lucifer?" There were a couple stranger angels in the room, one of which was lying on his side over the carpet with a bowl of grapes. There was a thurible hanging by him, too, burning incense; a smoky stream of myrrh, gently woody, rushed Lucifer's nostrils. Sighing, he felt his muscles lose their tension.

"Yes, that is my name." Allowing his two friends to have their grand reunion after only a few days apart, Lucifer moved toward the angel on the floor and sat. He was particularly good-looking, with long box braids cascading down the front of his shoulders, and dark brown skin, which had been painted over with some red, lace-like designs, especially along his face. He wore beaded jewelry that rattled when he moved. "You're pretty."

A grin. "That means everything coming from you. I'm happy to meet you. I'm Azazel."

"I'm Lucifer." He paused, blinked, then the both of them laughed. "You know that already. Forgive me."

"No need to apologize. I see everything they say about you is true."

"What does everyone say about me?" Lucifer shifted onto his belly and laid with his arms crossed, cheek against a forearm. "That I'm no good at delivering fruits?"

Another silky laugh. "Well, they do say that—"

"I might just cry myself to sleep—"

"They also say you're the angel of beauty, but you're shy about it." The angel plucked a grape from its stem then brought it to Lucifer's mouth, which accepted it eagerly and chewed before humming at the sweet tartness. "I can see that's so."

A bare foot landed not far from Lucifer's face, and he glanced up to see the angel who'd been in the air, still holding the chalk between two fingers. "Lucifer, we're glad to finally see you for ourselves. Though it's difficult to concentrate with such beauty in the room." The young angel flushed a bit at that. "I do need to stay focused on my work."

"What is your work?" Lucifer noticed that the debating angels were still at it, waving their arms and pointing at the diagrams. "What are all those numbers?"

"Have you seen the universe?" the angel said cheerily. "Do you think that made itself on its own?"

Lucifer raised his head instantly. "Oh? You create the universe?"

"Not create," Azazel answered, fast, as if he needed to correct Lucifer very quick or face repercussion. "Only God creates."

"But organizing, arranging, painting the colors on the planets," the standing one continued, "that's our duty as angels. Have you seen how uniform it is? It takes a lot of... arithmetic."

"That's wonderful." Lucifer smiled, then returned to looking down and away. "When I saw it, I told my friend Baal that I felt like living among it forever. It must be difficult to have it agree with you."

"It is!" shouted both of the debating angels, apparently only able to agree about that one statement.

Azazel fed Lucifer another grape. "Speaking of the universe," he said, directed to all the others, "I heard Gabriel won't come by, after all. He's traveling through Andromeda, helping put stars into place."

"That's a shame," Rosier sighed as he moved to sit on a divan, and the angel standing by Lucifer agreed.

Asmodeus had followed behind Rosier but didn't sit, instead

speaking to the angel he'd been conversing with earlier. "Phanuel, is Michael around?"

Michael. That was a nice name.

"He is, but he's probably busy." He waved a hand around, as the figure of another stranger came in through the door. "All archangels are the same! They do nothing but work. It makes no sense to me! I'll never understand them."

"Oh? What are you saying about archangels?"

And Phanuel shut his mouth and scrambled to his feet. He doubled over in a deep bow, and Lucifer blinked in confusion as the other angels in the room followed, save for Azazel. Already on the floor, Azazel simply bowed his head respectfully as Lucifer hurried to sit up and follow suit, but not without glancing at the angel who had just come in.

Eyes red-orange tourmaline and onyx hair, darker than that, braided around his head like a crown, with two small braids near the front cascading onto his shoulders, all adorned with just a handful of golden cuffs. He wore small, hooped earrings, also gold, and that was all for ornamentation. Over his tunic, he had a simple maroon cloak, held together by a chain in the front. His skin was pitch dark, his nose was long, his mouth was pressed into a fine line. "Good day to all of you as well." A deep voice, soothing even if he spoke flat.

"Uriel," said Phanuel, smiling mischievously with his head still bowed, even as everyone else moved back to their earlier positions. "Forgive me. You know I was only teasing."

"I'm not offended." Uriel stepped forward and ran his gaze, piercing, over the room until it settled on Lucifer. He blinked. "You're the new one."

Lucifer waited for Uriel to point out his beauty, but he didn't. "Yes." Warmth gathered at his cheeks. "My name is Lucifer."

"I know."

"Ah."

Uriel brushed past them to the angels still at the blackboard and immediately asked various things at once about their galaxy-construction efforts. He turned his back on Lucifer as if he were of no importance, and Lucifer supposed that was true. He was only one of thousands of angels, and 'one who doesn't even know if I'm good at anything besides being beautiful.'

Sadness snuck onto the young angel's face; Azazel shoved yet another grape into his mouth. "Don't worry over Uriel," he whispered, leaning in. "He's like that with everybody."

Asmodeus appeared so suddenly, sat at their side, that Lucifer jumped. "Absolutely. Even I'm not his friend." He had somehow acquired a ceramic cup of yerba mate that he took a sip from immediately after.

Lucifer swallowed the grape on his tongue, almost without chewing. "He's intimidating. Phanuel called him an archangel, right? That's what Raphael is."

"Yes," said Azazel. "Archangels are... our princes. The princes of Heaven that keep everything orderly. The real enforcers of Father's will. It all sounds like so much work to me."

"I could never be an archangel," Asmodeus mumbled. "If Father ever asked me, I'd tell Him a field of corn could do a better job."

Lucifer heard one angel ask the other what time was.

"There they go," laughed Phanuel, and Lucifer turned to, finally, perceive him decently enough: olive skin and almond-shaped, emerald eyes, with pronounced cheekbones. His hair, black as ink, framed his face, falling in feathery layers to his waistline. He wore chains carrying rubies and sapphires and obsidians; on his hands were rings, an excessive amount, amethyst and carnelian.

The two angels who'd argued earlier began debating again: they said, time is just distance, it's all relative; no, it's true everywhere; no, only here. They gestured at the stars and their moons, each rolling on their belly over the bed of the dark abyss and pulling time around themselves like bedsheets, not unlike Lucifer at the beginning of this chapter.

This chapter of an infinite life.

Heavenly days, it can be said now, were clocked to a certain planet's struggle against its sun's doting hold — an insignificant measurement but, in such a wide universe, there wasn't significance anywhere else. Time was thus an imperfect system, for eternity, but if the angels could create a perfect thing, they would be God, and God they were not.

Nor, they'd all insist, did they have any interest in being God. And time itself mattered little — the tracking of events and lives — when nothing had ever ended and never would. In time, too, it would begin to feel like there had never been a beginning either.

An angel said that he thought hours to be flat; no, they were curved; no, they were cyclical and haloed on their heads.

But our Lucifer was caught up in the first mention of Earth, so he turned his head and asked Asmodeus, who snickered and replied, "Hm. Well. It's a big green sphere."

Imagining a great lime, Lucifer said, "Ah." The conversations continued all around him, but listening was fruitless when he didn't know himself, much less the world outside him. Still, he smiled, watching Asmodeus laugh along with Rosier about whatever they talked over as Phanuel began to speak with Azazel, who moved his hand from between the bowl of grapes and Lucifer's mouth to tug his scarf back. He tousled the young angel's hair, then scratched his nails along Lucifer's scalp soothingly.

Nothing was happening, just enjoyment of company in the luxury of Heaven, the paradise where nothing ever happened.

One can't help but think they were all secretly unhappy, that all angels held a preeminent desire for destruction, but that isn't true. If you choose to believe, the angels were quite content; watch — Lucifer's eyelids had drooped, and he was thinking, 'Father, you are great. You are great and kind to give me everything like this. I want to thank you.' He was made wise, after all, and thus felt a downy warmth in his chest, this nostalgia; the wise know to be nostalgic for the good times even while they're happening. Yet: 'I would do anything to see you. If angels are like this, then what about you? Would you put your hand in my hair? Would I be worthy? I want to be. Where are you?'

He thought of Earth again. Earth. Earth. The center, the angels said, of a centerless universe, so important they had mapped themselves onto its turns.

Faintly, the strums of a harp returned him to reality, but Lucifer didn't turn to see the musician. Sitting up, he noticed the notes of the song — treble clefs — skipping circles around his head, then blinked a few times. Asmodeus was shouting, in the midst of telling a story —

"Weep, you angels!" — and being met with unrestrained laughter, including from Rosier, who was accusing him of exaggerating.

"Are you okay, brother?" Azazel asked, his hand still in the air by where he'd been massaging Lucifer's scalp.

Lucifer nodded. "Yes." Hours had passed, though he wasn't sure of that and had simply grown restless. He reached to adjust the scarf that had fallen to hang by his neck, then got to his feet. "Thank you for the grapes." Tempted to ask if Azazel was the angel of affection, he decided it was better not to initiate a conversation by accident.

"Lucifer, you're leaving?" Rosier's frown was evident in his voice. "Should I go as well?"

"No. Don't leave because of me," Lucifer said. "I'm just a little tired." And, perhaps, bored. Angels don't get bored, but Lucifer was barely learning to be an angel. "I'd like to rest," he added. "I will clean the home while you're here."

Rosier laughed as kindly as he always did. "We'll clean together once I return. Do you remember the way back?"

"I'll find it somehow." Lucifer turned his gaze to the exit and began to make his way towards it.

When he stepped outside, he didn't walk in the direction of the lake. The young angel wandered, instead, looking all about, letting himself be overwhelmed by this inordinate magnificence. It was redundant, almost — all this beauty. City of redundancy.

Lucifer looked past some archways into what was not unlike a bazaar — there were dozens of shaded stalls on either side of him, with various angels having set up their craftsmanship — clothing, furniture, seasonings. He listened to the scraping of a carpenter chiseling wood and the chirps of chattering angels. Nothing was being sold; there was some basic trading, but the primary exchange occurred between goods and smiles. Lucifer had no need for anything, so he stared, solely, at fellow angels and their labor.

Creating — though only God can create. He found a pillar, put a hand on its polish, nearly hid behind it. His thoughts were returning to him, like he'd woken from sleep watching this. But consciousness is often born from production, by our relation to production; to live is to create. Lucifer saw four angels working a massive iron cast bowl with steaming broth and round grain rice; hearty smell beckoning, he licked his lips. Consumption is creation, too.

One of the angels noticed him and, laughing, shouted for the youngest angel to lend a hand. He flushed, wanting to apologize; his muscles had tensed, as if waiting for a strike. Waiting for something, anything — for an event to entice his life into action. Lucifer forced himself to relax, let ease make its way out of his body, take his hand, smile, then lead him toward the four angels and their contentment in paradise.

He wasn't sure what the problem was, wasn't sure why he foraged for a sudden narrative to his life, a purpose. But we're always looking for narratives, looking for meaning, looking for God. Even the angels.

CHAPTER 6

S omething of Earth fascinated him, began to seep into his
dreams.
Lucifer traversed Heaven, asking for stories of this faraway,
utopian place where God might live, and the angels said it wasn't a
lime; it was like Heaven, but it wasn't. It had beasts, proportions of
greatness, that roamed the grasses — and it was so unbearably green,
they all said — broken apart by massive bodies of turbulent water.
Where Heaven was still and calm, Earth was explosive and wild.
Anyone who'd ever been led the way down — and they always said
"down" — described intense battles between mountain-tall creatures,
tackling one another and ripping open their throats. The young angel
had gasped, but they'd all insisted it was true. They're not like us, they
said, they're beasts, they only know how to be beasts.

"Lucifer, play us something!"

The young angel in question startled, looked up and away from the
small, circular table, which had floral lace designs stitched into its
mantle. Two angels, who'd been passing by, were coming closer, and
now Lucifer wished he'd earlier asked to eat inside Azazel's home rather
than sit out in the front garden. "Play something?" He knew what they
referred to — the timbrel and pipes he'd begun carrying around,
strapped to his hip and perfectly visible when his back was turned to

the street, as it currently was. "I—" He looked at Rosier, who was with him as usual, but the angel of fruit was in the middle of chewing a seasoned mango slice, and Azazel had left them a few minutes ago. With no other recourse, Lucifer turned back to the angels who had called to him. "I can't."

"You can't?" one said back.

"I'm not really," Lucifer replied, uncertain, "I'm not really very good."

They all laughed, even Rosier, at Lucifer's phrasing, as the angel who'd shouted walked closer to lean against the table. "But I heard the Lord gave you those instruments."

The other stranger responded, "For just decorative purposes, perhaps." Oddly, he seemed to mean it kindly: "You do look nice holding them, youngest brother."

Before Lucifer could even frown, Azazel came out of his home, saying, "Hey, you two, leave that angel alone. He's easily frightened." Then, Lucifer was looking away, embarrassed and asking himself if he really came across that way. "And what are you doing here?" Three empty glasses clinked as Azazel settled them on the table, his other hand preoccupied with a tall, long-necked opaque bottle, which he tilted to splash a vinous sea into one of the cups. "Is it Samyaza?"

"Yes, we wanted to ask if he's home."

"I wouldn't know," Azazel snorted. "He's mad at me." Earlier, he'd mentioned having nine other housemates. "But go ahead and check, if you like." The angels gave thanks before moving past them toward the front door, but Azazel wasted no time in changing the subject: "Do you want me to serve you, Lucifer?"

Lucifer nodded, quickly. "Oh, yes, thank you." He reached back and drummed his fingers against the flat side of his timbrel. Recently, he'd taken to practicing alone in his bedroom, trying to find rhythms but still struggling. In the process, he'd discovered something else: when he blew onto the pipes, he felt the organs inside his body tremble and release tiny songs of their own. Perhaps, he thought, the Heavenly Father had placed instruments within him too; he'd begun to hear them ring and whistle with sweet, elated breaths.

"Have you ever drank before?" Azazel asked, filling another one of the glasses with wine.

Lucifer was prepared to say he'd definitely drank before, but Rosier spoke over him, "No, I've kept him away from alcohol. God bless."

Azazel laughed, the sound like bells. "What do you have against a little drunkenness, Rosier?"

"Nothing," Rosier mumbled, then brought another mango slice to his lips. "I just don't want him to start getting too attached to it so early in life. Asmodeus had a century where he was having too much every day, and it was a struggle to get it away from him." He paused, then teased, "Maybe I should intervene in your case, as well."

Azazel joked back, "Wait another million years. I just discovered pulque." He filled the last cup and set the wine bottle down before reaching to hand Rosier a glass. Then, Azazel handed one to Lucifer. "Here, brother. Have a taste."

The youngest angel took it, stared down at the surface, then looked back up, thinking to ask what was special about this drink before deciding he'd rather not be teased for his questioning. So, Lucifer sipped. It was sweet, though it had a dryness to it, and he decided it was good; noticing this, Azazel smiled in encouragement. Lucifer had a little more, feeling himself loosen around his shoulders, then snickering, saying that maybe he would become like Asmodeus. Rosier's groan made a grin bloom across Lucifer's mouth, as he reached to clink his glass to Azazel's and the two downed their drink together, laughing. Then, they had another, and another.

It wasn't long before, "Earth," escaped Lucifer's mouth.

"Oh no," Azazel said, "don't ask me. I've never been."

"Neither have I," Rosier said, though he had told Lucifer this already.

"I want to see it..." Lucifer hiccuped, eyes lidding. His body had begun chasing after itself with every movement, like he were a shadow, trying to keep in step with its captor. He raised his arm, to reach for an olive from a little porcelain plate, then actually raised it a second later — delay. And he noticed he was giggling too much, rocking to try and center his weight. "Who gets to go?" The olive was in his mouth; how did it get there?

"Definitely not an angel like me," Azazel sighed.

Lucifer propped an elbow on the table, held his cheek in his palm. "What kind of angel are you?" He asked himself the same question.

"I'm the angel of body painting." Immediately — he snickered. "Want me to show you?" Azazel had nothing more than a fine brush and red dye in a silver capsule with him, but that was all he needed. Swift, he used Lucifer's face as a canvas, transfiguring him into an art piece itself. It was during this moment that, abrupt, the elbow still set on the table slipped, and Lucifer knocked his glass over. He saw his friends jump to grab it for him; Lucifer was a few seconds late. Apologies tumbled out from his mouth but were met with suppressed snickers.

"Brother, you drank too much." Azazel smiled. "It's alright, you'll only have to have some water."

"It's best if we walk home," Rosier said. "The last thing I want is for Lucifer to fly right into a building." With a chuckle, he stood and moved to Lucifer, taking his arm. "Come on then."

"I'm alright," Lucifer replied, but his mouth felt distant, and his weight continued to stumble. "I'm sorry for spilling your wine. I'll come back to clean it."

"Nonsense." Azazel waved a hand. "Go rest, Lucifer."

Rosier continued hugging Lucifer's arm as they walked down the road, and though the young angel wanted to apologize once again, the shorter one spoke: "I'll take you to the Fountain of Life. If you drink some water there, you'll feel better soon." With his free hand, Lucifer tugged down the hood of the cloak he wore over his head, wishing he had told Azazel not to decorate his face at all.

They arrived, and Rosier was kind enough to cup his hands full of water before letting it drip onto Lucifer's mouth. He drank it down with shut eyes and felt coolness travel down his throat before making its way throughout his entire body, from the tips of his toes to the top of his head. He made a soft noise, feeling already a little more grounded — coming to realize he'd already forgotten the way they'd walked to get there. Yet still, he sighed in relief, sitting on the edge of the fountain and looking for, rearranging, finding, himself.

Rosier rubbed circles into his back. "I shouldn't have given you so

much. I take full responsibility. I'll make it up to you tomorrow."
Lucifer mumbled apologies, saying it was his fault because he was
certain that it was, but Rosier didn't respond to that. Instead, he
reached for the hood of Lucifer's robe and pulled it down, before his
fingers skimmed delicate through the youngest angel's hair.

"Hm?" Lucifer lifted his head some but didn't move to stop
Rosier. "What are you doing?"

"Keep still for two seconds please." The angel of fruit split the sea
of golden threads, then crossed each river over one another, creating a
pattern, weaving a braid. Lucifer allowed it, finding the tugs on his
scalp a bit pleasant. "I haven't taught you how to braid your hair. I'll
teach you soon." He let go of the finished product, though he hadn't
tied it, didn't have a ribbon with him, and it would come apart soon.
"I'm tying better luck into your hair," a laugh, "and maybe a little love
too."

"Love?"

"Yes, love," he teased, then Rosier leaned to press a simple kiss to
the top of his head. "Oh—" Lucifer looked up at the same time. "Hello
Phanuel."

The angel was alone, dressed in just a cotton tunic that hugged his
wider-set hips, but he seemed chipper. "Hello, brothers." Phanuel
came closer, an eyebrow raising before one end to his lips curled. "I see
Lucifer had too much to drink?"

Lucifer pouted his lips. "I'm feeling already much better. I just
need to walk some more."

"What you need is to eat something," Rosier told him. "Once we're
home, I'll feed you some soup."

"I always did wonder," Lucifer whispered for no reason at all, "*why*
we're supposed to eat."

Phanuel laughed at this. "I see he's back to normal already, but if
it's food you're after, I was actually about to go to a fight. Michael
wanted me to go support, so I asked him to save me a few seats up
front. I think it could do you some good, Lucifer. Have you ever gone
to a match?"

Lucifer shook his head, mumbling that he hadn't, though he'd
heard a word or two about the expansive amount of ball games, wheel-

less chariot racing, and wrestling sports that angels played in the stadiums — so many perhaps because angels craved to hurt one another. "You said there would be food?"

Phanuel laughed. "Beans, probably, but it'll be exciting." He nodded at Rosier. "I'm sure Asmodeus will be there as well."

The angel of fruit visibly lit up but continued to hesitate. "Oh, I'd love to, but it depends on what Lucifer wants."

"I wouldn't mind." Lucifer decided to not be so difficult for once. "I'd like to see Asmodeus too."

Phanuel clapped, grinned. "Let's go then," he said, turning and beginning to lead the way, "before anyone takes our spots."

Rosier leaned closer and the three began to walk, saying he'd met Asmodeus at a chariot race. Two hundred thousand or, maybe, two hundred million years ago, but who can count so far? And, at this, Lucifer tilted his head, imagining the angel of friendship doing anything other than lazing on a divan, but his attention was drawn away before he could ask the details.

The amphitheater they approached was impressive, devouring a massive block in the city of Heaven and composed of columns fashioned from travertine and tufa, with each of the eighty archways in between appearing to be an entrance. Moving inside, there were crowds of other angels, some heading toward the large stairways that climbed up into the five horizontal sections, but Phanuel led them straight forward. They came upon open-air seats, carrying plush cushions and ceramic plates of food, in one of the rows closest to the arena. It was sandy and flat, populated by a handful of chattering angels, seemingly setting the rules for the marathon of fights. All around was the scent of sizzling, maybe over-seasoned, food and of perfumes and sweat — which itself was like petrichor — and briskness.

Still, Lucifer didn't concern himself with as much awe as one might expect. The instant they sat, he reached for the bread and beans and rice, stuffing it all into his mouth until his cheeks looked comically full. He could hear his friends laughing but paid it no mind, moaning heartily, going through the plate, nearly licking it clean of crumbs, only looking upward when a horn blared loud above. Suckling on the remnant of flavor on his fingers, then, he watched the angels near to him stand. The roar of a cheer rippled through the crowd, fists flying up into the air, some wings fluttering in excitement, striking yammering victims on the face. Thundering drums and trumpets followed, a hundred, casting a wide net of music over the amphitheater. At Lucifer's side, Rosier waved madly at Asmodeus, who was many rows above, too busy singing and shouting with others to notice.

Ahead, from one end of the arena, walked an angel onto the sand, in a simple, short tunic, a wild grin on his upturned face. His sun red hair was tied back, and he faced the crowd, waving a hand when the angels cheered for him. Then — Lucifer finished his plate — the musicians, of which there seemed to be on every line of seats, playing their instruments with remarkable cohesion, grew even louder, alongside a booming chant overwhelming the building enough to almost make it shake. From the other side of the arena, another angel appeared, a brunette, who smiled, smaller but much prouder.

A horn sounded again, belonging to an angel flying over the stadium. Instantly — the two angels at the center rushed one another. Lucifer saw the redhead reach over the head and under the shoulder of the other, like he meant to lock his arms around his neck, but the brunette evaded it with little more than a step to the side. He moved to duck beneath the arms of the redhead to gain control, grabbed him by the torso, then rammed forward to send the other to the ground.

Lucifer gasped instinctively but didn't hear it over all the noise — only felt his breath robbed.

The brunette's wings, vast and earthly, shot out from his back to flap once and fling himself back onto his feet, far from the redhead. His chest rose, sunk, as he huffed sharp through his nose, but his face was set, hardened as stone. Lucifer gulped down what felt to be crystal, only to hear others clapping, so he did the same. Various names, too, were shouted out, but he couldn't decipher which belonged to the standing fighter. And from the corner of his eye, he noticed Phanuel, pumping his fist in the air and letting out an enthusiastic cry. Initially, Lucifer felt embarrassed to attempt it, but the cheer would come out naturally soon enough.

The one on the ground jumped back onto his feet and rushed the other again, but he shot his own wings out, flapping twice, moving forward, and high — kicking one leg out with a spin. Lucifer nearly screamed as the attacker made slamming contact with the brunette's shoulder, but the redhead's victory didn't last long.

As he attempted to shoot himself back, the brunette grabbed the ankle of the other and, strongly, flung him off to the side. The brunette fell and tumbled back; the redhead hit and rolled harshly over the ground.

Lucifer jumped up and cheered some more, not sure why, but his heart had begun racing in his chest, beating so tough he could feel it in his skull. He remembered the stories of beasts battling on Earth; he wondered if they were like this; he thought of Earth, Earth, Earth. When both the wrestlers moved back onto their feet, Lucifer reached for some food from the plate of Rosier, who laughed, and cracked a pecan between his teeth to settle his soul. He could only manage to sit atop a leg, ready to leap into the air once more at any moment.

They circled each other — the fighters — over the sand, the redhead with his wings still outstretched behind him. The sprawl of feathers, pointing like daggers. But, now he was bloodied, scratched fine, and panting, mouth wide open, sweat dripping down his brow. The brunette responded to it with a grin — smug, like victory had just been assured — before they rushed each other yet again.

There were holds, and there were strikes, and then in one moment, the redhead held the brunette in a chokehold, beat his wings hard so that they both barreled high into the air as the other thrashed. Then, he hurled him to the ground hard enough sand was kicked into the audience.

Lucifer shielded himself with his hood as everyone shouted out, but he didn't take his eyes off the one on the ground for a second. He whispered, prayed, under his breath, "Get up — he'll finish you if you stay there. Rise up again, defend yourself." With a sharp intake of breath, he cut himself off.

The redhead swooped down, maybe to go so far as to crush the other's bones, but the brunette rolled out from under him. The redhead couldn't react in time: he struck the ground, fell over it, and skid clumsily, before the other angel came up behind him. He shot forward with his wings, grabbed the redhead, and dragged him, squirming, over the sand before casting him up, flying after quickly, grappling again, then pulling him back down.

Unlike the redhead, the brunette didn't fling the other, he grabbed him by the head and fully dug him into the ground. *Crack* — something breaking, sharp, gutting out white through skin on the back of the angel's throat. In Lucifer's own, he felt his pounding heart and a shocked cry caught. He couldn't stay still, the gruesome sight — gurgles and bursts of blood — blooming out into thrill.

Perhaps, the redhead sought to get to his feet again, but the brunette stood now straight, brought one foot to his opponent's neck and pressed down, as he pulled one of the arms back as well, upsettingly opposite to the direction it was meant to be. Again, *crack,* and a howl from the victim, guttural and shrieked. More bones escaped the cage of flesh to join the host of Heaven. And even if the angel screamed, there must've been something pleasurable about it, about the release, the escape from skin.

The winner faced an adoring crowd.

Lucifer finally saw him well. He was indeed brunette, but a shade removed from black and tousled in curls that fell past the nape of his neck. His skin was brown as bronze, kissed by a handful of darker specs — like he were a mountain itself with touches of a wildfire's ravage. The hooded eyes — those were hazel, but only between the soil browns and leafy greens. And no, there aren't words for the full of his lips, or even the hill on his nose bridge; there are words, but they begin to fail, they become repetitious. He was tall, mountainous again, and broad everywhere; this mountain of an angel.

Lucifer's heart had returned to his chest. Here, it swelled and invaded his blood, as the angels were rushing the stadium, cheering, "Michael, Michael, Michael!" And the winner met them with a great bout of laughter, his grip leaving the mangle he'd left of his opponent.

There are some that can be described forever — each strand of hair, every line on a knuckle — and surely, Lucifer could have seen himself doing that, even now. This was his, this is our, first drunkenness. This heat in his face, this rush; he was leaning forward, breaths refusing him. Lucifer uttered it delicately, feeling his lips shape around the name and tasting honey sweetness, "Michael, Michael, Michael."

A laugh. It turned the angel's head to catch Rosier eyeing him with a silly smile and tilted head; Phanuel had disappeared, maybe having flown into the arena like so many others. He said, "Don't bother, brother." He got to his feet and nodded at the redhead, who was now being helped to sit by Michael. "He has to go take that angel to Raphael or one of the lesser healing angels. And then everyone will want to invite him to eat." He paused, appearing to remember the extent of Lucifer's youth. "He's an archangel."

"Archangel," Lucifer repeated before, in his head, whispering it again, again. 'Archangel Michael, Archangel Michael, Archangel Michael.' He sought to gather himself, but he was lost, slipping through his own fingers. "He looks like the greatest of them all, the strongest and proudest angel in Heaven!"

CHAPTER 7

I n Heaven, there were a few angels of honey, who went about meticulously collecting the nectar of flowers before bringing the small vials to a building they shared with those that prepared sugar. From the nectar, the angels used thin needles to knit out the honey, only then to gather the sunlight-seeming dribble into crystal jars. Lucifer had a few times followed behind and ducked behind fences, curiously watching them work, each one with his own stitching pattern, each offering up different honeys, different flavors.

Licking soft lips, remembering this, the angel of beauty held a woven sack of pink cacti fruits and stared at the prickled green pads of a cactus bursting a flower from its head. It was rather tapered, pointing upward in red-magenta, yellow stamens barely peeking through, eyeing the angel. Blinking in response, Lucifer felt his hand drawn out, tugged toward the petals, soft as the tips of his fingers brushed them, filtered through them — thinking of nectar. The softness was, first, welcoming, but the cacti soon stirred from its sleep and launched itself at the angel, who startled backward in fear but far too late.

He later found himself over the water basin of his home — needle-thin thorns staring back at him from his fingers.

For hours, Rosier had sat with him, sighing, trying to pick them out, but Lucifer's impatience made him frown and huff at once before leaving his side. He danced damaged fingers over the ripples of water, instead, coaxing with words, little pleas for help. But he was not the angel of water, nor the angel of fruit, nor the one of honey — he remained scarred.

Asmodeus had arrived — must've let himself in — and leaned against the doorway, arms crossed. "Well, there are two options. You speak to Raphael, or you bury yourself in some dirt and hope the roots of a tree tear you to a thousand pieces." As was common, the alleged angel of friendship was hardly clothed — a maroon robe barely tied together at his waist.

Lucifer furrowed his brows. "If I go to Raphael, I'll faint from embarrassment. It's better I stay here and argue with the water."

"Then burying yourself it is?" Asmodeus teased, but soon enough, Rosier appeared at his side — the final angel who took Lucifer's concerns seriously.

"You can try going to the bathhouse. The water there is..." Rosier sighed. "Don't make that face." Looking directly into the mirror over the basin, Lucifer faced his own grimace. "I can go with you."

"If I must, I'd rather go alone." Lucifer had spent all his time alive so far avoiding the bathhouses. "I know I'm being ridiculous." It was frustrating — knowing your emotions were erratic but that knowledge not making them leave you. "I'm not so young anymore either." Every angel has this embarrassing moment: when they start saying this phrase far too early. "I should go." Though, Lucifer feared being stared at. His face was one thing, but a naked body was another — even he couldn't stand so much as accidentally glancing at it when he washed himself.

He always did it in this room he was currently in, with just some of the soaps he'd been gifted, a towel, and a pumice stone. Once, Rosier had tried to convince him to simply go to the bathhouse, because Lucifer continually left puddles they had to mop, before they discussed the issue in length and Rosier had sympathized enough to stop pressuring him. That, of course, didn't stop him from sighing to himself whenever he caught Lucifer waddling his way to the basin with a basket full of trinkets.

The angel of fruit held in his eyes a delicate, pitiful look. "Are you certain, brother?"

Lucifer laughed but couldn't fight his frown. "I know I can't keep this up forever." He would certainly live forever, after all. "Can you tell me where to go?"

Asmodeus was the one who gave him directions, as Rosier went to Lucifer's room nearby, got on the tips of his toes beside one of the many towers of gifts — still, Lucifer hadn't arranged everything — then returned with an unused large, thick towel. Lucifer, meanwhile, heard where the bathhouse was, not too far, and wondered how Rosier had gotten lucky to live somewhere so convenient. He took the towel from his housemate with a soft breath, reasoning it might serve him well to leave the house, regardless.

Lucifer left them and, not surprisingly, heard the beginnings of an overdramatic argument between his friends as he shut the front door behind him. An amused smile twirled his lips as he clutched his towel, comforted in the cotton against his thin fingers, even if the spines on them dug in harsher. He willed himself to walk the way he'd been told, meeting a crowd of large mushrooms crossing the road before him, though one of these great beings paused to wave its gills at the youngest angel, who flushed rosily and waved back.

The building — Lucifer came upon it with his usual nerves beginning to return, tingling like there were bells beneath his skin; it was composed of painted marble, upheld by bulked pillars, chiseled into complex contours at their peaks. In most respects, the bathhouse was still rather simple, except for a dozen statues — of animals the angel didn't yet know — the way in. There was a front door, beat out from gold, that a stranger had just held open for someone without arms, but when he saw Lucifer, he smiled and gestured invitingly.

Whispering a word of thanks, Lucifer nodded and climbed up some steps, then moved inside.

He caught the earthy colors of a mosaic floor first, depicting what appeared to be suns and, again, animals. Coolness on his bare feet, Lucifer felt the angel who'd let him inside brush past before his gaze flickered upward to note ten other angels in the narrow room. They reached for cubicles raised high over painted benches, where some sat, all chattering and laughing, their jewels rattling as they removed them — all in various states of undress. Instantly, Lucifer clutched the towel to his front and pivoted to look away, but the other side of the room was no different, and now fire rushed his face, heating him until he was sure he was reddening like forging metals. He scampered, then, to a corner, shoulders tensing tight, all his breathing having left him so suddenly.

'Did they see me? Are they seeing me now? Will they tease me?' He glanced back, tried not to be so obvious. Most of the angels were too concerned with passionate conversation to notice him and others were walking past an archway, a mouth leading deeper into the building. Some of them held a towel still, but there were others who stood as naked as creation.

One angel met Lucifer's gaze, then turned and whispered into the ear of another.

The youngest angel turned downward to stare at his feet with widening eyes, as he racked his brain for something to do. 'Regret, regret, this is regret,' he named the itch of feeling, stirred up from his belly, coiling his spine. All Lucifer could do was exhale, slow. He set his towel down on the bench, then took a hold of his robes; with trembling fingers, still pinpricked and stinging with thorns, he pulled. They slid from his shoulders, and then the rest of his body, simply enough — all there was to do was untie the golden string at his hips. Left in an embroidered tunic — the same one Father had him dressed in on the day of his making — Lucifer pulled it over his head, careful as if he were deposing himself of a crown. Immediately, he reached for the towel, draped it long over one shoulder to try and cover his front and back.

Then, his jewelry rattled, reminding Lucifer of its company.

He wore so much of it, hanging from his ears and his neck, but also from his wrists and his upper arms, his waist, tight, and his thighs and his ankles. They were even in his cloud of hair and over his head, around his fingers. It would take ages to remove it all, but he wasn't keen to hurry to where the bath might be, so he dragged on this moment excruciatingly, dreadfully. Every adornment came off — Lucifer unclasped, pulled, yanked, then organized it all on a cubicle above until all that was left were his filigree earrings. There was no choice but to continue forward, after that. Being without his gems, however, felt infinitely more vulnerable, and Lucifer hugged his towel close, adjusted it, breathing slow.

Head lowered, trying not to tremble, he walked past the angels who'd whispered of him; there were gazes on his back, like hands, like nails scratching at his skin and asking to peek beneath.

The next room was wet, hot, dense steam radiating from the ground and the walls, carrying with it the grapple of a thousand fragrances interlaced. Like the undressing area, there was mosaic, though much more ornate. The ceiling carried with it sweeping, overlapped paintings of figures among nebulae, a story of angels and stars, but unorganized, formless, like a written epic that was only fragments now — perhaps, that was exactly what it was, but Lucifer didn't ponder this, looking instead for somewhere to sit. It was difficult; this room was much rowdier than the last. Angels were reclined upon benches or the ground, joking and talking about every mundane, meaningless thing there was. Hundreds of oil flasks, on low tables, were scattered along the length of the space, angels often reaching for one, or maybe a few, before slathering their bodies in them, some even smoothing it onto their wings.

By the entrance, Lucifer settled on the damp floor with his legs crossed, still hiding himself with his towel. He tried to avoid looking, really did. He tried and tried.

There was one angel near to him, humming delicately, as he ran a hand up from his opposite wrist to bicep, which was toned and taut, nearly as taut as his waist. Unlike Lucifer, he carried on with no shame, as if he didn't know he were naked at all. He shifted attention to his shapely, curved thighs, rubbing oil there as well, something earthy. When he lifted his head, and Lucifer hastily ripped his gaze away, he asked a friend to help with his back. Lucifer reached for the flask closest to him, unscrewed the top, then tilted his wrist so the clear, maybe lightly golden, oil fell onto his other hand. A soft, rumble of a groan. Lucifer glanced up, before he could stop himself, and saw the same angel smiling as his friend massaged the stiff muscles of his upper back.

There — a sweet taste on his tongue, in his body itself, umbilical almost, lightened Lucifer's head like water turned steam. He shifted where he was and felt a weight settle on his chest, ribs creaking. Eyes falling shut, he tried to thoughtlessly coat himself in slippery oil, holding a subdued lavender scent. But, even blind, he saw the bodies of the others, he heard the tiny huffs of pleasure and leisure, and he grimaced at the hands of the herbal smells taking and drowsing him.

Wondering why he'd ever thought it was a good idea to come here, Lucifer sensed a stare again, shot his eyes open, and he turned — saw an angel in the middle of stretching, standing up at his side. The angel smiled, pleasantly, not at all aware of the pain boiling Lucifer from the inside. "Are you alright?" he asked. He made no attempt to hide himself, so Lucifer settled his gaze on his chest, but it was supple. "Do you need help? You're very beautiful—"

Breaths all sprinting away — "No, I'm okay, but thank you, thank you—" Lucifer scrubbed himself fast, feeling the cuts of thorns cry out but caring little. He finished and stood, wrapped in his wet-now towel, then clambered between the angels lounging, a few who chuckled, confused at him. But past the next archway, he came onto the main section of the bathhouse, a great atrium where there was only light bearing down, shimmering onto, a grandiose crystalline pool, overborne with fifty angels at least.

This room made the last seem quiet — joining the clamor of talk, there were musicians sitting at the edges of the water, fingering their instruments and singing so lovely, in the tilts of their annunciations, their little rhymes, it made Lucifer stumble. A few angels were even eating, though nothing more than simple finger food not likely to make a mess, while others drank liquor that they passed around in chalices — all this in between the washing, which was done with refined soaps and scrubs. Cleaning, here, treated like it was celebration; and maybe it was — a festival for the broken cradle of Lucifer's heart.

But, he couldn't turn back. Lucifer held his towel, frowning, listening to his feet padding against wet marble — *pat, pat* — as he made his way around the pool, by shaded colonnades, coiled by vines and their berries. Searching for a desolate corner and coming upon a lonely section by a muraled wall, he crouched, then sat. He quickly removed his towel, leaving it by the edge, and slipped in. Gasping, shuddering — warmth embraced his body everywhere, shaped around him, squeezing. An exhale teetered out of him, but it was in loose pleasure. In one of the shallower parts of the pool, he could touch the ground easily and feel the water come up to his waist, but that was hardly a blessing.

Lucifer tried to avert his gaze away and did, but his thoughts remained on the bodies he'd just seen. 'Beautiful,' he thought miserably, 'they're beautiful.'

On the matter of bodies, it's easier to state all the things angels aren't — undone, unbecoming, unsightly. They had the figures of a hand's work — God's hand — on where they could be defined — lines of muscle — but ever more prominently on their soft touches, whether they were built tougher or lither or heavier. Each eye like it had been finely painted, and all their wet hair falling in drenched straightness or curled around their faces, necks, shoulders. Every movement quite perfect, elegant, like watching clouds drift upon the surface of their sky. Free from their mouths came little huffs of air, like lost gusts of wind. And their fingers, the brief drags of them on their skin — like the trickles of rain on earth.

Lucifer's eyelids were weighing down; the oils of the angels had filled the room with a sleepy aroma that had him rock in place. The lull of singing didn't help; Lucifer, who was facing the wall and praying no one took note of him, glanced over, intending to watch the musicians. He saw, instead, water rolling in beads down the shape of bodies, glistening, tracing the arc of their backs. He saw droplets, gathered at their eyelashes, dripping down their faces, stumbling past plump lips.

"Lucifer!"

Jumping, stumbling, the youngest angel wanted to cover himself, but there was no time. Baal had hopped down onto the pool right beside him, splashing the other, making him yelp. "Ah!"

"Oh, forgive me!" Baal rose from the surface, grinning, then shaking his head so the curls sprung water out every which way. "But I've never seen you here before. Do you go to the other baths, usually?"

Lucifer nearly burst into tears, though it had been a while since he did that, at the water's devastating clarity. Even if he hid himself, he would look silly; that knowledge, of course, didn't stop him. He turned his back on Baal and wished he could wrap his arms all around himself, and even attempted it. "I... usually bathe in my home. I've never been here." Baal's eyebrows raised; Lucifer sensed it. "I'm sorry." He wasn't sure why he apologized. "I feared that I would be stared at."

"For good reason." The water rippled as Baal presumably inched closer. "Even though I've seen you before, I'm still taken aback by your beauty, and nakedness... does add to that, I suppose."

Lucifer tried not to stare, again he tried, but his mind was a wooden room where a candle had just been knocked over. Clenching terror drew his attention up Baal's form, from what he could see through the water, to his abdomen, to his chest, to his face. His shoulders rising and falling in stutters, water was almost steaming around him, he knew his face was rosy. It was all too much, all falling over him — the angels, the smells, the soap suds. Was this desire? Desire for what? Desire to return home and be stored away in a chest never to be seen or touched?

"Are you okay, Lucifer?"

"Yes— Yes, I am."

"You're staring at me strangely," but then Baal chuckled, "and you seem to be having trouble breathing."

"I'm not sure," Lucifer answered. "I would just like to bathe." He could feel they'd drawn a bit of attention, so he looked, noticed there were indeed a handful of angels who stared, who stared at Lucifer. Hurried, they turned away but murmured to each other. What were they saying? They kept glancing back, looking at him, taking him in — in where? In their hands. Their mouths moved; Lucifer read them: 'Over there is the angel of beauty, take a look at his body, see how the Lord made him, his hair, his hands, he reminds me of a rose, but thorns are prickling my eyes.'

Baal spoke again, softer, "I see." When Lucifer faced him again, he saw a tiny smile. "You're uncomfortable." Lucifer's shoulders slacked, just a little — the joy of a person naming your troubles. "I can help you wash quickly, then we can leave."

Lucifer swallowed, feeling as if a stone traveled down his throat. "Thank you, but there's more than that. I have some thorns, in my hands—" He tried to raise them from the water, but one by one, the bristles began to fall away, right before the both of them. "Oh."

Blinking in surprise, then in awe, Lucifer whispered, "Never mind, then." He heard the other laugh once more.

'You're making yourself suffer,' Lucifer scolded himself, 'and why?'

Baal, as promised, helped him wash, rubbing soap into his muscles with gentle digs and strokes, and Lucifer's fever lingered, but the uncoiling tension was nonetheless sweet. It unraveled him, teased him loose into unfurling like a blooming flower. "I," Lucifer said quietly, "listened in on these angels the other day." He'd been visiting Asmodeus, handing him a couple raspberries wrapped in a handkerchief and laughing when the older one said Lucifer looked a bit like a raspberry himself; a red scarf was over his head. "They were saying something about Earth..." He'd heard the loud gossip from around a corner.

Baal stepped away, hum dancing from his lips. "Oh, you've never been, have you?" He patted Lucifer's shoulder. "It's difficult to describe but," a pensive pause, "it's a place our Father creates life in." But there was life in Heaven already. Why create more somewhere else? "I haven't been in a while."

The youngest angel nodded. "Thank you." 'God lives there, on Earth,' he reasoned in his head. 'He has a house there.' He said, "Thank you, Baal, for helping, but I'll be leaving now."

"Of course. Will you let me walk you home?"

Baal seemed very sweet; Lucifer considered he'd like to be around this angel some more. Smiling — "I would like that." After they exited the pool and dried off, they walked together to the dressing room, where they pulled on their clothing and accessories wordlessly. And it was only after Lucifer had placed all his jewelry back on that he felt at ease again. 'It's nakedness,' he told himself. 'That's the problem. I'm averse to nudity.' Once the two had begun down the road, Lucifer mumbled, "Baal, you said you'd been to Earth?"

"A few times, at archangel Michael's direction." Michael — that had been the angel at the fight, the strongest angel. "I remember, I think, three thousand years ago, I got swarmed by beasts. It was terrifying, but it was exciting too."

"How can I go to Earth?"

Baal pursed his lips, then crossed his arms. "You'd have to ask an archangel."

This question was harmless, nothing but curiosity: "What if I wanted to be an archangel?"

The angel of flight laughed, but in surprise. "You'd like to be a prince, brother? But you're so beautiful; it's hard to imagine other angels taking you seriously." Lucifer's simple smile wilted into a frown; maybe Baal noticed, maybe he did not. "But don't worry, Lucifer. I can tell the Lord has great plans for you. Looking at you — I can feel His mercy."

CHAPTER 8

" I have an idea." Lucifer was sprawled over the couch, his head over Rosier's lap. The latter angel was learning to embroider, humming thoughtfully as he threaded oranges and reds through a beige fabric, creating the lines of limbs, four of them, and then a body with a bushed tail. A fox, a creature Lucifer didn't know, whom he figured to have been thought up by angels — one of many earthly souls the divine can only dream of.

Lucifer wasn't doing much personally, playing with his own robes and resting after a longer day of work, and his friend answered, "What's this idea, brother?" Lucifer said he would visit Earth. "Earth?" Rosier stopped his work, though didn't put it down, before letting out a breath, slow until it became a sigh. "Lucifer." It wasn't a harsh inflection, which Rosier seemed perfectly incapable of, but it was firm. "I heard the Lord asked us not to visit so often anymore." Lucifer asked why. "I'm not sure. I didn't ask, but Azazel mentioned it was because angels wouldn't stop fighting the bloodthirsty beasts there."

Bloodthirsty — Lucifer had never heard a word like this; he picked it apart literally, thinking of filling a wine glass with blood and sipping. Would it drunken him, too? A frown forming, not quite liking the direction of his thoughts, he said, "Baal told me that he went with one of the princes. If I befriend an archangel, then he would let me, wouldn't he?" It would definitely be easier than asking God, who was so good He would surely say yes, but He was nowhere to be found.

Rosier furrowed his brow, in what was nearly worry. "Brother, you can't befriend someone only because you want something out of them."

"That's not what I mean." A pout settled itself onto Lucifer's lips, then a huff as he shifted to sit up beside his friend. "You know all I can think about is Earth, so why shouldn't I be allowed to go? Maybe it's what the Lord made me for. Maybe I'd be helpful there." There, in God's house, on Earth; he could worship Him there. "Or," Lucifer added because the blinking expression of his friend was unsettling, "do you suggest I shouldn't?" Rosier looked about to speak, before the sharp sound of shattering plates — the distinctive crack of porcelain — turned both their heads.

Asmodeus emerged from the kitchen soon thereafter, his hands settled on his hips, a purse to his mouth, thick brows scrunched together. He blinked, looking at the two. "I think someone broke a few plates."

"*Someone?*" Rosier scoffed. "Is this 'someone' named Asmodeus?"

"Well, he might be. I'll have to do some investigation."

"I'm rather certain it was Asmodeus."

"Have you asked him? Perhaps, you ought to have more faith in your old friend. You two stay there. I'll look for the culprit—"

"Wait," Lucifer said quickly. "Asmodeus, you're the angel of friendship."

"Oh?" Asmodeus said, as if he hadn't known.

"Yes," replied Lucifer. "Are you friends with any archangels?"

"Raphael is a good friend," Asmodeus answered. "But I'm not close with the others."

Rosier finally set down his work, perhaps in exasperation. "Lucifer, there's nothing wrong with befriending an archangel, so long as you don't expect anything in return. I don't think there's any problem with you going to Earth, either, but archangels are busy. You shouldn't distract them from their duties to our Father."

"I'd like to be Uriel's friend," Lucifer told them; he had schemed this all already, his first scheme. "He seems lonely." This was in comparison to Michael. The archangel. Lucifer had snuck into wrestling and other sport matches a copious amount of times, partly for the violence, and the wonder of its healing, and partly to admire the hands doing the harm. Michael, built like a fortress, who stood tall like one, too. "I—" Lucifer thought of the last time he, in the midst of trying to cheer the loudest, saw the chief prince, face kissed in blood that wasn't his own, a perfect smile peeking through. "I want him to relax."

Rosier, worry slipping into amusement, replied, "Are you really the angel to be telling others to relax?" Lucifer flushed at Asmodeus' rowdy laughter, but he'd made the decision already. He hadn't seen Uriel since that day in the observatory, all that time ago, but the memory of his voice was crystalline — the monotone, the flat reverb — and so was the way he hadn't mentioned Lucifer's beauty, not once. It had become another fixation, then, for him to seek out Uriel. The last hundred repetitive, beautiful days, he'd spent arranging this new desire — though one could argue all of Lucifer's desires were really the same desire. Uriel could take him to Earth, Uriel could introduce him to Michael, Uriel could bring him to God.

Angels cannot be devious, but they come close. Lucifer was giggling to himself, some other time, as he filled a basket, with sourdough bread and wine grapes, and planned to bring his timbrel and pipes, too — all to try and seem as amicable as possible. When he left, he wore a scarf over his hair and smiled with a modest bow when any angels approached. He asked, a bit nervously — nervous despite having come up with a script of all the likely responses he'd get — "Have you seen Uriel?" Each time, angels looked between each other curiously or called out to a friend at the other side of the street; always, angels answered that they didn't know.

Lucifer thanked them, then continued on his way. He flew, he walked, he traveled through a good portion of the city, becoming frustrated with its consistent rearranging and asking himself if he'd already walked certain streets or if they were working against him. Reaching a bridge — by then, it had been hours — Lucifer finally groaned in surrender, stopping at the highest point to look over the edge at a river beneath. The surface was clear enough that he could see straight to the pebbled bed, along with the bundles of fish, who traveled in waves of white, orange, black, carrying along with them their favorite small trinkets that angels had dropped into the river.

The youngest angel watched them, smiling at the sight of a fish held tight by its ruby necklace, before reaching into his basket and retrieving a sliced piece of bread. When the water shuddered in fight, Lucifer quickly reassured it, "It's for the fish!" Plucking off some tiny pieces, tossing them down — not long after, the animals rushed to devour the gift, knocking one another, bumping, even biting. Lucifer stared curiously until a few of the fish poked their heads out of the water to look back at him.

"Oh, the fish are pretty," sighed a caramel voice beside him.

"I know," Lucifer replied. "I could watch them forever." He turned just as the stranger moved to lean over the safety wall.

He was about the same height as Lucifer, with pale skin and pecan brown waves of hair. The eyes on him were wide, smoking gray, and he had a button nose, dotted with the same freckles that were tossed along all of him not concealed by a thick, golden-embroidered — much more elaborate designs than what Rosier had been doing — robe. It fell to his ankles, right above bare feet, which carried, too, some of his jewelry — chains that cradled soft-colored stones. And there were white lilies all in his hair, petals touched by a passing breeze. His smile was toothy — "I could too. Can I have some bread to feed the fish with you?"

"Oh," Lucifer inexplicably flushed, "of course." He took another slice and broke the bread in half before handing the larger portion to the stranger.

The angel thanked him, then tore his piece into smaller bunches before scattering some into the river below as Lucifer had done. "I didn't know they liked bread so much." The fish ravaged. "I should have guessed. You see, one of my closest friends adores fish, but I've never taken the time to learn anything about them. It makes me feel so rude— Oh, I'm being rude right now, aren't I?" Lucifer dropped his piece to the water before quickly trying to deny it, but the angel waved a now bread-less hand. "My apologies. They call me Gabriel."

"A beautiful name for a beautiful angel." Something about it sounded familiar, but Lucifer couldn't be sure.

Gabriel laughed. "You must be the angel of flattery. You're the beautiful one. Lucifer, right?"

Lucifer had just brought the last piece of bread to his mouth to chew briefly, then swallow, before he jumped. "You know my name?" Gabriel nodded. "How is that?"

"I think most of Heaven knows of you these days, brother." Gabriel turned and leaned his back against the wall. "That said, I'm always by this bridge yet I've never seen you. Are you lost? Have you come to the west seeking something?"

"Someone, actually. Uriel — do you know where he is?"

"I do! Maybe. Uriel does nothing but work."

Perking up — "Oh, are you his friend?"

Gabriel laughed another time, the sound making its way out of his mouth like bells. "I like to think so. Do you really need to speak with him? I can lead you to his home, though that's all the way in the north. He might not be there now, but he does go and sleep, allegedly."

"In the north?" Lucifer sighed some, realizing how lost he was. "You don't have to lead me. I'll try to find it on my own."

"No, I wanted to get to know you anyway." Lucifer's face grew warmer. "But is it alright if we walk? My wings are tired from traveling through the stars for so long."

"The stars?"

Gabriel, gesturing upward, told him of a galaxy, composed of clusters of coppery red. He said he'd jumped from one moon to the other, his feet leaving deep craters, on the way to a planet, which he'd grabbed with both hands before flying off to place it around the proper star. By then, Lucifer and Gabriel had begun to walk, begun to chatter relentlessly as angels do, and every now and then, a few strangers would approach, but Gabriel always ushered them away so that the two could continue uninterrupted. There was a pleasant flutter in Lucifer's chest at the gesture; Gabriel made him feel like he was interesting, which Lucifer had never really thought of himself as — unfortunately beautiful, clumsy, and naive, yes, but never compelling.

Gabriel described each of the infinite celestial bodies above them in all their fiery, rocky, misty massiveness, and they talked about little meaningless things, as well:

"I like the white lilies in your hair."

"Thank you! I like them too. White lilies symbolize purity, they say."

"What is purity?"

"Not sure! I suppose that symbolizes something too."

Lucifer frowned. "That's a bit confusing, isn't it?"

"Well, Father is very complicated about the nature of things."

"I wish we could ask why things are the way they are." He said these words carefully, prepared to be told to simply live and stop asking so many things, to close his mouth, to beat the timbrel God had placed on him as just another decoration. An adornment for the adornment.

Instead, Gabriel whistled a tiny tune as they walked an upward path, then said, "Well, you can try."

"How?" Lucifer listened idly to the jingling of his timbrel, sitting snug in the basket hanging from his inner elbow; it was laughing at him. "Not to say that I'm worthy, but I'd like to know where He is."

A startlingly straight-forward answer: "Sometimes our Father sits at His Throne, sometimes He's in Eden. He hasn't come to Heaven in a million years."

"A million years?" Lucifer's heart grew heavier, heavier. "Why?" Did He not like Heaven? Perhaps, did He not love it anymore?

Gabriel shrugged. "Maybe you could ask Him, if you ever run into the Lord along the streets."

Lucifer remembered all the ways in which he wasn't worthy, all his mistakes; they flooded into his mind and made him flinch. "I'd be embarrassed to stand before our Father in the state I'm in, brother." He hadn't meant to say that, but he kept speaking, not sure why, "I'm ashamed of myself. Every time I wake, I look upon my reflection, and I ask who I am, and I never know what to say. My name is Lucifer — that's all that I know. I know what the Lord dressed me in and what He handed to me, and inside, I can feel the detail He put into me." These whistles between his words, these beautiful things inside him. "And yet, I'm lost. I want to know what He made me for, so that I can uphold His splendor," he wanted purpose, Lord, he wanted purpose, "but I don't know. I don't know anything at all."

Ahead, there was a gray limestone building with a particularly high peak, composed of pointed arches holding up a vaulted ceiling and mullioned windows, sliced into shapes, variously colored to portray faces, stars, plants, flames, and eyes, most prominently — infinite irises and pupils. The most notable window sat above the great double-door entrance: a large, circular structure crafted from hundreds of panes pressed together. And those swirls and twists carved on the grayed walls — Lucifer's head spun trying to comprehend them. He saw, also, the curved details, minuscule, built into the doors — could only breathe in shock.

Gabriel spoke: "Brother, I hear your worries." His voice was warm, almost physically so, as if he were a quilt coming over your shoulders. "Would you like to step into the cathedral for a bit?"

'Cathedral?' "What will we do in there? What is this place for?"

"It's to worship in, to ponder, to meditate, to speak to Father."

"Will He hear us better in there?"

"He can hear us anywhere, but it's nice to have a place dedicated to it. Come along." Gabriel walked ahead, and Lucifer thought to remind him that they'd been on their way to Uriel's home. With this, he also fought the urge to tell Gabriel he'd changed his mind, about everything; with horror, he realized he'd wailed about his troubles to a stranger. Lucifer frowned, opened his mouth, but the other angel was already stepping past the ajar doors. With no other choice — following after him, holding his breath in his mouth.

As they moved from the west end into the central nave, Lucifer stared up at the ceilings, held by exceptionally wide pillars, coming together into peaks that looked even higher from the inside. Many of those columns twisted into pointed arches that divided the nave from rooms off to the sides — north and south transepts — and between the ceiling and the arches were two sectional rows. The highest contained windows, the clerestory, beaming in light far above eye level, but tainted by the colors of the glass, so that the brightness bathed them in rose reds, blues, greens. The second row was a gallery, its settings engraved with some floral aspects, generally wide and spacious enough Lucifer figured he could go stand there if he wished; with a blink, he noticed there was one such angel there already, basked in lapis lazuli from a window, sweeping where he walked.

There was a more circular section at the head of the building, but it was empty. As he looked through the aisles, walking behind Gabriel, Lucifer noticed that, apart from the golden seats, settled on a marble floor, everything was quite desolate. There were a few scattered angels, and there were candles, in their brazen holdings, but nothing else. It gave the cathedral the impression of a façade — all the decor of a place of worship, sitting empty of holy objects and blessed souls.

Gabriel spoke in a whisper, "Shall we sit?" He had been leading him to one of the pews, steps echoing off the floor, and stopped beside it with a gentle smile.

Lucifer thought of prayer. He couldn't remember who it was now, perhaps a stranger at a gathering, but someone had told him that angels were supposed to worship through prayer often. They didn't do it often, but when they longed for things — they prayed. And they longed for things often.

"Oh," the young angel breathed. "I suppose so." The air of the room was thin; he found himself struggling to reel it in as he sat, then shifted so Gabriel could settle at his side.

"You sound like you have many troubles, brother. Forgive me — I had to mull it over. I didn't want to give you a bad response."

"You didn't need to give me a response at all," Lucifer replied, nearly grimacing. "I didn't mean to tell you all that."

"But I'm happy you did. Lucifer, does it really hurt you not to know what you were made for?"

"It does," the angel said truthfully, because he had no choice. "All the others seem to know how they should worship God, but I feel like a disgrace to Him. They call me the angel of beauty, and maybe it's so, but then what do I do? Lay over a carpet, eat grapes, and let all of Heaven set their eyes on me? I can't; it doesn't feel right." He allowed his head to droop forward so that he stared down at the basket he'd planted over his lap. "Should I pray that He gives me an answer? Or do you think the Lord is unsatisfied with me?"

There was hesitance, then — "I remember when you were created, Lucifer. I saw how our Father sewed you from coppers, how He handled you when you were burning coals and when you were settings of gold. He embroidered a nose on you, a sweet mouth on you, then the outline for a pair of eyes before He placed suns there. He sculpted your face with wet clay; He opened you like a citrus and planted a garden of budding flowers inside. Then, He weaved your hair from the streaks of three stars and your wings out of four wandering crescent moons." He breathed but was not finished: "And your hips — those came the tides of a sea, the same one whose pearls He took to carve your feet and hands. There was so much jade, so much marble; He fit it into the last places you were hollow. When He was done, I watched Him breathe life into you, then cradle you as if you were His first angel, before He settled you into fire and let you simmer." Gabriel gasped and took his arm. "No, don't cry, Lucifer!"

Voice wobbling, teetering over an edge — "You say all those things, then expect me to hold myself together? I feel like I—" He sniffed, reached to wipe an eye with the back of his hand, but soon enough the burn streamed from his cheeks to jaw. Hoarse, a gasp dropped from his mouth, having scorched its way out of him. "You say all those things, and now I feel like I'm falling."

"Falling?"

"Falling from up above, from Andromeda." He hugged the basket in his hands and felt shivers rock him. "Falling because the weight of your words is too much, it's too much. I think I'll burst like a star."

"You *are* a star, brother," Gabriel teased, then took Lucifer's face in a palm, swiped away a tear with his other hand. "Father told me. He said, 'Look at my morning star. My Lucifer.'"

Lucifer saw it: the Lord kissing his face, calling him His. "Gabriel," escaped his lips, "you were really there when Father created me?"

"I was." Gabriel grinned wide. "I'm an archangel, didn't you know?" Lucifer's heart stopped, eyes widened, mortification turned him red. All the effort he put Gabriel through to find Uriel, but a prince had been before him the entire time. "I fed you the fruit of Life, then the one of Knowledge. I'm happy to see you again. The way God spoke of you, I always knew you were going to be special. You're wise, Lucifer, and blameless in all your ways. And you are so beautiful, I can't find the words."

"Thank you, Gabriel. Thank you, thank you." Lucifer trembled, wanting to throw himself at this angel and embrace him tight. "You must be the angel of kindness."

"I'm not," the prince laughed. "But you could be. I think it'd suit you. And, between us, I think you're much more than the angel of beauty, brother. I hope you figure it out soon and see that you're right where you belong." Lucifer belonged, here, in Heaven. "God has great plans for you, you'll see, but I ask you stay modest. Stay humble."

"Yes," Lucifer answered, not feeling his mouth, not sure he'd said it. "I promise." His happiness was too much.

Then, Gabriel leaned forward and planted a gentle, friendly kiss on Lucifer's cheek. "Let's leave now, shall we?"

"Of course, brother."

CHAPTER 9

Mﬤ ore time passed, breezing along with the leaves. The
Lucifer whom you've come to know so intimately could
now smile a bit easier and sit on tree branches in groves,
napping and fiddling with his hair and sighing dreamily. He could pick
fruit without any tussling with plants, and he eventually convinced
Rosier to run a booth in the bazaar. He could dance, though his limbs
were still a bit too stiff, and he tapped his feet too quick, and he got the
rhythms wrong. But these imperfections were adored by Lucifer, who
knew he'd grieve the day, soon, that he mastered to dance and would
have to find something else to learn. He'd grown to understand those
angels who gathered wondrously by any leaf that stumbled onto the
never-changing roads and thought, 'This little thing, this little irregu-
larity, this little miracle.'

Make no mistake: Lucifer heeded Gabriel's advice, above all. When
compliments came, the young angel lowered his head and said, "Thank
you, but it's the work of our God." He continued to cover himself,
visited the bathhouses when they had the least amount of angels, and
he sat in the darkest corners of rooms, so as to not distract others from
their labors through his mere appearance. The angels who saw him
must've thought this was the end of Lucifer, the end of his growth —
thought this angel would be a sweet soul who didn't know his own

beauty for eternity. Indeed, had it been any other angel, the story might've ended here.

But, when no one saw him, Lucifer went out looking for Uriel again, twelve separate times.

If nothing else, he was persistent — traveling to the furthest northern point of Heaven, searching among the mountains of pink limestone for a hand-hewn, fantastical house — Uriel's. Near it, there were various other buildings carved, hollowed, into the great towers of rock bursting through the sandy ground, many of which were the homes of angels who greeted Lucifer each time he walked past. The youngest wondered what they considered of him — though he would find out soon — coming so often to the house of hefty pillars and statues at the end of the path. The gilded door was always shut; the etchings of twinkling stars upon it always said, "He is not here," or "He wants to be alone."

"Please," Lucifer always sighed. "Let me in. I want to be his friend."

One of Uriel's neighbors, one day, told an angel about Lucifer's strangeness, who told another one, who told Asmodeus, who stopped Lucifer midway on his final trip. Before Lucifer could even open his mouth, Asmodeus had put his arm around Lucifer's shoulders and turned them around. He began guiding him home, saying, "Let's go back, brother," and Lucifer realized that he was acting odd, acting different than the other angels, and there existed no greater horror. He knew his place now; he had to stay in place now.

"I'm sorry," he murmured, then leaned against his friend, who rubbed his back and kissed his hair. "I'll prepare some tea, once we're back. If you're not too busy."

Lucifer found enjoyment in brewing tea, sweet lavender and chamomile, and he liked serving wine and working dough with his hands. He loved watering all the plants of his house, and he enjoyed wrapping himself in blankets, and he found that maybe being a simple, thoughtless adornment was not so bad. He avoided his reflection. He liked the friends he'd made, enjoyed having them over and talking and talking.

The fact that so much time had passed only surfaced in his mind when Gabriel came to visit one day. He hadn't seen him since that day in the cathedral. Lucifer instantly gasped, ushering him in, hurrying to prepare some butterfly pea flower tea, blue-purple, before bringing it out to the other. Gabriel accepted it, though said he would only be with him a moment. "You can't stay longer?" Lucifer frowned immediately. "I'd love to catch up."

Gabriel had a twirling smile on his face. "Another time. Today, I have a message."

"Oh?" Lucifer stepped back, watched Gabriel lift his cup and blow at the surface. "A message from who? Could it be?" His heart — already stuttering at the possibility.

"It is." Gabriel made a soft, amused noise. "Our Divine Lord sent me," and Lucifer was sure his blood was somehow leaving his body — with it, his soul, "to deliver the news that He wants you to visit His garden."

"Of course," Lucifer barely managed to say, was having difficulty standing upright. "But His garden? Where is Father's garden?"

The archangel sipped his tea, smacking his lips, then blinked in surprise. "Oh. That's good." He stared at it, drumming his fingers on the paint of the porcelain, as Lucifer thanked him quickly, softly. "Yes, well, I can take you as soon as you're ready."

Father. God. The God that had made Lucifer. "Now. I can go now —" No. He stopped himself, putting a hand on the warm robe he wore before realizing that wouldn't do. "Wait, give me some time to prepare —" He was stumbling backward, already, trying to remember what he'd worn on his first day living. It had been a tunic, but which one?

Gabriel hid another smile with a sip of his tea. "I'll wait here."

Lucifer sprinted. He barged into his room, threw open drawers and the wardrobe, and scampered to find what were most likely the clothes the Lord had dressed him in. He, also, rushed to use the basin to wash his face, then clean his body as best he could with soaps and a pumice stone. He talked to himself incessantly, rubbing rich, aromatic rosehip oils into his skin, feeling incredibly disgusted with it very suddenly and wanting to grab his flesh and remove it in a way he hadn't felt since he was an infant. And just as he considered crying, Rosier showed up at the open doorway.

Stammering, the angel of fruit said he'd spoken to Gabriel, and Lucifer nearly fell to his knees to praise the Lord for sending him help.

Rosier had Lucifer sit, then he ran a brush through his hair smoothly before collecting some sections from the front, twirling the strands around his fingers to give them a twist, before tying them back so that Lucifer's face was perfectly visible. "He spent so long making it," Rosier remarked, and it might've been a tease but his tone was too sincere, "I imagine He wants to see it well." He pinched Lucifer's cheeks to give them a natural blush before telling him to stand. Together, they layered on all the jewelry God had adorned him in, then they returned downstairs.

Gabriel had been waiting for more than an hour, but he said it was no problem as Lucifer doubled over in an apologetic bow.

There was nothing else to do, after this, but leave. Rosier bid him a sweet goodbye and good luck simply. And Lucifer, trembling as he walked, holding his own hands, tried to settle his breathing, which kept flapping about his chest. He swallowed, prayed quiet that all would turn out well; he prayed to God, though he knew this was an odd thing to pray to Him about — there was no one else to pray to. Gabriel led the way, walking along a series of paths that Lucifer wasn't too acquainted with, and in a pattern that he'd never tried. When the walls of Heaven, the open pearly gates, began to approach, Lucifer, anxious, scratched his front teeth against his lower lip.

"I'll leave you alone with Father."

Lucifer had a few times flown upwards into the universe, had wanted to go to Earth, but now he wondered if there was anything else past the walls — another city, another Heaven. He dropped his gaze to the golden road and saw it slowly consumed by cobblestone, in just patches initially, and then dirt. The tips of his fingers brushed one bar of the titanic gates, and it was smooth, cold and uninviting — an odd feeling to embrace what was paradise.

"And then I'll return for you once I feel the time is right." Gabriel looked back to him, a certain stream of light beginning to come in from outside Heaven and illuminating one side of his face, casting a flaming shadow on the rest of him. "How does that sound?" He smiled, as innocently as he always did.

Lucifer swallowed. "That's alright with me." He looked ahead and saw, now, soft whiteness invading the ground in batches, its consistency resembling steam. "Where is Father's garden?" In between this intruding material, there was blueness, not very different from a sea. He wondered if they'd climb onto a canoe soon.

"Between Heaven and Earth. We'll fly," Gabriel said, as if he'd heard Lucifer's inner musing. "It's not so hard, but don't get lost because I'm not a good scavenger, and don't fall because I'm not a good catcher." Lucifer laughed, quiet, before he watched Gabriel spring out his wings at the same time he jumped through a space between two clouds.

For once, Lucifer didn't hesitate. He dived into the sky, ushering his wings out to catch himself, and flapped — stared at the way his feet hung over the thin winds. Barely, he could see something miles below, some illusions of green. But he recuperated; he looked to Gabriel who was not far beneath, then smiled back. They traveled through the air, Lucifer not lagging behind much, as they shifted to just a hint beneath the clouds and glided. He kept looking below, recalling everything he'd heard about large creatures and fights and Earth, and he thought about asking Gabriel if they could take a detour, very quickly, for a slight moment, so that Lucifer could touch the soil and let himself be frightened by the beasts of legends.

But Lucifer knew better, by this point. He followed, swerving between the hanging limbs of yawning, tossing clouds, and didn't speak another word to Gabriel. Eventually, they came upon a collection of leaves, branches, flowers — this isle drifting along the open air above Earth.

The grass met Lucifer's feet, sharp and cool, as he fluttered his wings to slow, then pulled them back into his body. There was a little stumble, as he gained footing, but then he straightened up. And he inhaled, great, felt air rush past his lungs to splurge into his blood. The crisp of the green blades overwhelmed him, and as he spun around, taking in great, bountiful trees, his eyes growing wide, his mouth falling open. A noise of awe escaped Lucifer before he twisted to ask Gabriel about this place and about God. "Oh—" The archangel remained in the air. "You're leaving already?"

"Yes! Good luck, brother!"

"Thank you!" Lucifer waved high over his head just before the archangel beat his wings, strong, and shot upwards to disappear among the clouds. It was then that the youngest angel felt a brush against his ankle. Thinking it was just an attention-hungry flower, Lucifer cast his gaze down. What he saw was a furry, colorless creature so curled into itself that it had a rounded impression, and it was long-eared, sniffling and hopping — a bunny, a rabbit. There's no other way to describe it: Lucifer's heart combusted. He reached and scooped it into his arms, smiling great, so struck with tenderness and care at once — he almost went blind.

"Hello," he told it, thinking the animal would respond like an angel, before seeing it twitch its pink nose in response. And it did speak back, though its vocabulary was not particularly impressive — not that Lucifer could judge the rabbit for it, since he was still working on expanding his languages himself. It was while in conversation with this rabbit that other animals, plenty, began to venture out of the tiny, crowded city of nature.

Lucifer allowed the rabbit to hop away from him. Then, anxious in his fiddling hands, he went to a pair of deer, but relaxed as they instantly began speaking to him profusely. When he heard singing, he looked up to a batch of round, blue birds and complimented them with thrill; and a family of them swooped down, frightening him for half a second before laughter invaded; they grabbed his robe with their beaks and tugged him along deeper into the garden. Other creatures welcomed him, one by one, great and small ones alike. He was shown to a pond, where he greeted each fish individually, then sat with the frogs and listened to them chatter. Butterflies swarmed him next, urged him down another path, where he met bears, wolves, owls. Hummingbirds settled in his hair and bees gossiped into his ear.

Time — all of it was lost. Lucifer settled on mossy, flat boulders, introduced himself to all the living things in the garden and eventually felt a legged, slithering creature make its way up his ankle. He looked upon the snake, then smiled, moving to peel it off and carry it on his shoulders for as long he could. When the crows chattered to him, Lucifer wondrously told them they seemed much more intelligent than all the dutiful, though lovely, angels he knew, and they squawked in their laughs. Settling the snake atop a branch, he said hello to the spiders there. After that, he returned to the deer, for a while, before finding time to walk alongside tigers.

When he stumbled upon a vast field of flowers, he couldn't resist the urge to run to it. Lucifer flopped down, laying, tittering, as flowers nuzzled his body everywhere in an attempt to welcome him as the animals did. There were sweet purple bee balms, bearded irises, and hyacinths, and then sunny garden mums and daylilies, and vibrantly yellow marigolds; some soft pink geranium fought its way forward to flutter against his cheek in kisses. He rolled around in the warm affections of the flora, shut his eyes, let himself take in pleasure and feel it spread throughout his body. He breathed delightfully, smiling — thoughtless, consumed by happiness.

"You are enjoying Eden," came the voice of the Lord.

And, instantly, Lucifer shot up, eyes opened, as if he'd been sleeping. His Father didn't face him, but His being still overwhelmed the angel so much he had no choice but to get onto his knees and bend so his forehead touched the ground. He said, "Heavenly Father— Lord— How great the Lord is." Each word heavy, long like it dragged. "How great and powerful you are." Shivering, he crawled, upon the flowers first, then the grass, toward Him — lips finding the blades of green by His feet, not daring to get too close. He peppered kisses, this action coming naturally to him; kissing, kissing. "The Most High." Fumbling for words, all the syllables clambering over one another so it became incoherent drivel.

"It pleases me that you like the bed of flowers. I prepared it for you."

Rushed by a rage of emotion — emotion, emotion, emotion — "You are good and merciful, God Almighty." The blistering presence of power made his body seize up; he couldn't shift from his position even if he wished to. "I am not worthy to be here before you. Glory to you, glory to the bed of flowers." Something inside Lucifer, beside the burning ravaging him — something had just clicked right into place. He continued, whispered, "Praise be to you."

"Lift your face from the dirt," and quickly, Lucifer did, "face me so that I can see my creation."

"Yes, Father." The intensity was so much Lucifer trembled where he was. He averted his gaze and moved to sit on his knees, facing the Lord. He felt himself be examined, but it was nothing like how the angels did it: he felt enveloped in His authority, in flames so cold they began to burn. He couldn't help but keep moving, restless, his heart beating erratic and his vision hazy. And yet in a harsh instant, his breath disappeared; God had put His hand on him.

This was not mere flesh — the Lord's skin was feather-soft but blazed with all the heat of the universe still, sizzling, a vacuum pulling in, bringing Lucifer closer. God dragged His fingertips along the curve of his jaw, then took his chin. He lifted, and Lucifer looked up at Him adequately for the first time, and the angel finally kept still. "As beautiful as the day you were created."

Lucifer couldn't speak; he was boiling.

"I know you wanted to see me earlier—" Lucifer's heart swelled, for He had heard his prayers, "—but I knew you to be too young, and now I see you have grown little since your creation. You are still so rife with innocence. Your eyes are wide. Frightful."

"Please forgive me, Father."

"And you still do not know who you are."

"I am yours, Father." It came so naturally it ached. "What I am is yours."

"And what do you do?"

"I worship the Almighty God, the King of Kings."

The Lord seemed satisfied with that answer, and His hand on the angel, painfully slow, inched back and away. "The animals in the garden adore you. They tell me they would like you to visit more."

"If you would have me, Father." Lucifer chased after God's hand, feeling terribly alone without His touch, as if he were starved of water and tasted it in His fingertips. "I will come into your garden every day and worship, worship until you tire of me." He clutched the grass by his knees, felt it between his fingers, kept attempting to look at Him but was too weak to hold His gaze for any more than a second.

"I would never tire."

"Then I would worship you eternally."

His Father turned away, beginning to walk — ordered, "Come with me," and Lucifer scrambled to stand. Straying behind, knowing he was not worthy to walk at His side, not yet, perhaps not ever, Lucifer knew his subservience, and he was overjoyed with it. "Do not hang your head so low. Lift your chin." Lucifer did as told. "Look at all you see." He did so; he had done nothing but taste his surroundings since he'd arrived. "This is the Garden of Eden." Lucifer repeated the name, and the letters were sugar in his mouth. "The Earth will become like this at the appointed time."

"All of Earth will become your garden?" It felt like a reasonable assumption, and Lucifer smiled in the warmth of his Father's short, pleased laugh, rumbling the way thunder did.

"That is so. Eden will fall to the Earth, but for now, it remains in the sky."

"Father, they tell me Earth is full of beasts. Is it true?"

"It is."

He opened his mouth, then hesitated. Lucifer flickered his gaze to the ground again, as certain creamy white honeysuckles, trailing up high stems, brushed against his side, tugging on him. Nerves coming undone, he wondered what he was doing — asking questions to the Most High. He berated himself, wished he had brought a scarf so that he could cover himself with it.

"Lucifer." In went his breath, like cracks tearing through glass, and came to a stop — 'my name, my own name in His voice.' "There are questions you have for me."

In between God's words, there was the sound of buzzing, bristling — nature teetering and bustling. Lucifer heard the ruffles of the honeysuckle as it tried to attach itself to the hand he hung vulnerably by his side, then lifted his eyes to the Lord, who stayed turned away. "I could spend all of eternity here, asking questions."

"Eternity always begins somewhere — ask me what you meant to a moment ago."

Lucifer clasped his hands together, interlocking his fingers, and he spoke quietly, compliant, "Why did you fill the Earth with beasts, Father? Will they be replaced by these animals in the garden?"

The answer wasn't immediate; Lucifer had always thought hesitation to be such an angelic thing; on God, it seemed both reassuring and frightening. "Not precisely, every animal will wander into the Earth in its own way — you see how different they all are."

"Then why did you make the beasts?" Lucifer didn't think before asking, remembering the rabbit he'd held and the story Baal had told him of a beast nearly tearing his limbs off. "What is the purpose of creatures that only harm, that destroy?"

"Only harm? Destroy? Lucifer," said so sharp all of the young angel's organs rattled, "you should not concern yourself so much with gossip or exaggerated tales. All of my creation is good."

Startling, stumbling — "Forgive me, forgive me." Lucifer fell into a slight bow of the head. "I didn't— I did not know— Please, Almighty Lord, I did not know that I was not supposed to. You are merciful— I—"

"You stutter and you shiver — for an angel, it is unbecoming, like you are attempting to be no more than an animal." The Lord faced the angel, but He commanded, "Bow lower. Have you no respect for your Father?" Lucifer heaved internally, but only internally, holding his own hands tighter and lowering his head. "More." Lucifer bent at the waist, wondering if that was enough, thrashing in his own mind, being whipped over and over for his shame. He wanted to wail — 'Father, Father, be merciful, please have pity on me, please forgive me.' "Crumble to the ground, if that is how you feel." And Lucifer fell, he fell, he fell to his knees and brought his forehead to the grass again, hands planted over the greenery before his head. "Do you not see your own clothes and your castings, the jewels I set on you, and the beauty I have gifted you? Your golden timbrels and pipes? See your splendor and remind yourself that it is I who created it, who has made your fair heart and your perfections."

Lucifer whispered, murmured all the words he knew: Father, Lord, King, God, Creator, Father, Lord, Most High — everything, he gave Him, he gave Him all of his tongue, all of his voice, all of himself.

Yet, the Lord was unsatisfied: "Do you believe?"

"I believe," the angel said, voice so weak he thought to repeat it. "I believe. Oh, I believe in you, Lord." And he believed in His creation, the plan He had for His creation, and Lucifer thought he was so good now, so good at knowing what an angel ought to do.

"Ask me another question."

"Another?"

"There are many in your soul."

Lucifer shut his eyes, swallowed, trying to find his heartbeat, but it had left him. His mouth — when it moved, it did so on its own: "I want to know if I am yours. I said that I am, but I want to know if it is true, if I am really yours. Your angel."

"You want to know if you are mine."

"Yes, Father. Not an angel of beauty, nor of anything else, but an angel of God Almighty, Creator of Heaven and Earth, and all that I see." He trembled, even knowing he'd just been scolded for it. "Because, Lord, what is there to be, if not yours?"

Instead of answering, God returned Lucifer to the bed of flowers and said he should take the chance to lay in it some more.

CHAPTER 10

Hearty spice invaded him, coming in through his mouth, skippering and totaling to fall down his throat. His lips parted, the soft sigh of delight leaving him, and then he smiled wide, bringing his spoon away from his mouth and back to the metal jug in his other hand. From it, there was steam drizzling upward from the stew of cooked fava beans, with olive oil, onions, cumin, parsley — this he had acquired from an angel preparing food in a cart to hand out for no other reason than to be kind.

Lucifer was seated on a lower step of the stairway up a hill — it was a mount of a meadow, and its grasses rustled with breaths, and one angel was picking gold off the sunflowers. Nearby was the amphitheater that Rosier, Baal, and him had left just a few minutes ago, Lucifer skipping ahead and humming with barely a thought in his pretty head. The streets remained crowded, the mob of angels discussing the end of the ball game they'd all bore witness to.

Baal fell victim to the same conversation topic, grumbling, "I can't believe Michael lost." He was plopped beside Lucifer, eating from the same sort of jug.

Lucifer raised a brow, initially, then laughed, bright as wildfire. "Oh, you bet on him, didn't you!"

"I bet with Phanuel," he replied, placing the metal spoon in his mouth and leaving it there so his following words were muffled. "He said that I'd clean his house if Michael lost, and he'd massage me every day for a week if he won."

Rosier, who sat at Lucifer's other side, laughed along with the youngest. "Phanuel bet on Michael losing? I thought they were close friends." Lucifer hadn't known that, but he supposed that made sense: Phanuel always had the best seats reserved whenever Michael would be participating in anything. This time, it had been a sports game — players passing a ball around with their hips, legs, arms — and Lucifer had become the sort to be swept away by the energy of the crowd.

When they cheered, so did he, and when they threw their drinks into the air, he did too, but he had trouble following the rules. Often, he forgot to look at the ball; his gaze would settle on Michael instead, the Michael who would be up front, leading the team, or passing the ball up so that a flying angel might strike it another direction. Lucifer always watched him, cheered for him, had begun rattling his timbrel to cry and catch his attention. And yet — Michael hadn't taken note of Lucifer. It was as if God Himself were there, always twisting the prince's gaze just a finger-width away from the angel of beauty.

"*Well,*" Baal went on, annoyance making him grumble, leading Rosier and Lucifer to share a look of amusement, "Phanuel tells me that he's really only good at strength, and that Michael is blinded by too much confidence." Lucifer almost pouted, thinking this was unfair, as an angel like Michael surely had every right to hold himself in such high esteem. "And he's not a good leader, he told me. He's too proud."

'Proud?' Lucifer looked up, innocence making him tilt his head. He'd never heard the word, but it didn't seem so bad. It only sounded as if Michael knew himself, believed in himself. Certainly, there could be nothing wrong with being a bit proud.

"At least the game was exciting," Rosier said, likely because he'd earlier mentioned he wasn't fond of the bloodshed of angel sports and often avoided going.

"Yes, it was exciting," Lucifer agreed, setting his cup of stew beside him on the stair. "I was rooting for Michael and his team, but as long as everyone enjoyed themselves," he chirped, "then I don't think the ultimate winner matters too much."

Baal turned to look at him, chuckling. "Since when do you say wise things like that, brother? Have you become a philosopher?"

"Oh—" Rosier's exasperation made Lucifer flush instantly, "—you don't know the worst of it! If only you lived with him. Since he returned from Eden," weeks now, "he's been spouting all sorts of things like that. Yesterday, he was talking to the tree in our patio about existence, and earlier today, he asked me why Heaven has walls, and *oh,* he keeps talking about our Father!"

"I didn't think I that annoying," Lucifer mumbled, a frown having settled on his lips. He donned no headscarf on this day; in fact, he wore just a long tunic and his hair loose — scandalous for how he usually carried himself. "I can't forget it. I see the Lord even in my dreams now, and Eden. Eden! It's such a paradise." Baal reminded Lucifer that they lived in paradise. "Paradise like here but different." When he saw Rosier open his mouth, he continued quickly, "He planted a bed of flowers for me." He'd already told Rosier this, but not Baal, and he was delightfully taking advantage to tell this story again. "He let me sit with Him, and He let me ask Him everything I've ever wondered. I would do anything to see Him again. He was kind to me. So, so kind to me."

Rosier smiled, soft, then mused, "Maybe you'll see Him soon. One never knows Father's will."

Lucifer couldn't stop gushing: "He's so incredible. I want to say it over and over. When I met Him, I saw every sun and moon on His face, and His steps sweetened the dirt so that it tasted like honey." He remembered the mud on his lips. "When I kissed His rings, I saw all the stars on the gems. And I touched His robes, I remember, and I saw that it was made of time, time itself, smoothed out. All the light that has ever existed was falling from His eyes, there was light of every color, more than I thought existed," and then, he stopped. A hand found the timbrel strapped to his hip. He padded his fingers over it, without thinking.

"Lucifer?" Baal called, concern trickling from him.

The angel tugged the timbrel free from where it hung, weighed it in his hands — patted the flat part, shook it, heard the rattle. His gaze rose to see the crowds lingering on the streets, and he remembered the first day he'd encountered Heaven, and he remembered the songs, how angels played music and danced. Lucifer had never sung before, never thought to, but the moment he parted his lips, it came naturally, "Holy God, we praise your name." His voice was melodic, finding rhythms in the air — coming alluring and sweet and spiced, smooth. The words had been inside him somewhere, had been waiting to be released: "Lord of all, all in Heaven adore you, infinite your vast domain, everlasting is your reign."

Nearby angels turned their heads, half staring amusedly as the other half, reverently inspired by Lucifer, sang back to him: "Holy, Holy, Holy Lord God of hosts!"

Lucifer stood — it was a manic fervor — as he made a steady beat in his hands, stepped forward. He sang, "Of the Father's love begotten, are the words beginning to be. He, the source, the ending," a breath, guttural yet dry, "He, of the evermore things, non-forgotten!" Shifting his weight from one foot to another, practically hopping between them. He smiled and sang to those angels who had moved closer to hear him — maybe a dozen, perhaps two dozen.

The angels sang back at him, joyously, and some had instruments of their own, lifting to string them or beat them or raising them to their mouths: "Holy, Holy, Holy Lord God of hosts!"

When they danced, Lucifer led them. He moved along the ground, swift, as music planted itself into the air, and he spun between its roots, roots that turned heads of even more angels. Then they, too, were joining in the hysteria. They cheered for the beautiful angel shaking his tambourine, then bringing pipes to his lips. After he blew, he sang again, and the masses sang back, and all of God, surely, was burrowing into Lucifer's body, making him heavy and sway, dizzy. His hand found the smooth marble of a platform, and he hopped, flapped his wings to boost himself; he did this only to steady, but now he saw the many, many angels looking to him.

It wasn't sneaking glances, little glimmers to catch his beauty; now they stared with respect, awaiting his command. 'Lord,' Lucifer thought. 'Through you, by you, they—" But he couldn't finish this muse. He continued to sing, letting them join, teaching them that this joy could be God's, that they could worship Him like this, that they could praise and adore Him like this. All of him felt an instrument, in God's hand, his threads being strung, but he was smiling widest that he ever had.

"In you," he sang, "our Father, I rest my hope; let me never be put to shame!"

But, Lucifer couldn't last long, not after one song became many, not after the final verse. Breathlessness made him stumble, his body slumping as if to faint. Helping him down from the platform was Baal, who had re-appeared at his side; perhaps, he had joined the singing, but Lucifer didn't know. He flickered his gaze, caught Rosier too, and smiled exhaustedly. Baal was laughing, "Lucifer, what have you done?" Lucifer wasn't sure, but he was happy in his gasps for breath, in his sweat.

Rosier spoke, "We should go home, or else we'll get trampled." It was true: all the angels had gotten caught in the fervor, which had reached out of Lucifer's own body and grabbed each listener, invaded them with the madness of worship. But at Lucifer's loss of leadership, the wave splintered into disorganized psalms, into dancing, into melodies growing steep, rhymes getting lost. The angels had turned into the madness itself.

"Help me walk," Lucifer whispered, eyes searing in exhaustion. Baal didn't hesitate, one of his arms finding Lucifer's waist and holding him against his side as they began to move through the sea of angels, many who saw him and praised him, all speaking at once so that Lucifer couldn't decipher the words of any singular soul. That is — until he caught a certain voice. He looked back, back as if into a memory.

So far away in the crowd was Michael, with that proud grin of his and one hand in the air, but he called out to the youngest angel still. "Lucifer! Lucifer!" Even with all their distance, their gazes met and locked. An intake of breath, then the exuberant shout: "Lucifer — the Lord has never made as fine an angel as you!"

The abyss formed from the ends of his vision. "Lucifer?" His lithe body — a furnace — surrendering to its weakness. "Lucifer." Rosier's voice barely seeping in — Lucifer slumped against his friends, fading into the darkness like the one preceding life. If angels could die, it might be like this, like falling to sleep, returning to the time before. Like every angel was the flames of the universe's beginning, the expulsion from emptiness. "Lucifer!" And they would all return to nothing, one day.

But if that is the case, it didn't happen then.

Lucifer would go on to wake, so jarringly as this, in his bed many hours later, not remembering having fainted from overexertion or even being tucked in. His legs kicked, then, at the covers as he swung up and sat, looking all around as if searching for the prince who'd had the audacity to kill him as he had. Instead, he saw clutter, so much of it — all from the fateful first days he'd spent as an angel. And this juvenile room was, suddenly, an embarrassment. He rolled off the mattress, stood, tied his hair up.

'Never let me be put to shame,' Lucifer had sang. 'And now,' he thought, 'I will no longer shame you, Father.'

Restlessly, this angel worked through the gifts that remained — mostly textiles and art pieces, which he decided to fill the last open spaces of his walls with. He draped two more carpets over the floor, then placed three more embroidered cushions on his bed that didn't quite match but there was no helping it. The basket of petals holding the scars of his first blood — he placed it beneath his bed, far enough that no one would see it.

Then, Lucifer sat before his mirror, atop a cushioned chair. He took a cedar wooden hairbrush, the bristles soft as they threaded through his blonde, wispy hair, scratching gently against his scalp. Looking to the mirror, hoping to see the beautiful angel — only for the new joy of his heart to grind to a halt on the ends of lips, turning down, slow. His shame had not left him; his nose, his eyes, his mouth — like shards of glass on his feet.

Lucifer set the brush down, then beckoned his wings free. When he brushed them, he used a curved gilded comb, dragging it delicately between the feathers, smoothing and settling them into place. He thought that maybe shame would always linger, but God had now offered him salvation from this through love, through singing for His love. So, Lucifer was joyous, he was, and smiled again. He took the mirror by its edge, then turned it away, facing the window to reflect paradise.

It was better that he couldn't meet the features of his face. The beauty of them was violent, the need of them, the need of them to take. To grab Lucifer and save him — what is there to save him from, in Heaven? — from himself. But perhaps it was too late, even now, to save Lucifer; too early, before creation, it was too late.

Lucifer headed for the door, beckoning his wings back into the cage of flesh. Remaining in a loose, cotton, wondrously soft tunic, yawning, he made his way to the stairs, then the kitchen. He scrubbed dishes clean — two cups and a plate — then set a small stock pot, drizzled with olive oil, over the flames he lit on a ceramic stove. He went for some vegetables. They felt nice in his hands, their texture was sturdy — the sensation pulling him out of his head. Squash, celery, carrot, chayote — the slices he subjected them to were slow. Then, he added everything to the pot, along with a bundle of spices to season. He allowed the vegetables to sweat for a few minutes, stirring with a wooden spoon, then added cuts of onion and smiled as the sizzling scent drifted up into his face, kissed him. Mixing in some more, then adding garlic — pausing again to enjoy the smell — bay leaves, the juice of a few limes, jalapeños, and broth. He covered the pot and left it to boil.

Lucifer told himself that he enjoyed cooking, and he did. He enjoyed plenty of things about living, in fact. His hand lingered on the handle of the pot's cover, but he smiled, a little delighted that this was his life, after all.

The tiles were pretty — the paint on them so detailed. There was a window that looked into their patio, and their patio had trees whose bark crisped when he scratched it. And sometimes his housemate Rosier would rear them to drop fruits into Lucifer's hand and when Lucifer tasted them, they sweetened his mouth so whole he thought he might cry. How kind the Lord was, to let them spend an eternity happy, to worship Him through joy. Even this quietness, this simple living, could be worship too, right?

When his friends arrived, they found Lucifer like that, in the kitchen. It was Baal, Asmodeus, Rosier, and Phanuel, and they asked him various things at once, and Lucifer smiled, and he told them, "I'm the angel of worship." They all faltered, looked at once another, but then appeared to believe this, nodding, affirming it.

Using the top of Rosier's head as an armrest, Asmodeus said, "But the singing, Lucifer — something like that has never happened before. Everyone is talking about you. "

Lucifer's cheeks warmed before he turned his attention back to his soup. "I hope all kind things."

Asmodeus replied again, though Rosier was writhing, trying to escape from beneath his friend's arm, "Kind or else, I wouldn't go outside if I were you. They'll smother and ask you to sing again."

"I can confirm that," Phanuel said. "That's why I'm here, to smother you and ask you to sing.

Lucifer laughed softly. "Not now, but maybe once I've recuperated from the emotion of it all." He hoped to speak to God soon, maybe he would seek out Gabriel, and hope to send the message. "Oh, Phanuel." He turned his head. "You're Michael's friend, right?"

"Well, I would say so."

"He called out to me, when I was leaving—" Michael with his hand in the air, shouting for Lucifer's attention, catching it tight, so tight he still had it. "I want to speak to him. Do you know where he is?" But Lucifer's question started strong and ended soft, as Phanuel was already frowning.

"Father sent him away."

"Away?"

"To another galaxy, a far one too." Phanuel shifted from one foot to the other. "A little under a hundred million years, if he were to ride on a wave of light."

Lucifer could only stare, everything within him having ground to a halt, so Baal was the one who replied, "Do you know why the Lord sent him so far?"

"No," Phanuel said, "it was really sudden."

"We won't see Michael," Lucifer murmured, "for a hundred million years?"

"Michael," Phanuel reassured, "can fly a lot faster than that, so it could be sooner that he returns. Don't look sad, Lucifer. I spoke to him before he left. He told me he'd seek you out once he returned."

"He did?" It soothed his heart, mellowed it until Lucifer was smiling again, though gently. "I hope he's back soon then." He continued with his meal, adding, "And I hope to sing again, but I would just like to do nothing for a while. Rosier, is it okay if I don't help with the fruits until I'm ready to go out again?"

"Of course it's okay." Rosier had apparently surrendered and simply stood with Asmodeus' arm on his head. "You can stop helping with the fruits altogether, if you're busy worshipping now."

Lucifer didn't deny it. He moved to serve his soup finally as he realized this title did indeed fit him, but not all of him. 'Angel of beauty, angel of worship,' he called himself, finding the two together made him up, like he had found both halves of his heart. Complete, at last.

When the youngest angel returned to bed, he bundled in his quilts and snuggled into them, ready to be lulled back into sleep before his thoughts wandered and stumbled onto the archangel from earlier. Michael. He still didn't know him — 'only from crowds, have I seen him' — but something, indiscernible, of the prince beckoned him. He recalled the first time he'd taken note of Michael, winning the wrestling match with just a single drop of sweat falling from his brow. All Lucifer wished was to meet him, to speak with him. He couldn't explain it, but it was all that he wanted.

Lucifer felt drowsiness tease his eyes shut, and before long, his thoughts returned to the Father he'd sang so earnestly for. He remembered Eden, and he remembered the touch of God on his jaw. He wanted to see Him again. 'I want so many things, but I want to know if you are happy with me now, Lord. I want to know if I have made you proud of me. I want to know if this is what you intended for me always.'

Thereafter, Lucifer was in a dream, standing on clouds, seeing his Father, the air so shaped that all the simpler things fell into Him. The rival cosmologies, themselves, stemmed out from His shadow, every truth real for Him, their dimensions creeping from His outline. In proximity, there was the shape of the earths; Lucifer touched them.

When the Lord gestured for the angel to approach, He offered the seat at his side, and Lucifer crawled to it, sitting, feeling snug in all the wings that composed him. Smiling — for he felt comfortable in a way he never had. One of God's hands went to caress his head, as if he were His child — and he was — as Lucifer could only breathe, brokenly, some affectionate words.

The bodies of the universe presented themselves, but to see the stars is to see the past, and thus the Lord and the angel watched the birth of creation together. He explained to Lucifer how its wheels turned, and He described the patterns among the sheet of the abyss, which He lifted to wring out the waters from before He set it back into place, and He revealed that it was not quite an abyss at all, that it was all alive and breathing in tune with them.

In the distance, some siblings ushered along some gas to mold into a sphere, before setting it on a course around a star. Lucifer asked if he could ever build a planet too, because he thought it would be nice to create. And initially, the Lord didn't reply, but then He revealed that Lucifer should remain close to Him.

But Lucifer, smiling cheekily — from every mouth — replied that God was everywhere and that at the ends of the universe, he would still be at the Lord's side.

The Lord said Lucifer was best suited to sit beside His Throne.

The angel, watching His Father judge creation, asked what he should do. He wished to say that he'd learned to sing, and he could sing beautifully. Worship — it came very naturally to him. Lucifer asked if the Lord was pleased with him; within, pain was swelling the same as a distant sun that was beginning to burst. Was he good enough? A deluge of red trickled into the whites of his eyes, and water began to seep from the crevices; the angel asked if he was loved. If the Lord was really loving.

The Creator said: "When I speak, may you hear love always, above all." Lucifer moved closer, having been ushered to do so, but pain was boiling, and he parted his lips, gasped, trying to wade through melted vision to find his Father again, thinking the source of creation could adore him back. And great palms, hefty, heated, cupped the most beautiful face of the shivering angel. "You are loved the way you are, and you are all that you need to be. You are even more than I wanted of you."

The angel wept little words of gratitude, though his voice broke and continued breaking. He thought this tenderness should never end, this conditional love; if he knew death, he'd ask to be killed here. Instead, ease washed into him as the Lord, our God, pressed His lips to the angel's heads. Slowly, slowly, the crying stilled and ceased. What followed were His arms, coming around His creation, who was infinitely small but eager to embrace. Between them — the weight of the universe. Soon, Lucifer would tell Him about his life, about all his tiny dreams and worries.

"You are loved, my morning star. See how I love you. The angels and you are what matter most to me."

'Do not ever let me go,' the angel pleaded. 'Hold me tight, Father. Do not ever let me go.'

CHAPTER 11

The angels had their antiquities, but a civilization can't rise without one having died, so it can't be said they had civilizations.

Azazel's voice: "Heaven has never been so loud."

But they come close, as angels often do. They had epochs, each an eon — so when new periods came, they were ushered in with enthusiastic vigor. That's how they welcomed this one.

Lucifer hadn't meant to eavesdrop, had only been passing by, carrying home a basket of paprikas and lentils. He heard his friend from around a corner, speaking to this angel named Moloch and another named Mammon. He didn't know them well, though Moloch was the angel of gift-giving, while Mammon was the angel of gold. They sang frequently with Lucifer out in the streets, but Lucifer had never noticed them, for a hundred other admirers chased after his music, as if trying to catch it with their own hands.

Walking away quick, drifting away from the squawks of gossip, Lucifer shook his head to himself, distracting his mind by thinking of all the duties that remained for his day. He had to prepare something to eat, then travel to Eden to serve Father wine and sing for Him, and he had promised Baal to go flying after he returned. Then, he had to visit a gathering hosted by Phanuel, prompted by the invention of a rubber ball by an angel who was going to argue for its use over the traditional painted stone spheres for sports. These would cause less injuries, he said, but part of the fun was the gory injury — hence why there would be a debate. Afterwards, Lucifer would visit a small bathhouse with Rosier in a less populated corner of the city, which Lucifer dreaded, but he was an angel of beauty too, and shame was his punishment for it.

'Busy, busy, busy!' — but he didn't mind; it was pleasant to always have something to do.

Lucifer traveled home, did all that needed to be done, then stopped to have some simple slices of peach, along with a cool glass of hibiscus tea. As he ate, he braided back the front portions of his hair but allowed the majority to keep cheerfully cascading past his shoulders. He slipped on sandals, retrieved his instruments, before stepping out onto his balcony and standing there a while, timbrel and pipes on his hip. He waved, down at one of his neighbors — Orcus, angel of soil. After this, Lucifer leapt into the air, spreading his wings.

Most angels required the guidance of Gabriel to find Eden, still, but Lucifer no longer. He'd gone so often now he could find its direction in his veins, or maybe it was his arteries, which had rearranged themselves to mimic the path to God. Some had begun to say Lucifer had yet another title: the favorite. The angels claimed their Father had never invited any one angel to visit so much, nor had He been served wine by the same one so regularly, nor had He ever planted a bed of flowers for one. They said Lucifer must be His favorite, and that they stood witness to Lucifer being tended like a flower, teased to grow in the direction of archangel-hood. Always, Lucifer negated every accusation of godly favoritism — they loved him for this — but in private, he hoped it was true. If only out of hope to serve the Lord more intimately.

He descended from the clouds into the hands of greenery that made up the now-familiar grasses, trees, trees with ripe fruits, fruits being reached for by grazing animals. The tips of his wings tilted downward into a graceful glade before flapping once to stop, then twice to hover before landing on his feet. Lucifer smiled. Nature caressed his legs in greeting, and a pair of dragonflies buzzed by his ear to welcome him back. Walking, continually brushed by the flowers and creatures that knew him well — he crouched to kiss the heads of the lambs that came to see him, then got on the tips of his toes to do the same to the elephants.

By the time he came into the open meadow by the Trees of Life and Knowledge, there were a dozen angels there, beside Father, who was seated on a modest throne — arguably, a simple seat — facing away from them, watching a waterfall. Before Him was a table, made of every type of bark, with a royal purple covering and a large silver chalice with every manner of gem built into it. Additionally on the table — a tall crystal pitcher, filled to the brim with blood-red wine that rippled over the surface with life. A glance within, and Lucifer saw the crimson sprawl of stars, blooming roses; and Lucifer saw himself, before he bowed. He bent lowly for his Father, then turned his face to the other angels.

Lucifer leaned into their kisses on his cheeks, uttering words of thanks. Most of these angels — Ishtar, Seir, and Gemory, if some names should be picked out — were well-known to the youngest angel now, as they made up the rotating choir the Lord had made for Himself. Lucifer didn't yet lead them in song, however; he returned to the Father and greeted Him, "Lord Highest." And he took the pitcher, so massive in both hands he had to hold it against his body, then tilted it downwards. The wine — streaming into the chalice; it fell in curls before Lucifer set it down again.

God took the chalice and brought it to His mouth.

Lucifer watched, pleased when his Father made a noise of approval. Stepping back, the angel stood with the others, pulled his pipes from where he had strapped them. He blew into the tubes and listened as the angels began to sing. Unlike those joyous songs Lucifer led out in the streets of Heaven, this was not the type to dance to; instead — a soft one, full of praise for all the creations in Eden. Lucifer had written the psalm, of course, as he had written all of them.

'I'm happy.' He had been nothing but happy for perhaps a year now. The sweet rhythm of life had settled. He couldn't tire of what had been his fate all along — felt nothing but grateful he could spend all his existence at the Lord's feet, praising Him, serving Him.

He tried not to think of Michael, who was still up in the stars somewhere. There had been weeks, not long after the chief prince grew absent, that Lucifer traveled through meadows and orchards, climbed onto the highest branches of the tallest trees, staring upward, waiting for the moment Michael would descend magnificently into Heaven, holding an entire universe on his back. But a soon return wouldn't come, and his duties had taken over, and if there'd been hope, it had dwindled. Hope, it seemed, ought to wither sometimes; Lucifer knew his gaze should remain on God, who was his solace, his comfort. His love. He was happy, at His side; he couldn't be happier.

The song finishing, Lucifer watched as two angels, Seir and Ishtar, went to feed the Lord the small dishes they'd prepared. They stood close, bringing to His mouth cuts of sourdough bread, marinated in oils or spreads, as Lucifer and the other angels took a minute to rest. They sat, they laid, waiting for their Father to speak, as He always did. Lucifer relaxed over the grass with Gemory's head on his lap, but he didn't let his attention drift; he quite loved the Lord's parables.

"In the days of an earlier universe, behold, there had been two moons and their planet. And an angel, who was sat atop their sun, was painting those stars that live on the fringes. But distracted by his own thoughts, the angel's paintbrush slipped, and he had come to block out the planet of the moons. Becoming frightened, the moons ran in opposite directions." Lucifer scratched his nails against Gemory's scalp slow, soothing. "It was only after they reached the edges of their galaxy that they realized what they had done, and the moons missed each other terribly. Turning around, they went looking for one another, but they could not find their way back because their planet had disappeared. They asked the stars for help, and the angels told the moons, 'If you cannot find your planet, then you must be very careless.' Fearing to be laughed at, the angel who made the mistake did not admit what he had done."

Father paused, to be fed, then continued, "Now his shame created a suffering for the moons called purposelessness. Unable to find each other for millions of years, all they could do was cry, cry icy rocks that still stream across the universe today. And for all that time, the hum of their sadness could be heard from every point in the skies. It was only when that angel confessed, that something could be done, and to his surprise, his brothers did not ridicule him. They comforted him and promised help. Together, the angels painted the planet again — this time, more vibrant — and gave it a ring so that the moons would always recognize it."

The story ended, and the angels rose to their feet so they could sing for Him once more. This time, it was a cheerful song; Lucifer shook his timbrels and moved from side to side, barely resisting the urge to start dancing. Singing, singing, singing — he could barely decipher time to have passed, only realizing that they were on their twelfth psalm when the Lord began dismissing them. At this, the angels each took a turn kissing His rings. Lucifer was the final one, walking up and getting on a knee to it, his lips lingering, his chest warming. To touch God — it was sweeter to Lucifer than sleeping and even sweeter than waking.

"Thank you, Father."

The Lord replied, "You're becoming more beautiful, Lucifer."

Lucifer raised his head, blinking eyes that widened. "I am?" But his Father maintained His gaze on the waterfall, away from the angel.

"There is nothing more beautiful than worship. Your splendor is like none other of my creations."

A smile stretched upon Lucifer's face before he stood, bowed deep for what must've been the hundredth time. Whispering just a few more praises, Lucifer stepped back and turned to follow the other angels who left, though not without glancing back at the few who stayed. The lonely God always asked some angels to remain and keep Him company, and for their work, He gifted them new precious stones they could fashion into jewelry.

Taking to the air, Lucifer planned a long nap, but arrived outside his home to find the angel of flight at his doorstep, being awkward with his hands, as if he didn't know how to stand naturally. When their eyes met, Lucifer suppressed a sigh and said, "Oh, I did plan to fly with you, didn't I?" He forced a smile, albeit weak.

Baal knowingly chuckled. "I can see you're tired, Lucifer." He went up to him, draped an arm over his shoulders just as Lucifer shrugged his wings back into his body. "We can spend some time on the ground, instead, if you wish.

Lucifer leaned his head against his friend, liking the little affectionate gesture. "But I made a promise to you. If you just let me rest a little first, then we can still go." He paused, then laughed quietly, "Yes, you can come inside."

Another chuckle. "Thank you. But go sleep, younger brother." Despite his words, Baal wasted no time in stepping into the house with him and asking his favorite question: "Did Father tell you a story today?"

Lucifer, quite briefly, told Baal the tale of the moons, adding, "And I believe that's His way of saying not to hide our mistakes, for we may cause suffering on accident." Moving away from the other angel, he went to one of the couches, flopped onto his belly over it, and his muscles loosened as he sighed.

"Oh, you're so wise." Baal's teasing voice came from right by him. "I thought he was explaining why some planets have rings."

"Well, that too. Maybe." Lucifer's voice came muffled, as it filtered out from the pillow his face was smashed against. "But that wouldn't make any sense, would it? Unless every one of those planets lost its moons." Occasionally, Lucifer wondered why their Father couldn't just be literal about the nature of things. Always, it was metaphors, allusions, words designed for interpretation. The first falsehoods.

"Hm. Should I make some coffee? Tea? Chocolate?"

"No. You're my guest."

Baal, smile evident in his tone — "Please try to forgive me for disobeying you. I'll prepare something to eat while I'm at it. Do you want some cinnamon in your coffee?"

"No, Baal, you shouldn't," Lucifer said, not making any move to stop his friend. "But yes. A lot of cinnamon please." And their suppressed laughter filled the air.

There was some shuffling in the kitchen, and Lucifer heard the clank of pots, rush of water, then the crinkle of a fire. He shut his eyes and listened to his friend work and the beats of his heart. Once, Lucifer had asked if these thumps in his chest were necessary, and God had replied that they were not, and maybe He would take his heart out, and Lucifer partly longed for that day. He imagined it beating, held tenderly in the Lord's hand. His mouth parted, and he thought of sharing this thought, but then he predicted Baal to look at him curiously and ask if something was wrong, and Lucifer would say, 'No, what can be wrong? In paradise, nothing can be wrong, and nothing can be wrong with me. God loves me. He would not make me wrong.'

When Baal's voice returned, it said, "I just remembered. I had something to tell you." Lucifer, groaning, sat back up and leaned into a cushion as Baal settled beside him with a silver tray on his lap. "Do you know about the building Asmodeus is working on?" Lucifer nodded, taking the ceramic cup that was warm on his palms and smoking richness from its brown surface. "He told me they want to plan a feast for when it opens, and he's inviting you to help."

"I don't imagine I'm good at planning something like that," Lucifer replied before blowing at the surface of the coffee to cool it, then sipped a tiny amount. And it settled his heart, just a bit. "But I'll be happy to go for the festivities, though no singing. These days, I'm so spent."

"That's alright." Baal leaned back into the couch and turned his face up to the ceiling. "But you do have the loveliest voice in Heaven, Lucifer. We all love to hear it."

Lucifer couldn't resist — "Well, maybe only one song." There was a little chuckle between them. "And please keep track of how much wine I have."

"Yes, yes." Baal drank some coffee himself, hiding an amused smile. "Anything else you need, Father's favorite?"

The younger angel pouted his lips. "I'm not fond of being called that." When Baal told him it was true, Lucifer replied that it couldn't be; he stared at a plate of sweetbread on the platter, any appetite in him dissipating. "I'm not an archangel. I'm sure someone like Gabriel or Michael is His favorite." Michael, the Michael who remained lost in the cosmos.

"You'll become an archangel, brother." Baal nudged him with a fond smile. "Soon, I think. That's why everyone wants to be your friend."

"Is that why you are my friend, Baal?" Lucifer teased.

"Yes, because you are God's favorite, and because you are beautiful, and I want to be best friends with an archangel." Baal drank from his cup again, then added, "Your personality is tolerable most days too."

Lucifer couldn't contain his laughter. It was just another simple moment in his repetitive life; but he was happy — happy, happy, happy.

What else could an angel be but happy?

CHAPTER 12

The end. This is where he often begins the story, though he's never told it. He's heard them say that his life really began here, because Lucifer surely couldn't live unless he was adored. And it was sweet to believe that there's ever such a person who starts our life, that everything before them was unnecessary — the belief that life begins with love. Our first love.

But see: Lucifer was at a river with a wide bucket and two baskets crowded with clothing. Humming, doing laundry along with a dozen other chattering angels, two singing a work song — beating tunics against smoothed rock to dislodge the stains. He had just emptied the bucket filled with river water, mixed with natron and oil to soften its composition, into the shore. After this, he raised it, sat it atop his head, then struggled to lift the baskets too. It wasn't far that he walked, wobbling, before Asmodeus dropped down from the sky, taking the bucket.

"There you are! I've been looking for you!" He wore a nose ring, as he'd apparently picked up jewelry-making as a hobby in the last hundred years.

"Oh, I was on my way home." Lucifer sighed in a soft relief that Asmodeus would help carry everything now. "Is there something you need me for? I don't have anything else to do today."

"God is good," Asmodeus replied cheerily. "That's perfect — do you remember that gallery we wanted to host a feast to celebrate?"

"Is it finished?!" A thousand times before he'd been told to prepare for the opening, only to be told that it would take more time. "I remember you were having trouble with the garden. Did you figure it out?"

"*Well*," replied Asmodeus, in such a way that said he hadn't. "The important part is over with and that's what matters."

Lucifer frowned. "You shouldn't leave any job half-finished."

"Yes, yes." The older angel gestured dismissively. "Tell me what you think of the flooring, since that was the real hard work of your dear friend Asmodeus. That's an order, God's favorite." He spoke again, before Lucifer could interrupt, "And don't be so uptight. You're too young for that."

Lucifer barely suppressed a huff because he was definitely not young anymore, he thought; he knew who he was, was so sure of it that he took any indication otherwise as insult. "I never did ask," he said, to diffuse his annoyance, "how old you are, Asmodeus."

"Eleven billion."

"Oh."

Asmodeus laughed, heartily, at that. "Though before Earth, we didn't measure age, so I've lived longer without a sense of a time than with. To have it now feels wrong still. And once you've lived this long, it becomes difficult to care about any one thing or the other; life becomes forgettable."

Lucifer frowned. "How do you ground yourself?"

"Rosier makes some excellent pie."

They arrived home, then Lucifer went to string everything up to dry on the patio as Asmodeus went to go bother the angel of fruit he loved. Lucifer, meanwhile, went up into his room and stood in the center for a while, hands on his hips, pondering. 'Should I dress well?' *Tap* — he stepped and approached his extravagant wardrobe, a little unplaced intuition taking his hand and making him brush the silk material of some drapery. 'I should cover up so as not to distract anyone.' But, it was a feast, he told himself, and a little attention wouldn't hurt. Just a little.

Surrendering — he reached for the silk robe, colored lapis lazuli and draping to cascade sweet from the form of his body. Then, Lucifer swapped his small earrings for dangling filigree ones and clasped on more jewelry so that there wasn't any part of him that didn't rattle when he moved. He decided to braid his hair back and away, with some loose strands to frame his face in brushed out curls. And he thought to smear something on his lips to make them rosier than they already were, before realizing that was likely taking it too far, and adjusted his robe to not accidentally expose more skin than he wished. He remembered Gabriel's advice all that time ago, about modesty and humility.

Still, he found himself going to the kitchen, picking apart a pomegranate, bringing the seeds to his mouth, trying only to paint his lips as he ate — 'just a little, barely noticeable.'

When Rosier and Asmodeus, in the living area, saw him, they startled but didn't say a word of Lucifer's appearance, instead glancing at each other, then ushering Lucifer to come with them outside. The three took to the sky thereafter, the oldest leading the way, climbing high so that they could see the finished gallery in its glory. Asmodeus' hand pointed it out to the two — premature, before the tower had even come into proximity — and it would seem to be wholly unnecessary. Any angel would be able to recognize the novelty of the spherical, convoluted, and jade mechanism at the peak of this square-base, marble building. It was both a clock and a navigator — told time, distance.

They dropped onto the steps leading toward the entrance, Lucifer hearing Asmodeus say that they hadn't figured out a purpose for this building yet before Rosier suggested oil paintings. It was often the case that angels simply built, then found each creation a purpose later. 'God must be like that,' Lucifer thought, 'like us angels.'

The youngest found himself, had lost himself, moving into a low ceiling-ed place, nonetheless adorned with magnificent frescos and chandeliers. Steaming, the spices of a feast struck him next — they trailed from the long tables that had been set along tile flooring, nearing the grand staircase that led into what was likely more luxurious architecture sitting empty and eager for furniture. In between the not-enough seats, there were angels reaching for the pots. And the following is an account of what they ate: black beans — spiced with coriander, garlic, cumin, chipotle — rice of the aromatic variety with mustard seeds and turmeric — loaves of bread that were mushroom-shaped and kissed amorously with poppy seeds, fried artichoke, and steamed corn-dough dishes.

When the angels saw him, you'd think God had walked in. Lucifer hardly had a moment to speak before he was ushered in by various strangers, though some claiming they met him since he was young. "I haven't seen you since the day you walked the streets of Heaven for the first time!" Lucifer couldn't recognize him, glanced away momentarily, only to see that Rosier and Asmodeus were preoccupied greeting a mutual friend. Turning back to this angel who'd taken to holding his upper arm, he heard: "Would you like some berries, favorite of Father? I picked them myself."

"I'm not His favorite," Lucifer replied, soft, "but I'll accept." He did his best to smile, knowing he'd quite asked for the attention this time, and this must be his punishment. Another angel offered him a chair, and Lucifer thanked him, bowing his head, settling down. "I'd like some wine, if there's some— Oh, I'm sorry—" Two nearby angels had rushed to get him a glass, only to trip over one another, but everyone laughed, so he laughed too. On his lap, he twiddled his thumbs.

But, eventually, ease settled in — manifested from the music and the alcohol Lucifer now understood the use for. At the first sounds that left the singers' mouths, Lucifer raised his head, smiled, and began clapping his hands to the rhythm. He stood up, too, hoping someone would extend a hand to him to dance, but if any of the other angels had the courage — they couldn't satisfy his impatience. Asmodeus waved him over, and Lucifer hurriedly escaped the incessant compliments of those around — be assured that he blushed oh so earnestly at each — to rejoin his friends. He sang with them, danced. And it was like this that time stopped — like this.

Their neighbor Orcus stood before him, and over his shoulder, Lucifer caught the smear of movement, swift. Past a window, some thirteen feet away — someone had just moved to stand on the outside end and position himself among the greenery. It was an angel, smiling at Lucifer, as if they knew each other. It was an angel who looked tattered: face streaked with some speckled ash, curls of hair loose and disorderly, maroon robes torn at the hems beneath a heavy charcoal cloak beaten as thoroughly. His arms were crossed, and his head lightly tilted — beckoning Lucifer to come closer, to come *know* him. It was the eyes — earthy like Eden — that struck in Lucifer who he was.

'Michael. Michael. Michael.' His heart twisted into a battering ram against the front of his chest; he swung his gaze back to Orcus, who was halfway through turning his head, likely to meet the culprit of Lucifer's bewilderment. "Orcus!" He grabbed his shoulder, halting him from catching the archangel outside. "Tell me — there's a garden out there, right? I just saw a glimpse of it. Do you know the way in?"

"Lucifer?" Rosier, at Orcus' side, called, but Lucifer paid him no mind.

Orcus blinked before gesturing vaguely to his left. "The corridor there. But I'm not sure if the garden is finished— Asmodeus might know better—" Lucifer couldn't stand still enough to hear more; he broke off into a full sprint in that direction, hearing his neighbor's fruitless calls, Asmodeus' laugh, and Rosier's little sigh.

Rushing into the narrow hallway, not catching any of its detail, Lucifer's eyes locked on the door at the end, before he caught a flash of a mirror to his right. He slid to a stop, stumbled, stepped back, then looked at his reflection. It was a mirror, so small it only reflected his top half. Fluctuant breath stumbling from his mouth — he cursed himself, 'What have I done? My clothes are too thin, and they frame my body too closely, and I'm not even wearing anything beneath. What if Michael is calling me out to the garden to scold me? What if he'll tell me I've upset the Lord?' He licked his lips, still faintly red from pomegranate and, now, wine.

With a swallow, he continued down the corridor and pushed open a door out onto a raised patio, beneath a pergola dripping vines to nuzzle the top of Lucifer's head. Light raining onto him — its petrichor like honey and the scent of peonies. He made his way to some steps, onto a forked cobble walkway that split fields of flowers toward a circular marble fountain, cradled by benches and tall yew and boxwood shrubs. There were families of myrtle trees too, but Lucifer didn't look to them, because he could see Michael by the fountain, facing it. An unruly overflow of daisies moved along the water, so many that they spilled onto the cobble by Michael's feet.

Soon enough, the petals were spilling over Lucifer's sandals too. And he said, attempting to be steady but failing so miserably he shook nearly as much as his voice, "Michael. Would you like to come inside? The garden isn't quite finished. My friend Asmodeus told me. Look, the fountain is making a mess here."

Michael seemed to hesitate, before he turned to Lucifer, and they were facing each other, seeing one another, for the first time since that day years ago when Lucifer had led all of Heaven in worship. Up close, finally — Lucifer felt all of himself melt like precious metal into a cast. "You know my name," Michael said, and his voice had a mellow reverb to it. "That's a shame. I wanted to introduce myself." Lucifer opened his mouth, but Michael was grinning; it revealed little dips in his cheeks. "I am Michael, archangel of God, angel of strength."

'Angel of God,' Lucifer thought.

CHAPTER 13

"My name is Lucifer." The angel fell into a deep bow, bending nearly at the waist. "I'm the angel of worship and the angel of beauty." His voice was soft, like it was running itself out of him, leaving him alone, vulnerable. "It's an honor."

"Don't bow for me."

A flinch tempted to rush Lucifer; he sensed Michael inch closer. "You're an archangel."

"I'm your brother." A warm hand — taking Lucifer's shoulder. "An angel just like you, an angel that has wanted to meet you for many years now."

Heart tripping in his chest, Lucifer wondered if the other felt the terror that tore ravines into his veins. "Why are your clothes torn, Michael?" He raised his face, slowly brought himself to stand straight but weary. Michael was unraveling him beneath his palm, 'and he doesn't even know it, does he?' His gaze climbed along the stature of the angel, noting every exhaustion on Michael's features, tugging them as if to try coaxing him to bed. "Have— Did you just return from your trip?"

"The moment I landed," he laughed, both full and breathless, "I flew through all of Heaven, asking everyone I saw, 'Have you seen an angel named Lucifer? Do you know where he lives?' They told me about this feast, so I landed outside. And then I heard singing, your singing, the same way I did just before I had to leave. By Father's will, I saw you right through the window." Lucifer couldn't help a smile as the other removed his hand and plopped down onto a stone bench by a shrub. "You're as beautiful as I remembered."

"Michael." Lucifer interlocked his fingers before himself. "I'm really— I'm honored, but you were gone for so many years." He settled to sit beside the other, staring down. "Go rest, please."

"Don't you worry, I will, but I wanted to come know you first."

"There isn't much," Lucifer spoke a little too quick, "there isn't much to know about me." His fingers wandered to fiddle with his rings. "I'm a young angel, not so young anymore but young still." He thought of his conversation with Asmodeus earlier.

"But I heard someone say you were Father's favorite," Michael replied, quirking an amused brow. "Isn't that true?"

"It's not," Lucifer said. "It's a misunderstanding, just rumors. Personally, I don't think angels should joke about knowing the will of the Lord."

"But surely the angels say it for a reason?" Michael grinned and leaned a little closer; Lucifer realized they were facing each other now, taking one another in, close. "They've never said anything like that about me or the other archangels. Why do you downplay your importance, little brother?"

"I don't!" But Lucifer flushed with warmth. "It's only that—" He stopped at the sight of Michael's tilted head. "What? What is it?" He shifted, just to try and thrash against the constraints holding him in his mind. "What's so amusing?"

"You don't act the way I expected."

"What did you expect?"

Michael laughed and looked away from him again, but Lucifer caught foliage in his irises, saw millions of trees, rustling, anxiously. And Lucifer relaxed because he knew that the two of them were nervous, only one was better at hiding it. "I'm not sure. All that time up there in the cosmos — I had nothing to do but think about you. I mean that." Lucifer held his hands tighter, dug his nails into skin, as if that would stifle the tightness of his stomach. "Father had me order a few angels in rearranging a system of planets, and it's good work, but tedious. I wondered what life was like in Heaven, and the angels tell me that Heaven is noisy now."

Lucifer chuckled. "I'm apparently noisy."

"Well, I did hear you from out here," Michael teased, and the other angel looked away, quick, cringing in his embarrassment. "But you have a nice voice, so why not? And you're beautiful enough that I'm sure you can do whatever you like." Before Lucifer could speak, the prince changed the subject: "You said you were the angel of worship?"

"I—" Lucifer coughed, as if that would expel all the desire to tell Michael that maybe they should never talk again. "Yes. I lead angels in psalms, and sometimes we dance in the streets too. I'm blessed that our Father also invites me to Eden regularly to serve Him." Lucifer paused to consider those blessings, and the new one he had before him — shaped like a strong angel with charming, compassionate eyes. "I'm not His favorite, I don't think that, but Father has been very kind to me."

"Interesting." Michael drummed his fingers on the bench. "Because I think you're one of the greatest angels I've met." He waved a hand, instantly, when Lucifer burst into splutters of denial. "None of that. Father says the most important duty for an angel is worship, and that makes you the most important angel." Perhaps catching the scorch over Lucifer's face, reaching even his ears, Michael continued, "Can I share a secret with you?"

"Secret?" he echoed. "You have secrets, Michael?"

"It's not much of one. Can I share it with you?" It was obvious now that Michael masked nerves behind his smile.

"If you so trust me—"

"Then I'll be clear: I'm not very good at worshiping." He saw Lucifer's expression. "It's true. When Father asks me to praise Him, I'm awkward. I never know the right words, and I fumble, and I'm probably a shame to Him." Michael looked to the daisies by their feet, kicked them a bit. There was something endearing about it; this large angel who just couldn't keep still. "That's why when I saw you singing out in the streets, I was amazed. I'd never seen anything so— I don't know how to describe it." A delightfully saccharine laugh. "You can see now how I struggle with words."

"Please," Lucifer said; his breaths felt hollow, like all the many things inside of him were suddenly missing.

"Please what?" Michael raised his head a little, slanting it to him, and their gazes were soft, but somehow that was as overwhelming to Lucifer as a pierce into his heart. "Are you embarrassed?"

"Of course I am," Lucifer confessed, shaking his head, attempting to laugh away anxiety. "I don't know how— how to respond to your kindness."

"Will you respond to it with friendship?"

Lucifer jumped again but saw all the sincerity in the other's face, which had come even closer to him. "Friendship?" Without meaning to, only vaguely aware of a desire to escape captivity, he shot up to his feet. He blurted, "Michael, you are an archangel—"

Michael appeared to be all amusement again. "And you are Lucifer, angel of beauty and worship." He stood too, sturdier. "I want," then he hesitated, possibly searching for the right word, "I want to learn from you. Teach me how to worship, brother. I can see you'd be a great teacher." Lucifer noticed how Michael was taller, maybe half a head so, forcing him to lift his chin each time he meant to meet his eyes comfortably.

"Michael." 'Michael, Michael, Michael.' All his vision was blurring around the archangel, so that Lucifer could only see him, him alone. "Do you mean that? Really? It isn't a joke?"

"Something has to be done about your insecurity," Michael teased, and Lucifer laughed, quieter, but feeling all the tension in his muscles become water tumbling down. "Yes! Yes, I want you to be my friend. Yes, I want you to teach me all that you know."

Lucifer couldn't help a smile, but a golden gleam soon caught his eye — this long handle behind the angel and near to his head. Studded with a few gems and precious stones, it contained a rounded pommel end, holding a thick, dark tanzanite. From the smooth grip, there were long guards extending to the sides and, downward, reflective silver of some sort.

Michael blinked at Lucifer, then reached behind himself, grabbed the handle, and brought the object between the two of them, holding horizontally, as if an offering. Lucifer could only stare, lips parted a sliver. "Oh, forgive me, I should've stopped by my house to leave this before coming. I didn't mean to scare you." The young angel trailed his eyes along the beveled groove on the flat side of a thick, long blade that came together to a sharp point at the very tip, so sharp it seemed to be slicing through the air itself.

"What is it?"

"Oh! It's a sword. I suppose it's no surprise you've never seen one before. Do you want to hold it?" And he pressed it forward into the space between them, Lucifer raising a hand but only letting it hover over the stretch of the weapon.

"It's a big knife," Lucifer reasoned, aloud accidentally, only to purse his lips when the angel's rumbling laugh followed. He took the sword with one hand, at the handle, then placed his other there, as well. As Michael removed his hold, too fast, Lucifer felt the weight of the weapon strain against his palms before it tugged him down, all of him. He stumbled and gasped, but Michael hastily reached to take the guards, sustaining the sword off the ground.

"Oh— It's heavy, I'm so sorry— I forget that—" Michael's proud facade crumbled as he pulled his weapon from Lucifer's hands entirely and reached to slide it into the golden sheath strapped to his back. "I should have realized—"

Lucifer was not the type to interrupt, but he didn't like the look of shame that flickered over the other. "What is such a large knife for? A sword, you called it?"

"It's to fend off the beasts on Earth." Michael breathed with some drizzle of relief. "If you ever visit, you'll see why we need them."

"I wanted nothing more than to see Earth for a long time," Lucifer said, a bit offhandedly, not thinking. "I'm happy in Heaven and happy with Father, but I would still... want to see what it's like."

"It's an interesting place, an indescribable one." Michael nodded, seemingly to himself, then told him, "I'll take you to Earth, whenever you like."

Viserally, as if the memory had been gutted out, Lucifer remembered how he'd tried to befriend Uriel with the intention of having an archangel offer such. "Thank you," stiffly, "but my place is in Heaven. I wouldn't want go anywhere without the Lord's permission."

"I see."

Lucifer swallowed, wondering if all his disquiet was annoying the other; 'maybe I should be proud like him, maybe simply try it.' "I'll let you know," he said, wondering how to sound casual and relaxed, for once, "if I decide you can go with me."

That was too much — Lucifer knew his face was too flushed for Michael to believe he wasn't putting on a silly act; he couldn't even meet his eyes. And yet Michael laughed, wonderfully, "Oh, I do hope to convince you that I'm worthy."

Lucifer tried to stand up straighter, puff out his chest — realized he looked ridiculous. He turned his nose away and breathed. "We'll see about that." 'If my voice trembles anymore, I might break down into tears of embarrassment.' "It'll depend on how our friendship evolves."

"Of course, of course." Michael had a grin in his tone. "But then that is a yes that you'll be my worshiping mentor?"

"I suppose I'm saying that. However," Lucifer looked back at the older angel with a little smile tugging at the ends of his own lips, "I want to learn from you as well."

"Anything." Instant response. "Anything you would like to learn from me."

The eagerness seemed to catch them both off guard, but Michael's words laid between them. It pulled them closer, somehow. "Teach me to wrestle. I've gone to a million matches in the stadiums." Lucifer saw Michael's eyes widen and his eyebrows curve, teasing something, strangely, like regret. "You say you were enamored with my music, but that's how I felt whenever I saw your strength. I want to learn to be a fighter, to be strong the way that you are."

"Younger brother." The tenderness made Lucifer soften, grow weak against all his will. "I'm sorry I never saw you there. I was so focused that I didn't look into the crowd. Of course I'll teach you. I'll teach you until you've become the new angel of strength."

Lucifer shook his head. "Don't apologize. I'm just happy that we can finally meet." But, slowly, he sat on the bench once again, and

gripped his robes, and remembered how thin they were. Vulnerable —
he felt exposed and vulnerable still.

"Lucifer."

"Yes, Michael?" He let his head fall, allowed some discomfort to
creep onto the surface of himself once more, as his fellow angel sat at
his side. They were back to how they had been minutes ago.

"You're so ashamed of yourself." Lucifer blinked, wondering if his
emotions were really that noticeable, getting angry at himself for it, for
definitely irritating the prince. "I don't see why. If I could, I'd praise
you the way that you need, but I can't, so instead I'll tell you to enjoy
your beauty."

"My beauty?"

"Be proud, Lucifer. Take pride in what you do and your body."
Michael smiled, and all the worries inside Lucifer, again, fogged into
the amber sky. "Be kind to it, because you're being kind to the Lord's
creation." Lucifer didn't know what to say, didn't know how to
breathe, suddenly. "Can you promise me you'll consider my words?"

"I do promise." Lucifer nearly trembled, barely saw Michael nod.

"Well, I can't be here much longer. I have to tell everyone that I
arrived unharmed — at least, Raphael. Then I'll sleep for days, hopefully not weeks."

Lucifer thought of the time that had passed — years he'd spent
waiting to meet Michael, in inexplicable and desperate longing. There
was something so inevitable about this, as if he'd seen it coming, as if
angels could really taste, just a little, omniscience. "When may I see you
again? I want to see you again soon."

Michael was radiant against the forever brilliance of Heaven. "Not
long. I'll find you. And if I'm told to take to the stars again, I'll just take
you with me."

CHAPTER 14

Frowning, he enveloped the warm roll of bread in a handkerchief before settling it into the basket on the counter. "Baal," he sighed, "there's more bread of mine in that cabinet over there." Tossing his head. "Feel free to have as much as you'd like. I'm ashamed. Nothing can make up for how rude I'm being. You're right — I should never leave bed again."

Baal, who was seated on one of the counters, paused his leg-swinging to laugh. "It's really alright, brother. I'm no archangel, and I know you look up to Michael."

"I do, I do, but you're my friend. I barely know Michael. It's just that, well, Father is always giving him things to do. This is the first time since the gallery opening that we'll really have time to talk. I'm sorry."

"Don't be! We see one another every day." He hopped off the counter, nudged Lucifer, who laughed quietly. "So don't spend all your time with Michael worrying that you've hurt my feelings."

"Thank you, Baal. You have a heart of gold." Lucifer recalled Michael's golden jewelry, in his mind's eye. "You remind me... a little of Michael. Strong, I mean to say — though you're all soft underneath."

"I'm not soft!"

"You're soft! You're like a pastry full of jelly."

Baal was scoffing, but his cheeks tinged in pink. "I'm no such thing. I'm like a block of chocolate — bitter and tough."

"You're like chocolate cooked in sugar," Lucifer answered with a great smile. "Hm. Rosier is like a peach cobbler, and Asmodeus is like a spongy, sweet muffin."

"You're so disrespectful, Lucifer, saying these things while they're not here to defend themselves." But they were both laughing. "What is wrong with you? Are you hungry? Maybe you should be the one eating the bread."

"I'm not hungry! I'm only making good comparisons."

"You're lucky you're not the angel of comparisons."

"Is there one?!"

"Maybe, but we can be sure it isn't you."

Laughing, Lucifer was walked to the door by the other, each exchanging promises, between teases, to see one another again sometime soon. Baal suggested meeting at the bathhouse, and Lucifer suggested they meet anywhere but. The angel of flight planted a kiss on his cheek, then unfurled his wings behind himself and flapped strong enough to fling downwards a breeze that ruffled Lucifer's robes, before disappearing off into the sky. The most beautiful angel, on the other hand, stayed where he was for a moment — on the street, feeling his heart stutter and fumble. Then he tugged down on his patterned headscarf and tried to recollect the details of what he'd been told by an angel Michael had sent: 'Far south, the furthest you can go, until you see the streets grow narrower, a little rockier. There will be a house at the end of the city, with an open gate.' And he flew.

He did his best to think of nothing as he did, only to search for the place he'd been told to go: the home of Michael, in the southernmost corner of Heaven, where a river fed into a great rocky shore of a sea that shimmered as it reflected the perpetual, ample light above. Rolling waves, crashing against massive gray peaks and jagged boulders, where a few angels either laid or sat, some chattering, some luxuriating in silence, whereas a few others were in the water, three diving from the extreme heights they flew to — Lucifer saw this with sweet relief. He noted the walls of Heaven too, but they were far off into the distance, ingrained in the water and slicing the horizon in half.

Gliding down onto the same traversing golden path that ran through Heaven as arteries, he found that the buildings were close together in the south too. They marched up a steep hill, toward one house that sat quiet. "Oh," Lucifer said to himself, taking his basket with both hands. The home was guarded by a simple, single-colored facade exterior wall, holding an open gate door, peeking out a front garden that was unruly and lively, and the roof was flat but not empty. Stacked, stumbling, there was furniture all over it, between the pots that were placed on the edges, spilling over with various herbs and vines to fall onto the walls of the house.

Stepping past the gate — which was painted white but made of iron that had been meandered into flowery shapes — Lucifer hummed curiously at the staircase that greeted him immediately. It appeared the heart of the house was the second floor, rather than the first. Climbing up the steps, looking around, the beautiful angel asked himself if he'd ever come near to this place; surely, he had. It wasn't familiar, but he'd traveled everywhere back when he delivered fruits with Rosier. What if he'd left a basket of pears outside Michael's home thousands of years ago without realizing it?

The door was open. And the first thing Lucifer saw, as he moved inside, weary as strained hem, was a table, oak wooden; this is because there was an angel laid upon it as if it were a bed.

But, beyond him, there was a living room, large, with some couches and cushions on the floor, various other tables and candle stands and tapestries. A collection of minerals was scattered around, the sort ingrained into the stones that created them. Against the wall, there was a great model of the sun, made of painted metal, beyond description and beyond comprehension by virtue of its complexity, though one might note that it was composed of mirrors, or it was perhaps eyes, or it was perhaps a million golden teeth in an ever-shifting mouth.

"Lucifer!" Out of some corridor emerged Michael, carrying a smile and what appeared to be some brooms and various other cleaning instruments. He just about waddled with it all, coming into the living room and snapping, "And you, Phanuel! Get up!"

The angel on the table instantly shot upward to sit, and Lucifer realized with a startle that it was indeed Phanuel, with his hair disheveled and his clothes nearly slipping off his body in their entirety. He was alert, but fluttering his eyes, saying, "Hm? How did I get here?"

"A wave knocked you off a rock, and you hit your head." Michael set everything in his hands haphazardly on a couch then brushed himself off. Though tangled, his hair was raised with a tie on the back of his head, strands spilling. "I dragged you back in here. How are you doing? Does anything hurt?"

"My head," said Phanuel.

Lucifer frowned. "You should go see Raphael, brother." He moved toward him and set his basket on the table but instantly regretted it. Phanuel's gaze flickered to the bread poking out from the cloth, with a hungry swirl in his eyes, but Lucifer had only brought a single roll of time-extensive kitchen labor — for Michael. He'd thought he was going to be alone with him; 'I hoped to be.'

He fought the urge to be bitter. He knew better than that. Phanuel was Michael's friend, after all, and it would be impolite to kick him out, scandalously so. And yet Lucifer still couldn't bear to move his hand, take the bread, offer it to Phanuel.

"Lucifer is right, brother. Go see Raphael, just in case."

The youngest angel nearly sighed in relief.

"We can fly you there, if you wish."

"No, I think the walk will do me some good." Phanuel rolled off the table, stretched, then slapped his hand on Michael's shoulder. "But thank you for bringing me in and for laying me on your table like a vase."

Michael laughed. "I only meant to place you there for a moment. Forgive me."

"You do call me the angel of forgiveness," Phanuel responded, grinning easy, before he went toward the door, moved toward the youngest. "Oh, brother dearest." Thereafter, Lucifer's biggest fear came to pass: "I hope you don't mind, but I'm starving and..."

"You may have it," Lucifer said, forcing a smile well enough that it reached his eyes, but beneath his skin, he had just burst into shrieks so sharp they cut him. He reached into the basket and handed Phanuel the still-warm loaf. "Please, enjoy it." Though he hid his agony well, a part of him wished he hadn't, and that the other two could see the suffering in his gaze, but they didn't. Phanuel thanked him again, took a bite, and moaned, smacking his lips, before ruffling Lucifer's hair through the scarf — which he had spent an hour styling and was now most definitely ruined.

"Mm, you're a marvelous baker. Thank you!"

"Of course." He said it probably too stiffly that time, but Phanuel continued not to notice. "Thank you... for enjoying."

With a bright, and a perhaps silly, smile, Phanuel finally went to the door. "I'll go ahead and leave now, but we can all spend some time together later." He stopped. Again. "Ah but it's really great to see you invited Lucifer over, Michael. Our younger brother always talks to me about how much he admires you."

Flames rushed his face, and Lucifer nearly screamed, 'Be silent, Phanuel! Be silent! Be silent!'

"Oh?" Michael was smirking and quirking a brow. "He does? What does he say?"

Phanuel opened his mouth before his gaze flickered to the younger brother in question, who was looking at him, desperate, nearly trembling as he tried to tell him wordlessly to close his mouth and leave. Phanuel blinked, and he laughed, "You can ask him yourself." He put his hand on the door. "But hey, Lucifer! Thank you for the bread! And make sure to ask Michael why he talks so much about you too." Michael's face instantly stumbled into a warm tint. "See you two some other time!"

The mischievous angel left their presence, chuckling to himself. And the two who remained stood there in silence the taste of sulfur, Lucifer wondering if he should sprint outside before he was interrogated, but Michael coughed, cleared his throat. He muttered, "He must have hit his head very hard."

"Yes, yes."

"Can I offer you a drink?"

"You don't have to, but— Water would be good."

"I'll get you water." The kitchen was small, connected to the living room, not at all separated as Rosier and Lucifer's was; and Lucifer realized rather instantly that Michael seemed to live alone. Phanuel's house was elsewhere — Lucifer had seen him enter it once — so as Michael went for a small pitcher of water, opened cabinets for a glass cup, and served it, the younger angel couldn't help but notice there weren't many dishes, not utensils, not much of anything. "Pardon the mess in here. I promise it's not usually like this, but since I was gone so long, some angel helped themselves to welcoming me back with a feast, but I fell asleep just a few minutes in."

"You live alone, Michael?"

The archangel made a humming noise as he went over to the table Phanuel had been laying over. "That I do." He handed Lucifer his cup of water, then plopped onto a chair. "I promise this house is lavish," he accentuated the word, as if he enjoyed saying it, "when it's clean. I hoped to make it presentable before you arrived, but Phanuel was being a bit bothersome."

"It's alright." Lucifer sipped the drink, cool on his lips, before looking across the living room's hundred things, then to the kitchen again. He saw that the bulk of furniture was made of dark wood but carved and painted to uphold all sorts of geometric signs. The countertops were made of rough granite, with clusters of coppery colors, and stone chiseled with glyphs from, perhaps, a more ancient time. From the living area — a pair of open doors ushered in a rolling breeze and led out into an extended balcony, peering out over the sea, with two cushioned seats and a table. There was a small silver censer there, holding some burning incense smoking upward. "I can help clean—"

"Nonsense. You're my guest." He waved a hand. "Sit with me. I want to talk."

They hadn't done so since their time together in the gallery's garden. Lucifer took a breath and pulled back a chair before moving onto it, feeling oddly small, looking away from the other. "I did want to ask how you've been since your return. Has Father told you of any plans to send you back up?"

Michael shook his head. "I've hardly spoken with Him, to be honest with you. I did speak with the other archangels about things, developments on Earth and developments here."

"Developments?" To Lucifer, it always felt like nothing changed, despite the developments he had himself ushered in. "What sort?"

"Well, you," Michael laughed as the other angel flushed. "And the new buildings, new inventions, new foods. We are always developing, creating new things, finding new ways of going about our days, or theorizing about ourselves, about how we work, and about how all else works."

Lucifer set his drink down and smiled, soft, without meaning to. "I suppose that's all true."

"Do you feel that nothing ever changes, Lucifer?"

Confronted like this, Lucifer could only blink, then tilt his head to the prince. "Have you read my mind?"

This deep, gentle chuckle — "Maybe, but in all your time alive, haven't you felt yourself change? And if you change, then all the world does around you." Michael leaned back into his chair; it creaked. "You know, Gabriel told me how Father seems to adore you."

Lucifer tugged the scarf from his head and smoothed back mussed hair. He noticed the loose strands that tumbled down from Michael's bun; all he did was stare, though he longed to reach out, tuck them into place. "Ah." He shifted. "Gabriel. I miss him. I haven't seen him in a long time."

Michael smiled, faint as dying flame. "Raphael also sang your praises."

"Raphael is very sweet."

"And Uriel..." Michael hesitated, and Lucifer couldn't resist a little laughter. "He said you are a decent singer, that you are very good at worshiping. He even admitted that you're somewhat pleasant to look at." He kept on smiling as Lucifer kept on laughing. "It's the nicest thing he's ever said about anyone, I think."

"I'm so honored." He saw Michael's amusement. "I do mean it. Uriel seems like a kind angel, beneath his hard shell. Maybe shy, shyer than me."

"You'll have to forgive him. He's too old, one of Father's first angels, likely the first. He's seen more than you can imagine. But no — I still think you're shyer." With that, Michael swung back onto his feet and waltzed over to his kitchen once more. "Didn't I tell you we have to do something about that?"

Lucifer planted an elbow on the table, so that he could hold his cheek against his palm, and found himself equally amused and nervous

— his ankles crossing to keep himself in place. "But what if I enjoy being so timid and so humble?" What if Lucifer enjoyed hating himself?

"I'll have to convince you otherwise." Michael pulled, from a cabinet, a tall opaque bottle and another glass, which he subsequently served himself wine into. "But let's stop being distracted from the reason why you're here."

"How can I be distracted?" Lucifer would find Michael always made him laugh. "I have no clue why I'm here!"

"Have you forgotten, brother?" Michael grinned back at him then reached to place the wine where it had been. Turning to lean against one of the counters, he raised his cup and sipped, just barely brushing his lips against the maroon-red surface, testing for taste, texture. "Mm." His gaze flickered from his drink back to Lucifer. "I asked you to be my mentor, and you agreed. Do you remember?"

"Of course I remember." Lucifer could feel a smile wiggle across his lips, squinting his eyes; he raised some fingers and placed them over his mouth, as if to hide. "You also said that you'd teach me to wrestle."

"Mm, right. I did." The archangel stared, tapping a nail against his glass. "Very well, Lucifer. Let's meet three times a week for two hours. You teach me songs, and I teach you to fight. But where? Do you have any ideas?"

A hum; Lucifer thought of how Phanuel had eaten the bread he'd brought for Michael; he considered that he wished to be alone with the other. "How about... that garden where we spoke? Outside the new gallery?" He remembered the fountain, the way in which daisies tumbled out of it, having invaded the waters; he remembered how flowers had been in the Fountain of Life when Baal taught him to fly. Then, he remembered the universe, fantasized of Michael among the stars, lying on two planets as if they were his bed, and he would have a sun as his pillow, nuzzling his jaw. "It's unfinished, but I don't think anyone would interrupt us." Michael had thought of Lucifer — all those years in the sky.

Michael drank some wine again, slow, considering, before he replied, "That was a gallery? For art?" Lucifer told him that it was, and one end to the archangel's lips twirled. "I suppose it's no surprise that's where I found you then." Lucifer raised his head, not quite stammering because no words left him, and he had no idea what to make of what the smirking Michael had said. "Let's start soon. Tomorrow. I'll meet you there at midday."

"Yes," left Lucifer's mouth numbly, then he repeated himself: "Yes. We can fight first, and then we can lay on the grass and sing." That sounded a bit fun, a bit sweet. "How many instruments are you skilled in?"

"None," Michael said. "Why, how many can you play?"

Lucifer blinked. "Oh—" He was compelled to cower, as he always did, but beneath Michael's gaze, he felt strong, felt sturdy, felt like he could stand tall against the waves beating against the rocks outside. "All of them."

A rumbling chuckle. "All of them? Is there anything you can't do, angel of beauty?"

For the first time in his short life, pride unraveled in his chest; and Lucifer smiled, delicate and sweet as honey.

CHAPTER 15

They were shouting his name from across the bazaar. Lucifer was perched on top a closed clay pot, sitting near to Rosier and flipping through bundles of paper on which he'd drafted a new song for his Father. Once he saw two angels rushing over, and Lucifer hopped off to stand straight, hugging his work to his chest. He looked at them curiously, then laughed when one of them bowed and cheered, "What a delight to be looked at by the most beautiful angel in Heaven!"

"Did you come only to compliment me?" Lucifer became strongly aware of his appearance anyway and reached to ensure his two thick braids, joined together at the back, had stayed in place. He couldn't afford to look disheveled; after all, Eden was waiting for him.

"I heard a rumor that Michael's training you." This angel was Azazel, face overbrimming with henna. "Are you planning to be a fighter now?"

The other piped in, "But should you really be wrestling? I thought Father made you to be beautiful, and fighting is such a dirty thing."

"I don't think it's dirty," Lucifer argued, though half-heartedly. "Even then, none of you are fulfilling your roles all the time, so why should I be beautiful always?" He teased that these two ought not to worry over him regardless and that an angel fighting was a beautiful thing in its own right, but neither of the angels before him looked convinced.

Azazel said, "That might only be the case for you, brother. Next time you train with Michael, could we go watch?"

Lucifer nearly opened his mouth to tell them that he wouldn't mind, before remembering that he would. "I'm sorry. Michael and I train alone." They deeply enjoyed the privacy, something neither received much of, given their popularity, which only increased when they were seen beside one another.

Lucifer had heard all the rumors already: 'I saw Lucifer and Michael walking the streets together,' 'I caught them talking and laughing not once or twice but four times this week,' and 'Even if they don't say it, the signs of friendship are all there!' Once, Michael had mentioned that he'd heard the gossip too, and Lucifer had waited to see if he would say more, but he hadn't. 'That's alright.' It was nice not to concern themselves with the rest of Heaven. It was nice to exist as only two angels in a universe, however momentarily.

The beautiful angel of worship had begun to frown, apologetically. "We don't want to be distracted, is all, and I don't want for you two to see me humiliated." The angels laughed and denied that could ever be the case, but Lucifer shook his head and affirmed it. "He pins me to the ground over and over; it's embarrassing." He pursed his lips, then chuckled a bit to himself. "But if all this gossip is really so rampant, I need you two to do something for me."

Azazel raised a brow and curled an end to his pretty lips. "You would like to amend the rumors?"

"Precisely," said Lucifer. "Make it known that not only is Michael training me, I'm training him as well. I've been teaching him to sing and worship our Father. And, as I am, he's embarrassing himself terribly." The two angels before him laughed, as well as Rosier, who was handing someone a basket of fruit and trying his best to look as if he weren't listening in. "Am I clear?"

"Crystal, brother." Azazel, snickering, pat his friend on the shoulder. "We'll correct everyone and leave you be now." Turning, he took the other with him, and Lucifer smiled as they walked away.

Then, he caught Rosier's amused smile, in the short second the angel brandished it shamelessly before he twisted his face away. "What are you smirking about, Rosier?" Lucifer leaned against the pot he'd sat on with giggling amusement. "You think I don't know what everyone is saying?"

"I don't doubt your intelligence, younger brother." Rosier emphasized the *younger*, as if to remind him. "But you're so strange. Don't you want the rumors to cease? But here you are, spreading them further."

"Angels will talk no matter what I say. It's better I correct the gossip than try to stop it. And, they're not saying anything untrue or offensive, are they? Michael and I are, indeed, teaching each other our talents and failing miserably."

Rosier hummed before reaching to grab his belongings, set by the ground. "And what about the rumors that Michael and you are friends?"

"I will not comment on those."

"Is it true? Are you and him friends?"

Lucifer waved a hand, but the simple question had done enough to make a scattered blush rise over his cheeks. "I have to go see Father now. Oh, and then I'll be busy after that a while." He had plans with Michael; this time, they'd promised to bring a little cider, just so they could relax over the grass a while — talk. "But I'll join you for dinner." Michael had said he enjoyed hearing the younger one ramble; Lucifer didn't know why he had so much to say whenever he was with him.

Rosier gathered some cloth bags into his arms, then snickered, saying he would invite Asmodeus to join them. They met in a short embrace before each took off in opposite directions — Lucifer walking with unstable breaths, so small you could hold them in your palm. He turned his attention back to God, once again clutching his writing close. It was always easy to settle back into this, this worship: once he set his mind to love, it ignited his body whole. Watch — he smiled, wide like he wasn't sober. All of his heart — weighting with adoration for the Lord, and soon enough, it began to burn.

He folded his papers, slipped them into a pocket of his robes, then flew up and out of the city, then downward to the clouds. There, he saw a few angels, sat on the white hills, chattering. 'Maybe,' he thought, 'Michael and I should spend some time here together too.' As his feet brushed the grass of Eden, he further considered, 'Or not. I don't want him to think I can't live a day without his company.' He walked, seeing the Lord's garden as no different than always. 'It's only without God that I can't live.' He went one by one greeting the animals, petting them when they walked past, and feeling the plant life welcome him as well, either with wavy gestures or affectionate caresses.

When Lucifer arrived at God's usual seat beside the waterfall, he bowed deep enough to kiss the grass, then got back onto his feet so that he could say hello to the choir of angels. He hugged and kissed them, then turned his attention to the Father. As always, He faced away, but took a moment to stare at Lucifer, a brief one, but a moment nonetheless; angels often whispered of that — their loving Father, who looked at Lucifer the most of all His creations.

With a bashful smile, the youngest angel went to serve the Lord. He took the large pitcher, bowing his head respectfully, greeting Him, "Our great Lord, Father of all things, your angels praise you. Holy, holy, holy that you are." He poured wine into the Creator's chalice before pressing his lips to the table.

"Sing for me," the Father said.

Joy in his eyes, Lucifer nodded and opened his mouth. He sang, wordlessly, only sustaining a range of pitches — inside him, he could feel the rattle of the instrumental organs the Lord had placed there in his chest — to bathe the holiest garden in a voice like sugar. This he did, until his Father drank from His chalice, indicating He had heard enough. Lucifer cleared his throat soon, thereafter, reached for his timbrel and rattled it, and he parted his lips again. In worship, he left the angels in a fast, jovial song that had been worked on for days and written to dance to.

The Lord smiled.

When the time came for the angels to feed their Creator, they stepped forward with pre-prepared bowls of fruit. Lucifer had already sat on the ground, eager to rest and hear his Father speak, when he was ordered to come closer. It was so sudden that Lucifer startled and the other angels looked to him with curious tilts of their heads, but the angel of worship didn't hesitate before rising up again. This was an honor, and Lucifer knew this as he nodded at the command to feed the Lord. The beats of his heart thundered as he reached for a single berry, taking it with two fingers. Barely managing not to shiver — he placed it into the Lord's mouth.

"In a keeper's garden, there was once a dove, so pure its feathers held neither spot nor pattern. And so beautiful was the bird that no one would dare touch it. For it was known that the handsomest creation is that uncorrupted by hands, by affections — consider how paint chips when caressed."

Lucifer's mind wandered; it'd never done before but now it did. How would his training with Michael go? It had been weeks and, still, there was only minor improvement to be seen. He could remember with intense vividness the first time they'd met in the garden: Lucifer — unsure of himself, clutching his tunic — and Michael — stretching and grinning, looking excited beyond belief. And proud. Michael was always proud — 'the angel of pride.'

The Father's words snuck into Lucifer's reverie: "But the dove itself did not know this. Catching its own reflection in the mud, it began to wonder what might happen if it dirtied itself. And, from the inside, this bird began to stain itself with its own affections. Misleading itself, the bird wondered if there was another garden past this mud, one the dove could make for itself. This because he had grown dissatisfied in this garden, where the others knew better than to adore him."

Several minutes were spent on hand and feet placements. And once they'd begun to wrestle, they gripped one another's bodies, digging their heels into the grass, as they staggered, trying to tip the other over. Michael taught him how to throw punches, kicks, and emphasized all power came primarily from manipulating your center of gravity and weight.

At one point, Lucifer believed he'd had a tight grip on Michael's waist, and he tried to lunge at him, to topple him to the ground. Michael had responded with a much stronger surge forward. Falling, Lucifer had panicked and flailed, even attempting to force his wings out of his back. The two — grunting and rocking. Michael's hands had taken Lucifer's wrists and held them over his head, his weight coming down on the younger's legs. Lucifer's heart, erratic at that point, had tangled by his ears as he breathed heavy, sweating, panting, trying to squirm, but Michael looked down on him with no more than a smirk.

Michael — taking both of Lucifer's wrists with one hand, holding them sturdy with no hint of difficulty, still over the other. And Lucifer had cried, "This isn't— This isn't fair— You're the angel of strength." Enervated gasping — breaking up his words. "I can never beat you." Their faces had been close, so close that their breaths brushed their lips; and Lucifer, feeling nothing but fire and newborn, tight confusion in the pit of his stomach, could only stare up at the other, wide-eyed, feeble.

"Wrestling and fighting are not only about strength," Michael had said, red-faced, panting but not nearly as much as the other. By his head, the pinks of a bowering myrtle tree. "If that were the case, I would never lose, but I do. You'll find your own strengths to beat me, eventually. I promise." His eyes had been great redwood, shaking with the bouts of a storm; something between the two of them felt hot — forging metal.

"The dove," said Father, "would fly into the mud one day with another bird, which it had deceived to think like him. And they became dirtied together, amid searching for the other garden beneath the mud. And they found so much pleasure in rebelling that they couldn't see how their feathers had grown filthy, nor realize they would never dry. And they dug, but there was no other garden, there was no other paradise, and the doves would never be pure again."

"But I still don't think I'll ever be able to win," Lucifer had said up to Michael, noting the way the older angel had blocked the light above them. A shadow draped onto Lucifer's body, running its hand up his sides, feeling him.

"I have all of my hope in you," Michael had replied, before moving off him, then taking his hand, pulling him back up onto his feet. Their palms had fit nicely together.

Lucifer blinked, looked up as he slowly fed his Father a cherry, and he waited, waited for the Lord to end the story happily, waited to be told the doves asked for forgiveness and were granted it, but no such reassurance came. The angel found his mind roughly jerked to the present, and when he was sent to sing with the others, as usual, he had to fight a frown. His mind whirled with the tale of the dove, unsure what it had meant, unsure what they were supposed to take out of it other than confusion and a sort of impending anxiety.

'Have we done something? Is He unhappy with us?'

It wasn't until the Father started to dismiss angels from His presence and from Eden, not in any different a fashion as He usually did, that Lucifer began to fear the story had been targeted, that it had been directed at himself somehow.

The Lord told him, "Lucifer," and his heart petrified, "stay with me."

The retreating angels stopped, glanced back at Lucifer — because it was not typical for God to ask only one angel to remain to keep Him company — but they didn't meet his eyes. Turning away and hurrying, the angels all flew up and away from Eden, until the angel of beauty was left there with nothing but his body and his soul. He didn't have an idea what to do except move to stand beside his Father, bowing lowly, affirming, "As you wish, Lord Highest."

"We have not spoken in a while. Tell me how your heart has been."

"My heart? I do not know — I am full of love and adoration, but that is expected of the angel of worship, is it not?"

"That it is. Have you been happy?"

"I am always happy, Father. Your mercy endures forever."

"Stand up straight," and Lucifer did, with some hesitation, "and pick up your chin, show me your face." As the Lord turned to see him, the angel obeyed but remained his gaze by His feet in respect, feeling unworthy of anything else. "It is very clean but go rinse it with the water of the pond."

"Yes, Father." He didn't falter in following orders, walking to the bank, with all its rocks, fed by the shimmering waterfall before them. Lowering into a crouch before moving onto his knees, Lucifer scooped some of the water in his hands. He delicately brought them to his face and wet his skin, shutting his eyes, massaging as droplets cascaded down his front. Instantly, he worried the Lord would scold him for dampening his clothes, but instead, he heard an order for him to return to His side. Lucifer stood back up and attempted to pat his face dry before his eyes fluttered open, soft.

As he walked back, his Father said, "There is nothing more important than remaining clean. An angel that becomes impure becomes unworthy to live in paradise."

Lucifer stood by His side, unsure, not understanding. "Impure? What does it mean to be impure?" In his head, he cried, 'Have I become impure? Have I become ruined?'

"To not know impurity is to be pure," the Lord replied simply. "Do not tremble, Lucifer. You have nothing to fear."

The sound of his name in God's voice made Lucifer still; he whispered, "Forgive me, Father."

"But you must keep it in your heart that you shall always remain clean, in all ways. Your mind and your body belong to me — see what goodness has produced in you, what eagerness to clean yourself, what earnestness and longing and concern to worship has. Thus far, you have proven yourself to be innocent. But your eye is the lamp of your body and when your eyes are healthy, your whole self is full of light. When they are soiled with filth, you become full of darkness." And He would wave his hand, indicating to all of that which composed the garden. "Everything in Eden, everything on Earth, and all that lives between the stars or in Heaven was founded and established by me. Ask yourself who might ascend to the mountains of the Lord." Lucifer swallowed dry, nodding. "Who may walk on the fiery stones along the holy mount of God?" Trembling again. "It is the dove with clean hands and a pure heart."

Lucifer could not hold himself up; he fell to his knees, let his head fall forward so that his chin pressed to his collarbone. He cried, "Holy, holy, holy Father. Great and boundless. Creator of all things." He clutched at his robes, heard the crinkle of the psalm he'd written. "I am your servant. Please have mercy on me."

"You have my mercy." But the Father didn't tell him to stand. "And you have my love, Lucifer."

It took everything Lucifer had not to burst into tears of affection, even if his knees pressed onto prickling rocks. He thought, 'It is good to bleed, right?'

"All that I say comes from a place of love." 'Is love meant to pierce?'

"If it's an angel of beauty that you are, you must know there exists no greater beauty than that of a well-kept garden, that which Eden is now and Earth will become in time. During your creation, I planted a garden inside you with young flowers that I can see now are still not bloomed." Lucifer couldn't fight the urge to put a hand over his chest, as if he'd be able to feel for them, and breathe hollow, searching for the sound of shifting leaves where lungs might be.

"I want to be good for you," came the soft words from between Lucifer's lips. "I want to be perfect for you." 'I was made for you.' "All I wish is to have you speak fondly to me."

There was the distant sound of grass, crunching as someone stepped upon it.

"Today, you are all that you need to be, Lucifer." And the angel lifted his head a little. "You do not need to search for yourself any longer. You are complete, I made you so."

"Thank you, Father."

Then, a simple suggestion: "You might enjoy seeing Earth. I know that is something you have longed to do." Lucifer's heart — withering into gratitude. "Go with my blessing."

He, earnestly, jumping, kissed the Lord's rings, wishing to make tangible the extent of adoration in his heart. Lucifer worshipping unconditionally — a million years he could've spent there — but the noises of crushed grass, someone approaching, were unrelenting. Lucifer glanced backward — saw an angel he didn't initially recognize step out from between trees, with expansively fiery wings pulling back into a body.

It was Uriel, with his hair down for once, in long cornrows. The archangel saw him but said nothing, as he continued toward the Lord.

As if from a distance, Lucifer heard the Father dismiss him, and he nodded and kissed His hand again, then stood straight Lucifer turned on his heel, though not before seeing Uriel go to sit beside God's chair. The old angel rested against it, shutting his eyes, as the Father's hand went to the top of his head. He patted it, comfortingly.

CHAPTER 16

I n a previous dream, the Throne had appeared to him as emerald, and it did so again — but this time fractured. And He who sat upon it was jasper and carnelian. Too much has been said already on the Lord's cosmology, that which He wore as skin — Lucifer noted it again — but there was life on Him too. His head was often molded upward to resemble a corn stalk; from His chest, there was a canyon of divorced continents; and when His eyes weren't stars, they were the gazes of every insect that'll ever roam.

In the future, they'll think Him many gods or they'll think Him none at all — already, Lucifer wondered if God always had so many faces, if God considered Himself one thing, or if He, too, was rummaging for identity, for purpose. God, looking for God.

Not enough has been said of God's servants, His handmaidens, who were made up of hundreds, thousands, of wings all beating against one another, interlocking wheels of molten gold encasing living moons and carrying enough eyes to fill an ocean, and stretched thin faces stacked on bulky ones, furred. Their thousand eyes were always burning, and when Lucifer hurried to stand among them, those flamed gazes always looked at him as if he didn't belong. Lucifer would only touch his flesh in response, wondering why he wore it, as if he had dressed improperly for the occasion.

Each of these angels tore through the dimensions, through the dark, but their abstractness paled in comparison to the God on the Throne, who Lucifer couldn't see now. He tried again, but what he saw was collapsed, contorted into itself enough that all fell inside, that nothing could escape — not even light.

Then — *tic, tic, tic* — knocks, so many of them in quick succession that Lucifer had no choice but to startle. His eyes shot open; he felt the many pillows either beneath his head or surrounding his figure or clutched to himself. Having wanted to consider his dreams, he breathed, slow, but turned his head when the knocks came again, but they were more like taps, clinking on glass. Lucifer rose to sit, groaning and feeling blankets, sheets, quilts, slip down his body. He reached for the curtain by his bed, realizing the sounds were coming from the window behind. Curiously, he tugged it aside, streaming brilliance into the bedroom.

A grin embraced him; Michael was laughing as he tapped against the window again with his knuckle, his rings making that little *tic* noise. And Lucifer leaned forward to see that Michael had somehow perched himself on the tiny windowsill, on the tips of his toes, his wings half-spread out behind him so that he could balance. He'd seen the archangel's wings before, but he remained stunned by their span and the deep, brown feathers along the top slowly transitioning to a thick row of whites, before the lines of dark wenge wood at the bottom. "Good day to you, brother," Michael called out. "May I come in?"

"The window doesn't open," Lucifer laughed. "You'll have to come in through the balcony."

"Will you let me in through there?"

Instead of answering, Lucifer smirked, then pulled the curtains to cover the window, and Michael, again. He hopped off the bed, stretched his arms over his head and hummed to himself thoughtfully. He purposefully hesitated a minute before going to the closed entrance to the balcony — heard some rustling on the other side. He opened the doors, saw Michael tucking his wings back into his back and running a hand through his hair to smooth some curls away from his face. "Good day," Lucifer greeted, unable to keep a smile from dancing upon his mouth. "Is there a reason you've broken into my home and woken me up?"

"Broken in?" Michael laughed. "I asked permission. Now, may Lucifer, Father's favorite and most beautiful angel, allow me into his room?"

Lucifer turned up his nose, looked away, and hummed, mischief twirling his lips. "And why should Lucifer do such a thing?"

"I come with an open heart and wish to make an earnest request of him."

"You promise that it's earnest?"

They were both smiling. "It's a little self-serving."

Lucifer shifted back. "Well, you've caught Lucifer's interest, so he'll spare you a few minutes of his time, so long as you treat it well."

"How kind of you." Michael stepped inside, looked around, then seemingly wondered aloud, "So this is your home. It's very nice."

"I'm curious how you found it." Lucifer plopped back onto his bed with a yawn, leaning back onto the mass of pillows. "Was it Phanuel who told you?"

"It was Phanuel after he asked Asmodeus to remind him."

"Mm. I'll have to scold Asmodeus for exposing others' secrets so easily." But Lucifer's heart softened as Michael went to sit beside him, leaning into the cushions as well; he couldn't help but think this was the sort of thing friends did: sit in bed together and talk.

"I'm sure he wouldn't have told so easily if it were under normal circumstances." Michael flopped back with a relaxed sigh. "I told him it was an emergency."

"Emergency?"

"Yes — I had to see you immediately." Michael turned his head a little, looking at him, a crinkle of glee by his eyes. "Word spreads so quickly in Heaven, as I'm sure you know." Lucifer had assumed the chirps of rumor had flooded the city already, but he was disappointed to hear it confirmed, nonetheless. "Father told you to visit Earth."

"He did," Lucifer reaffirmed, "and did you hear that I'm planning to leave tomorrow? I'm happy you came by. I don't know how long I'll be gone. Gabriel said he'd take me, but he warned me it's difficult to keep track of time between Earth and Heaven."

"I spoke to Gabriel."

"Oh?"

"I told him I would take you to Earth myself."

Lucifer shot up to sit upright. Swift, he turned and raised an eyebrow at Michael, who was smiling widely, proud, proud, always proud. "But Father said Gabriel should—"

"I spoke to Father already. And, I had a wrestling match planned for tomorrow, and then a chariot race the day after that, but I canceled it. I canceled all the plans I had for this."

"But—" Lucifer spluttered, scrambling over to move closer, wanting to grab and shake him. "You can't be serious, Michael. Why would you do all that? Did you hit your head?"

"I've never felt better, brother." Michael was still laying back comfortably. "There are not many greater joys than seeing angels experience things for the first time. You need someone to protect you, too, and I don't doubt Gabriel's abilities but, don't forget, I made this promise to you. I'm fulfilling it now."

Lucifer wanted to take this as lightly as the other was, but there was a star-recalling burst in his chest of emotion — tenderness, fondness, intense longing to embrace the other for his easy kindness, to squeeze him as tight as he could. "Don't laugh at me, Michael, but— This means a lot to me. You're really too nice to me—"

"No, don't say that." Michael sat up finally, shuffled even closer so their legs brushed against each other. And he leaned toward his face and spoke firmly, "You're a great angel, Lucifer. Don't say things like that. You act like you don't deserve kindness." Lucifer wanted to tell Michael he'd always thought this, had always had this little, unintelligible feeling in his head. "Well, you deserve a lot more than that. I feel like I have to invent new ways to be nice to you."

"I'm sorry—"

"No, don't apologize. You're a sweet angel, and I like to spend time with you. Don't argue with me." Lucifer smiled, feather-soft, noting Michael was getting just a little better at complimenting already. "Let me take you to Earth, let me show you all that it is."

"I could never deny you." Lucifer, feeling more gentle and warm happiness than maybe ever before, stood and said, "Come with me to the kitchen. I baked some bread earlier — please try it."

Laughing — "If Lucifer insists."

"Lucifer does insist." Standing, moving to the door, the beautiful angel lingered there. "Come. I want to leave this room. I had a strange dream."

"Tell me about it," Michael replied, chuckling, getting to his feet, and Lucifer hesitated only because he didn't want to be thought of as strange himself. "I hardly ever dream, personally—" the younger one couldn't imagine that, couldn't remember the darkness, like the one of infancy, anymore, "—so tell me about yours."

They talked, though Lucifer did most of it, and Michael listened. Occasionally, a glimmer of curiosity or confusion shined through, and Lucifer feared the prince would berate or laugh at him or leave him, but he never did. He laughed, fondly, kept replying, "Tell me more. No, I want to hear you say it. I like how you think," as if he thought Lucifer's strangeness was a little beauty too.

But then Michael bid farewell, and Lucifer went to work preparing the couple belongings he'd bring before going to spend some time with Baal, who laid on the living area's carpet with him. Asmodeus arrived too, served everyone drinks, pausing to fling grapes across the room that Rosier attempted to catch with his mouth. Lucifer rested his head against Baal's ribcage and mumbled if Baal had any advice to share, to which the older angel told him that Lucifer should fly high and quick, slip between branches, but stay on the ground to avoid the winged-beasts.

"But I wouldn't worry," Rosier told Lucifer quickly, "since Michael is going with you, you have nothing to fear." That only made him worry worse; what if Michael suffered an injury because of him? "What you should be concerning yourself with is that I'm going to be living alone for days! Who's going to have breakfast with me?"

"If you'd like," Asmodeus offered, "I can move back in for the time Lucifer's gone and make a mess of the kitchen."

"It'll be like you never moved out then," Rosier grumbled but playfully.

Then, Azazel — having definitely heard the rumors and helped spread them — was at the door with a warm corn flour drink and wishes of good luck, and after laughing with him a while, Lucifer decided it was time to rest again. He went to pack a cloth pouch with another pair of clothes, a few rolls of bread, and some flasks of water he gathered from the basin. Then, there was nothing to do but sleep again. Sighing, pulling on the drapes, falling back onto the bed, Lucifer rolled onto his belly.

He laid a while like that, eyes shut, face smothered against a pillow. He remembered Michael — those confident eyes, those strong arms — a ditzy smile quivering Lucifer's lips, then his wings unfurling to curl up close to his body, hugging his form. 'Stop, it's not right to think of another angel so much.' It was strange, it was wrong. Lucifer forced thoughts of the Lord, hoping he'd see Him again, in his sleep, and sit beside the great Throne.

Instead, he dreamt of Michael.

And himself, standing on the grass of an unfinished garden outside a gallery, but it was not a dream — a memory. Michael, embarrassed, saying he'd make a fool of himself, and Lucifer, blowing into his pipes, smiling. He told Michael to loosen his muscles, to dance to the music, but the archangel couldn't grasp moving his body with no tactic, no training, no goal. Left without recourse, Lucifer said, "Follow my lead." He kept playing his instrument, swaying, then hopping, spinning, before allowing the waves of the rhythm to take his hips. He danced around the other, hearing Michael whine and complain that he didn't quite understand how dancing translated to worship.

Lucifer wasn't keen to explain, and Michael made a dauntless effort, but he couldn't loosen, couldn't get himself to whirl about, not yet.

When the decided time came — Lucifer awoke with a delicate drag on his soul he couldn't comprehend, wings still clutching him. He arose, dressed in the tunic and robe he'd prepared in advance, then said goodbye to the flora in his bedroom. He skipped down the staircase, slipped into Rosier's room to tell his friend that he was leaving already — stopped.

Rosier was fast asleep, curled up like an animal, though he'd promised to be awake to see the other off. But Asmodeus was also there, laying on his side, draped in the same bedsheet as the angel of fruit. He was awake, propped up on an elbow, his hand cradling his jaw. Both in greeting and dismissal, Asmodeus waved his free hand. And Lucifer stood there, puzzled momentarily, before realizing he didn't have the time to waste pondering this. He simply smiled, instead, stepped closer, and pressed a kiss to Rosier's forehead, then Asmodeus' cheek, right by his smirk.

In contrast, Baal was awake and out on the street with a great grin. When Lucifer reached him, Baal hugged him tight and wished him luck before walking to the center of Heaven alongside the youngest angel, fiddling with his fingers. There, the prince already was, sword at his back — the same one Lucifer hadn't seen since their first meeting in the garden.

Michael, like him, carried a cloth bag slung securely along his torso, paired with what appeared to be a rope of bulky, golden chains Lucifer didn't see the use for. Gabriel and Raphael were there as well, at either of Michael's sides, though Raphael supported his weight on a wooden cane with both hands. It was thick, almost to the arm-width of a lithe angel, with carvings along the sides, painted in reds, blues, oranges, blacks.

Lucifer realized he'd never seen Raphael walk before.

The angel Uriel was standing away, just enough that he looked to be an observer of the scene rather than a participant. When Gabriel and Raphael greeted Lucifer and told him that they'd keep his name in their prayers, Uriel opted to nod, simple, at him, though respectfully. Lucifer smiled at that.

"Are you ready?" Michael asked, moving to the youngest angel's side with his wings already outstretched behind him.

"As much," Lucifer gulped down his nerves, "as I will ever be." Pulling out his own wings, Lucifer followed the chief prince seconds after he'd shot upward into the air. And he tried not to turn back to see Baal and the empty spots where his two other friends should be, succeeding, and then wishing he hadn't. By the time he finally looked behind himself, Heaven was a distant city, like Venus' brilliance becoming a faraway star. The space beneath became clouds, and in between them, Lucifer saw hints of Eden. He knew this path well, but

Michael, up ahead, didn't descend yet, and it wasn't long before the familiarity of the sky began to reshape into something else, something thicker.

As the archangel glided downward, Lucifer flapped to catch up, opening his mouth to ask if they were nearly there, but as if prompted, Michael pointed at the world they approached.

It was greenery, life that shouldn't be at all foreign to angels, but here, it was. Great trees sprouted from the ground, hanging so many hefty leaves and hulking branches that the air was dense, so dense Michael called out that they'd have difficulty landing. But Lucifer couldn't reply — his gaze enveloped by life, by the abundance of shifting foliage that he saw in every direction, descending from the massive arms of trees they approached and in the traces of the faraway ground Lucifer caught between them. Something about breathing was wet — humid — stirring out a gasp from him, who fumbled trying to accustom to its weight, along with the heat. Air rushed, beating against him, and yet he wanted to fan himself.

When there was a sign of clearing, however small it was, over the jungle, Lucifer hurried. He landed before even Michael, reeling in whatever breath he could. Feet staggering, he stumbled and twirled. Looking all about, eyes wide, mouth agape. Plants he had never seen before, open to show him their wild colors and asymmetry — but not flowers, not yet. He turned up to the towering trees, bearing cones and scale-like leaves, and sensed ferns brush against his legs, along with horsetails and mosses. He just barely caught sight of what seemed to be tiny, minuscule insects on the ground, many known, and Lucifer almost sighed in relief, but that was only temporary.

Movement, on a tree — Lucifer nearly yelped out loud at the realization it was a beetle, black with a hardened shell, familiar but different. Something was off about its composition, like someone had rebuilt it from an imperfect memory, and it was massive. Then, there was a flash of 'a creature that isn't a bird' — with a wingspan maybe the size of Lucifer's arm, distinctively un-avian features on its face, despite the bright feathers that doused it, and a long beak that swooped down to snap across the body of the beetle. The small legs of the victim — spasm-ing before the creature shot back into the air with its meal.

Lucifer stumbled, heart itself shivering. He turned over to Michael, wildly, hoping for an explanation, but the prince was stone, careful eyes set on the wild tendrils of jungle before them. Lucifer breathed, through his mouth, but Michael's hand raised quick, silencing him. There was no other choice; Lucifer followed the archangel's gaze, slowly, hardly moving — just his head.

Immediately, he couldn't see it. He thought it was only leaves, merely rustled by the wind, but there were two flickers, quickly — a blink. What followed was a low rumble, sizzling with reverb, growing and growing, not in mere volume but number. Lucifer's pulse entirely stopped. Out from the trees, into the small clearing, stepped the clawed foot of the creature, and its body followed — bipedal but with its abdomen horizontal, shorter arms near the front, leading to sharp claws — a large head before itself. From its mouth, opening wider than Lucifer's width, there were rows of teeth, coming to points like the tips of kitchen knives. Its feather-y composition did nothing to detract from its unusual smoothness, instead camouflaging it among the ferns.

From its sides, more beasts emerged, until there were four, or maybe five, but Lucifer's breaths were coming quicker, unstable. His heart had begun beating again, but with such force it rocked him. Barely, he heard the clink of Michael reaching back to unsheathe his sword. In a whisper, he told Lucifer, "Climb up a tree."

"What—?" Lucifer was interrupted by the sudden strike against his ears of a screech, roaring out from one of the creatures. He heard Michael snap the order at him this time. Lucifer, jolting, flapped his wings, enough to shoot backward into tough bark clumsily. He gasped but gripped the tree, just as one of the beasts had seen him. Lucifer scrambled, using both his wings and his grip on the branches to make his way up as fast as he could. Hearing Michael's yells of force, then the rips of a sword cutting through 'something wet, something that splatters like a fruit.'

Lucifer climbed, clambering, shaking so much now his vision blurred as he looked back. He'd turned to see the archangel but instead saw a beast lunging forward, nearly closing its jaw around one of Lucifer's legs. He hoisted himself up with a short, frightened cry, hugging a tall branch and trying to continue up as hastily as possible.

He panted and trembled, desperate to hold on, but saw that the beast had managed to claw its way up some of the bark — was coming closer, coming nearer. Lucifer wanted nothing more than to scream, wings stretching out again instinctively, before he hissed when they smacked into the sprawl of leaves and branches above and tangled themselves there.

He squirmed, reaching behind, trying to tug his wings free, but the beast kept scampering to him. Watching, wide-eyed, confused, all of himself scattered in disarray — Lucifer had never felt fear like this, nothing close. It completely paralyzed him; his bones locked, his mouth went dry.

He hadn't noticed Michael had gone quiet, that the creatures Michael had set himself up against were silent. Lucifer only saw a flash of light before golden chains came around the approaching beast. They seared into its skin, tightened, choked it out as it shrieked and shrieked. And Michael was above, somewhere between flight and standing on the beast's head. He had leapt into the air, at some point, and now held the ends of the chain with one hand — raised his sword up high with the other.

With a great, overpowering shout, Michael brought the sword down, and the raptor's head came clean off.

CHAPTER 17

"In the beginning," Michael said, "our Father created all the heavens and all the earths, all at once. But the folds of the deep tore, and everything burnt up into light. From those flames, He created the angels. The first few were not right; they ripped into streams, over and over, as the Lord weaved the sea out of the sky." He glanced back at Lucifer, a mere flicker of the gaze. "It was from those angels that came the creation of pain — created from their feelings of incompleteness. Everything fell into a dark age that lasted 250 million years. In all that time, the angels cried out to God that He have pity on them. They begged to have their bodies stilled and their thoughts all stopped; and Father, in His mercy, took one angel and laid him to sleep on the black water of the abyss. He settled his heart and molded him for another million years, and then He hung him up, enormous and hot, and he was the first star. Father did the same with all the others, promising that angels would never know suffering again, that as long as we worship, we would live in paradise with Him for eternity."

Lucifer flickered his gaze upward into the blue sky, brushstroke-d with white intermingled bodies, moving along, slow. As expected, he couldn't see the stars from here; he couldn't see his eldest brothers. "That's why Heaven... is paradise?" He stepped, careful, along the branches, up high on the trees with Michael. "That's why Father allows us to have lives of pleasure?" Smiling — "He is great, great and merciful."

"Indeed." Michael stopped, then gestured for Lucifer to come nearer. "I hope that provides you with some reassurance. Father is good, and these beasts have their own role in His greater plans. Perhaps one day, they'll be with us in paradise."

Lucifer had wailed earlier, "What happened? Heal the beast! Michael!" because he hadn't yet developed an idea of what happened if something was hurt and didn't heal. He knew only of the sports in Heaven, of how injury was always temporary, of how bleeding was a blessed touch to life. Ripping himself free from the branches his wings had tangled themselves in, he'd cried out in pain; and blood had splattered, onto his robe, onto the bark. He'd fallen to his knees and put his hands on the creature, waiting for it to writhe, to beg, but it was still. In the present, he said the archangel's name, soft, then, "But what if we tried healing it?"

"You cannot heal a dead thing, Lucifer."

"But—" He grimaced. "I can see you're getting frustrated with me."

"I could never be frustrated with you."

"I don't understand." Lucifer kept craning his head back, as if he'd catch sight of the limp creatures they'd left behind many minutes ago now. "How can something be and then stop being?" He heard a shrill squawk, sensed another one of those un-avian creatures pass above. "Where does it go? It must go somewhere."

"Not everything is eternal. Only Father is, and the angels because of His covenant with us." Michael took a step closer, but Lucifer couldn't meet his eyes, staring at the branch they both stood upon. "Don't concern yourself so much with beasts, for they're beasts." He gestured, calling Lucifer's attention before them.

Obedient, the angel of beauty shifted his gaze to see a towering wall of boulders, patched with green moss, water tumbling down its side into a large semi-circular pool on the jungle floor. It was warm — Lucifer could tell just by looking at it — with waves lapping at a pebbled, grassy bank. There were no large beasts around, only small creatures Lucifer recognized as perhaps related to the ones he was familiar with in Eden — rodent-like and furred — though they often skittered away whenever beasts, of the smaller varieties, sprinted past. Below the surface — fish, though not many, moving along.

"Beautiful, isn't it, brother?"

Lucifer opened his mouth to agree, but turned back to Michael and immediately stopped at the sight of crimson stains, like wine, splashed onto Michael's once beige robe. The blood wasn't wet any longer but hadn't caked into the cloth quite yet. "Michael, take this off." He couldn't stop his hands; they reached out and gripped the prince's arm, and Lucifer said, "Let me wash it. It's my fault, I was the one who had to be saved."

A chuckle, hearty but not long enough to hurt. "Your robes are dirty too. Really, we should both wash up. Did you bring any spare robes?" Lucifer nodded. "Good, as did I. I brought some soaps as well."

"Soaps?"

"Yes."

"To wash our... bodies with?"

"Yes?"

Lucifer blinked once, then twice, and as the realization of what Michael was intending settled, a warm flush blanketed his cheeks. "You want to bathe? Here?"

Raising a brow at him, Michael began to laugh a bit livelier. "Yes. Is that a problem, Lucifer?"

Lucifer was shaking his head, a little too much, hearing his earring jangle — clink, clink. "Won't it be unsafe?" He cleared his throat. "We could get attacked again."

"The skies are clear." Michael nodded at them. "As long as you fly straight up and don't run into any branches, no beast should be able to reach you. The flying ones aren't likely to attack an angel, but if you get unlucky, you still have nothing to worry about — I'll have my sword nearby." Before Lucifer could respond, the archangel had already hopped off the branch, falling for a few seconds, before landing easy. Soon thereafter, he made his way toward the water, setting down his chains, sword, and pouch on a great boulder with a flat top.

Lucifer stepped down, as well, but hesitated when he saw Michael already tugging the stained robes off his body. Underneath, he wore a simple, sleeveless tunic, embroidered with cool colors at the edges. It wasn't long before he gripped this too, pulling the cloth over his head. Lucifer looked away instantly, or at least attempted to — but he caught a glimpse of Michael's back, his spine as he curved forward, the muscles of his body stretching. He heard the shuffling of Michael setting all the drapery aside and rummaging through his bag.

"We can try using the soaps to wash our clothes, too." Michael must have removed his sandals because the noise of his footsteps was softer. What followed was the sound of subsequent splashes, two of them — Michael stepping into the pool. The sigh Lucifer heard tumble from the other's mouth was low and drawn out, bristled at the end — pleasured. "It's warm." Wet ripples and turning. "Oh. Lucifer, you don't want to join me? If not to clean up, you should at least come relax."

Lucifer swallowed, rough as if his throat had dried and cracked, staring at some trees that he'd been looking to for a while but only really saw in that moment; 'the leaves are large and disordered, untamed, nothing like Eden.' "Are you sure it's safe?" What was he supposed to say? 'Michael, you see, I'm terribly ashamed of my body, so much so that it's transferred to being ashamed of all bodies.'

"Of course it is. Is something wrong, Lucifer?"

He didn't want Michael to think badly of him. "No. I was only looking around. Earth is magnificent." There was nothing he wanted less than to be away from the other, too. "But I'll wash now." One of Lucifer's hands went to the golden tie by his waist, holding up his white robes, and he undid it. The material immediately slipped, tumbled down one shoulder, and dragged down his arm. Still staring at the trees, he gripped his robe before pulling. It cascaded from his body, collapsing to circle his sandaled feet, and he was left in a tunic.

It was not unlike the ones he always wore — thin, made of just one cloth, falling to his mid-thigh — but royal azure, with lavender embroidered by the collar. Lucifer hesitated, again, as he had done and couldn't stop doing. He reached for the ends of his tunic, tracing some lines of embroidery there, and pulled it over his head. The rattling of his jewelry made him sigh at himself, wondering why he'd bothered to wear so much. Michael had it easier; he wore about half as much as Lucifer did, and it was all simpler golden arrangements. Perhaps it was because Michael was a wrestler, a fighter, who couldn't afford all those weak things.

Lucifer painstakingly removed all his adornments, set them down on the boulder, before placing his clothing there too. He noticed the couple streaks of blood on his robes and tunic as he laid them but, removing his sandals, simply turned his head away. Michael was already running a green, olive oil slab of soap up an arm, having moved to the center of the pool, where the water came up to the hills of his ribs. Facing the rock wall, the prince stared up at the water crashing down, his hands cleaning himself distractedly to create froth that gathered on the curvature of his muscles, his chest, his thighs, and tangled itself with hair.

Lucifer breathed as he put one foot in the water, feeling the wet warmth nuzzle his skin. Moving into its body, he dipped his head for a moment, shutting his eyes, then broke through the surface again. His hair became heavy on his scalp, draped on him like silk. "Brother—"

Michael faced him, then outstretched a hand, where he held the bar of soap. "Need some help?"

"No. But thank you." Lucifer knew he should offer his own aid, but he couldn't stomach it. Gaze drifting to the water, he saw it was just clear enough to show his body in shamelessness, and he flinched. The compulsion was strong — to run and cover again, but he stayed where he was, rubbing the soap against his limbs, his collar, his abdomen.

The noises of Earth were a comfort: the off chirps and squawks and far cries of beasts, the buzzing of insects, and the coos of the winds; all that was alive, and all that, according to Michael, would die. Lucifer's eyes fluttered shut, as cleansing lulled him into thoughtlessness, thoughtlessness that lulled him into ease. He hummed, mimicking the song of a distant creature, wondering if it felt the way the angels did, if all things that existed felt, even what didn't move or breathe. Some angels believed that there was a vital, non-physical element that divides the living and non-living things — a soul. Extending his hand to return the soap, letting it be taken, Lucifer breathed and didn't believe this.

He felt as if he could sink into the ground to intermingle with it, and he could find a soul there; he could even find a soul in stones.

Lucifer didn't notice the eyes on him for a while — when he did, it was because he'd moved to splash his face. He noticed Michael, gaze caressing the shape of his figure, as if his eyes were a mouth, and he was tasting Lucifer like champagne.

He startled, crying, "No, don't look at me—" And he wrapped his arms around himself, stepping back, mortification turning him red, hot, and twisting his stomach.

Instantly, Michael blinked, as if he'd just woken from sleep. "Oh, I'm so sorry." His head shot up to face the sky so that he could look away from the other, but now he looked silly and only made Lucifer feel ridiculous. "Is this fine?"

Frowning deep, Lucifer said, "No. I'm the one who's sorry. It's only that I feel vulnerable, like this, and when someone stares, even when I'm clothed, it bothers me. You know that I'm ashamed of my body." Beats of silence followed, in which Lucifer chewed upon his bottom lip, then quickly washed off the last of any suds before beginning to trudge through the waters. He headed for the bank, the weight of shame dragging his feet even as he tried to move quickly. Heart beginning to sprint, thoughts racing around his skull — 'He must dislike me now. He must think I'm unreasonable.'

Michael spoke, just as the level of the water had reached Lucifer's hips: "Can I say something to you, Lucifer?"

Lucifer, of course, stopped. 'I am weak, so weak, I am the angel of weakness.' "Of course." He turned halfway, hugging his own body as if he could blanket it entirely with just his arms.

Michael's eyes were soft again. "When I asked of you, angels said to me that your beauty was so great, one could take a glance, but never stare. That your face alone was as dangerous as too much wine, that you made their heads hurt and their visions blur." He laughed, shakily, as he moved closer; with a tug on his heart, Lucifer realized the other was horrifically nervous. "I learned that their words were true. When we wrestle, when we spend time together — the pain you give me is indescribable. But I also thought, 'How terribly lonely that must be, to be so beautiful that others think of you a thorn.'" His arm extended out, fingers brushing against one of Lucifer's wrists, before taking it. Michael pulled downward, making the other expose himself, then simply held him, rubbing his thumb over the veins. "And how worse it must be to think that of yourself."

Something in Lucifer's chest was shattering, but slow — a carnivorous, pulsing ache.

"So," Michael continued, a grin taking his mouth, "I've decided to help you. From now on, I'll carry some of your burden. Give half your beauty to me, Lucifer, and stare at me all that you wish." Just like that, the tension coiling Lucifer's muscles stuttered, then unraveled itself; the younger angel laughed quietly. "Go ahead. I'll do a twirl, if you like."

"Angels are equal," Lucifer replied, smiling back. "You give me half your strength, then. And also brush my wings."

"Only if you brush mine as well."

"It's a deal." Lucifer put his other hand down, and he wasn't covering himself anymore. He peered into the Earths in Michael's eyes; it was like wading through another dense jungle, but once Lucifer found Michael's deep pupils, he caught his face reflected; he saw that his splendor was infinite. "Now let's finish bathing, lesser angel of beauty."

Michael responded by splashing the other lightly, and Lucifer, in usual overreaction, retaliated by flinging as much water as he could at the other. It developed into a brawl quickly, which became a wrestling match, which became Lucifer flailing as Michael tackled him into the pool. The fight didn't last much longer after that. They recovered themselves, climbed onto a boulder, different from the one holding their belongings, and laid upon it, soaking in the heat of the great sun above.

And they were silent a while, lying beside each other, Michael so still, with his eyes shut, Lucifer was sure he'd fallen asleep. Raising a nude body up halfway, he turned onto his side. He watched the angel of strength, watched his chest rise then fall, and the wet curls of hair stuck to his face and neck. Lucifer's head felt light; with a sweet smile, he realized all of himself felt light.

When they groomed each other's wings, they did it tenderly. They picked out all the hints of dirt or debris, crisped against their fingers, and Michael cleaned the dried blood from Lucifer's feathers. The prince preened him smooth and hummed a song the younger one had taught him in a time that felt distant; and it was distant, because Heaven was far, and time was only the present, and the present was only Earth.

Michael's fingers touched, ever soft, the nape of Lucifer's neck — shivering, breathing — and he asked, "Can I braid your hair?"

Lucifer whispered, "Yes." He shut his eyes and felt the pleasant tugs on his scalp as Michael gathered all his hair in the back, split it, then worked two braids out that he eventually joined back together with a tie.

When they stood to dress, Lucifer felt Michael's hand drag up along his back in such a mild, natural way that it could have been accidental, or something they always did.

It was only after the angels pulled on their clothes that Michael pointed at some enormous beasts — much larger than the previous ones and donned with spikes along their back — that were approaching them again. "But don't worry," he chuckled when Lucifer looked about to take off into the sky. "See their flat teeth? They're not interested in eating creatures."

"They don't kill?"

"Only if they must."

"Then are they really beasts?"

The answer wasn't simple — instead of delving on it for too long, they searched for a clearing and wrestled again. Lucifer had learned to dodge, to sidestep and evade when Michael tried to seize him. He'd learned to roll back onto his feet after attempts at a pin. He'd learned how to balance on his heels or on his toes when the other shot for a takedown. And on the ground with Michael, Lucifer learned to grapple the other from behind, using his legs to hook the inside of the archangel's thighs, while clutching his throat tight in a lock. Michael usually rolled and escaped, but Lucifer was getting better at holding it.

Lucifer couldn't beat Michael yet, but he was getting closer, closer.

They broke away, heaving, but rested only a minute, only enough to savor their full laughter. Then, they sat, and Lucifer clapped his hands, tittering still, as Michael tried to follow the beat with the timbrel. Grumbling, "I feel silly."

"Keep complaining, and I will make you dance with me."

After an hour spent singing, Lucifer forced him to dance anyway. Like the younger angel, Michael was improving — slowly, but he was. All that strength in him was learning to come loose with music, and it sweetened Lucifer's blood to know; it was not unlike watching his friend learn to relax. He jumped and cheered when Michael had begun laughing and enjoying the rhythm. He took Lucifer's hand, grasped it tight, and the two danced together. It was clumsy, shy still, but sincere in every wrong step and embarrassed laugh.

Yet when the sky lost its sea, Lucifer stopped where he was. He looked above into the molten rock that began to rip through, then watched in wonder as he noted streams of pastel pinks and yellows, along with some hints of the recognizable blue. The sun seemed to be walking away, heading toward the horizon, so fast that Lucifer waved his hands in the air and cried, "Brother! Brother, where are you going?"

Michael laughed, so much that he almost doubled over. His hand went to Lucifer's upper arm; he couldn't seem to stop touching him. "The Earth is so big, Lucifer. The sun is off to visit the rest of it, so it'll be dark for a while. But no worries. When it's dark, the lights of all the stars will be visible to us, and they'll guide us."

Lucifer didn't believe it, but with Michael, he flew to some high ground that broke off into a cliff, overlooking more jungle and more land that seemed to stretch infinitely; unlike Heaven, there was no wall. And, together, the angels watched the sky become a reflection of the intimate universe Lucifer had flown into so many times before. Sat at the edge of the steep, Michael gestured at the constellations he knew, each by the milky wave of light traversing the night sky, and named them each.

Then, Michael told him they should rest. It made sense to Lucifer: it had grown dark, and angels enshrouded themselves in darkness to sleep. Earth, however, was bustling with predators and sleeping atop a tree wouldn't be very comfortable, so they searched for any place that would be suitable for angels, who lived pampered lives, to relax. They returned to the pool where they'd washed and found a grotto nestled by the waterfall. Giving thanks to their Father, immediately, they moved into it, passing by a few mammals that scurried along, before Michael went to cast fire on a few charcoals.

Lucifer was already yawning by then, plopping down on the jagged floor and rubbing an eye. He mumbled, over the crackles of nascent flames, "So I suppose we'll be sleeping on the cold ground here?"

"Didn't I tell you to bring a blanket?" At Lucifer's pursed lips, Michael sighed. "That was my mistake. Well, mine is quite large, as you can see." It was a miracle Michael had managed to fit it in the pouch he pulled it out from; the blanket was a dozen feet long at each side and thick, too. "We'll share it."

Lucifer hesitated. Sleeping so close to someone wasn't anything he'd done before; still, it was chilly enough that Lucifer's skin prickled, and he remembered Asmodeus in Rosier's bed before leaving. Maybe it wasn't strange at all, maybe it was a perfectly mundane thing for an angel to sleep snugly with another.

Using their clean clothes, bundled, as pillows, Lucifer and Michael crawled under the one blanket. Their shoulders pressed together oddly, but it didn't seem to be a bother to Michael, who yawned loud and turned onto his side, curling up a little; his wings peeked out from behind him. At the closeness, Lucifer's heart immediately stumbled and tripped, but Michael's serene face inches before his own, and the brushes of the archangel's legs against his own with each shift — it ushered in this unfamiliar feeling. Something quiet but needy for more.

He discovered himself wanting to be afraid, feeling that he should be, knowing he should taste distress like his first visit to the bathhouse, but Lucifer could still hear Michael's words from when they bathed. He thought of thorns, remembered those in his hands so long ago. The prince's eyes were shut; Lucifer thought of tracing the bridge of his nose, his mouth, with his index, to see if he would prick him.

Instead, he fell to sleep too, smiling fondly, feeling cozy, as the archangel wrapped his wings around him. Lucifer attempted to do the same. When their first morning came to be, they were both caught smothered by feathers. Lucifer cooed, a bit like a bird, as he awoke, and Michael teased him ruthlessly.

On the second day, the archangel took him out into the ocean and walked out into the water. When Lucifer was reluctant, the prince laughed, "Have faith in Father!" and then they were both running out over the surface of the sea. On the third day, they wrestled over some open land, rolling about and catching leaves in their hair and green stains on their clean clothes. On the fourth day, they watched the beasts and stared curiously at their eggs. On the fifth day, they forgot to watch the dawn together, staying tangled in their makeshift bed and talking; Michael revealed that he was the last chosen archangel, and Lucifer told him about the fruits he used to collect. On the sixth day, Michael taught Lucifer how to hold his sword.

And on the night before their final day, Lucifer and Michael hadn't bothered to ignite any fire and laid in the dark, waiting for sleep to creep in. Their legs had crossed over one another — rivers converging — and their sides pressed flush together. When Michael's hands reached, touched Lucifer's tunic, the younger one thought he was being urged to move, but the fingers were hesitant, drifting along, saying to come closer. At the same time, Lucifer felt Michael's hands already inching away, and so he stretched out his own touch, placed it on Michael's wrist softly, telling him to continue, that this was nothing wrong.

The night was loud, composed of coos and buzzes and howls. And it was dark — Lucifer didn't feel seen and being caressed was nice, so he allowed him to continue, rubbing a thumb encouragingly along the prince's arteries. And Michael's strength must've left him because his touches were delicate, soft presses, all along Lucifer's figure but lingering by his upper half. Was he trying to mold him, like clay? Was he shaping him into something new? Lucifer thought that he wouldn't mind that, as he breathed, nerves making it tremble, and put his own hands on Michael, touching his belly, where he found some softness, and his chest, which he let his fingers stroke.

'Touching each other,' Lucifer thought, half-dozing already, 'like we've never known another angel.' His eyes must've shut, but he had trouble telling; Michael's thumb pressed into his throat, coaxing a muscle to loosen. 'Maybe you're as strange as I am.' Smiling — tiny, timorous.

When the morning of the last day came, they didn't speak of what they'd done. Instead, they thought to rest after such a hectic week. And they did, sitting and talking about God, who they agreed was great, and about angels, who were in love with living. What was living? It was this — the breeze, the tap of your hand against the chest of a friend leaning on you, the slice of a citrus to share, the sun streaming down from between the leaves, the shade freckling onto your body, the little kiss of a prince on your jaw.

One day, Lucifer will fantasize about having spent an eternity on Earth with Michael, having built a house and settled somewhere between the mountains. But today, he stood and readied to leave. The two angels tried to take in the Lord's barely-conceived garden, for the last time, but they could hardly see anything more than each other.

CHAPTER 18

T his is how God shows His displeasure: He doesn't drink, He doesn't eat, and He doesn't speak. If Lucifer didn't stand before Him, he might've taken the silence to mean God had left them. He might've come to believe God had never existed, and the angels had made Him up as comfort for their occasional troubles or as an explanation for their existence. This is unimaginable: consciousness without a weaver; this is a horror. So if Lucifer had ever the choice, he might've decided to inspire the Lord's hate, rather than His quiet displeasure. A hand that strikes from the dark is at least proof of a hand. It's kinder to be beaten than to be left untouched.

But Lucifer returned to Heaven from Eden, unsure what to make of the missing parable today. He landed on the gilded street, then he touched his lips, perturb made palpable along a frowning mouth. It's likely Lucifer would've stayed there, worrying over God's uncommon silence, infinitely, but Asmodeus appeared soon enough. Coming up to him from behind, taking his arm, the angel of friendship tugged the startled Lucifer along, saying, "I heard Michael is looking for you."

Then, Lucifer was smirking. "Is that so?" He walked along with his friend. "Should I go out and find him? Eden was so tiring today; I think I'll rest instead."

Asmodeus, who donned colorful ribbons woven into his braids, laughed. "But isn't Michael your best friend?"

"Oh? Is he calling me that?" Lucifer bit his lip to try and keep from smiling too wide, but his eyes squinted in joy. "Mm, he shouldn't get so ahead of himself." Of course, the two hadn't discussed their relationship in length; it, really, was nicer if they didn't. Lucifer enjoyed the rumors, and he enjoyed sitting beside the archangel without wondering what their closeness meant. "I also wanted to spend some time with Rosier today."

How much time had passed since Earth?

Lucifer couldn't be sure; all the days had melted together, so it could have been years now, or perhaps months. The only indication that any time had passed was Lucifer's grown familiarity with Michael's corner of Heaven. The couches and chairs of his friend's house had become familial, as the plants had, and as the sea had. Michael had doubled the number of utensils, plates, cups in the cabinets of his kitchen. The two had learned little things about each other; Michael loved a dash of honey in his tea and daisies and listening to others play the piano; he preferred to dance with others rather than alone; and when he slept, he kept his wings out and mumbled without reason. He loved the moon as dear as he did Earth, and he sometimes traveled down just to lay over the craters. Michael liked gentle things, softness, in between his strength and pride.

When Father created him, Michael confessed to Lucifer once, an infant lamb had been made along with him, and he awoke with it cradled in his newborn arms.

"Well," Asmodeus broke into his thoughts, "do you want me to walk you home?"

Lucifer was still considering his options, but the decision was soon made for them. Up ahead — it was a crowded hour for the streets — was Michael, among a group of angels, who were all speaking to him at once about various things, all the while the archangel kept nodding but also asking profusely if they had seen the angel of worship. It wasn't long before Michael lifted his chin and saw who he was looking for, far enough away that he had to shout. Slyly, Lucifer hummed before turning up to Asmodeus and asking, "Should I run away?"

Snickering — "Go. Hurry before he catches you."

Lucifer grinned and didn't hesitate; he waved back at Michael before spinning on his heel then breaking out into a sprint. He heard Michael call after him, bewildered, yelling what was wrong. 'Is he going to chase me? Would he actually?' The answer was immediate. Soon, the beats of the archangel's sandals sounded against the golden road, far behind but coming nearer, closer.

He turned a corner, stumbling a little as he tried to slip between oceans of angels — many of them seeing him and saying, "Lucifer? Lucifer, what are you doing? What are you running from?" — but it wouldn't be long before Michael rushed past them as well.

Lucifer didn't let a building in the way stop him; he put a foot on the edge of a fountain, then launched himself into the air with a flap of his wings. He flew forward, upward, fast, but there were many angels there too, and as he dodged both their bodies and their questions, he thought he wouldn't be able to outfly Michael, the same way he couldn't quite outrun him either. He landed hastily, pounding bare feet against the flat roof of a building.

A thud not far behind alerted him to Michael, who had dropped onto the house and exclaimed after him, breathlessly, "Lucifer! Why are you running from me?!" But the younger angel answered him with a laugh and a look he threw over his shoulder — a sugary, teasing smirk. Lucifer caught a glimpse of Michael's confusion wind into humor.

The chase didn't continue for much longer, as Michael was indeed faster and stronger, 'but not smarter.' Lucifer felt Michael's hand brush his shoulder as they were in between buildings and, heart punching against his sternum, he took the chance. He reached back, grabbed Michael's wrist, and fell into a crouch. Michael tripped over him, enough that he carried just the right momentum for Lucifer to fling the archangel easily over his head.

With his wings, spreading behind him quick and striking against the air, Lucifer shot forward. He grabbed Michael with both hands and drove him into the narrow alleyway between the two homes, drove him right into the ground. Michael cried out, sharp, as his back was slammed into it, and Lucifer hissed as he landed, and he stumbled — that was the fatal mistake. Michael was able to maneuver them around, roll over, grabbing Lucifer by the wrists, as he often did, and pin him to the floor.

Shouting out in frustration, Lucifer kicked his feet. "Almost!" He heaved, so much he could barely see the angel above him, "Almost! I was so close! I had you!"

"You had me," Michael laughed, hearty, between his gasps. "You really almost had me."

Lucifer flopped, going limp beneath the other with a surrendering pout. "Count your last days, Michael. It won't be long now."

Michael grinned, bright as constellations. "Mm, we'll see about that." But his hands went to Lucifer's warm cheeks and, in a quick swoop, he planted his lips against Lucifer's forehead; then he did it again, and again, pressing one kiss after another until he had done perhaps more than a dozen. "Mwah, mwah, mwah." Lucifer thrashed, flushing, embarrassed, thinking, 'As if the humiliation of defeat were not enough!' And yet, of course, he didn't really fight him off; even in shame, he couldn't bring himself to deny Michael's affections.

"Release me! Release me!"

"That's for making me chase after you through every street in Heaven." Michael loosened his hold on the younger angel's face, chuckling. "Tell me what has gotten into you — why did you run from me?"

"I wondered if you'd chase me."

"Are you happy now that I did?"

"Delighted."

It turned out Michael had been looking for the younger angel because there was a fight that he insisted Lucifer must go to: "You don't have a choice. I'll carry you there if I must."

Lucifer, snorting, brushing himself off, roamed back onto the street. The archangel followed him, and if the two were notorious for anything, it was closeness. Michael often put his arm on Lucifer while they walked, and Lucifer did the same to him. When they were seen sitting together, they were cooped up, usually pressed to one another, sometimes with Lucifer whispering all the gossip he'd heard that day into Michael's ear. They didn't care who stared, and they didn't mind what angels said about them, about the curiosities of how they had grown friendly so quickly. All of it drowned in their honey gazes and the tender shape of their words.

It became that Lucifer felt strange without the other; he recognized it as a kind of dull pain within himself instantly, and it made him restless for the prince, for his voice, laugh, those dark, curly wood shavings of hair that Lucifer could run his fingers through eternally.

Michael's own fingers brushed Lucifer's wrist, which so often felt shamefully dainty beneath the archangel's strong grip, before he conquered, took, held his hand. Lucifer made a noise of irritation, as if Michael's fondness were a chore to put up with, but he held his hand back, tighter.

"Phanuel is busy helping his housemate with something, so you can take his seat at the front."

Lucifer felt the shadow of the greatest amphitheater drape upon them. "Will you win today?"

"You think I'd dare lose before you?"

"I'll be cheering for your opponent."

The archangel's laughter was warm and hearty as they made it past one of the archways, where angels rowdily bumped into one another, heading to find whatever seats might still be open. And Lucifer thought to ask if maybe he should leave instead, see Michael later, practice wrestling with him alone in the gallery garden. He parted his lips, felt a little breath skitter out. His eyes were on Michael, who was looking off and shouting at a faraway angel if the arena had been cleaned; their hands were still interlocked. "Michael—"

"Lucifer!"

The angel of beauty jumped and turned his head, saw Baal waving an arm, standing by one of the other archways, and Lucifer sighed a bit, unsure if it was in relief or not. He turned to the prince, whose attention had shifted too, and told him, "I'll go sit with Baal. Good luck. Don't get too beaten."

Michael blinked at him, then up at Baal, who remained where he was and extended his salutation to the archangel as well. "Oh—" Michael smiled and waved back. "Of course. But come find me afterwards?"

Lucifer's lips curled. "Perhaps." Their hands broke away from one another, a residue of warmth left on the younger angel's palm, a tingle on his fingers, a sense of incompleteness. But he swallowed that inexplicability and turned away from the prince, heading for the angel of flight, who greeted him with a wide smile. Before Baal could speak, Lucifer asked, "You've come to watch Michael fight?"

"Well, I had nothing else to do, really." Baal nudged him, then began walking at his side. "It's been a while since I've come, also."

"Do you ever wrestle, Baal—?" Lucifer cut himself off to smile and bow his head at an angel passing by, complimenting him as excessively as usual. "Oh, thank you, thank you. It is God who is great, but thank you!"

Baal snickered at that before he replied, "I fight some, but not plenty." On Earth, Michael had told Lucifer to lift his chin and look upon his body with greater confidence. "Wrestling, in particular, I haven't done in a very long time, especially not publicly." But Lucifer still grimaced at his beauty, felt as if he were forcing fingers into flames. 'Is this really alright?' "Um, Lucifer?" 'Can I allow myself to be admired? Can I admire my own body?' "Lucifer?" 'Not all pain is bad — it is good to bleed, I was told once. Maybe, the agony my beauty brings on others is something to—'

Thump — Lucifer walked straight into one of the pillars, flailing, stumbling. His hands slapped onto the stone, and he heard the rumble of laughter behind. He didn't bother turning around, screwing his eyes shut, mumbling to Baal, whose chuckling was beside him, "I apologize." His cheeks were flames, his body was cowering.

"Don't think so much," Baal told Lucifer, instead, with a surprising tenderness. "Or you'll get lost in your mind one day, and I'll never find you again."

Lucifer tittered, feeling his muscles come loose. "How dramatic." He turned back to him and said, "Come. Let's go to the first row. Phanuel's seat is free. Hopefully, whoever usually sits at his side is gone too."

That was indeed the case. After they settled in and ate, the stadium roared to its usual life — the two competitors were walking out, making a show of it, doing a twirl, and posing. Michael looked right at Lucifer as he did it, and he gave him a grin that Lucifer didn't return, opting to turn up his nose instead — still learning to do that but enjoying it, giggling about it. When the chants flowed out from the crowd, next, along with the blares of excited drums and horns, all Lucifer did was clap. He didn't get swept away by the fervor, not in the manner he used to. That was melancholic to realize — all the excitement of youth was fading away, revealing something unknown; it was exciting, also.

'I feel aged. I feel as if you've aged me with your own hands, Michael. Ripened me. Like a red fruit, at the edge of a branch, hanging at its peak. Beautiful — and just about to fall.' A little laugh, his own thoughts embarrassing him. 'Maybe I'm the dramatic one.'

"Oh, it's a tournament," Baal, munching noisily at a loaf of toasted bread, told Lucifer. This meant the winner would accumulate prizes for each round they won. "We'll see how long Michael lasts. He's good, but last year, he only got up to third."

"We'll see," Lucifer echoed, smiling, reaching back to toss his hair over one shoulder. Then, he stood and clapped, cheering the name of Michael's opponent.

There were some murmurs immediately after — rumors, definitely, that the angel of beauty and the angel of strength were bickering, but he didn't mind. It was fun; gossip was fun; this was all fun. Lucifer plopped back down, fiddled with his hair, trying to smother an amused snicker in his throat. He felt Baal lean closer to ask if Lucifer knew the opponent angel, and Lucifer plainly admitted that he didn't. He, in fact, had no idea what he looked like. He hadn't taken his gaze off Michael for a second, had hardly blinked.

The tournament passed by at the speed of comets, each fight coming and going with hard grapples, and tough lunges, and the occasional snap of a limb. The violence which angels could employ on one another — it would only be shocking if there existed repercussions, if there was no healing. Instead, it was a marvel. Gashes, open cleaves of skin, spilt blood attached and coming loose from jutted-out bones. And for Lucifer, who had now met death, it seemed paradise was not, thus, absence of pain, but promise of mending.

When Michael won the first round, and an angel with a trumpet flew down to hand him two necklaces with great ruby pendants, the archangel took them quick, then flung himself into the air with a great beat of his wings. He landed on the perch before the first row of seats, right before Lucifer. Still panting for breath, brown skin flushed, tears of sweat stumbling down his face. Lucifer stared at him, lifted an eyebrow, before Michael chuckled and draped his prizes over the neck of the younger one.

"And why," Lucifer breathlessly laughed, "are you putting your winnings on me, exactly?"

"You make a good trophy display," Michael teased, grinning. "Now, kiss my cheeks for good luck. I'll need it for this other round."

Lucifer, feeling the curious eyes of all the angels on him, scoffed and turned away, denying him the kiss. But he was warm inside, burning up, feeling as if he were being grilled. It made his legs restless, his hands link together.

Michael did the same for each round won, layering every necklace and bracelet on Lucifer so anyone who saw him risked being blinded by the sparkle of a hundred jewels. And, as Michael had promised, he didn't lose, though it hadn't been easy. By the final fight, Michael was scratched, scrapped, sliced, pouring ichor from every injury; he had an eye swollen almost shut; he had a great canyon of red across his bottom lip.

After pinning the final opponent, and the announcer angel called victory, the prince stumbled. He received a massive, golden coronet, filled with jaspers, trembling. At the sight, Lucifer was incapable of stopping himself — he scrambled onto his feet, forgetting to wish Baal farewell, before he drew out his wings and flew, flew before anyone else could rush the arena. He hurried to Michael's side, caught the archangel as he'd begun to lean over.

"Heal him," the announcer simply huffed, flapping his wings so that he bobbed in the air. "That's all he needs."

Lucifer put an arm around Michael's back, other hand clutching his bicep. "Heal? Me?"

"Yes," the angel said, thin brows furrowing. "His injuries are many, but they're not so serious. Go on." He seemed hasty, waving his hands for Lucifer to go already. The reason why was clear: angels were flocking over, asking if Michael was okay, if he had taken it too far, if he needed help.

"There's," Michael mumbled, weakly, husky, into Lucifer's ear, "a room over there. Take me to where I walked out from."

"Yes," Lucifer said, not thinking, "yes." He startled as Michael, grimacing, reached to plop the coronet on Lucifer's head. "Ugh, that can wait, Michael—" But the crowds were already becoming oppressive, so Lucifer tugged the other along, quick, walked with him, hearing the announcer tell everyone to scatter. He headed for where Michael had indicated, the entrance into the arena, finding a dark, simple backroom, where a few angels wasted no time in pointing Lucifer in the direction of a corridor.

Walking there — it became very quiet, all of a sudden. The sound of sand scrunching beneath sandals and the weight of air assaulted Lucifer, as the two moved through the narrow way toward a quaint, square room in a corner. It had a long, rectangular basin of water, beside a small wooden bench. There was a table, too, that upheld some flasks of oil and some soaps in a tiny golden platter. Lucifer, swallowing, brought Michael to the bench, let him drop onto it, heavy, with a grunt.

"I—" Lucifer swallowed. "I'm no good at healing. Should I find Raphael?"

"It's just some scratches," Michael laughed lowly, lifting his head, then smiled with exhaustion playing upon his lips, caked with blood. "The water will heal me. Just help me wash." And then he planted his hands on his knees, stood right back up, raised brawny arms over his head in a stretch. He yawned loudly, and that rumbling groan of a noise warmed Lucifer's face, again, and his gut. "It's been a very long time since I've gotten beaten this bad, is all."

Lucifer sighed shakily but nodded. "Yes, it has, hasn't it?" He went to the basin, finding a linen cloth that had been draped over the edge. He dipped it in, whispering a hello to the water, then returned to Michael's side. "I don't think I've ever... seen you so injured."

"If only you were the older one," Michael snickered, with ease turned dulcet. "For a while, I thought I was the angel of pain. I didn't know how to use my strength. I was always hurting myself and those around me by accident. I broke Phanuel's ribs more times than there are stars in God's firmament. You and I — we've met at a good age." Lucifer agreed. "I'm blessed we didn't meet when I was too young."

"It's difficult to imagine," Lucifer whispered, unsure why, "that you've ever been young." He raised the wet cloth in his hand, brought it to Michael's collarbone. There was a jagged slice there, likely from when Michael had rolled along the coarse arena ground. Lucifer tugged on the collar of Michael's plain white tunic, and he dabbed the towel along the line of crimson — blood like melted ruby — his gaze flickering down. Rising and falling with the chief prince's steady breaths — his chest, ample, plush almost, muscular; beads of sweat rolled down, as if dripping along hills.

"We have all been young once," Michael replied.

"Has our Father ever been young?"

"Well," laughter, "there is that one exception."

"The Lord is fascinating," Lucifer said. "He is so unlike anyone." 'I wonder if He is ever lonely.' He lifted his gaze, then dragged the soaked towel along a gash by Michael's chin. Droplets of water, right before him, stitched the skin back together, and there was the pale line of a scar for just the flicker of a second. Michael became pristine again, there, as if no injury had ever tainted him. But Lucifer's mind had wandered some: he was remembering Eden earlier, how the Lord had been silent and refused to touch His offerings. Lucifer thought to pray soon. He loved God, and God would surely inspire him to write better psalms; definitely, the problem had been Lucifer's music not being good enough. Lucifer couldn't muster any other explanation.

Michael spoke, voice barely above a murmur: "You heal very tenderly, Lucifer."

"I don't know how I'm doing it."

"The water likes you. Perhaps it's because you're beautiful."

Lucifer listened to a ripple, two ripples, of the water basin. "It used to hate me, once." He reached to scrub one of Michael's biceps, feeling the hardness of it, the curve. It made his heart flutter, skip, like wings — he didn't know why — and his soul wear down until it softened.

Michael, the archangel of strength — something about that strength made Lucifer unsettle, made him flush. This little need, overbrimming — to pull the prince just a bit closer, to feel at home in his warmth, to press his cheek to that chest and coo, like an angel singing to the mounts.

"But it'd be difficult to hate you," Michael replied, his voice rumbling, shaking the Earth, with amusement. "If someone asked me to dislike you, I don't think I could."

"Because I'm so beautiful?" Lucifer teased, his smile light. He gazed at his muscles, again, thinking a bit about how God had created Michael, lovingly carved the details — the dips by his smile, every eyelash, each curve of his knuckles, a dark freckle at his hip. Creation as an act of love.

Michael opened his mouth, then shut it, then reached, took Lucifer's hand, the wet cloth slipping from the younger one's grasp; then, he squeezed cold, nimble fingers. "How about—" The tremor returned to the prince's voice, but different this time. "How about we go have something to drink?"

"I'm not—" Lucifer looked away, but he felt Michael eyeing his neck, branding him. "Not finished."

"Afterwards," Michael responded. "You like rose tea, with a loose-leaf black base. It's your favorite. Let me prepare it for you."

Lucifer felt there were stars beneath his eyes, scorching, asking to drip down from his tear ducts. "You remember?"

"Of course I do."

"Thinking so much of another angel — how embarrassing for you," Lucifer teased and delighted in Michael's splutter. "But yes. Tea would be nice."

CHAPTER 19

"Rosier?"

"Mm?"

"I have a question."

The angel of fruit was laying sleepily on the couch, wrapped up in a patterned quilt. Have you ever seen a drowsy angel? Their eyes are always shut, or nearly there, their mouths pulling open into long yawns. They curl into themselves like flowers frightened of the dawn or like they're insects, like they're really quite small and hiding away from all the large things of their world — the suns, the moons, and the Lord, their God.

"It's been a long time," Rosier mumbled, a rumble of laugh in his words, "since you've asked permission to ask a question like that."

"Has it?" Lucifer moved to sit beside him, though taking half the quilt and pulling it over himself. Settling his head by the cradle of his friend's neck, letting his own eyes flutter shut, saying, "I'm sorry. It'll be quick. I can let you sleep in a moment. Did you deliver fruits today?"

"I did. Do you remember when you used to deliver them with me?" Rosier smiled, turning to plant a kiss on Lucifer's forehead. "All you would do is cry and complain."

Lucifer was grimacing. "Don't remind me, brother."

"Well then," Rosier replied, "do you remember the first time you went to sleep? You were so scared; you told me that you were afraid you'd wake up somewhere else." Lucifer didn't have that memory; and he frowned, wishing someone had told him to remember. "And then another time, you asked if God dreams." This Lucifer could recall quite well, though for no reason; 'how odd it is that some moments remain with you and others slip away.' He thought that if he were ever to tell the story of his life, he would include this scene.

If he were ever to tell the story of his life, Lucifer decided, he wouldn't speak a word about any of the bad things.

"I have to confess now," Rosier continued, "that I've never met God."

Lucifer lifted his head immediately. "What?"

His older friend was still smiling, though blinking away the dozy from his face. "I've heard Him. There weren't any fruits in Eden yet, barely any animals. His voice came to me from a bush, and He asked me to plant His fruits into the soil, and so I did. I helped them grow, and I spoke with Him, but God never revealed Himself to me, like you tell me He does to you. He's never touched me. If the Lord had already made Himself a flesh body then, He didn't show it to me." Lucifer, frowning, wondered aloud why God wouldn't meet the angel where he was. "He knows my heart," Rosier said. "And I'm satisfied with very little. I've already known Him in rearing fruits. To meet Him in a flesh — I don't need that. I can feel that's not Him. But— You wanted to ask me something, didn't you? I'm sorry. I got distracted."

Lucifer nodded, slow. "Well, it relates to God." He cleared his throat. "You said you don't think that's Him in the flesh?" Rosier was shrugging. "Why do you think that isn't Him?"

"Flesh is God's creation," Rosier replied simply. "God cannot be something He created, can He?" Lucifer supposed that made sense. "What did you want to ask about God?"

"I," Lucifer said, then began to question if it would even be worth asking. "Have I been acting differently?" he opted for. "The Lord was very kind today to me. He let me feed Him, but something feels different, and it must be me, right?"

Rosier blinked. "What feels different? Is it different in a way you don't like?" Lucifer wasn't sure yet. "It could be that you're simply older now. Do you feel more confident leading His choir?" 'I do,' Lucifer answered to himself. 'I do.' "Maybe the Lord is meeting the new Lucifer for the first time." A little chuckle as he raised his arms in a stretch, moving off the couch. "And deciding whether He likes him or not." Lucifer didn't respond, running these thoughts in his mind, when Rosier asked him if he wanted to go on a walk with him.

"Thank you, but I invited Michael over," Lucifer murmured. "He'll be here soon, I think."

"Oh." Rosier looked away, then back at him. "Don't you think...." Lucifer raised an eyebrow, but Rosier shook his head, changing his mind about whatever it is he was going to say, before stepping back. "You said he's coming over?" Yes — Lucifer said that he should be. "I see. Do you think he'd like something to eat? I brought some papaya." It wasn't long after those words that someone was knocking at the door, and Lucifer said he'd answer it, leaving his friend and the quilt, abandoning them both.

After the door was pulled open, Michael smiled. It was the first time they hadn't come up with an excuse to see each other. They hadn't said, 'I want to practice,' or 'I need you to come to an event with me'; it was, 'I want to see you,' and 'I want your company.' And so the prince arrived, Lucifer greeting him with a tease and Michael with a press of his lips to Lucifer's cheek. Against his skin, warmed as if it had sat on the sun, the words — "Hello. I'm furious with you."

Lucifer moved away from him, smiling more than he wanted to show, so he turned away, began leading the way through the inner garden. "Oh, what did I do?"

"I noticed someone cleaned up my kitchen while I was gone."

Lucifer bit his lip to smoother a laugh. "Mm. I hope you find the beast who did that soon." Perhaps Michael had meant to say more, but they met Rosier in the living area, in the midst of picking up the quilt and folding it in his arms. "Oh, Rosier, you know Michael, but here he is up close and in the flesh."

With a hearty laugh, Michael went up to the angel of fruit, shook his hand, and said, "So you're the housemate I've heard about. Lucifer has nothing but nice things to say."

Rosier smiled; there was a little relief in it, as if he'd been frightened of something. "Good. I have a lot of embarrassing stories about him so he should speak very carefully of me."

Lucifer scoffed and reached for Michael's wrist, then began pulling him toward the stairs. "Well, we won't be here long. I want to take him to the pomegranate orchards. If you'd like, you can come with us."

The ends of Rosier's lips twitched. "It's alright. I'll stay here."

Unsurprised, Lucifer nodded, assumed his housemate saw him, then continued up the steps, dragging the prince, who murmured joyfully, "I didn't know you had plans for us today."

"Well, we must do something," Lucifer replied, bringing him down the hall, pulling him past the open door into the bedroom. Delicate, he released the archangel from his grasp. "But if you want to stay here; I'm okay with sitting and talking, as well."

Michael moved away, beginning to wander, touching and lifting whatever he could in the crowded space. "You own a lot of things." It was a mere observation, but Lucifer reminded him that he did, as well. All the angels did; they had nothing to do but build and hold in Heaven. "That's true." Michael was approaching a mirror, the one facing the window; Lucifer had forgotten about it. Why did it face the window? "What's this?" The prince took it by the border, tugged it so that it faced them both; there had been a silk sheet hanging on one of its corners, and it fell to pool by his feet, as if he'd undressed. "Oh, this is beautiful."

Seeing only Michael's reflection, Lucifer agreed. He watched as his friend brushed fingers along the golden carvings on the border, tracing the outline of spirals appearing to rustle awake at his touch, curl and shudder. "It was a gift." He'd forgotten that, but he was remembering now. 'I turned it to face the window. Why?' "Do you like it? I could try and find out who made it." Carefully, the younger angel approached, feeling a certain tension in his throat, tightening.

Earlier, God had told Lucifer to come closer; Lucifer had felt very small; he felt very small again.

Michael reached, taking Lucifer by the shoulder, then tugging him nearer until Lucifer's reflection also appeared in the mirror, stared at him, was surprised just the same as him. The prince smiled, the dips near his mouth showing, before he said, "I would appreciate it, angel of beauty."

Lucifer scoffed a bit and was already turning his face away from the lace collar of his tunic and the filigree, flaxen suns dancing from his ears. 'You,' he thought, 'at least look very nice today.' Lucifer glanced back, and he found that the usual pain he felt was a little less, a little simmered, when Michael was at his side. Earlier, Lucifer had sang in the presence of God; he had felt confident; he felt confident again. 'I like when you wear that robe.' It was vermillion. 'I want to tell you that. Should I?'

Michael opened his mouth, then shut it. Lucifer had been expecting the prince to say something about Lucifer's shamefulness, but he didn't, and Lucifer was glad. He didn't have the energy to go through the script, the apologies. When Michael kissed him again, it was at his jaw, and Lucifer breathed a bit, as the prince said, "You're being quiet."

"I was thinking," Lucifer replied plainly.

"Thinking about what?" Michael was still very close; his breath brushing Lucifer's cheekbone. "Tell me."

Earlier in his life, Lucifer had been teased for his questions, and he had stopped asking them. "I just remembered something silly." Indeed, he had. "One time, I asked why we eat." He had been recovering from his first drunkenness — maybe. "Nobody ever answered me."

Michael was chuckling, and Lucifer expected the prince to tease him. Instead — "No reason. You would be hungry, but you could live an eternity hungry. Maybe we should try it, for a thousand years — not eat or drink." Lucifer smiled, despite himself, and said the hunger would hurt. "For you, I wouldn't mind a little pain." He wouldn't mind to be pricked.

'Oh, Lord, forgive me,' Lucifer thought miserably, 'I like Michael too much.' He liked him. He could admit it now. He liked him so much that he couldn't stop smiling. His heart was in his throat, but he spoke through it, "And why does God put us in these flesh clothes, when we could be something else. If I were God, I would let us be spirits." He thought of a dream he had once: "And we would have a thousand eyes and a thousand wings." Michael was laughing, but he tugged him a little closer, his arm hooking itself around Lucifer's neck, like he wanted to lock him there, beside him, forever.

"Where did all this come from?" Michael didn't seem frightened; Lucifer will say this was the first enamor. "Where is Lucifer?"

"Look for him," Lucifer turned and faced his friend finally, realizing how close their faces were, their noses almost bumping. The archangel was smiling, almost goofily, giddy, and Lucifer had this realization that he was liked. He loved, and he was loved.

"You talk confidently for an angel who can't face his reflection," Michael said, almost a mutter, as if he didn't want anyone else to hear, anyone else who might be in the room with them — God. Before Lucifer could respond, Michael had moved his free hand to Lucifer's face, cupping it, turning the beautiful angel's chin so that his gaze fell onto the mirror, back to the two angels there, one was supposed to be himself and one who was the prince of Heaven. "Which is a shame, because if he could feel what I felt when I saw him, I think he'd be capable of anything."

Lucifer almost said, 'Only God is capable of anything.' Instead, he whispered, his sternum feeling like it had been emptied out, "What do you feel?" Michael hesitated; his reflection's mouth twitched and a breath skittered out. "I taught you — the words." They had been words of worship, but he didn't say that. "I'm testing you now."

It seemed that, for Michael, actions were still easier than words. He grabbed Lucifer, this time by his hip and by his bicep, and then he pushed him forward, almost against the mirror, and Lucifer gasped, but stiffened, now so close to his reflection that he thought it was trying to put its mouth on him. Flames, agony, about to grip him — the disgust toward his body all rushing back — but then Michael was pressed up behind him, his face over Lucifer's shoulder, and he began to kiss his neck, his shoulder. He did it fast, as if trying to match the rapid beats of Lucifer's heart. And his grip was tight, like he wouldn't dare allow him to escape, an escape Lucifer would never dream of.

Fleetingly, their eyes met in the mirror, and Michael said, "No, don't look at me." Lucifer whispered his name, hadn't meant to. "Look at yourself." He did. "You're beautiful. Lord — the most beautiful angel. The favorite angel." Lucifer was trying to catch his breath, as if with both hands, but it slipped between his fingers. Michael's kisses were sweet, soft and full, as if Lucifer were himself a gift, as if he were an adornment — or, as if he were meant to be adorned. As if he deserved songs too. "Can you see it now?"

Lucifer thought, to himself, that his lips were plump, his nose had a delicate curve, his lashes were long, and his hair had a volume that enticed you to touch. 'I'm pretty,' a lost voice said in his mind, and it was true; he was the angel of beauty. 'My body is perfect.' Michael's hands found it, like they had on Earth, but his touch was fluttery, as if it would dart away when Lucifer showed any hint of discomfort. And then he lingered his lips by Lucifer's cheek, right by his mouth, his nose bumping against him again. 'This is all the evidence I need. I'm God's favorite. His favorite because I have this.' "You," Lucifer said, shuddering, "kiss me too much."

Michael burst into laughs but retaliated with yet another kiss. "Can't I kiss my friend?"

"Do you kiss your other friends this much?"

"A better question," Michael deflected, "is why you never kiss me, the way I do you."

Lucifer breathed out through his nose, feeling as if he'd expelled his own soul as he replied, "Another day." But, finally, his pulse was calming, and he was feeling like sleeping, and maybe he'd invite Michael to nap with him, and he would ask Michael if he'd dreamt. Lucifer said, quietly, "I'm still learning to love myself. Will you be patient with me?"

Michael said that he would, and that maybe this is the little pain he'd love to put up with for infinity.

CHAPTER 20

O ne has to wonder if God bores of all this — all this life. See, Lucifer began to worship God with new vigor. He danced amid Eden, leading the others in psalms, then staying with Him a while in beautiful submission. But — the Creator lingered His gaze, maybe thinking Himself an excess wheel in the mechanism of the universe, wishing He allowed Himself celibacy and never bore an angel or a sun. Lucifer's hand beat the drum, the silvers at the circumference of the timbrel rattled. The sun fell, past Eden, into the Earth.

And you, in His image — do you relate to Him? Do you relate to Him now, do you feel yourself an observer now, scratching at the pages? Do you watch the end approach impatiently or miserably?

When Lucifer left Him, God must've felt like this, with barely the restraint to grab the most perfect angel in the last moment that He could. But they say the Lord tires, that He rests on certain days, that maybe he was too exhausted to ever save Lucifer. Yet — they also say that free will is a creation of God, and one must ask, then, if He has ever had will — if He has ever been capable of choice.

Our Lucifer, meanwhile, hurried home, going for a fruit basket before flying back out. He headed straight for the meadow he'd earlier planned to meet some friends in and smiled widely. It was difficult not to be happy. It was a perfect day, in a perfect paradise. Earlier, God had asked Lucifer to stay behind a while, gesturing that the angel could go sit in the bed of flowers, so he had. He'd plopped onto them, then laid back, wondering if the Lord would speak with him, but He was silent. Lucifer, haloed by lilies, had watched a pair of butterflies in the air nuzzle one another.

He landed on a golden street that had broken off into dirt, tugging his wings back in, then stepping past an open gate. The shrubs turned their heads, along with the scattered flowers, and Lucifer noticed three angels nearby tossing a ball around, and four angels chattering by a tree, and one angel, sitting further in the meadow, with his head in the lap of another. Beside a family of honeysuckles were Lucifer's friends — Rosier, who was arranging the plates over a simple picnic blanket they'd set up, and Asmodeus, who was serving wine, and Baal, who had his hands in the air awkwardly, searching for anything to help with.

Plopping down at Baal's side, Lucifer planted a kiss on his cheek in greeting. "Hello!" he chirped, as the older one jumped, then set his basket down. He hummed thoughtfully before rummaging through it, picking out the apples, and setting them on one of the porcelain plates. "It was nice to go and collect fruits after so long." He tittered when Asmodeus, at his other side, tugged Lucifer closer, then nuzzled his hair affectionately.

The ends of Rosier's lips quirked upward as he worked at slicing a runny, golden fruit dessert, topped with pie crust — peach cobbler. "I hope the orchards were kind to you. The trees have been in a mood, to say the least." He breathed, unsteady, then served the dessert onto small plates before handing them out. Asmodeus, who released Lucifer from his hold, whined about wanting another slice already and promptly yelped when he received a smack on the head from one of Rosier's amber wings, which folded back into his body instantly after.

"Mmm." A sweet noise of delight skipped from Lucifer's lips as he forked some of the cobbler into his mouth. "Brother, this is incredible—"

Similar moans and praises, making Rosier grumble, came from Asmodeus and Baal, the latter of which was very quickly stuffing the entire thing into his mouth. It conjured the memory in Lucifer of his first days as an angel, struggling to fit all the presents he received into the house and Baal helping to eat the obscene amount of food gifted. Lucifer had become friends with him after that. A tide crept over — of how much time had passed, how long it had been since Lucifer's eyes opened for the first time in Heaven. It was heavy, something about looking back was heavy, like he was picking up all the universe, but Lucifer supposed 'that is my universe — my memories are my galaxies and my moons, and they are infinite, they are eternal.'

"Ah!" Baal jerked his hand away from Asmodeus' face, then held it.

Torn from his reverie, Lucifer blinked curiously, looking between the two at his sides. "What?"

"Why'd you bite me?" Baal asked, but there was no offense on his pursed lips.

Asmodeus shrugged before leaning back onto his elbows over the blanket with laughter. "Your hand was in front of my mouth."

Rosier rolled his eyes, poking at his peach cobbler with a fork. "Behave, Asmodeus, or I'll bite you too."

"Bite what? My ankles?"

Over the erupted bickering, Baal turned his attention to Lucifer, calling, "Brother, are you going to finish that?" He nodded to the dessert sitting idly on Lucifer's plate.

Lucifer smiled, bringing some of it into his mouth. "Forgive me, Baal."

The angel of flight laughed and waved. "Don't worry. Eat it, you spent all day with Father, after all. Did He say anything interesting today?"

Lucifer thought, then shook his head and said, "Not particularly."

It was only after he'd said so that he remembered. Those butterflies in the air of Eden — fluttering up against one another. Lucifer could still feel the bed of flowers gentle against his bare feet, and his shins, and his knees. The blue of the sky had been falling onto him, spilling into his mouth. The breeze — like daggers digging in deep. Thoughtlessly, he'd wondered to God, "There are two of every animal, Father. Is there a reason why?"

It was explained to him that animals were created incomplete, that each was fashioned, split into, an equal counterpart they'd adore for all of their days, from which the fruits of life would grow. And Lucifer, quietly, had asked if angels were also made in pairs. "Angels are perfect," He'd replied, "they are whole, and they are eternal." There was no need for them to devote themselves to anyone but their Father.

Lucifer wearily lifted his gaze, feeling a certain jigsaw sadness in his chest that he couldn't piece together. He tried, "You two," at Asmodeus and Rosier, "I have no idea how you're friends."

"Oh, Rosier hasn't told you?" Asmodeus laughed, though it was more of a cackle. "It was a couple million years ago. I was in my prime."

Rosier instantly cut in, "Prime for being reckless."

"I was in my prime. And I had just gotten interested in chariot racing. I was very good at it."

"You weren't."

"Well," Asmodeus refused to surrender, "I fell off in the middle of a race, and then I got run over by four other chariots." Lucifer and Baal hissed at the mere thought of what could've resulted of Asmodeus' body. "I looked even worse than you think. But our dear Rosier—" the angel in question huffed, "—flew into the arena, and he pulled me out before a fifth chariot got me. I don't remember what happened next, but I woke up beside Raphael—"

"You told me your name," Rosier mumbled, "before you fainted in my arms. There was so much blood in your mouth that I barely understood you, but you said, 'Nice to meet you, I'm Asmodeus.'"

"Oh, right, I remember that." Asmodeus smiled, but it was fond now. "Yes, I had to take a few days to recover fully, after that. Rosier wouldn't stop visiting to make sure I was taking care of myself. Isn't that cute?" Baal and Lucifer, cooing, teased Rosier, who was chewing his cobbler and ignoring them all.

But, so soon, hours had passed, and Lucifer made to stand, brushing his tunic off, telling his friends that he had to visit Michael.

Baal immediately looked incredulous. "But weren't you with him last time I saw you?"

"Oh, I know." Lucifer felt a little tinge of embarrassment. "But he asked me to visit earlier, and I can't say no to him." Something flickered over the brown eyes of the other, and initially, Lucifer was a bit confused, a bit upset. Was Baal annoyed with Michael? Why? It was like a slash against his stomach — the thought of anyone disliking the archangel.

"It's only that it's been very long since we've spent proper time together, brother."

And Lucifer frowned. He reached for Baal's hand and squeezed it tight, then he pressed a kiss to his friend's cheek, as he had done before. "Tomorrow, let's go fly together." He saw the other loose the tension in his shoulders. "I'm sorry if you've felt I've been forgetting about our friendship. Let me make it up to you."

With a soft smile, Baal agreed; he'd never been the type for grudges.

Lucifer bid farewell to the other two and started making his way back, going all the way to the meadow's entrance, before realizing he'd forgotten his basket. He turned, hurried to where his friends still were, but slowed at the sound of their chatter. He strayed by a nearby tree and nearly hid behind it, as he listened in:

"Who would have thought?" Asmodeus laughed, quiet. "Lucifer and Michael, inseparable by all accounts."

Mumbling, Baal's voice: "But it happened so fast, didn't it?"

Rosier spoke next: "Well, I don't think it's surprising at all." When the other two made a noise, he huffed. "It makes perfect sense, doesn't it? The most beautiful angel in Heaven and the strongest; don't you think they complement each other? Like the two halves of an apple. Sometimes Michael comes over, and I see the way they finish each other's sentences and how they do everything as if they're one. It's interesting."

Asmodeus chuckled. "Well, so long as Lucifer's happy, what does it matter? Angels are supposed to be joyous, and Lucifer definitely deserves some joy, doesn't he? I think he's quite sweet. We raised him well, Rosier."

"We?"

Lucifer managed to quietly slip away, thinking Rosier would probably take the basket home anyway. He took off to the sky and attempted to smother the words of his friends, but they echoed in his skull, empty and hollow. Not pondering the accusations, not analyzing them, he just heard them and kept hearing them.

Michael wasn't home yet. Lucifer didn't mind much, as his friend never locked the door and had given him permission to go in whenever he wished. He did so; Lucifer walked inside and wandered through the clean house, taking a moment to admire the great complex structure of the sun in the archangel's living area. After this, he went to Michael's room, where he encountered a hundred plants, spilling out from their pots and littering the ground and crawling the ceiling. They'd even crept their way up the posts of the wide, massive bed by a great window; it was open and letting in a soft breeze. From where he was, he could see some angels out in the water, enjoying it, enjoying paradise.

With nothing else to do, Lucifer climbed onto the bed with a tired yawn and moved beneath the covers. They smelled like oak, like Michael; the scent weighed his eyelids. And the noise of sea peppering shore with kisses lulled him to sleep. He dreamt of gentleness, of softness, of tender things only. Seeing himself laying on clouds, watching the blue ocean between Heaven and Earth — he dreamt of doing this when he awoke. Dreams containing dreams.

A hand through his hair, nails scratching his scalp soothingly, and his name, said fondly — it didn't take much to rustle him from sleep. He didn't need to open his eyes to see who it was, didn't need to do more than smile to indicate he was awake. "Lucifer," Michael's voice came again, now with a hint of amusement, "what are you doing in my bed?"

Lucifer tried to chase, blindly, after Michael's hand as it drew away. "I was testing it." The smooth laugh of the other made his heart flutter. "It's almost as good as mine." And he opened his eyes to see the archangel, moving from the bed to a window and staring out at some of the high waves. "But I suppose this makes it so you're allowed to sleep in my bed too."

Michael chuckled. "Correct." He turned back to face the other, then quirked a brow. "Are you planning to get up?"

Lucifer huffed, tugging the fluffed duvet so that it went over his head. "I might stay here a while. Hope you don't mind." Unbeknownst to him, Lucifer's legs were now mostly exposed, and Michael didn't waste a second before grabbing him by the ankles. He tugged forward until Lucifer, groaning, was dragged halfway off the bed, duvet slipping over his body so now all of him was exposed too. He gripped the bedsheets, so that Michael wouldn't pull him onto the floor, and he grumbled at the other, who released him with a grin. Simply twisting around to crawl back to where he'd been before, Lucifer slumped back onto the mattress.

He flushed when Michael's voice became gentler. "You're tired."

"No." Lucifer shook his head, now worried his playfulness had been mistaken for irritability. "I was just waiting for you— I didn't know what else to do. I thought about washing your clothes or preparing food, but everything is clean, and I assumed you'd already eaten." He shifted to sit up, tucking his legs half under himself, setting his palms on the duvet to steady — physically, mentally. Michael was sighing. "No need to scold me. I didn't do it; I came to sleep instead."

"Yes, I heard you snoring from the entrance."

Lucifer stopped, his eyes burst wide, his mouth dropped, feeling as if flames consumed his form at once. "Heard me what? I'm sorry— What—?"

Michael broke out into laughter, bright. "You didn't know?"

"No!"

"You snore!"

"No! Michael, be silent!"

Michael hopped to sit right by him. "You snore like a leopard — very loud, very rumbly. When we were on Earth, I feared one of the beasts would hear." Lucifer brought his hands to his face, hiding disgrace with fury, maybe this was the first fury "Oh, don't be so embarrassed. We didn't lose any limbs, did we?"

"I don't think I can continue my existence like this. Remember how the beasts disappear forever when they're killed? Can you slice my head off with your sword, Michael?"

Michael kept on laughing. "You and your dramatics."

Lucifer put his hands back down, muttering, "Well, did you know that you talk in your sleep? You speak strange, like you're saying ten words over one another."

"Oh?" Michael didn't seem embarrassed. "Interesting. No one's ever told me that."

Lucifer blinked. "Really?"

"I suppose you're one of the few angels who's ever seen me sleep up close. How do I look? Like the angel of beauty?"

Briefly, the younger angel remembered a moment on Earth: them arguing playfully, Michael grabbing him, hoisting him over one shoulder, and Lucifer kicking helplessly, screaming in embarrassment. The prince had brought him back to the grotto, settled Lucifer over the blanket, and chuckled that the angel of worship weighed nothing to him. Lucifer — laying there with all the fever of meekness, feeling like he'd just been kidnapped, feeling like he was about to be devoured, feeling happy, despite it all.

Tossing away the thoughts, Lucifer rolled his eyes with a smile and finally scooted off the bed, standing. "You joke, but you really are beautiful, Michael, even more than me." He noticed the prince was wearing more necklaces than usual, more adorned with glimmering gems — something he must have picked up from Lucifer. Maybe they were both changing each other, molding a new angel out of them both.

"Now, don't overdo it." The sound of a grin in Michael's voice.

"I'm honest, unless you're fishing for compliments. In which case, you're really too proud—"

"Humble me."

Lucifer turned back to Michael, but noticed a curve in the shape of the other's eyes — this exhaustion. "You're the one who's tired." Mellowing sadness made him ache. "Lie down. I'll leave if you're too tired to talk or wrestle."

Michael hummed, but light and kind, not doing anything to cover his fatigue now. "We can sing."

"You're suggesting to sing? Oh, Michael, you're not well!" Lucifer laughed, and the archangel did too. "Let me tuck you in, and then I'll let you sleep."

"No. Stay. There are those chairs on the rooftop. Let's go up there and count how many ripples there are in the water."

"We would never finish."

"It's alright. We have all eternity, don't we?"

Indeed, they did. Lucifer reached for Michael's hair and tousled the curls, as the other had done to him; he wished to braid it. Longing churned his stomach. He wanted to sit there with him, he wanted to hold him, he wanted to wrap his arms around the other until they were so close, he'd struggle to know where his body ended and Michael's began.

Lucifer agreed, and the both of them left the bedroom, climbed up a spiral staircase. On the way, the archangel asked if he might be able to lead the streets in worship soon, but Lucifer could only titter. They flopped onto one lounge chair together on the roof, scattered with pots of trees and flowers, overflowing onto the various furniture, none of which matched in style or tones. And they watched the sea, and they took in the brilliance of Heaven expanded before them, with all of its host and great constructions and pleasures and natures, flustered by the stroll of zephyr. Neither Lucifer nor Michael spoke much, but their silence was warm.

This, this here, could be worship. 'This—' Lucifer pressed an innocent kiss to the prince's sweet, divine mouth. This could be religion.

Michael smiled at him, rare timidity in his eyes.

All was as it should be, and they were happy.

INTERLUDE

He dreamt:

The angel of beauty sitting in Eden, between some white lilies and marigolds — both of which tended to him, as if he were made of porcelain, made to be delicate. In Lucifer's hand, there'd be the stem of a pink rose flower, that he plucked from sweetly, asking in a whisper, "Will he?" before the breeze captured the petal, tossed and danced with it. "Or—" the angel, slow, pulling another — the final petal, "won't he?"

Eleven stripped roses scattered by him already, all deep scars of *won't*, making the angel purse his lips and huff at them. There'd also be a handful of butterflies — wings fluttering with earth-patterns — all about his head, one in his hair, before they all skittered away without warning. It was so quick that it would turn Lucifer's head, before he hurried to his feet, straightening up, smoothing down his long tunic.

As if they'd never met before, the angel of strength moved out from between two trees and introduced himself, speaking slow as if this other creature in Eden would flee if he weren't careful. But, playfully, Lucifer would ask how Michael found him, and the prince would say he'd heard a hint of life, rebounding off the leaves, looked between the branches, then caught sight of creation so beautiful it burned. Lucifer wouldn't realize how close Michael was until the angel of strength had fallen to knees before him, snaked an arm around a leg, then pressed his cheek to a supple, pliant thigh.

Whispering — "I daydream of you, of loving you."

"How do you love me?"

"Like this." Yearning mouth — it'd press soft to the smooth of his tunic. "Like a flower, like a symphony, trapped in my throat, like you're an eternity, and I need you in my veins." Michael's other hand would reach upward, drag along Lucifer's back, as the younger angel smiled, letting himself be grappled along his hip.

But he'd kick and flail, wrestle, when the prince pulled him down onto the bed of flowers. Fighting off the affection, he'd smile and laugh at the assault of kisses to his face, turning his head away, not letting the prince catch his mouth so easily. He'd tease at Michael's insecurities — he knew them all, in this dream, for it was a dream, just a dream — it couldn't be real, could it? And yet his body would warm, was warming, fevering until he melted beneath him. Michael's gaze would possess him before his touch did. Hands slid beneath clothes, feeling for life, smooth and stiff.

But the younger angel, smiling wistfully, would reach for him too. 'Here, you're like the pistil of a flower.' Fingers searching, exploring — 'petals, here.' And their bodies coming, sliding, together. 'Running your touch up my sides, threading your soul to mine.' Limbs entangling and, then, songs of laughter again. Embracing, bringing their mouths to lock. 'Complete, He said, but I don't want to be complete; I'd rather be split and become full with you.' He'd part his legs. 'Split me, here.'

'I want to be soil. I want to be wet earth, needy to be sowed.' Curls of hair, soft against his pulsing throat. 'Make me mountainous, beneath your grip.' His chest ached, heat pooling there, dripping onto his belly, lower, lower. The hunger, the taste, was inconsolable for fruit, so ripe it tears its skin, and its seed in his mouth, in any place flesh could pull apart. There'd be tremors between them, but the prince, nuzzling inside, like a timid bee kissing nectar. Pain, body, tilted and arched, drawn toward ecstasy.

'There is another Eden, within me. I have it nestled between the heat of love. This is love.'

But when the sounds of heavy steps, approaching, came, they'd hastily rise. Gathering their clothes, taking each other's hands, and laughing, they'd run away from Him, as fast they could. So that He doesn't see, doesn't notice. Two angels creating love, creating.

PART II
ETERNITY

CHAPTER 21

The water was cool; Raphael felt it all the way up to his knees, where his long tunic stuck to his skin, drenched, as he moved along the river. One hand clutched a walking stick, the other held tight a woven basket. Repeatedly, he set the basket down on the close riverbanks, then bent to break his free hand through the unruly surface of the water. Of the bountiful fish — so many that they kept ramming into his bare feet — he picked out whichever seemed plumpest. He felt the shimmering onyx body squirm in his hand, flap its tail around in desperation, the stick of its scales, but he tossed it into the basket with the others. And he watched it stop moving, fall slow into the relentless sleep of death; it grew still over the mass grave of other fish. He took the basket again, pulled it close.

With a kiss to their wet bodies, Raphael wished them sweet dreams.

He didn't usually go out to collect fish like this, in the middle of so much he had yet to do, but he craved to leave his infirmary in the center of the city for a while and didn't want to visit Gabriel's house as planned quite yet. So, he decided to walk through the river, get himself some fish so that he could eat well later — though most angels didn't eat them, didn't even realize they could be. Raphael always took his time; there was nothing that needed to be handled more delicately than slaughter. After so many millions of years doing it, he still considered why fish could not live forever, if maybe it was because they were small. Then, Raphael asked himself if one day the angels might lose their privilege to eternity, if they might also end up in sleep, like their brothers in the sky.

But Raphael loved his Father more than anything. He knew that He was merciful and that He would never go back on His word, His covenant with the angels: eternity and paradise. He had faith. Raphael had nothing as much as he had faith.

Humming. Raphael heard it from nearby — maybe just a little upstream. The river was hugged by the dense greenery of the forest — not a great one, simply crowded, inhabiting this small plot in the western side of Heaven — so that looming trees blocked his vision of the corner the river turned. He walked slowly, quietly, even knowing the shifts of the water around would alert whoever was ahead. The archangel followed the curve of the way, settling his basket on his hip.

Between the branches of a tree reaching its arm out over the river, Raphael saw an angel draped over a flat boulder right at the shore. He laid on his belly, head and shoulders off the rock, so that his face was delicately raised above the surface of the water. The angel was beautiful, with some strands of wispy light hair tumbling from his braid, all the gems of their Father adoring him everywhere, and a long, draped robe of thin, light-blue sheer fabric, hanging loose from his body.

And Lucifer was staring at his reflection, fondness in the stars of his eyes, attraction in the sweet curl to his full lips.

Raphael breathed, first, but that didn't draw the other's attention, so he cleared his throat, stepped out from behind the tree branch, digging his walking stick into the mud. He called, "Lucifer, what are you doing?"

Lucifer startled but hardly did more than lift his head to look at the archangel. Laughing amicably, a small rosy flush settling over his cheeks — "Ah, I'm so embarrassed, brother."

Raphael moved a little closer to him, feeling the fish at his legs nuzzle and crowd around. "Were you—" He wasn't naive. "Were you staring at yourself?"

"Oh, I was! I'm sorry. If I'm bothering you here, then I'll leave quickly!" Lucifer moved to sit up, but Raphael shook his head.

"I was just curious. You're not in any pain or discomfort?"

"No! I'm very well." Lucifer smiled wide, with even wider, sociable eyes. "Honestly, I've never been better." His gaze trailed down, back to the water, and he crawled forward a little, so he was hanging over the river and meeting his watery self again. "But, to tell you the truth, being the angel of beauty is great pain sometimes. Everyone can look at me, take me in whenever they want, but I must find a mirror like this, just so I can enjoy my gifts the way they all do."

Something was wrong; Raphael felt a piece inside of him unsettle at Lucifer's words, as if the angel hinted at something confusingly morbid. "Brother, you shouldn't say things like that."

"Hm? Why?" Lucifer raised his head again, tilting it sincerely.

But Raphael couldn't explain it to even himself. "Father has always instructed us to be modest."

Lucifer blinked, then sat up again, and blinked some more. He didn't understand; 'Is this being immodest? Simply wanting to admire myself? Father made me opulent, and everyone gets to enjoy it, but I can't?' He feared voicing those thoughts, so he looked away, mumbling, "You're right." Because Raphael had to be right; an archangel could never be wrong. "I'm sorry if I came across as..." He wasn't sure there was a word for it — proud, maybe.

Raphael sighed, and Lucifer moved onto his feet. "No need to apologize; it's only a reminder. You're sure you are doing well?"

Lucifer reached for his cloak, which he'd discarded on the grass nearby, then pulled it on hastily, covering himself. With a swallow, he nodded. "Yes, yes. I'm sure, brother." He sensed Raphael wanting to come closer to him, but all Lucifer wanted, suddenly, was to not be looked at. Wrapping his arms around himself, he bowed his head respectfully. "I have to go. Thank you for speaking with me." He left it at that, then flew off in the opposite direction.

Raphael was abandoned with nothing but unease, and all he could do was think he'd let Gabriel know what he saw. Maybe Gabriel would tell Uriel, maybe Uriel would tell Father. Before long, he left the river as well, with his basket of fish and walking stick.

Elsewhere, Lucifer landed on a stone bench, tucking his wings back beneath his skin, then taking a breath. He adjusted the hair he'd accidentally trapped between his tunic and robe, before turning to see the cathedral he'd once entered with Gabriel at his side. It was an odd place to meet, but it was often empty, and that made it a nice place to kiss. By the doors, Michael stood, curls of hair hidden by the long, ivy green scarf draped atop his head; when he saw the angel of beauty at the other side of the courtyard, he smiled quietly, then slipped into the building. The door left ajar, the carving upon it blinked to Lucifer, as if to whisper that the archangel wanted him to follow.

He remembered what happened with Raphael, just minutes ago, how he was treated as strange for admiring his appearance, but that was supposed to be his role, his gift from the Lord. 'Am I not supposed to enjoy it?' Michael had told him to not be so shameful of his beauty, and Michael was as much an archangel as Raphael, wasn't he?

Lucifer headed toward the mouth of the cathedral, his own lips twirling up, his heart swinging in his chest as if on a pendulum, making his belly flutter. He shut the door behind him and, with relief, saw they'd chosen the right time — there weren't even angels sweeping the floor. And Michael stood alone in between some pews, in the raining light of the clerestory and the circular window above the door.

If there had been an altar, it would have been where Lucifer met Michael, where they kissed.

They kissed often now, had overcome the shy leaning closer and anxious glancing; they did it in gardens, in the meadows, behind fruit trees, beneath the water of the sea, in between buildings, flying far above them, under the shade and in the heat. But they didn't allow the other angels to catch them; in public, they snuck a kiss, when no one was looking. There was no reason why; it was simply great fun, something they didn't want the others knowing about. Once, Lucifer had kissed Michael all along his face then sprinted away as fast he could. It was fun, it seemed, to do things you're not supposed to. 'To tease, to deny.'

But now Michael was denying him. He pressed his lips to the corner of Lucifer's mouth, saying, "Hello there."

Smiling, gentle, wrapping his arms around Michael's waist and hugging him there — "Why do you need me, Michael? Do you want to practice?" The prince planted another kiss on him, at the other end of his lips. "Hm, now kiss me on the mouth."

"On the mouth?" Michael grinned. "I don't kiss my other friends on the mouth. Do you?"

Lucifer snorted. "Aren't I special to you?" He began unravelling his arms from the other, but Michael took his hands, gripped them tight, then tugged, making Lucifer stumble forward, forward onto Michael's eager mouth, forward into a sweet peck of a kiss.

This was the only way they knew to kiss — quick, just a touch, a tap. Pecking, like birds.

Satisfied and swollen with endearment, Lucifer said, "That's better." He liked being kissed, liked this strange affection. This queer liking, between them. "Thank you." And he imagined having brought a little handheld mirror, no matter what Raphael had said, and staring at himself, inviting Michael to appreciate the beauty too. 'Let's celebrate it, together,' he would say. 'It's a gift, after all. Come and kiss it for me. Kiss my little beauty all over.'

Michael's brows were curving, and his grip on Lucifer waned. He left him, stepping back. "Actually," the words were solemn, "I have news you won't like."

"Hm?" Lucifer had just reached to tuck a strand of the prince's hair back behind his ear. "What news?" He knew now that it couldn't be anything major because Heaven was, had been, paradise. "Is it about training?" Lucifer was excited to wrestle, already imagining himself and the prince tousling beneath the myrtle trees.

"I spoke to God," Michael replied. "He's sending me to Earth." Lucifer blinked, eyebrows knitting close. "It's no problem, but I'll be gone for a while." The other angel asked how long. "I'm not sure, maybe just a week." When Lucifer parted his lips again, the prince reached out a hand, cupped his cheek warmly. "Don't look at me like that. We're angels, and we enact the will of our Lord Highest."

Lucifer hesitated, then smiled, delicate. "Lord Highest?"

"Heavenly Father, great and powerful. The Creator whom we have paradise to thank for." Michael nodded, before adding, "And each other." He surged forward to kiss Lucifer's head. Pressing soft, his lips lingered, dragging on the angel's brown skin; a tiny, smacking noise.

Lucifer breathed out through his nose, imagined turning up his face and catching Michael's mouth again, but he remained still.

"When you return," Lucifer murmured, "you should lead the streets with me. In psalms, I mean." His gaze flickered up to his friend. "We'll thank the Lord for your safe return."

The prince stroked his thumb against Lucifer's high cheekbone, looking amused. "What if I return without arms or without legs?"

"God is good," Lucifer argued, turning to nuzzle his face against Michael's palm. "He wouldn't allow you to get hurt so badly. Even if He did, we could piece you back together — any part of you."

"Even my heart?"

"If you're so nervous, you can leave it with me, and I'll keep it safe."

"Tuck it in with you whenever you rest."

"Yes, angel of demanding."

The two were soon laughing, then shoving each other playfully and running out of the cathedral — the thumps of their bare feet on the ground deafening — before taking to the sky together. Here, they climbed up into the stars to grapple on another, wrestle as they plunged back into paradise, and then they traveled out of the city gates, however momentarily. Halfway to Eden, halfway to Heaven — two angels fell onto the comfort of a cloud, the larger one rolling over the other, the younger one smiling in bliss. Yet, they didn't kiss.

It wasn't until they'd returned to the gilded streets — walking along them, listening to the clamor of musicians in a small plaza, flapping their wings to strike at drums, fiddling string instruments with song — that Lucifer felt Michael's lips again, though they were soft and by his cheek once more. At the same time, the archangel's hand drifted up Lucifer's back, rising to his hair, tousling it between his fingers and loosening a petal that was caught there; it fluttered to the ground. Michael said he would leave him now, and Lucifer mumbled his farewell, aching to hold the hand that was drifting away from his hair, his body. He watched Michael's back until wings sprouted from it, and he left the other angel with one less flower in his hair and an improperly sad sigh.

Not far from his home, Lucifer walked the rest of the way, licking this lips, thinking of Michael despite just having been with him. When a nearby nectar-collecting angel shouted a compliment — "Lucifer, you're the loveliest angel to see!" — he almost didn't hear it but managed to turn, smile, and reply, "Thank you. I'm well-aware." Michael always said similar words to him, after all. He twisted forward again, hearing the angel's surprised hum behind him, but he didn't ponder on it, not in this moment, as he went to his front door, opened it.

In the living area, Rosier unfolded what appeared to be a gardening codex at the side of Asmodeus, who was sprawled over the same couch in what was probably sleep, though his contorted position might tell otherwise. "Oh," the angel of fruit said, turning up his head. "You're back." The house smelled of cinnamon, of warmth,

Lucifer laughed, sluggish, approaching. "Yes. I'm on way to sleep. I need it." He felt that he did, though he wasn't sure why.

Rosier nodded, then smiled, "Anything else Father's favorite also needs? A massage? I am here to serve."

"All I need is for you to wish me a very pleasant rest."

"I wish you the sweetest dreams you've ever had, brother."

"Thank you." Lucifer kissed Rosier's head, though not without glancing at the angel of friendship. Hesitating a bit, swallowing thickly — he decided not to say a word regarding the living situation, instead stepping back and heading toward the stairs.

Asmodeus had said the angel Uriel wasn't pestering him any longer on the manner of construction, had perhaps found an angel easier to order around or another duty to meticulously occupy himself with. And this, in turn, meant the angel of friendship was often in his old house, with Rosier, and saying nothing about returning, but Lucifer could read his mind well enough. Laying a hand on the railing, feeling its smooth polish — the immaculate craftsmanship of God's host — the angel, the youngest still, climbed, feeling his wings shift inside his own flesh. He knew; he knew Asmodeus was eager to return to his dearest friend and the house he loved. Lucifer understood that well enough now — wanting to be close to another — and he sympathized. To move out would be no trouble. Surely, any angel would offer God's favorite a place to stay, but there was only one that he had any interest in living with. He'd forgotten to ask in all their time together today, though a part of him had been hoping, praying, Michael would invite him first.

Before heading to bed, he decided to stop by the basin, washing his face and hands and feet, before returning to his room to undress. Lucifer did it slow, pulling his clothes off over his tender head, then running his hands over the plains of his body, seeing where it curved and where it lay flat, feeling the mellow heat of his skin like the lingering warmth on a tea cup. He felt as delicate as one too, as if he could chip paint off himself with his nails.

His gaze fell to the long mirror against the wall, the one Michael had pressed him up against once.

Lucifer remembered the encounter with Raphael and breathed, only breathed. He continued; soft hands traced his skin, rousing it awake, exploring this body loosely, something he had never fully done. Finding the dips of his waist, he thought of Michael, imagined the archangel's fingers roaming down his sides, up, then down. Then, he imagined Michael's mouth, writing sweet promises to where his chest met his stomach. Michael's fingers, finding his back, drawing out Lucifer's wings, reaching to trickle the inner feathers, shuffle through them — a soft gasp shuddering out Lucifer's mouth. Abrupt, his knees knocked together, almost had him stumble, as some fingers lingered right below his navel. His hips were shuddering, needing to rock forward, in desperate want of his hand.

Love yourself, Michael had insisted once, love yourself, love yourself.

Yet, he stopped, no longer wanting those fumbling touches, gaze flickering away, as he remembered God. He raised both arms to hug his own body, tight, instead, overwhelmed — cheeks warm even as he shivered. The Lord was watching, after all, was always looking after His creation so very kindly, and Lucifer didn't want Him to see. Even still, there was a stubborn memory, sitting in the back of his mind, of an inexplicable dream he'd had once, where Michael had followed him into Eden. Kissed him, reshaped him. But Lucifer suppressed this, didn't understand, and only felt his worry increase tenfold.

These feelings — they were taking on a life of their own, splintering out and gazing at him, and it made missing Michael unbearable.

'Don't go to Earth. I want to sit with you. I know our Father told you to visit, but—' He wanted to put his mouth to the archangel's again. 'I want to be with you.' Lucifer's gaze flickered upwards, caught his body in all its agonizing beauty. It was perfect in every respect, the Lord had made it so.

'But what does it mean for a body to be perfect? Perfect for what? What does it mean for beauty to be perfect? Because there are different beauties — I've seen how daisies are pretty in a way roses quite aren't. What am I for, Father? In what way am I perfectly made, for what purpose?' To *be* something so abstract as beauty — it was as if Lucifer weren't more than an abstraction himself, an idea, a fantasy, the figment of a lonely, longing imagination.

Lucifer dressed in a loose tunic before flopping onto his bed, where the excess cushions hugged him. He stared at the ceiling, wondered if the Lord was looking at him now, wondered what He thinks while watching the angels bustle around building all sorts of things, wondered what He thinks about the angels, always groveling and worshiping. Lucifer had nothing but smoldering adoration for his Father — of course he did — absolute obsession over Him, but he did sometimes just wonder.

Sleep seeped in until it invaded; it was darkness, and then redness, wet. He felt hands once more, but these hot as stoves, pressing to his skin all over, burrowing themselves beneath. Thrashing, he opened his eyes, saw a great beast hovering by his head, even greater than the ones on Earth — the size of the Earth, flaxen. It had three faces, snarling from them all. And from between their music, his reflection wandered out, came to Lucifer, put his mouth to his, then devoured him.

CHAPTER 22

His fingers plucked at the strings, tunes reverberating and dribbling Eden with a small symphony. The music drifted from a tall, golden harp, through the trees, toward some not-yet-red apples that hung from a branch. Sat on the flower bed, Lucifer strummed each of the chords, his eyes downcast, as he thought about many things at once, thought so much he didn't see the Father standing right by. It was only when he, on accident, brushed a string that sounded a jarringly high note, that Lucifer jolted, realizing his mind had wandered to a different time, different place. He raised his head, worried the Lord had heard.

He had. God was near to him, both hands behind His back, as He looked to the tree with green fruits, hanging low, low compared to Him. "Lucifer," came His voice, like that of a thunder strike, "you're not with me."

It had become that the Lord often asked Lucifer to stay behind, to spend time alone with Him. Usually, Lucifer sang, but sometimes they talked — Lucifer with his questions, the Lord with his answers, occasionally coherent but often not. And He gifted Lucifer all sorts of things: earrings, flowers, necklaces — a particularly nice ring, with a dazzling diamond and some emerald and sapphire, for his left hand.

The angel tried to swallow his nerves, but they tangled at his throat. "Forgive me, Father. I was just thinking to myself. It won't happen again." His fingers trembling, mimicry of the harp strings, he pulled a pleasant smile onto his face. "Should I sing for you?"

God didn't answer immediately, but then He did, slow, as if handing each word to Lucifer with careful grace. "What did you think of?" Why would God ask a question He knew the answer to? Lucifer thought, 'Aren't you in my head, my Lord? Aren't you inside me already?' "Tell me." There was nothing gentle about His voice, though had God ever been gentle? Life had continued, unceasing, for so long; memories were being replaced by new ones, and the first chapters of youth were more legend than experience now — stories.

"Oh," Lucifer breathed, not sure suddenly about what he'd been thinking of or if he'd ever thought at all. "Yes, Father. I was thinking of Michael, your chief archangel. An angel reported that they saw Michael on his way back recently, so he and those angels that went with him should return today." When the Lord didn't reply, the angel continued, "I'm excited to see him again. He's my dear friend."

"What have you done this week, in Michael's absence?"

His blinks were curious — "Oh? Well, I waited for him to return." He laughed, softly, trying to ease the tension hanging from the garden's trees and its clouds. "But I also went to fight in front of a crowd for the first time." The moment resurfaced to him, easily; it had been just a few days ago. "I met my friend Asmodeus and my friend Baal on a street, and Asmodeus had a stranger with him. He called himself Moloch." He wasn't sure if he was supposed to be going into this much detail, but it was a novel feeling to be the one telling a story in Eden, something that felt nice and, thus, should be good. "Asmodeus asked if Moloch could come fight with us, and I said that he could, so long as Moloch wouldn't be too rough with me." Moloch, jumping, had hastily insisted that he wouldn't, must've believed that the angel of beauty was fragile, was delicate. Trying to hide a delightful smirk, Lucifer had heard Asmodeus and Baal chuckle behind him; they knew he was anything but. Lucifer continued, "The stadium was hosting rounds of fights that day. Asmodeus and Baal went first."

In the backrooms, Lucifer had been with Moloch and a few other stretching fighters, who extended their warmest welcome to the youngest, as they always did, but Lucifer soon went to the opening into the sand arena and peered at the fight between his friends. Asmodeus had always been smarter, more experienced — an angel who, as you might have realized by now, had tried everything life might offer — and could guess your next move easy enough. "But his stance is imperfect," Lucifer had said to Moloch, "Look at how he tilts his weight to his left side, the wrong side." Baal, in contrast, was stronger and held a significant advantage in the air. "But on the ground," Lucifer had laughed to Moloch, "he's awkward." When Moloch asked, Lucifer had told him it was true he was trained by Michael.

"Do you have plans," Moloch had also said, "to become an archangel?"

"That's not for me to plan," Lucifer had replied. "Why? Do you think I would be a good prince?"

"All I'll say is that I would have a new favorite archangel."

Lucifer had laughed brightly, but in the present, he turned to God, and he continued, "Baal won, and then it was Moloch and I's turn. When I walked into the arena, the crowd was confused. They started whispering to each other. I think some of them laughed." The Father asked Lucifer if he'd been hurt by that, if he'd run away and cried. "I didn't. I've been practicing so much; I wanted to show them that I could do more than sing and dance." He could do more than bow and worship. "Moloch didn't believe in me either; I could read his thoughts easily with the faces he made. When the fight began, and he lunged at me, he touched me like I'd break." A smile slithered along Lucifer's lips. "Because he underestimated me, I was able to gain the advantage. In just six minutes, I had him in the air." One of the angel's hands left the harp, and he gestured wildly, showing how he had gripped Moloch's neck. "I dug him into the ground, and I broke his nose, and one of his eyes burst." Smiling — "It's Michael's favorite technique. He taught it to me."

There had been a cannon-burst of fervor, all around, like a volcano had erupted, had shook the Earth. To Moloch, Lucifer had teased, "Thank you for going easy on me, older brother." The defeated angel, in between the wails and throbs of pain, had laughed breathlessly. And Lucifer had stood, faced the awed crowd, and bowed for them, elegantly, letting them praise.

Softly, the angel finished, "We went a few rounds, and I won all of them. I was really happy, really proud of myself." When the Lord didn't reply, he shifted, turned to see the Father of the universe standing by a tree still, now with a flower in His hands, twisting the upper stem until it began to strain and tear. "I worked very hard," Lucifer whispered, the silence crinkling in his chest. "It's thanks to Michael that I've learned to be a little stronger. Thank you for him, Father." 'I really like him,' he wanted to say. "And thank you for me. You're merciful." He smiled earnestly, praying the Lord was satisfied with his swollen heart.

"Come closer." Lucifer didn't falter, scrambling to his feet, making his way over, breathing like the air was pliant and he had to smooth it small to release. When he reached Him, the angel bowed at the waist, golden strands of hair stumbling down the front of his shoulders. "When you are in Eden," the Lord said, speaking not sternly, but not kindly, "I should have your full attention."

"Yes, my Lord."

"What is an angel of worship, if he is not good at that?"

"I'm sorry, my Lord."

"Friendship is a beautiful thing. I created angels to be joyous, and nowhere easier can pleasantness be found than in loving one another, but you must not place any friends before God." Lucifer stayed where he was, tensing with each word that came from the Lord, eyes almost clenching shut from the shame stirring within. "A friend sharpens a friend, builds them, and encourages their character. When one falls, the other raises them from the ground and cleans their wounds. But they are not to be obsessed over, to praise in excess — never to glorify." Heart crashing against his chest, trying to break free — Lucifer shook so much he gripped his robes to steady. "Who do you serve, Lucifer?"

"You," falling from his mouth, quick, in between whatever it was clawing up his throat — desperation, but for what? "I worship you, Father." Lucifer's usual desires returned — those to fling himself at the earth by the Lord's feet and ask for forgiveness, to cry and hope his tears would subdue a drought of God's affection. No, he could never live without God. See how dramatic he is — just the hint of disappointment was turning him raw — but all those feelings teasing him to choke halted when Lucifer felt something land upon his head. It was a palm, the Father's, unlike any other hand, unlike anything.

Benevolent and infinite — His presence, dripping grace onto the soil. "My angel," He told Lucifer, "will you ever lose your youth? You tremble like when I made you — so tiny you were, curled up in my hand," the milky waves of a galaxy composing the lines of His palm, the Lord's face as the chasm of the universe's center, His eyes looking to the little angel He held, "a speck of light in the dark, but so bright, so much more beautiful than the rest." Lucifer's sigh, being drawn out from between parted lips, as if by a string. "But you need to leave the soil now, to mature."

Confused, the angel felt the Lord's hand trail to take his chin, and He lifted his face, before settling the flower He'd fiddled with into Lucifer's hair, tucking it by his ear.

It was a white lily. "Go now. Heed my words and sleep well."

Lucifer blinked, unsure, before he realized, 'He knows of the night terrors,' and then another voice in his head — 'Of course he does. The Lord is all-knowing.' "Yes, Father. Thank you." Finally, he straightened and took a second to kiss God's rings, cool on his mouth. "Please listen to Heaven soon, my Lord. I planned a celebration today for Michael's return, and we're all going to thank you." Lucifer smiled, sincerely — his eyes squinted. "I want to make you proud today." To make the Lord proud was good, to make yourself proud was not good; it couldn't be simpler.

"I will listen."

With this, Lucifer dismissed himself, turning to make his way out of Eden, and, finally, breathed easy. A sturdy flap of his wings and he rose from the grass, soared in between the clouds. He felt so much ease, suddenly, that his shoulders slumped, but it brought with it shame. 'Despite everything, I'm relieved to leave now. Yes, yes, the Lord's right that I should keep my attention on Him, but that can wait.' A determined sweep of excitement overcame him, and Lucifer flew into Heaven in a hurry. He'd begun to grin, thinking about the celebration that he'd planned, beginning to giggle to himself.

First, Lucifer had to change into something nicer, and he did — a fitted, partly sheer silk robe with wild, overlapping diamond patterns in cool violets and some dangling golden adornments threaded with azurite. Then, he hesitated, fingers brushing the flower petal in his hair — it didn't match his outfit. Slowly, he removed it, set it down by the bed. He added the finishing touches to his appearances, trying not to think about anything. Finding his reflection in the mirror, he smiled, feeling beautiful and happy about it.

Taking his instruments, Lucifer walked out into the streets, toward the already-crowded plaza at the heart of Heaven. 'I almost wish the Lord had scolded me some other time, so I wouldn't be late today.' He stopped short of being irritated at God, of course, but he was irritated nonetheless. Arriving at the center — his dearest friend was already there, half-seated against the edge of the fountain, both arms crossed, laughing loud in between exchanged words with Phanuel. But Michael, soon enough, caught sight of Lucifer, who was moving between everyone, heading toward him, with a heart grown so large it lodged in his throat. The prince was grinning, waving him over, then offering open arms. When they embraced, it was tight, one of Lucifer's hands going to Michael's curls of hair and clutching it like an object once lost returned now to be cherished again; and the prince put his face up against the warmth of Lucifer's neck and breathed low, hot.

Through a bright smile, Lucifer said, "Hello to you too." He stepped back, untangling himself from the prince, who wore that tattered, charcoal cloak he always did when he traveled. "How exhausted are you?"

Michael chuckled fondly. "I'm afraid that no matter my answer, you won't let me rest."

"You're right to be afraid," the younger one said, rattling his timbrel and turning to face the crowd. "I've taught you this song. Don't make any mistakes."

"Of course, beloved Lucifer."

Hitched breath — Lucifer almost combusted, right there, into a star of heat, but he held strong, even with every pinch of skin sanguine.

He cleared his throat, waving to call attention to himself and get started with the celebration. Everyone was turning to him, him and Michael; by the fountain, they were at the center. 'I wonder,' he thought, 'how they think of us, standing before them all.' He rattled the timbrel again, and with attention of Heaven, he began: "My eyes have seen the glory of the Lord, sound forth the trumpet never to call retreat."

There was a second of silence, of waiting, but then Michael filled it: "He fits out the hearts of His host before His seat. Oh, be swift, my soul, to answer Him. Be jubilant, my feet!"

The crowd sang back, delighted: "Hail His heavens! Hallelujah!"

Michael laughed, in what sounded like both relief and embarrassment, and Lucifer smiled in such warmth he challenged the sun.

Then, drumming, all at once but synchronized, as Lucifer had prepared. It was wonderful — all the neurotic planning coming to its fruition. In the process, he'd found that he could spend a thousand years celebrating his friend, could write songs for him, dance for him. Lucifer struck the tambourine against the palm of his hand, singing the next verse and beginning to sway as the music found its rhythm. Wind instruments soon poured notes into the air, and the strings followed.

When Michael sang again, the crowd cheered for him, cheered for him and Lucifer, who raised the pipes to his mouth and blew into them. The music moved him on its own, loosened his feet to strike at the ground; when he danced, he did it around Michael, who laughed amid the chants rising high around them. "Hail His heavens!" The angels still in their homes poked their heads out, rushing to join the growing stampede of celebration. "Hallelujah!" The usual madness of religious fervor.

But Lucifer, feeling the blaze of Heaven's eternal light on his body, his words, looked to Michael. The prince was saying, "Come tears for woes, hearts for pleads. I triumph still, if He abide with me," before he began to dance too, following his lead. Delight like honey filling his body — Lucifer was lightheaded but couldn't stop smiling; it was beginning to hurt, hurt good.

"Almighty Lord," he sang — Michael pulled him close for just a second, half of which he took to brush a knuckle against Lucifer's jaw — "Almighty God." Suddenly, all Lucifer was thinking — 'I wish I had

another eternity, so that I could spend it dancing with you, Michael.'
"Hallelujah."

Before the end of the psalm, it's worth mentioning the following: Lucifer, when Michael was looking away, faced the crowd and sang slower, beating his timbrel against the top of his head. He moved his hips, side to side, swinging, to the caress of his words. The attention of some spectators reeled in, they staggered their singing, gazes following the rolling waves of the beautiful angel's waist, where various chains studded with gems held him tight. Lucifer knew that, had he been stared like this before, he would have cried and hidden, but he was growing, 'dare I say, partial to their eyes,' to their attentions.

Nearly giggling, Lucifer danced over to Michael again, denying the angels his beauty now with glee. It was as he returned to the prince that the song culminated, but the streets of Heaven remained hysteric. All of everything was loud, only loud, and Lucifer couldn't find the room to breathe and slow his moving. It had to be Michael, who took him by both arms and smiled radiant, to hold him still. He said, between laughter, "Please, breathe before you collapse."

Lucifer had no intention for the festivities to end yet. He met Michael with a smile of his own and replied, "Come, friend, let's go to your house quickly, before everyone else gets there."

"You invited angels to my home?"

"There's going to be food and drinks, too, and music. I invited every angel in Heaven." Lucifer glanced back to the crowds, those still caught in the grapple of elated love for their Father. He watched them, thinking of how he had done this, made every angel take to the streets and sing with Michael and him. 'It makes you wonder who they really worship — Father or us two.' Instantly, he stopped, wondering why he'd thought that.

Michael spoke again: "Alright." Chuckling, as if it were a soothing caress. "Let's hurry so I can change into something more suitable."

Exhaling, Lucifer agreed, then the two snuck away, rushing to get the archangel into his home, his bedroom, and out of his clothes. He was quick — massaging oil against Michael's skin everywhere, scraping any grime off with a curved tool. He was delicate; he'd done this a few times before; Michael had done it once to him. They could clean each other skillfully, like they were each other's own bodies. Afterward, Lucifer washed the oil off with a basin of water and a drenched cloth, then applied some light, lavender-scented oil along the base of Michael's neck to perfume him. Finally, he went to the wardrobe and picked out a short tunic, embroidered so it was patterned heavily all over, and pulled an open, vermillion robe over him.

Lucifer stepped back, admiring his work for a moment, before deciding Michael would look elegant in a head chain. He went to the archangel's stash of jewelry, then returned; it fell loosely across Michael's forehead, but Lucifer tugged it back, adjusted it. Pausing, then noticing the other's face, so close to his, contorted in an amused little smirk — "What? I think you look nice."

"Of course." Michael reached out and shifted one of the turning spirals in Lucifer's earrings. "I think I hear some angels outside already. Shall we go greet them?"

"I'm sure it's just Asmodeus with the wine. But yes." He sighed, soft, finding Michael's closeness happily suffocating.

They left the bedroom and headed past the front door, greeting the visitors from the staircase before the gate. It was Asmodeus, as predicted, but it was also angels with barrels and sacks of every type of beverage and a few of the musicians who'd arrived early. Licking his lips, Lucifer blessed his foresight to clear out some furniture to create more space in the house, or at least the illusion of it. He welcomed each of the guests, along with Michael, and smiled at the kind regards they received before they led them inside.

Within minutes: all of Heaven had come over, attempting to squeeze into the building or idling on the outside, lush with refreshments among great pots of steaming, spiced food. Music — upbeat but not intensely — reverberated from each direction, too — this hefty sea of drums and bells that raised its tide far over them. All this Lucifer had fussed over, made every instruction as intricate and detailed as he could with a near obsessive desire to please. It was a desire incapable to be quenched. Many times, Lucifer craned his neck to look out the windows, asking Rosier or Azazel to go check on all the guests.

Lucifer would go ensure of things himself, but that would mean leaving Michael's side; he hadn't moved out of hand's reach since the return, and he had no intention of changing that. They went around the party together, conversing amicably with each angel, Michael's arm over the other's warm neck and shoulder, which he occasionally squeezed amid laughter. With their free hands — because Lucifer rested an arm across the other's back — they held glasses of crimson wine they drank wantonly from.

Eventually, Michael's hand found Lucifer's waist, and he held it loosely at first, as if only meaning to steady the other. Then, he fingered the chains of jewels there, as they spoke, to each other and to the guests. Timid until his grip grew a little tighter, confident — tugged Lucifer just slightly closer to him. And loudly, grinning dignified, he said to a stranger, "Oh, and look at this fine angel I found on my way back. He was sleeping between some blue stars, over a crescent moon. He's quite beautiful, isn't he?"

"He is, brother," the guest replied, laughing. "What do you plan to do with such an angel?"

"I'd like to keep him." Lucifer felt so much fever rush his body he nearly squirmed, but Michael's grip on him was sturdy. "Right here, attached to me like jewelry."

"Oh but you'll share, won't you?"

Michael responded with a twisted sort of smile, nearly a smirk; wordlessly, it said, 'I won't.'

After this, the archangel enjoyed introducing Lucifer to various angels who already knew them both; he gestured to Lucifer's natural beauty, as well as his drapery, his talents, his position, his sweetness. Lucifer tried to speak up a few times, but couldn't in all his remaining humility, as if his tongue had burnt on the heat of his face.

They sat on a couch at the center of the party, and they sat close. Lucifer laid his legs over the other and scooted forward, nearly settled on the archangel's lap, to feed him candies made of honey and dates. He leaned in, whispering all about the gossip of the week Michael was absent, and he grumbled, too, that Michael had embarrassed him just now. The angel answered with a laugh, before asking if he should beg for forgiveness. Lucifer didn't reply. It was not so bad, really — being desired — thrill in having what not everyone else did, what was craved but only you ate from your palm.

"Oh. Lucifer."

The beautiful angel turned his gaze, finding that he'd begun to smile absentmindedly. "Oh, Baal," Lucifer greeted the angel of flight, "how are you?" His friend wore a cotton tunic draped over his top half with just a hole for his head, along with earrings that jangled noisily as he shifted his weight from one foot to the other and swirled his own cup of liquor around, turning his wrist. Around them, there was chatter, some angels looking over, as if sensing the tension already.

"I'm well," Baal said, his lips twitching some. "I wanted to come see you." Lucifer opened his mouth to reply but the other angel continued, now turning his gaze to Michael, "And welcome back the chief prince, of course."

The archangel smiled, but it hardly reached his eyes. "Thank you." Lucifer brought a candy to his lips, not long before bringing another to Michael's mouth, which took it eagerly, chuckling. Then, the prince turned back to Baal. "I'm sorry if you want to talk to Lucifer. I'll let go of him eventually, I promise." Lucifer swirled the date in his mouth, tittering and waving a hand, not meaning anything by it; if he were drunk, it was lukewarm, but it was there still.

"No, keep him." Baal was all pleasantries — laughing and sipping his drink — but hollowed, bark-paper thin. "I just find it a bit strange." Lucifer swallowed his candy; Michael asked what was strange; Lucifer didn't like to be called strange. "The way you act as if Lucifer's yours, like he belongs to you."

The music was loud; it had faded to the background of Lucifer's perceptions long ago but now he found it overbearing. *Tu, tu, tu* — an angel beat a stick to steel, this clapper-less percussion instrument. "No," Michael said, too quick, then made a noise like he was clearing his throat but not sincerely. "You're mistaken. Angels belong to God."

Lucifer laughed, forcing it as well. "Yes, yes, we belong to the Lord. Come sit, Baal." 'Maybe you shouldn't have paraded me around like that Michael.' "Yes, here, on my other side. Let me move the pillow." 'Earlier, I was told not to praise a friend in excess or obsess over him.' Baal decided that he had something to tell Asmodeus, and he left them. 'Is it wrong that I enjoyed it?' He glanced at Michael, who had just called for someone to be kind enough to bring him another drink. 'Is it wrong that I enjoy you, a little too much?'

Michael invited him to dance, and they did. All the angels that saw them must've thought they looked lovely together. They talked, saying they wanted to be Michael's friend, wanted to be Lucifer's friend. All the angels that saw them — with trickles of envy clouding their features.

CHAPTER 23

They became looser with all the alcohol, as everyone did. When angels began announcing their leave, Lucifer stumbled to offer them favors in gratitude for their visit, which were taken with thanks in between the teasing for having been a fantastic host. Lucifer smiled each time until all the angels were gone, and the house was empty, though the disarray of empty pots and baskets mostly remained. When the youngest angel collapsed, he did it onto the couch, sat beside Michael once more, and his head flopped onto the older angel's shoulder. Lucifer groaned, rumbled and low, then Michael matched it with his own groan.

"Forgive me," Lucifer murmured, earrings ringing, yearning for the music that had left them, "I didn't mean for it to go on for so long."

"What's there to forgive you for? I had fun."

Lucifer normally would have joked, but he saw the exhaustion dragging down his dear friend's face. "You look tired." He thought of getting some water, so that their drunkenness could disembody from their muscles quickly but decided it might be best to sleep it off. "Let me help you to bed."

Michael didn't protest, though he usually did when Lucifer coddled him too much — meaning his fatigue had grown beyond words. Lucifer nearly flinched, berating himself internally as he took his friend by the waist and the arm to pull him up to his feet. Walking the prince to the bedroom, he began thinking, making the plans to return as soon as possible to clean the entire house, no matter how much the other might argue. He sat Michael on the edge of the mattress, removed the archangel's heaviest jewelry and pulled off the vermillion robe, then moved onto his knees to untie Michael's sandals.

"No," Michael grunted, "I-I can do that." He drew his feet up and removed the shoes himself, tugging them off then tossing them away. A line of frustration sketching itself between Michael's eyebrows, Lucifer felt a frown fall onto his lips, which were parting to apologize. The archangel spoke again, instead, "Thank you, for all this. I mean it."

Lucifer stayed where he was, and a little, embarrassed laugh escaped. "It wasn't too much?"

"I like it when you do too much." Michael rubbed an eye, then chuckled. "Who else would host the largest feast Heaven has ever seen just because I was gone a week? I fear what you'd do if I ever disappear for a month."

"I also fear what I'd do," Lucifer replied, quiet — less a joke and more genuine disbelief — then raised to stand once more. "I should leave you to sleep."

A few seconds of silence before Michael spoke. "No. Stay a while. I want to talk."

"You're tired. We can see each other again after you rest." Lucifer made his way to the windows, pulling on the drapes so that they escaped the glow, then came to be embraced by ample darkness. He remembered Earth, he remembered night, he remembered the softness of Michael's wings cradling him as they woke to watch the sunrise. "But," and a swallow, "you sang really well today. Thank you for joining me, and then dancing with me. It's nice to dance with you."

"I should be the one thanking you." Michael laid back on the duvet and yawned wide as a horizon. "I never thought I'd enjoy anything like that until you taught me. I owe you so much." A mumble: "This... new source of happiness." All of Lucifer melted, into something sweet, into loveliness. "Everything has been nice since the Lord made you. I'm happy you're here, here feeding me candies and tucking me into bed."

Lucifer laughed, breathless. "I've become so dependent on you. What would I do without my beloved?"

"Beloved?" Lucifer, smiling and scoffing, moved to the bed, settled down at the edge, right at the side of Michael. "Your beloved what, exactly? Beloved friend? Brother?"

"Simply my beloved." Michael smiled back, grand but sleepy, before he swung up to sit again. He shuffled closer to Lucifer and chuckled warm, perhaps at the confusion on the other's irises and brows and mouth. "My beloved Lucifer."

He took Lucifer's chin 'the way Father did, earlier,' but he didn't speak, 'and your eyes — they're softer than His.' Michael's gaze flickered like the flame of a lamp; it fell to Lucifer's body, dancing all around it. It climbed from the ends of his sandals, up his long legs, to the robe that was partly open at the front to expose the smooth skin of his chest to abdomen. There was heavy jewelry, as there always was: a particularly great pendant right beneath his collarbone, an emerald choker upon his neck, nuzzled by the wisps of his hair. Michael's thumb drifted upwards, brushed Lucifer full bottom lip, then slowly moved to trace his mouth, as the younger angel breathed delicately.

If it'd been years ago, Lucifer might have squeaked and rushed to conceal himself, but 'I'm no longer ashamed; you have taught me to enjoy this body, to love myself, beloved Michael.' He imagined the archangel's finger slipping inside, sliding against his wet tongue, imagined suckling on Michael's skin, trying to draw out his taste, his pulse. 'Will you kiss me? I missed kissing you.'

"Stay," the angel of strength whispered. "You live so far away, and I can tell that you're also tired."

Lucifer almost, almost instantly, said yes, but the risk of a nightmare stopped him; he'd had them all the last times he'd slept. 'Dreaming of things I can't think about when I'm awake, that I won't, can't, acknowledge.' He didn't want his friend to see him flailing, perhaps crying. Solemnly, Lucifer's head shook, and with a quiet voice — "I can't. I'll explain why another time, but I have to go home."

He let himself admire Michael back, and he thought, 'I like that I admire you, and that you admire me — that you're beautiful, and I'm strong. We're really quite fitting together; our features, they complement each other. I wish I could make you see it. Let's stand before a mirror together again. I want you to see how we're two halves of a single sun.'

Michael replied, "I understand, but please come see me early tomorrow, as early as you can." His hand fell from Lucifer's face, but it landed on his hip, where it had been during the party, and like then, he twiddled the jewelry there.

"Why should I?"

"I think I'd like you to be the first thing I see when I wake."

Lucifer breathed again, feeling his shoulders fall loose. All the blistering tension of the universe contained in his throat — undoing itself. "Michael." He imagined hearing a sleepy, croaky voice, being embraced by the simmering heat of Michael's tired muscles; them waking beside one another, Lucifer holding Michael tight so that he wouldn't leave bed, Michael's fond chuckle and silly, big grin. Then — he remembered Asmodeus was desperate to move back into Rosier's house; he remembered he'd been hoping for the chance to ask Michael about moving in with him. Lucifer unsettled, then looked straight at the other. "That reminds me— I thought— I wanted to ask—"

Michael was staring at his lips, eyes dazed with lingering drunkenness. His tongue darting out, licking his own mouth, as if he were dry and needed to drink, drink Lucifer. He leaned in and Lucifer, frozen, heard the prince's low, shuddering breath. When Michael brushed his lips against his, it was the simple tap of always, but slow and forward — like the press of ink to paper, like Michael wanted Lucifer's lips to read of him forever. Against him, he whispered, "What did you want to ask?"

Lucifer had forgotten already. "I wanted a kiss."

A sluggish smile. "I'll give you another." One hand roamed up Lucifer's side, drifted to his shoulder, and Lucifer shuddered before he found himself being pressed back, Michael's fingers having arrived at his chest suddenly. Michael, moving over him, like he was going to pin Lucifer in wrestling, but the younger one made no move to escape. Instead, as if he'd gone limp — Lucifer laid on the bed, breathing out through his nose, feeling Michael's mouth on his own once more, the tap. Next, the prince kissed Lucifer's jaw, then the pulse of his neck. The flutter of words there: "I missed you."

Voice having fallen to a shaky whisper, Lucifer replied, "I missed you too." 'Too much, too much,' he didn't say, feeling his back arch unwillingly. Pecks still, a hundred of them, landing onto his jewelry and onto the heated skin exposed by the parted front of Lucifer's tunic, falling open some more now. 'What are you doing?' Lucifer glanced at Michael, lost in all the curls of his hair, lost in his body. 'Are you hunting for new places to kiss? I'm out of them. I can't offer you more of me. I've run out of myself to give.' A soft, pleasured breath, then a loose, flimsy thought, 'But if I were like God, I'd create a new piece of me every day for you to kiss. I'd remake myself, chasing that mouth.'

A dull slam sounded, from outside of the bedroom, in the main living area — the front door. Michael snapped up, off Lucifer, who startled and felt his blood freeze. Michael's hand took his arm tight, holding him still. At the same time, the prince called out, strong, "Who's there?"

"Michael." Uriel's voice, always smooth and stern, always recognizable. "I need to speak with you."

The archangel clenched his jaw, looked back at poor, petrified Lucifer with wide eyes and a paling face, then replied, "I was about to sleep, Uriel. Return tomorrow."

"This is urgent."

"I see." Visibly, Michael chewed on the inside of his cheeks, nodded slowly, and moved away. He raised a hand to Lucifer, indicating he don't follow, before he made his way out to the living area. Half-shutting the door behind him, the chief prince walked out, but Lucifer raised his heavy body up and followed closely. Hand coming to the door edge, he peeked out, heard — "Did something happen? Is Father calling for us?"

"No." A hesitance, but ever brief, could barely be called fleeting. "This is about Lucifer."

"About Lucifer?" Michael's laughter. "What can be urgent to know about him?"

"Raphael informed Gabriel and I that he caught that angel staring at himself in a river, and that there was excessive pride in his eyes— An excess he'd never seen the likes of before."

"And what's wrong with staring at oneself? Don't you ever look in mirrors, Uriel?" Michael's tone was still humorous but strained now; his annoyance threatening to leak. "I don't understand why you would all worry over something so mundane."

"I saw you dancing with him earlier, Michael. Raphael and I have seen the way you hold him. I've seen your *mouth* on him. Gabriel might defend you two, but he's blinded by baseless admiration for Lucifer, and you— I don't know what has happened to you." A seizing breath, but Uriel continued, tone ice, "Arguing with Father to let you bring him to Earth this week? Talking back to our Lord like some sort of newborn, clueless angel?"

"It was not— I already apologized to Him."

"But not one of us sees a change in your behavior. The Lord made it clear He didn't want you to divert Lucifer's attention away from his duties, and He ordered you to regain focus in your own responsibility as our chief. But here you are, losing your judgment, drunk off wine in a feast, ignoring the fact that you were supposed to report to me as soon as you returned. And so I ask you again — what has gotten into you? What have you become? You are an archangel, Michael, and you are well-liked. All our brothers mimic what you do, so why are you acting this way? Do you want them to start emulating this erratic insolence you've been displaying? Do you?"

"No, Uriel."

"And it is even worse," laughing scoff, "because Lucifer is acting just as strange as you, and all the angels flock to him, hang on every one of his words. If you can't put yourself in order, then I implore you to control that newborn, at the very least." Lucifer gripped the edge of the door, confusion twisting his gut, marching fiery bile up his throat. "Take the mirrors from his home, have him write songs that aren't so loud—"

"Am I Lucifer's keeper? If you so wish to speak to him—"

Lucifer stepped out; he didn't know if Michael wanted this, but the words of both archangels had bristled his nerves and made him entirely shake. He was loud, purposefully, as he made his way over, seeing Uriel, noticing his stern, tight face, narrowed eyes. "If Father—" Lucifer uttered. "If Father is upset with me, then I will visit Him as soon as possible. I will ask for forgiveness and heed His advice. But don't you dare berate Michael for simply being my friend." 'You're jealous, Uriel. Because Michael is loved by many, while you are feared.' "Nor should you treat him like he is responsible for what I do."

"Why are you still here?" Uriel's voice was piercing. "And hiding in Michael's bedroom so immaturely?"

"I'm not young anymore," Lucifer said, feeling, though he'd never in his life had this urge before, like he ought to snarl. "I was helping Michael to bed, and I was on my way out. I'm evidently the one you're really furious at, so why don't you let me tuck my friend in before we take this outside? And then you can scream at me all that you like." Michael quickly put his hand on Lucifer's arm, by his elbow, saying his name softly, telling him to lower his voice and calm. Except, the flames continued to rage and rage; they had cast a wildlife within the forestry of his chest, rife with soils, waterfalls, and great beasts. It was all spluttering out.

Uriel didn't reply for a moment; his gaze fell to fixate on Lucifer's body. It was an ill-mannered stare at the same time as it was wringing — counting, tugging apart, every thread that composed him. His eyes settled onto Lucifer's hanging jewelry, then the faultless, sweet skin exposed by his robe — the same skin Michael had been near devouring seconds ago. But Lucifer stood proud, lifting his chin, letting the archangel taste his body; 'Be jealous, Uriel, be *jealous*.' When Uriel spoke, he did so sour, bitter: "In that case, you heard what I said. Remove the mirrors from your home, sing quieter, hang your head, and wear some proper clothes, will you?"

Lucifer's voice, dripping with brimstone — "These robes were a gift, the same way my beauty was. I have nothing to be ashamed of. Isn't this paradise? Why should I spend eternity disliking myself?!" His fingers twitched with the compulsion to grab things, throw them around, to even fling them at the other. "I will not apologize. And even if I'm the one responsible for Michael's behavior, I won't let him apologize either. We're friends. We want to be together." Before he could stop himself, the beautiful angel seethed, "You wouldn't understand."

Michael, whose touch had lost the youngest, tried to speak, but Uriel's fierce snap, cracking like a whip: "How wrong the angels who call you wise are! You look at me directly, speaking to an archangel like that!"

Lucifer, fuming, trembling — "Oh, you love that title, don't you, Uriel?" A little laugh, something between a giggle and the sound of chimes. "You adore it! You have nothing but that title you hold so dear, terrified that Father might ever—"

"Lucifer!" Michael cut in, slashing like his sword, and the angel froze. "Stop this, now." Sturdy, berating tone; it shook Lucifer to his absolute core, completely ripped his heart out through his chest. He watched it beat before his eyes, pumping and spilling blood onto his feet. "Please." Michael had moved even nearer to him, and his brows were furrowed, eyes alive with nothing but disappointment. "It's better if you go."

Lucifer shook his head, but all the fire blazing had dwindled instantly, dying out until he was a tiny flame, fighting the winds and failing. "No." A pitifully trembling voice, maybe his lip wobbling, but he couldn't tell. "I won't let him treat you without respect."

"I won't say it again," Michael said, cool as a cave, freezing. "This is an order from your chief prince." He had never looked at Lucifer like that — never spoken to him like that. It was making the entire house swerve and topple in Lucifer's mind until he saw nothing but whiteness, emptiness, confusion and terror, absolute terror. He wanted to reach for him, grab him, cry to him.

Uriel had a curl to his lips.

'You headless beast.' Lucifer was shaking. 'Michael has done what you asked. He's scolding me, trying to control me. You beast!' All inside of him was the desire to shriek, to launch himself at the other and wrestle him until he could get the bones to crack and spill a marrow of apologies. "Please, Michael..." And yet his voice was meek, hurting. 'What might my eyes look like? Do you see them swollen with pain?'

His beloved friend gave him a more reassuring smile. "I'll see you soon. I promise. Take care."

Lucifer gripped his robes, the weight of the heavens on his chest, and by virtue of that crush — breaths shallow. All he could do was step forward to try and embrace Michael, but the other stepped backwards. Flickers of distress over his face — Lucifer nearly felt himself black out as he stumbled away, shivering. "Yes, Michael," and he bowed his head the way he knew he was supposed to. And his face felt like it was melting off, as wax does from a candle. "Please sleep well." He longed to say something else, something affectionate. Part of him wanted nothing more than to cry for Michael to come with him, to come home, but Uriel was there, and Uriel was ruin. "Goodbye." He didn't take another look at Uriel as he walked away, but Lucifer felt the dirty smirk directed at his back.

Shutting the door behind him, there was a muffled voice that followed, "He is out of control, Michael. You can see it for yourself. Either you have him settle and learn basic respect and modesty, or I shall urge Father to do something about it. This is completely unacceptable."

Stinging. Lucifer took off into the air with eyes invaded by redness, and he felt his lungs shutter and beat; 'like my lungs are my heart, no, stop that, stop that.' It ached, a sinking feeling, to fly and to break out into cries that were useless to do anything besides rake his body. Vision blurred — his rasps made the rhythm of his wings fracture until he had to stumble onto the street. Devastation, curling deep, found his arteries, and his hands, raised to his face, couldn't mend them.

When he arrived home, Lucifer rushed through the house, up to his room. He slammed the door, staggered to bed. Flinging himself onto the sheets, grabbing a pillow with both hands, he buried his face into it. And he wailed, screamed with all this sorrow and embarrassment and fury built into an unstable mixture that was nearly making him spit fire. He punched his pillow, he heard Uriel's voice again, and he screamed into it another time.

All he could do was lay there in shame, and it was so until his pain put him to sleep.

CHAPTER 24

"Lucifer? Lucifer, what's wrong?"

There was blood over his eyes; this is what Lucifer believed. From his dream — metallurgic scents kept assaulting his nose, and his tongue was scalding, whipping to strike his mouth. His hands were curled into the bedsheets in fists, but he felt the linen of robes, instead — all half-ripped and strung half-removed from the bodies beneath. The bodies? Oh — they composed a mound, made itself of flowers plucked of leaves and petals, stems further stripped bare to reveal angels. Through struggle, before its rout, each of them had tried forcing their fingers through his skin, to brush nails on golden bones, but had come to scratch at nothing — like a cloudless sky, or the bare, naked heaven. When Lucifer put his own hands on them, he earth-cracked them, split fruit, seeds splattering out.

Beautiful angel with angels in his mouth, stringing from wet lips down to naked front, and he moaned, heady, when their sugar marched down his throat.

'Flesh?' Trembling, he'd met Michael's sunken gaze, clung to the great, winged moon that peered above. Kneeled on the wet of uncreated universe and holding himself tight to cannibalized angels, knowing finally to perish — Lucifer had cried up in four voices, "No — look away, Michael, look away." 'See, Uriel, what you have done?'

"You won't recognize me if you look. You won't know me." He'd begun scavenging for breath, feeling left behind by spirit, and thinking that flesh was not anything an angel should be.

Far past the horizon — a shapeless peak, beyond Michael, beyond the flat where the earthly spheres were perched, centric and eccentric. The single eye had been omniscient. But a beast, too — made of sharpened topaz and honey calcites, red jasper, then ambers, and citrine — had haloed Lucifer's head. And it had three faces, whispering and coaxing — coerced his supple body to spasm until he became pliant to its hand. 'Not him,' angel had told monster. 'Don't harm Michael.' He'd thrashed and shrieked — all those non-organs inside rattling with him — then gripped his own head, trying to pull the beast from his neck. 'Give me Uriel, give me any other.' Pleading, 'I'll devour anything you ask. If you want, I'd make ruin, out of this.' For Michael. 'Bring ruin to myself.' The fire-crack of a spine and wetness spilling forth, trailing down the curve of his back. 'God, if you listen, I'd create ruin, like you created me.'

Eating himself, Lucifer had awoken, rasping inhales as a fish, kicking out his legs and throwing his head around like he'd really detached it.

When Rosier called out his name again, dozens of times, reached for him in terror, the beast of the nightmare returned. Lucifer lunged at the other, took him to the carpeted ground and brought his hands to Rosier's throat. 'Shouting.' All he saw was his friend squirm as if a whip kept coming down onto his body, striking each muscle to make them jerk. A hand came up, attempted to swipe across Lucifer's jaw, but Rosier was no fighter; he tried to touch him, only, to call the gem of Heaven to his senses.

This pleasing pulse beneath his fingers — it intoxicated Lucifer; he clutched tight, brought the neck up, down, up, down.

But it was the banging of Rosier's head against the ground, those dull thuds, that made light burst in and rush through Lucifer's mouth and eyes. A blink and, suddenly, he was seeing his housemate beneath him, struggling, harshly trying to pull in breaths. He kept uttering Lucifer's name, trying to, asking him what was wrong, what was happening — and everything that constituted Lucifer shattered. He let him go, jumped away, crying out as if he'd been the victim of his own hands. Staggering and crawling — backwards until he slammed against the side of his bed. Lucifer shook, panting enough to make his shoulders rise and fall, rapid, then cried, "No, no—"

Rosier coughed and hacked, rolling over and holding his throat. He moved onto his knees, half-doubled over as he turned his head to look at the other. His mouth was open, reeling in air, but his hushed words were unintelligible. Lucifer could see his older brother's rounded eyes, hear his clammy voice saying, as it had been, over and over, "Lucifer."

"Help me," Lucifer blurted, wet droplets sticking to his eyelashes, falling, stumbling. "Help me, Rosier—"

Rosier remained still; he whispered, "What have you done? Did I —? Have I hurt you?"

"No, no, no," Lucifer wailed, bringing up his hands to cover his face as it became wrecked — the ruin. "Help me, Rosier, I'm begging you. Please help me—!" It cut itself off with a hiccup that finally coerced the other angel to scamper over, take Lucifer, before the younger one collapsed against him. Rosier pulled him closer to his chest, hugging tight — soft tunic pressed to cheek, settling in warmth. "Rosier," he cried and kept crying, as a hand went to running circles on his back. "Rosier, Rosier, help me."

"Tell me what happened, younger brother."

"I don't know, I don't know," a long, miserable drawl of the syllables, "please forgive me, please, I'm so sorry, I will do anything—" Reaching, weak and blind. "Here, let me kiss your throat. Let me heal it—"

Rosier shifted, turned down to Lucifer, then took his wet face with both hands; they were soft, tender. His lips pressed to the younger's warm cheeks, peppering upwards to catch all the tears as they trickled down. "Don't cry," he murmured, "It's alright. I forgive you, it's all okay, Lucifer. I am okay. We need to find you help."

'I love you, Rosier, I adore you.' "Michael," he breathed, "let's call him."

"What? Michael?" Rosier's mouth left him, but his hands remained. "No, Lucifer, we need to go to Father. He will tell us what's wrong, and He will heal you of this."

Lucifer stared, eyes wide, but couldn't conjure up an argument, and he wondered why he wished to evoke one anyway; the beast of his dreams laughed, knowing something he didn't. "But— But I don't want Father to see me like this. Where could I even go to see Him? I don't want Eden to witness me like this either. I can't go to Him, I can't. It's too shameful."

"Someone has to help you," Rosier urged, voice now cracked with worry. "And this is beyond Raphael. I've never— never in my existence have I seen or heard of an angel doing what you just did. Please. Look at me, Lucifer. Look at me. I'll take you to see Father. He is the only one who can tell us what's wrong."

'Please. I don't want to see Him.' But there was no other option. 'He will be upset with me.' Lucifer nodded and sniffed one last time, rubbing an eye free of its wetness, and then he rose to his feet with the other. 'Don't make me see Him, Rosier, please don't make me see Him.' Lucifer pulled on the thickest robe he owned, colored the purest white there was, and a matching lace scarf to cover his head. A veil — God had gifted it to him. 'Please don't make me.' Rosier had him wash his face, then the two made their way together down the stairs, leaning against one another. 'Don't, don't, don't.' As they escaped out through the door, Lucifer's hand took the other's wrist — unable to stop himself — "No. I can't go to Eden. Let me pray; prayer will heal me." Quickly, he stepped back, away from reach. "I'll go to the cathedral."

"Cathedral? Wait, Lucifer!"

Lucifer's wings had already sprung from his back, flapping once and flinging him up into the air. Not delaying for Rosier, he took off, lungs shuddering. Heading north. He knew the cathedral was nearly always empty, and he might have a moment to catch his breath — if it could still be found — before collapsing and sobbing as he planned. His head was beginning to feel light, with fear that shackled each feather and threw him around so that it was nearly impossible not to tumble into the couple other angels in the sky. When he landed, an exhale burst from his mouth and splintered. Lucifer stumbled and hurried up the steps, going to one of the doors, taking the handle, and grunting between the struggle to pull it open just enough to slip through. A dull slam, then sounding behind him.

As expected — alone. Lucifer made his way past the entrance, down the nave, toward the pews near the front. All he thought to do was fall into a kneel and clasp his hands together to pray. He did so, going past the very first seats and moving onto his knees over the cool tile, right before the empty front and center of the cathedral, the same place Michael had so sweetly kissed him before. Shining down to paint his colorless tunic in every hue there was, the towering stained-glass windows gazed. Lucifer didn't meet them, opted to remain quiet; he didn't think, didn't even place his consciousness where he was.

He unraveled himself slowly, in his mind, as if disrobing. Walked backwards through the events — running from his housemate, attacking him, dreaming of snapping angels in half and suckling their blood from their bodies, a monster appearing to him, as it did in every dream now, falling asleep, hurrying home from Michael's home, Uriel.

Fear, all he had was fear. He held himself and felt a shiver rock his body, curling forward, hanging his head. "What is happening to me?" he asked the cathedral. "I'm being chased by a beast, forcing me to do things I don't want." He didn't have a name for those actions; it was too overwhelming to even recall — because Lucifer was good, he was made perfect, he was supposed to be made perfect in all that was good.

Wickedness was a shock of pain throughout his body, delivering out of it. A cry erupted from his mouth and became a wail, "Please, Father," violence trying to convulse him. "Help me, help me." Unendurable pounding from within his own abdomen, crawling onto his legs and forming beads of tears — tears, again, crying, again — at the corners of his eyes. He groaned, desiring to curl into himself and shrink at the same time he was hysterical to escape. "My Lord, I need you, I love you, help me." A dull ache built on his spine, and pressure everywhere became stars stomping him slow, pressing down steady.

He wept. What else was there to do?

At this, the Lord revealed Himself; His booming voice called out, "Lucifer."

Between the sobs that had returned — mostly dry now, because Lucifer had exhausted himself — the youngest angel raised his head. He caught a breath, felt it scratch the innards of his throat. "Here I am! Father!" The colored beams of the windows greeted him back, and

God was between them, above them, above the cathedral and the sprawl of the universe. "Here I am."

"You're frightened."

Lucifer nodded, quick, raising a hand to rub at an itching eye "Yes. I am." The ends of his mouth were twitching. He hadn't wanted his Father to see him like this. He had run from Rosier, run from his lovely Creator. "I'm sorry." Lucifer knew now that had been the wrong thing to do. "I'm sorry I ran from you."

"You ran from your Father?"

"I thought— I don't know what I thought—" Lucifer's voice cut off, had run itself out.

The Lord said, "You have always thought too much, angel."

This tiny, weak smile, and Lucifer's relief — trickling into his body. "I have. I'm sorry." Some of his suffering had waned, he found. Reaching, Lucifer's fingers found where all his pains had been. "I'm here now. I won't make another mistake. I'll be a good angel, for you. It's all I want." He lifted his chin, then smiled, wistful, when God's own touch brushed his face, traced one of the half-dried streams that fell from the folds of his eye to his chin. "I want to worship you. When I worship you, I feel strong. Should I go to Eden?"

"Without you, Eden feels very quiet. Lonesome."

Lucifer almost laughed, cheeks warm and bashful. "I'll go soon. I'll sing whatever you like."

"No, Lucifer." The love of God was in the sweetness of His words, the caress of His tone, as He removed His hand. "Stay here. Tell me what's wrong."

The angel of beauty stared up at his Father, a little fear in his eyes, becoming crescents as he squinted in the light of Him. Surely, the Lord already knew; why would He ask Lucifer to expose himself? "In my dreams," Lucifer said, still, basking in the lingering touch of the Lord and the memory of His compassion, "there is a beast. Each time I sleep, it comes to me, Father. It settles itself over my head, and takes my hands, and makes them take other creatures so that I can eat their flesh." A short, pained yelp shot out from Lucifer's mouth as a burst of agony jabbed his torso. "Ow, something hurts, Lord, it hurts—"

"What else does the beast say to you?"

"He says—" Lucifer gasped in pain and hissed, gritting out, "He says to me, 'I will be above God, I will make myself like the Most High, remove Him from His Throne—'" A shriek now — Lucifer could do no more than double over, clutching at his robes tight enough to make the cloth strain to hold itself as one. "Help me! Father, please help me!" He shook his head, the rattle of his jewelry like sharp twists of needles in his ears. "Make it stop— I'll do anything for forgiveness, give you anything, my tongue, my eyes, my hands—"

"Breathe, Lucifer." He did, he did — unsettled, quivering, and so quick he couldn't hold it in. "Raise your head." He did. "And all your pain will cease."

At His word, it was so. Lucifer nearly wept again, this time in joy, as all the blood of his body warmed and fell into its place. "Praise be," Lucifer choked out. "Praise be to you, Lord Almighty." He thought that if he were in Eden, he would have thrown his arms around the Father, kissed Him. "I love you." 'Hold me,' he didn't say. 'Please. I'm scared of all the bad things. Why do you create the bad things?' He was shivering. 'Once, I asked why you create harmful beasts. You never answered me. Why do you create harm?'

The Lord didn't answer immediately. "The Beast is there." His kind hands left Lucifer, drawing away, and Lucifer wanted to chase the touch, but he was too exhausted now — too many things had happened at once, after one another. "Bringing harm to you, bone to bone, flesh to flesh, searching for your shackled spirit. From your own body," like a womb, "it has been delivered into Heaven."

"Who is the Beast?" came Lucifer's response, soft and unsteady with his confusion. "I can't bear another dream, not another thought. Guide me, Father, tell me what to do."

Outside, Rosier struggled with opening the cathedral door before stepping back to huff at his sudden weakness. A hand went to his throat, as he remembered his housemate's actions, and a surge of resolve urged him forward, told him to find another way inside. He flapped his wings, raised himself to one of the top arches of the cathedral, and settled onto a perch at the other side of a window. He pressed against it — 'There he is!' — and he saw his friend, before he saw God — non-material, non-compounded. Only barely, he could hear them.

The Father said, "I have always said that he who loves me will be rescued; I will protect him, for he acknowledges me, I will be with him in trouble, and I will show him salvation. But, angel, the Beast is not a creature I can cast from you." Lucifer — feeling the supernal-fire beneath his tissues drop cold. "You are the Beast, Lucifer."

"No— No, no, no! Father, I'm no Beast!" But he realized instantly that he was arguing with his King, so he fell back into a bow, this time his forehead landing against the ground. Crying out to Him, "I am yours! I am your angel!" He glanced up, saw some shadows from the corner of his eye, then shouted out, raising a hand, pointing. "There! The Beast is there!" He stumbled onto his feet and rushed away, but there was nothing — it had disappeared. Then, from the peripheral of his other eye, another head of the Beast. Lucifer cried out fearfully, stumbling backwards until he ran into one of the pews and fell onto it — crashing upon the seat, shivering, breathing.

"Lucifer."

"Forgive me, Father. Forgive me, forgive me!" Lucifer covered his face, terrified, and all the lights of the cathedral burned him.

"You are the Beast."

"Help me—"

"It's true that you are an angel of mine, but never have you been like the others. You, who I planted flowers for; you, who I spend time alone with in my garden; you, who I sculpted the most carefully; you, who is my most favorite, the anointed cherub. You, who is perfect, the most perfect in beauty and blamelessness." 'You're hurting me. I'm boiling.' "Do not cry. Reveal your face. You are above the other stars; you are the morning, and your blessings are innumerable. You will rise to a throne even higher than that of the archangels."

'But what is there — above the archangels? What could be between a King and His princes?'

"The superior are burdened with the hunger to harm, but mercy is resisting temptation, and mercy is what creates splendor."

"You're merciful, Father," Lucifer whispered to Him. What else was there to do?

"But you are an angel still, far beneath your Lord. You are to be submissive to your own Master in everything, to be well-pleasing.

Above the others you may be, but you are still among them. You are a ministering spirit as they are." And a few seconds of silence, as if the Father were waiting for a response that the angel didn't have. "You are not your own, Lucifer, you were created, you belong to me."

"But the Beast—" Lucifer tried to say, his legs pulled close so he was seated upon them on the pew, except the implacable gaze of the Creator bared down on him, seizing and grabbing him. He lifted his head, and again, the rain of the stained-glass dribbled onto his face. It showered his body — the reality of the Lord's words seeping into him, deep — so much crying he had done, so much that he was raw, as if he'd been scrubbed clean of skin. A final tear trickled down his face. It came to him: "It's me, I am the Beast."

Rosier whispered it to himself, "The Beast?"

The appetite to make suffer what can't stop you, this temptation familiar to the Merciful God. But Lucifer was good and perfect, and he didn't want this; he latched onto his innocence like it kept him above a pit of flames. He didn't want to be above the archangels, he didn't want to be more than any regular angel. He didn't want to be the favorite.

The Lord said, "Sing, angel," His voice all-encompassing, "and you will be saved."

Lucifer did so, fearing his God and loving Him — a long, somber note that rang out like an organ and echoed from the walls of the cathedral, sustaining until its decrescendo into a rapid intake of breath. God told him to sing again. Lucifer moved half off the pew, one bare foot on the floor, the other still over the seat, looking upwards, searching for salvation — another note, louder. "Sing." He clutched his robes and, for the third time, sang for Him, frantic adoration in his eyes; 'there are suns in them,' thought Rosier. "Sing." Again, again, even louder so that it rattled the organs of his body — and Lucifer's lungs began crying out to him. But he persisted, desperate, until the Father's voice came yet again: "Worship."

Within, something dislodged — a realization, almost, barely — Lucifer's hand raised to his throat, and he felt it strain against his touch. There was tearing, inside, with a striking sharpness. But he kept singing, he couldn't stop; he took another step forward, confused and terrified now, wanting to close his mouth, wanting to run away, but he couldn't. Wanting to plead for this to stop, but again, he was told to sing, and again, and again, until Lucifer became only the searing pain of his chest, neck, head; it was so much he could no longer see. And his song became unrecognizable to him, his voice running itself out from his mouth until—

One final time, his Father said, "Worship me." And Lucifer's last note was so high and forceful it could have been a shriek. It struck his body whole, raised him some inches off the ground, and made every part of him, every section of tender flesh, feel like it was splitting. And he did split — from the sides of his head great wings sprung out, as they did upon his back — all of him pulling so far he became, halfway, the form of his creation in that red-blazed blister. But it was like the creation of the universe — hot, quick; Lucifer fell to the ground.

And finally, the Father left the angel silent — having torn him.

CHAPTER 25

Vitriol burning his soul — eyes fluttered open; the oak beams of his bedroom ceiling. Before anything, there was wetness, all over, stuck to his clothes and caked into his skin, widespread enough he'd thought someone had reversed his skin, so that redness dribbled outside of him, to the floor, to the floor. Blinking, breathing in air, turning his head; Lucifer wasn't noticed by the others, not initially. Asmodeus kept speaking to Rosier, who responded, then answered the question of Azazel at his side, before turning his head to Phanuel. Bustling movement — two dozen angels — you'd imagine it was a feast in the bedroom.

Lucifer thought his ears might bleed and, without thinking, he wailed. He didn't do it too loudly, or that hadn't been the intention, but the cry ripped out of him, as if it'd been trapped in his throat all this time. And what followed were the tears; the emotions came afterward. It was all backward: the scream first, anguish second, the realization last. God, between the colored lights of the cathedral, saying something, something, something. 'To sing? To worship?' There had been a rip, of some kind, and shredding, like shoving both thumbs into an orange, splitting her.

Oh — he was still screaming. His throat was sore, but he was shrieking at the top of his lungs. 'Like this I'd been when I sang to

Father.' Hands fell to him — Lucifer felt them, coldly — and the faces of friends emerged in his vision like the ripples in a lake.

"Lucifer!" Rosier cried, scampering to his knees beside him on the mattress. "How are you? Tell me how you feel." His face was contorted in worry, as it had been when he kissed the tears rolling down the angel of beauty's face.

He was being helped to sit; Lucifer trembled when hands came to his sides and lifted him up; he shivered so much he thought the world was shifting all around him. Baal, Baal was there, his brows curved in worry, as he set Lucifer up against the headboard. Baal was saying, "Lucifer, please don't move much. You're still injured."

Lucifer opened his mouth, but nothing came out.

"Raphael just left," Asmodeus explained, as if the youngest angel had asked. "He's— Well, he's going for some water from the Fountain of Life." There was none of the usual humor in Asmodeus' tone; Lucifer's heart shriveled. "He's having trouble healing you. We don't know why."

'How could Raphael have trouble healing me?' Lucifer felt as if his head were about to roll off his neck; his weight — it rocked and it teetered. He was warm inside, and that heat was clawing up to fog behind his eyes. 'Why am I hurt? Why did this happen? I was singing to Father. Didn't He like the way I sang?'

Over Rosier's shoulder, Lucifer could see part of his tall mirror by the door. His hair was crisped with dried blood, hanging loose over his shoulders — tunic still damp — and his skin might have been there, but it was difficult to tell. All his beauty — obscured by what appeared red muscle escaping the body. 'What? Why?' Another wail, gutting itself out of him — and he shuddered, hard, fell back onto the mattress, heated like a star, feeling like he was about to burst. He was convulsing, nearly, trembling.

"Lucifer!" said Rosier, and Asmodeus, and Baal, and Azazel, and all the others in the room.

One of them demanded, "Tell us what's wrong."

He rasped, shaking more, not wanting a hand on him, wanting to screech. Lucifer tried words, and he felt his mouth move, trying to say them, but nothing was coming out. Where were his words? Had he forgotten them? His tongue was a beast in his mouth — 'a Beast, is that the Beast the Lord said was within me?' Lucifer heard a familiar voice past the balcony doors and turned to look, even as his mind kept reeling. 'Lord, is that the Beast? Did you remove it? Thank you.' Hiccuping — suddenly Lucifer was hiccuping. 'I love you, Father. You wouldn't hurt me. Because I love you. You love me too, right?'

The balcony doors flung open, banging; Michael forced his way through the crowd of angels in the room and rushed forward.

Lucifer was thinking, 'Why did you do this? Father, I'm in pain. Can you take it away? You're merciful. Let me sing again.' Everything ached, slow like rot. 'I'll try again.'

Hasty, Michael sat himself beside Lucifer, beside Rosier, on the bed. He took the youngest angel's hand, said quickly, "Lucifer. You're safe. Look at me."

Lucifer did as told, blinked, and the voice of the archangel flooded into his blood. When he breathed, it was easier. 'Michael. Michael.' He opened his mouth, tried to speak again, but nothing came out. 'Michael. I'm sorry. Please— Don't see me like this. No.' Michael's eyebrows were curved in distress. 'Don't look at me.'

"He was found like this," Baal said. "Someone dragged him out from the cathedral."

"The Lord must have done this," added Phanuel.

"Did Lucifer do something wrong?" Azazel, just about cowering, said next.

"He must've," came the voice of another angel.

"The Lord is punishing him," said yet another.

He did something wrong. He's being punished. Lucifer made Father angry. 'But it wasn't me. It was the Beast.' Lucifer turned his attention to Rosier, even as he held Michael's hand a bit tighter, and he continued thinking, 'It's okay, Rosier. Don't look so worried. I won't hurt you again. It will all be better now. That was why Father did this. Let's trust Him.' He leaned back, sighed, shaky, and tried to find the strength to relax. For the millionth time, Lucifer attempted to speak, but the soreness in his mouth became a blister. All around, angels kept whispering and chattering and mumbling that Lucifer must've done something terrible, he was asking for it, he had done something to invite punishment — that could be the only explanation.

"I'll speak to God," Michael broke through the chatter. "I'll find out why He's done this and what we can do to remedy the situation."

Rosier whispered, "Lucifer seems to be having some trouble speaking," and Lucifer nearly wept in relief someone had noticed.

"Well, he's ripped everywhere," Asmodeus replied. "But I'm sure Raphael will be able to fix that once he's returned."

"Yes," Michael said, before addressing the crowd . "Everyone, there's nothing to be worrying about." Though he said this, Lucifer caught sweat on Michael's brow. "Go to your homes already. Let us archangels handle everything, as well as Rosier." He turned to the angel of fruit in question. "Or— If you'd like, I can take Lucifer with me, to my home, and I can—"

"Michael." Like ice — Lucifer felt himself seize at that voice, the same one that had caused the tears that sent him running home after the party. "There you are. I was looking for you." Uriel stepped forward from the door, and every angel moved out of his way, even if it meant stepping over the feet of each other. His face was stone, lips pressed fine, his eyes narrowed into slits — and the plain boredom of his demeanor gave the impression that Lucifer's appearance was shameful rather than frightening.

Michael's jaw visibly clenched. "What can I help you with, Uriel?"

"The Lord requested you go speak with Him." Uriel moved closer, and he lingered in the middle of the room. "I believe He plans to send you away to Earth."

Lucifer's heart dropped, somewhere deep, and Michael stammered, "What? Send me away? But I just returned—"

"You heard me. Don't have me repeat myself."

Michael opened his mouth, then shut it, and for a moment, Lucifer thought the chief archangel was losing his voice too. But Michael tore his sight away from Uriel, and he put his other hand over Lucifer's. When he spoke, it was hushed: "I'll be back. I'll fix this." His gaze rose and caught Lucifer's own, and the two stared at one another. Lucifer felt his heart rise again, sit snug in his throat, the beats strangling him. "Whatever's gone wrong, it'll be corrected."

"Michael," Uriel called, voice tight. "He said He wanted to speak with you immediately."

"I will," Michael continued, still to the angel of beauty but more hurried, "make everything perfect again."

'I want to dance with you,' Lucifer thought. 'I want to sing in the streets with you. Let's return to that.'

"*Michael.*" Uriel, again.

"All will be well," Michael said. "I'll protect you, Lucifer, from anything. Like I did from that beast on Earth." A shaky, nervous laugh; it made Lucifer want to shriek for the third time. "I'll save you. I'll always be here to save you." He squeezed Lucifer's hand tight, and then he stepped back, away, the mattress crying out after him. But Michael turned, fast, with a roll of his shoulders, and walked toward Uriel.

Lucifer watched; he could do nothing but watch, even when Rosier's own warm hands replaced Michael's. He leaned against his housemate, feeling deflated and weak again, feeling the same way he had when he awoke. 'Save me? Michael, do you mean that?' He stared at Michael's back, stared at his shoulders, saw him come up to Uriel and look at him gravely but make no move to argue. 'No, but there is nothing to save me from. The Lord has expelled the Beast.'

"Everyone," Michael said, "leave Lucifer to rest already. Please."

At this, angels indeed began filing out, even Asmodeus, who frowned, and Baal, who did the same. They went out through the balcony and out the doorway, and Rosier tugged Lucifer a little closer as everyone spared their pitiful glances to the angel of worship who'd been left a mangle worse than any of them had ever seen. A display of power, perhaps, on the Lord's part. But Lucifer thought nothing like that, and he rested his head against Rosier's shoulder instead, wearily noting how Uriel and Michael left together, not saying anything more. 'Will you really leave to Earth, Michael? Will you? You can't save me, if you're so far away.'

The silence prickled once Lucifer was left alone with his housemate. He felt, almost numbly, Rosier rub his back, then reach to scratch lightly at the angel's scalp. Beginning to fiddle with Lucifer's hair, twisting it, braiding it, breaking through the blood, Rosier whispered, "I'll sit with you here a while, until Raphael returns and fixes you."

Fixing Lucifer — Raphael turned out unhelpful in that regard. He was able to piece Lucifer's skin back together, and over the course of a few days, he'd restore the youngest angel's ethereal beauty, but his abilities would falter when it came to Lucifer's throat. He said there were jagged cuts on the inside — "We have other forms inside us, you see; you must know that already. As a cherub, you have another pair of wings. I-I suppose it unsettled inside you, ripped you from the inside." There was nothing he could do, but life marches forward, never has the pity to retrace itself.

The next time Lucifer stepped out of his house, he wandered, not with any place in mind to go. He felt the gazes of angels flicker to him, then away — like when he was infantile, if you remember — but there was a new expression there, one he couldn't find a name for, and not knowing a word — it made him feel exceptionally young, too. Coming upon an unfinished staircase, leading up a hill — maybe there would be something at the end of it, but for now there was nothing except horizon — he climbed. Anxious, he thought that there were infinite things in Heaven but none that were appealing to him now, and when he reached the peak, saw the pulsing ends of the city, he found, 'All there is in Heaven is horizon.' A horizon cut by walls that had no reason to be there.

But the angels had no reason to be either.

"Brother!" The voices of Rosier and Baal, who were scrambling up the steps behind him, before the latter one said, "Hey, don't run off without telling us."

Lucifer stared at them.

Before Baal could ask, Rosier explained, "His voice has been missing." And that was surely why Lucifer was now thinking a bit too much, stuck alone with his thoughts, unable to release them, like a lid placed over soup, steaming, close to boiling over. "But next time he goes to Eden, I'm sure God will find it." Lucifer already missed God, missed singing for Him, so he nodded and Rosier smiled, though strained. "Let's go home." Taking his hand, leading him, like Lucifer didn't know the streets. "You too, Baal. There's some extra fruit." There always was, always was extra in Heaven.

As they walked, angels watched him again. One of them took the chance to quickly sketch the prettiest angel's figure on the bark paper his paintbrush caressed. Another angel whispered something to his friend, but Lucifer didn't know what. Upon returning home, Lucifer found even the words to his psalms refused to leave his mouth. And in many ways it was like the purpose he'd found, the worship, was gone and he was indeed a little angel again with nothing to do but lay in beautiful misery. But he smiled at his friends, let them kiss his cheeks in greeting when they visited. After all — he'd always told God that he offered Him everything, and now God has taken some of that offer, and Lucifer had been sincere with his promise, so this should not bother him. He had asked for it, so why be upset? 'I love you, Father, I do. This is not much a punishment. I always said I was your servant, and now I'll learn to worship without words, if I must. You'll see I'll never make you unhappy again.'

Michael returned the day before Lucifer went to see God, and he took him to a meadow, and they sat, hidden behind a tree, and Michael kissed him on the mouth. Limply, Lucifer had leaned into him, his warmth, nuzzled the prince's nose with his own. He imagined insects in the grass, half-lidding his eyes and catching his own reflection in Michael's pupils. Shame waking from slumber in his chest — he frowned, and the prince mirrored it, then kissed along his throat. Like an Earth beast, wanting to tear the head off its opponent with its teeth. Michael said he would speak to God, and Lucifer took his hand, squeezed the fingers.

In Eden, the Lord had Lucifer lead worship with his timbrel, not mentioning the muteness of His most beautiful creation.

'I'm sorry,' Lucifer told him in his mind. 'You're still upset with me. Whatever I did, I won't do it again.' Maybe Lucifer knew already the problem, but he suppressed even the thought. He remembered the first time he'd come to Eden: God had scooped him into His arms and shown him that there was something beyond the flowers, the flower bed, and the flesh on him, and the strings of the cosmos. You remember it too — God holding the youngest tight. Tighter. Then, the Lord had parted a fruit and allowed the juice to dribble onto Lucifer's lips.

The nightmares continued — ending always with flailing and sweat and a shivering body he wanted to crawl out of. 'I want to worship you forever.' Labors of pain — grappling him, whipping him — each time the angel of beauty awoke. Dreams, at the danger of leaking into life again. Life — though there was hardly any of that in Heaven, only spirits in disguise. 'Was this because I started thinking less of you? I won't do it again. I adore you, I do. I'll love you forever. I'm your angel. There is nothing else to be but your angel.'

"Here," said a friendly stranger, one mid-day. "I knit you these scarves, Lucifer. You used to wear them so much, over your hair and all. I think you can use them to cover the marks on your neck. You'd look very beautiful."

'Please don't hurt me again.'

CHAPTER 26

More time passed, uneventfully.

Asmodeus was kind enough to feed Lucifer some blackberries. He had stumbled onto — though a more appropriate term would be 'found' — Lucifer settled on a thick branch of a massive olive tree. His head had been against the trunk, eyes fluttered shut, mouth parted with soft breaths. From his body fell the bundles of his long robe, tumbling down the branch itself, and his hair had been messily splayed out over his shoulders, one strand over his face, stuck to his lips. When Asmodeus landed on the tree and gently rustled the younger one awake, Lucifer'd revealed downtrodden, tired eyes. And Asmodeus had noticed that the bottom of Lucifer's feet were caked with mud, dried to the soles.

Lucifer, with nothing to do but stare at the basket of berries Asmodeus held, had been offered them. Instead of speaking, he'd opened his mouth wide and listened to his friend chuckle as the fruits were placed on his tongue. Sweet, tart, bitter at once. They crunched nicely between his teeth, and Lucifer wondered if he should stay there a while, sitting and being fed as if he didn't know what a blackberry was. There was amorous pleasure in that, in pretending to know nothing — he did that a lot these days, in between the worst of his depression.

Before Asmodeus arrived, the beautiful angel had spent some time seated on a gigantic lotus flower that floated along a smoky body of water. Heaven was always shifting, contorting itself new environments like you'd tilted your head, saw them at a new angle — certain objects big like it was a trick of perspective, an illusion. Like Heaven itself was an illusion. This area Lucifer had found was strange in that particular way. The lotus, pink like a pair of lips, had beckoned him closer, held some of its petals flat so that the angel could lay upon it and stare into the still, golden sky. Doing so, he'd listened to the ripples of the pond around him.

Then, the flower had said, 'Angel of beauty, your feet are dirty.'

'My feet are dirty.'

'Remove yourself; I fear you will stain me.'

'But don't you,' Lucifer had thought solemnly, to himself, 'fear for me, who is stained?' He'd replied, 'Please don't make me move. You are the only soul who can listen to me.' Flowers had souls, surely; how else could they talk? 'Hear me, speak to me.' Everything weighs with soul.

'Leave me, angel.'

'Let me wash my feet in the water.'

'You'll soil the water.'

'Why am I soiled? Why am I soiled?'

All he'd wished to do was lay on the lotus, his mind twirling with dreams of nothingness — even awake, you see, he dreamt now. Instead, he was cast out from the pond, made to find another place to rest in the forest, and found himself a tree that pitied him. As he flew up to the branch, he'd thought again of the distant walls of Heaven and the open gate. Months ago, the muse had come of what might happen if he simply walked out one day and never returned. But in that moment, it didn't; he fell asleep, and he had nightmares because he only had nightmares.

Then, Asmodeus was feeding him berries.

"Your feet are dirty, Lucifer." Lucifer nodded at him, bending a leg closer so that he could grab his own ankle, tilting it up so they could both see the sole — blackened, browned, some shards of grass nearly piercing skin. "Is that from here?" Head shake. "Oh, you must have just returned from Eden." Nodding again. "How about we go get you cleaned up? The bathhouse shouldn't be so crowded right now. Is that alright with you?" Lucifer didn't answer, simply allowing for Asmodeus to assume he agreed. At this, the older one helped him down until both their feet were on the ground — Lucifer's bare and Asmodeus' clad with henequen sandals.

Though, Lucifer was afraid to see his reflection in the water of the bathhouse. Yesterday, it had turned to him and said, "Father is very kind. This is your fault."

'But I gave Him everything.'

"No, you didn't. What if Father is right? And you're the one who's wrong. He is so much greater than you. You don't know anything. He knows what's best for you. He loves you."

'He hurt me.'

"You deserved it."

Cringing — Lucifer didn't know why he kept struggling to place himself in the present, in his own body.

The two angels left the forest and returned to the golden streets, the weight of the timbrel and pipes hanging from his hip making Lucifer's feet drag. At his side, Asmodeus spoke — of all sorts of things, of his plans to see Rosier and maybe have dinner with them both. He said he had been learning to paint, that he was no good but that he enjoyed it — 'And that is what angels were made for, right? Enjoyment?' He had just beaten Phanuel's team at a sports match; he had played on Michael's side.

'I want to see Michael.' It had been too long — an entire day, almost. 'It's making me ache, I want to see him.' Michael, the only angel capable of striking down each of Lucifer's spiraling thoughts, frightening his despair enough to make it flee, and tying his soul back to his body. It made Lucifer miserably desire him, his touch, his kisses into his hair.

But Lucifer could share none of those thoughts; muteness continued sitting on his tongue and rubbing its eyes tiredly, sadly. It may have been hundreds, thousands, millions of years of silence — but time didn't walk the way that they did. She danced all around, swinging her hips and giggling at Lucifer with the knowledge of how he might regain his speech one day, or how he might not, but only Father knew, and only she knew. She, who was Father. And so it was difficult to know how much time had passed or if any of it had gone by at all.

He thought of the bathhouse; he remembered having gone there countless times. Lucifer, eyes heavy, lifted his gaze to consume the great building coming into the street before him like an intruder. He knew that, once in the past, he had told all his friends that he liked to bathe alone, and that had been true then. 'Is it true now?' He couldn't be sure. 'Why did I always want to be by myself? Was I ashamed? Why was I ashamed? Why would Father want me to be ashamed?'

Asmodeus asked, "Lucifer, shall I leave you here alone or do you need help?"

Lucifer gestured to be left be, smiling when Asmodeus pressed a kiss to his cheek in farewell, but there was laden, quiet pity that Lucifer caught in his friend's gaze. It was enough to upset the youngest angel again, as he made his way up the steps to the entrance.

Arriving in the familiar undressing room — there were four angels there, conversing as they pulled their clothing and ornaments over their heads, probably not realizing all that they had, 'but that is what happens when you make for yourself little ministering spirits that only know pleasure, Father — they don't appreciate things, and they don't realize all their joys come from you, and that you can take it all away.'

Lucifer bowed in greeting at those who saw him, calling, "Lucifer! Do you need any help? It's nice to see you. We're here if you need anything." His hand rose, initially, to tell them, 'No, I can remove my own clothes,' before he stopped.

'Do I really wish to be alone with my thoughts any longer?'

Curiously, Lucifer instead settled his lips into a pout and gestured for two of the angels to come closer. *Help*, he mouthed, and both of his victims jolted. Still, they didn't hesitate, not much; they glanced at one another, then came forward, a pair of hands going straight to the golden string belt as another pair reached to remove some of the jewelry from Lucifer's hair. Soft breath, spilling from his mouth, he watched as drapery was pulled open and apart, delicate, as if they were peeling a citrus.

And the disrobing was simple; he had no tunic, wore nothing beneath his robe except his skin. 'If they wanted to wrestle me right now, they would win; my arms are tangled in sleeves.' One angel skimmed up his torso, taking the chains of precious stones to remove them, but his hands were fiery, and they ignited skin beneath his fingers. The other angel moved onto a crouch, lowering his head as he reached to take Lucifer's shins. He tugged one leg up, to pull off the adornments around his ankles and feet and upper legs, one by one, and then he set Lucifer's foot down. He did the same with the other, as the standing angel finally freed Lucifer from his robe.

It conjured in Lucifer a memory of earlier that day, of his time in Eden. The Lord, as He nearly always did now, had dismissed His host, except for the angel of beauty. Then, He'd ordered, "Because I have dirtied my feet walking along the garden, you will wash them until there is not a speck of dirt left." An obedient nod before Lucifer had been made to kneel, so that he could scrub clean the Lord's feet with water from the lake and the ends of his own attire.

"There, all done," the standing angel laughed. "Oh, you don't have a towel, do you?" Lucifer noticed that the one who'd crouched on the tile floor lingered his gaze on the thighs just freed from the constraints of jewelry. "Do you want me to lend you one?" Plump thighs, kneaded to perfection by a creator.

Lucifer raised a hand to indicate he didn't need it, and by instinct, nearly lifted his other arm to cover his newly exposed body, before he stopped, again. 'No, let them see me.' A little smile — and he moved both hands to his back, held them. 'I have nothing to hide. I'm the most beautiful creation, after all. Let their gazes lap me and try to taste honey off my skin.' Twitch, right along one side of his face. 'Better this in their eyes than pity, better this than tragedy.'

He entered the next room and saw that there were half a dozen angels scattered, on the floor or on seats, but they all looked up, they all saw him, in between the smoke of burning incense. 'And they're all praying to come nearer to me, to touch this waist and squeeze it, so that they can be sure that I'm real.' One end of Lucifer's lips curled, sweet, as he moved onto the mosaic floor and plucked a flask from a tray — lavender. 'Then they avert their eyes, embarrassed, but they can still see me in their minds, wondering if I might feel as good as I look.'

"Lucifer, do you need any help?"

A nod, before Lucifer extended his wings out behind him and looked at the three new angels who had made their way over. He handed one of them the oil, then stretched his legs out before himself with a soft, easy sigh. When one angel began work smoothing oil onto his wings, ruffling those inner feathers and the slim space of smooth skin between them, Lucifer shuddered and felt a crackle of fire within his chest. He leaned into the hand that went to his scalp, to run itself through the threads of his long hair, and another simmering noise escaped as the third angel took one of his arms. Together, the three rubbed lavender into his body, working his muscles until they softened beneath their nimble hands and mellowed Lucifer so thoroughly he nearly went limp.

His mind was whirling; the eyes of angels kept accidentally catching his own, and they were graying, they were flickering like the dying flames of a candle. Wavering, they moved between confusion, fear, and deep, guttural want. Every sound Lucifer let seep from the tip of his tongue made them visibly tense, and so he kept doing it — 'See, Father, how there are ways to speak without speaking? You took my words, but not my hums, my sighs, my sweet groans.'

The fumes of the room begging to make him faint, eyes falling half shut, he lost himself in their caresses. He shivered, leaned, and tilted over each touch. Something was good, delicious for his body like candy swirling in his mouth — coiling him up, making him tighten like a screw. And everything was hot, warm, and stuffy. It could have been that his lungs were taken in a fist, but he breathed, he breathed. He unfurled between their fingers and came apart in strings.

"All done," one angel laughed, deep, and pinched Lucifer's cheek as if to make light of the situation by harsh force.

'How silly,' Lucifer grumbled in the hidden palace of his mind. 'He's whatever the opposite of intelligent is.' Because he felt creative, he tried, 'Moron. Stupid. Imbecile.' And those words came to exist, as simple as that. Breathing — good, he felt good — Lucifer pulled himself away from those wonderful hands, then bowed thankfully to hide the smirk that had begun to snake onto his mouth.

'I wonder why they stare at me like that. Are they confused? Are they scared? They're the strange ones; all I'm doing is bathing.' But he was dizzy and seeing double. There was *power* in this, he was realizing, and maybe that was what was good; he felt like he was wrestling it away.

Making his way to the pool in the great atrium of the building, he felt the luster of Heaven fall upon him. He wished it would dim, however momentarily, so that Lucifer could be the brightest thing in the bathhouse and everyone's attention would turn to him — none of the nervous glances or timidity. Yet, it wasn't necessary. There were only about twenty angels in the water and one musician, strumming an instrument by the edge of the pool. Seeing him, they greeted Lucifer with gestures and soft smiles and calls of his name. 'Lucifer, Lucifer, our wonderful Lucifer.' Then, as expected, they looked away.

With a tinge of amusement, Lucifer climbed down into the pool and moaned delightfully slow and languid as the hot water enveloped him. He fought a victorious grin as the feeling of the angels gazing returned to his nude body. 'Them, just like those in the other room, like those who undressed me, always, all of them, devastated by how much they desire to abduct me and pin me to the walls of their homes like a portrait, or onto their beds like a quilt, or onto their bodies like an earring.' Instead of taking their offers, 'I' simply gestured for them to bring over soaps, 'and little obedient angels that they are, they bring me of every type, of every kind.' And yet, still, he denied their touch, finding power in the denial, in their dutifulness.

With a candied glee, he mouthed a thanks to the small crowd of angels that'd formed around him, took a rose-colored soap, then rubbed it between his palms to make it foam and bubble. Slow, he ran it down one arm, before scrubbing the other. The suds kissed him, slow, needy. Humming, he bent to do up each leg, and the inexplicable, good feeling returned. It returned ravenous — knowing that many angels were watching carefully, licking their lips, feeling hot desire in their guts to hold Lucifer like a tangerine and suckle on him.

All he could do was smile, wistful, as if he didn't know everyone was eyeing him; 'as if I don't know anything, as if I'm an animal in Eden.'

He walked away, to where the water was shallower, by a wall, so that he might tempt them. 'Tempt them into what? I don't know. I don't care.' With a blink, he noticed the pool was quite smitten with him, too: the water clutched tight around Lucifer's hips, as possessive as the sun holds its rays. A breath in, and he massaged soap into his hair, threading his fingers through it. Then, he washed his own body again, delicately, running his hands along his skin easy and slow. Quiet noises, small hums of melody, tiny lip smacks of pleasure. 'I can feel them coming closer, like the predators of Earth, looming out from the trees, those who want to tear me open and devour me.' Devour like he did to the other angels in dreams. 'Come, come, I can sense your hunger. Come bite into this body and taste liquor. Come groan on my supple flesh, and I'll have you in my mouth too. Let's eat one another. Already, you're coming nearer, forgetting yourself, seeing me, only me, desiring only me, me—'

"Michael!"

Shattering — Lucifer spun around the instant an angel before him said the name. His heart battered right out of his chest and splurged blood into all the water, that was now cracking and snapping and cold. Everything inside Lucifer felt expelled. His eyes landed on the archangel, standing right by the pool edge, looking down at him with his brows furrowed. Unlike the rest, he was dry, he was dressed, his wings still stretched out behind him, as if he'd just landed. That was definitely the case — Michael had dropped in from the open ceiling. And all Lucifer could do was stare with round, horrified eyes up at his friend. 'Did he see? How much did he see? Is he angry at me?!'

Michael crouched and, in one great sweep, grabbed Lucifer under his arms, promptly hoisting him out of the pool. Instead of setting him down, however — even with bathwater falling in rivulets from the beautiful angel to puddle the floor — Michael gripped Lucifer around his back and bends of knees. He carried him easily, like that, as he began to walk away from the pool. The rampant blush of, not only being seen like this, but being held against Michael's body made Lucifer nearly catch fire. Instantly starting to thrash, he kicked his legs uselessly in the air, knowing he probably looked ridiculous; it did nothing to help the scorch on his face. Throwing his hands in the air, trying to shove Michael's shoulders and chest so that he let him go —

the archangel only held him tighter, provoking a pitched cry as the younger one startled.

Lucifer was forced to pass by every soul in the bathhouse, like this — 'I can't meet their eyes, I can't, this is the most disgraceful thing I've ever heard of,' — before Michael plopped the younger angel down on a bench in the undressing area. He grabbed Lucifer's clothes and harshly, roughly, began to tug them back onto their proper place. "No towel?" — a grumble. He was hasty with the jewelry, throwing it all on, hardly allowing Lucifer the time to grab the instruments and adjust his earrings so that they wouldn't prick.

Then, the prince took Lucifer by the upper arm and pulled him, stumbling, outside. The glare of Heaven slashing Lucifer — if he could speak, he'd cry, 'Take me back to the darkness! Take me back!' But Michael didn't seem particularly keen for banter. Lucifer knew he should probably apologize, in the gesticulating way he'd come to rely on, but his curiosity hungered. Did Michael see him toying with how much everyone adored him? Did he notice the hungry need in their eyes? Had Michael ever felt that way when he saw Lucifer? 'You have, right?'

Walking, Lucifer came to realize Michael wasn't at all like the angels they had just left behind. He never quite lost his reasoning whenever he touched or kissed him, he never really shuddered with timid want, never panted like an animal. Of course, Michael loved to take in his body, to watch, to stare, to even put his hands all over him, as if he were going to mold him as wet clay. But he looked at him differently, calling for him always differently, uttering his name fearlessly, taking and grabbing Lucifer in a way no other angel had the pride to do.

'You do not desire me.'

A pleased smile on Lucifer's lips, as he lifted a tender gaze to his beloved, stern archangel's face.

'Because you know I am already yours.'

CHAPTER 27

Raphael dragged his body away on the mattress, then pursed his lips in thought, and Michael, speaking for Lucifer, as he tended to, said, "What is it, brother? Do you see any change?"

"I've told you this before."

Lucifer raised a brow, finally closing his mouth, then tilted his head up at Michael, who stood by the bed, where Raphael and the youngest were. Gingerly, Lucifer felt the familiar sheets in the familiar building, all the memories of his first moments as a newborn ravishing him. Raphael had his hair down then; now, it was tied back in a thick braid, interweaved with ribbons and beads. Lucifer also hadn't been completely soaked before; his hair was currently tumbling down his front, dampening his robes and neck. And Michael, of course, hadn't been there. 'I wonder if he'd remember where he was, maybe he was on Earth, maybe he was on the moon he likes so much, maybe he was gossiping with some stars.' Lucifer remembered stumbling to the wall, just minutes after he'd awoken from whatever came before this, touching the paints — the sensation remained, dryness on his fingers.

Raphael had described Lucifer's birth as a spectacular genesis, hadn't he?

The angel of strength spoke again: "Please, Raphael."

"Only Father knows when Lucifer will be able to speak again." Lucifer swallowed, raising the tips of his fingers to brush lightly against the skin of his throat. "But—" Raphael reeled in a deep breath, then set it free, and Lucifer saw his dearest friend's eyes flicker with hope. "Those deep wounds I used to see are healing over very nicely; each time you visit, I close them some more. And I would say this won't go on for much longer."

"That's incredible to hear, thank you." Michael, nodding, settled his hand on Lucifer's shoulder. "Really — you're incredible, brother."

Raphael's tan cheeks tinted softly. "No need for that. It would be better if you speak with Father about it. Have you ever tried?"

Michael looked away, immediately changed the subject: "We really do have to get going, brother. Thank you again for all the help." Raphael frowned, but Michael kept finding different directions to look and, before long, took Lucifer's hand and tugged him off the bed. "We're meeting tomorrow with Gabriel and Uriel, right? I look forward to it." And once Michael had pulled Lucifer onto his feet, he put an arm around his waist and held him — tight, as if the angel needed the support to walk.

'Of course Michael can't convince God to help me,' Lucifer thought.

'He blames himself,' Raphael realized, his hands settling over frail knees.

With nothing but some hurried goodbyes, Michael led Lucifer out from the room and into that corridor where he'd caught his first glimpses of Heaven from the tall windows that reached even loftier ceilings. It was the place where the mirrored self had tried to coax Lucifer closer, but he didn't spend much time reminiscing. Instead, he maintained his gaze on Michael, who was looking ahead, who refused to look at him, noticeable tension in his jaw, at his temples.

Lucifer was really just relieved to return home already. Raphael no longer looked at him kindly, only somberly. He'd run into him and Gabriel, once. Gabriel had said, "Ah, your eyes are so sad, Lucifer. Is something wrong?" Of course something was wrong. "Don't worry.

Father is all-knowing. I'm sure this is part of His plan to help you. All will be well! God is good." And every angel reassured Lucifer with the same words: God is good, trust Him, He loves you. They wiped his tears with those words; they frowned when Lucifer continued to cry, as if the youngest angel was being irrational.

"Maybe," his reflection taunted once, "you are being irrational."

As they stepped out into the light, Michael mumbled, "You really should have brought a towel." Then, he used the back of his hand to push all of Lucifer's hair over onto one shoulder, and Michael's knuckles brushed the warm, damp skin of Lucifer's neck. Something there went aflame, and they kept walking, walking, walking — two pairs of clean feet padding against the ground, almost in unison. "Once I get you home, I'll brush your hair, make you something to eat." 'Michael is too fussy now.' "I'll make sure you're asleep before I leave."

Lucifer began digging his feet into the road, taking Michael's arm and tugging. Making a face, of a pout and narrowed eyes, he tried tempting the prince into a nearby orchard by nodding his head at it. 'Take me there,' he wanted to say. 'Throw me over the grass and put your mouth on mine. If the angels see us, let them! Let them live woefully forever, wishing they were us, that they could love like us.'

"Let me take care of you instead," was the reply, and then Michael dragged the beautiful angel away from the lascivious fruit trees, both of them frowning.

Lucifer wasn't very enthusiastic about being coddled. It used to be that he was the one who did the coddling. He'd often made the trip to Michael's home just to clean it, wash his clothes, then prepare him some bread and tea the way he liked, and Lucifer enjoyed helping the other bathe and picking out his jewelry; he'd quite liked the thought of an eternity of just that, of looking after Michael and receiving hearty affection in return. Yet, since what occurred in the cathedral, Michael had become the pamperer of the two. He was always after Lucifer, spoiling him with whatever he wanted, fluffing his pillow, brewing him a buffet for every meal, doting after every strand of hair that went out of place. Holding him consistently, obsessively, as if always at risk of a permanent separation.

The other angels didn't ease the worry. Instead, they gossiped that it was Michael's fault that Lucifer's voice had been stripped. No one knew what had taken place in the cathedral, but they knew Uriel had scolded Michael the day before the punishment. Jabbing their fingers at the archangel, the rumors claimed Michael had snapped at Uriel and failed to heed his warnings. All the angels said, 'Prince, look at what you have done. You have taken away the most beautiful voice in Heaven. It's your fault. Aren't you our angel of strength? Look at what you have done.'

They met Rosier and Asmodeus in the living room. Asmodeus was often there now, having practically moved back in, while Lucifer spent so much time in Michael's house that he had practically moved out. With Lucifer's voice absent, however, nothing had been organized formally; once, Lucifer had tried to communicate with the Lord through a scroll, only to be immediately barred from writing itself. But perhaps it was better like this; Lucifer didn't want to wake Michael every day, kicking, whining, from those endless, spiraling nightmares and didn't want to stand the sight of Michael, distressed, eyes hefty with pain, thinking he had caused this, that God was punishing him by punishing Lucifer.

The archangel rested his hand on Lucifer's back, greeted the two angels kindly, before walking Lucifer up the stairs.

Lucifer recalled the feeling of Rosier's neck against his fingers. It could happen again. It always could — though Rosier had learned to wait out in the hall when he heard the worst of Lucifer's flailing and cries. It was only after the angel of beauty calmed into quivering, quiet heaving that Rosier would come in, with a steaming cup of bougainvillea tea. And they'd sit in silence together.

Michael brought him to the bed.

'Father. This morning, you asked your choir to sing for you, so I led them with my timbrel and listened as the others sang. And all your angels danced joyfully, frolicking through Eden as you've always intended for us. I mouthed the words I had written for you, standing in the flower bed you made for you. But, did you see, I felt the last of me extinguish; it came to me that it was no longer your name I prayed to.'

Michael was scolding him: "Lucifer, now that we're alone, and don't think I didn't see, we need to discuss your behavior." Lucifer was already groaning, shifting away from the other before flopping onto his back over the plump pillows. The prince remained sitting beside him, looked about to continue talking, when one of the many tendrils of vines by the bed took hold of Michael's bicep. He startled, a bit befuddled, then laughed as all the flowers rushed to nuzzle his face, smother him in their graces. "What are you all doing?" — chuckling, cheerful.

Tender gaze. 'They missed you,' Lucifer wished to say. It was nice to see the archangel in his bed, it always was — Michael being kissed by smooth lilacs, white and purple.

"Stop that, stop that," Michael chided playfully, waving away his attackers. "I'm trying to be angry with your keeper."

He didn't like it when Michael was upset, but Lucifer had nowhere to run. Thus, he grabbed his friend by the front of his robe, pulled him down so that the archangel escaped the flora and fell to lay on his side beside him, on the mountains of cushions and blankets. Warmth, softness, enough for any angel to fall asleep instantly, but Michael wasn't any angel, so he made a face, huff, at Lucifer that said, 'Don't try your charms on me.' And he took the younger angel's chin with a certain sturdiness.

"Open," the archangel ordered, but Lucifer kept his mouth closed. "Lucifer." He couldn't help a silly smile, neither of them could. "Don't be difficult."

Lucifer decided to comply, though normally he would have fought, kicked, and made the other wrestle him; his lips parted no more than a feather's thickness.

"More." Another feather. "Lucifer." 'I like it when you say my name like that. Say it again.' "Please?" 'I like it when you say that too.' He conceded, truly, this time — opened his mouth wide and did his best not to laugh as Michael leaned to peer inside. "Huh. I don't see anything. I have no clue how Raphael does it." A sigh and shift back, removing his hand from Lucifer's chin but lifting it to skim his knuckles against the other's cheek, swiping away some strands of gold. "Should I brush your hair?"

Lucifer smiled, amusedly, and nodded, moving and flipping his hair pompously as the other laughed. They maneuvered around so that Michael sat behind him, against some propped up pillows, his legs spread, and Lucifer sitting between them but facing away. He sighed delightfully as his friend ran down a hairbrush, taken from atop a nearby cabinet, smoothing out any knots in the drying threads and allowing the scalp scratches to fill the silence. Then, Lucifer hummed, as best he could, a little wordless song. The archangel braided his hair slow, expertly, because he'd become quite good at it, and he tugged on the finished product. Lucifer half-twisted back, breathing slow, meeting the other's eyes.

"Do you remember this one time, we were both by my house — we wrestled on the water before a wave hit us," a small laugh, "so yes, we climbed onto a boulder, and we sat a while. You looked over the edge, and then I looked with you, and I saw your face beside mine. I thought we looked very nice together, I wanted to tell you that, but ah! My pride. I couldn't do it." An insecure, timorous smile. "You asked me if the sea knows it's alive. You asked if it had a face, with eyes and a mouth, and where we might find it."

Breathing in, Lucifer's eyes found Michael's lips. He stared at them, considered they looked soft, softer than the pillows, softer than the petals of a cardinal.

"I never told you this — I always thought your mind was as beautiful as your face. I'm only saying it now because you can't tease me." Lucifer tittered a little. "Don't tease me in your head, will you?" 'Something inside me is softening down, making me pliant like water pooled in your palm.' Nodding. "Thank you." Michael patted Lucifer's back twice, gently. "But also—" He cleared his throat. "Whatever you were doing in that bathhouse — don't do it again, okay?"

'Why?' Lucifer fully turned his body around; he was still between Michael's legs, but now facing him, quirking an eyebrow. He feigned innocence, or at least attempted to, but one edge of his lips twitched, wanting to giggle at his friend's demeanor and the light flush along his dark cheeks, as if a butterfly had settled there. 'It's my body. I can do whatever I want with it.'

"Just agree with me."

'Oh?' Lucifer gave him a grin. 'Jealousy? The chief prince is jealous?'

"Come on, you, I'm serious." Michael inhaled deep, then turned away. "I've had a long day. Fighting was exhausting, and the crowd pressured me to go more rounds than I usually would, so don't be so much trouble with me—" Lucifer, quite suddenly and forcefully, planted both his hands on Michael's chest and shoved him down onto the bed. "Lucifer!" But he cut himself off with a sharp breath, as the angel of beauty clambered onto his upper legs, sat, then placed his palms on the archangel's shoulders. What came next was a low, rumbling groan; Lucifer had begun to rub slowly, molding, massaging. "Ah, thank you."

Kneading Michael loose beneath his hands, Lucifer wanted nothing more than to press their bodies flush together, to feel every part of the other, cosmically heated and shifting and beating and sturdy and soft. 'Michael, Michael, Michael,' 'I want to say it forever,' 'I can't stop, it's sweeter than honey on my tongue.'

Michael's wandering hand, finding Lucifer's thigh, slipping beneath the robes, by the tunic that had ridden up — tracing the chains strapped there, the cool gems stuck to intricate bends of gold, then brushing feverish skin.

'Yes. Hold me, squeeze me there, nuzzle me open.' Lucifer opened his mouth, feeling as if wine poured out from between his lips, and released a sweet, languid sound.

The quiet noises of Michael's pleasure burned coals deep in his gut, rising smoke to cloud his vision, and before long, Lucifer moved, moved to rest on top of the other. He heard, felt, his friend stiffen, but then those muscles ebbed all that tension, and he became lax, open. Lucifer swallowed as the other's warm palms took his even warmer cheeks, the tips of fingers tapping by his temples, and they looked at each other, gazes brimming so heavily it became difficult to see the details. 'Michael's jaw, his nose, his mouth, his eyes, his brows, his lashes, his mouth, his neck, his mouth, his mouth.' Swallow. 'My entire body throbbing in beats like a heart. Wanting to be yours.' Every breath dense, steaming and boiling. 'Help me.' Closer, Michael leaned closer.

'Devour me like a pomegranate and stain your tongue.'

His full lips pressed, reluctant, to Lucifer's forehead. Michael kissed both his cheeks next, delicate as a caress on glass, breathing, weak, "Lucifer." Then, his mouth found the angel of beauty's, and Lucifer nearly crumbled like a wilted flower. "I'm sorry."

'Please.' Lucifer trembled, fighting tears of desire and confusion, confusion at the wildfire making his legs restless and confusion at his own mania. His hands trembled as they traveled up the body of the other, finding once more Michael's supple chest, firm and strong. And he anticipated the prince pulling back — he did, for a moment, to swallow hard — but Michael leaned back in, as if chasing, seizing.

This was different — unlike any other kiss they'd shared. The prince bestowed it soft and slow, weighting their eyelids until all there was between them was taste, saccharine, innocent, youthful and ancient. "Mm," Lucifer managed, pressing forward with a kiss himself — a peck, that Michael matched. And their lips began to move slow, to drag on each other as if trying to take them somewhere — a little experiment of dance and fight. Their noses bumped; little smiles tugged into their kissing. "Mmmm." The archangel moved his hands from Lucifer's cheeks, brought them down to the high of his waist, just about his ribs, and hugged him tight there. "Hah—" A tiny gasp, nearly a laugh.

"I feel drunk," Michael murmured against him, then shuddered. "Your mouth— When you were created, your lips must have been laced with liquor."

Their legs tangled, devastating timidity falling away to expose the angels in all their vernal love. The flowers in Lucifer's belly rose, yawning, looking all around, searching for the culprit who'd rustled them from winter slumber. Longingly, the angel thought, 'Kiss me, kiss me, kiss me!' with nothing less than hysteria. 'Kiss me more.' And he caught an unknown, guttural torture — want — in the earth of Michael's eyes as they both leaned to, indeed, kiss some more. Like this, they found their bodies moving on each other, following the lead of their mouths, rubbing like palms together, trying to create heat.

"Lucifer." The beautiful angel made a sweet whine in response, grating himself on whatever parts of his friend might be the hardest, sturdiest, perhaps sharpest. As if he could find some piece of Michael that would stab him. "That feels nice." If only the prince could enter him, could spread his very skin, move inside, so that their souls would kiss how lips do. "*Ugh—*" Like he was pained, Michael kept grunting, but he didn't stop rolling his body, tidal, over Lucifer's own. Smiling, the younger one touched the collar of the prince's drapery, fingers already trickling beneath to flushed skin. His back was arched, his waist still in the prince's tight hold.

But this couldn't last long enough — the sound of chatter was suddenly quick approaching, at the other side of the door — Asmodeus and Rosier coming to check on Lucifer.

It turned Michael's head, and then he was shifting, his grip on the other angel becoming looser, limper. 'No! Don't you dare remove your touch from me! I'll die! I'll be the first angel to die!' Michael, abrupt, pulled Lucifer back to him, drawing him to his chest and holding him there, tight. Blinded by the robe of the archangel pressed against his face, Lucifer heard the creak of the door, and then Rosier's gasp, before his whispering apology for interrupting Lucifer's sleep, then Asmodeus' quiet laugh. Next, there was shuffling and the door being closed with a thump, but Michael didn't weaken his embrace on the angel of beauty. He put his chin on top of Lucifer's head, imprisoning him to the quick thunders of his heart, dull against Lucifer's cheek.

They melted against one another, bodies pressed close and fitting so snug Lucifer thought they must have been fashioned for each other, no matter what Father said about wholeness. He wrapped his arms around Michael and did his best just to feel him, but his own pulse continued to race, in time with the raises and dips of the prince's sternum, and Lucifer wanted nothing more than to shake his head and scream.

'I wish I could get even closer to you — I wish we could sink into each other and become one.' Lucifer clutched Michael's clothing. 'What is inside of you, archangel? Did Father plant flowers within this body too? I want to peel you open and suck the nectar from them.'

"Lucifer." 'Michael.' "I can't stay to sleep here." 'Stay, stay, stay.' "Let me go." But Michael didn't push him away; he surrendered in all the weakness of God's strongest creation. "The bed is small." 'Let me rest my head on your warm chest, or you can sleep on mine.' "Mmm." 'Stay.' Michael, weak, tugged the blankets closer.

Lucifer smiled, in a wistful daze. 'One time, I dreamt of us,

Michael, in Eden. We were over the flowers, and you touched me, remade me. I thought that I could adore you more than the sky, than the heavens, than the Earth.' He let his eyes flutter shut. 'In vain, I love you; in vain, the dawn streaming onto you, beside me; in vain, I want to be yours, your angel. Angel of love, angel of Michael.'

CHAPTER 28

U riel only ever felt comfortable around the Lord's Throne.

Unlike the others, he walked the streets of Heaven stiffly, his entire body tense at all times, feeling awkward with just two legs, and worse, with clothes, no matter their weight, and with fine hair and jewelry. Whenever Father sent him away, he spent most of his time in the vast libraries of his home, seated curled up over some cushions on the floor, and he'd either be writing a book or reading one, or re-reading, memorizing it. All the curtains would be drawn; he always preferred the darkness, broken by the timid rays of a single candle, used most often while he painted the mosaic calligraphy of each word into endless manuscripts or carved glyphs onto stone. He was the only angel who knew every language, every script.

Occasionally, Gabriel would come by, tell Uriel that Raphael recommended he not starve himself, and then he would try to let in some light as Uriel quickly went to cover his head with anything he could. "Brother," Gabriel always laughed, and he had a friendly little inflection to his speech that Uriel was no fan of, "why are you the way that you are?" 'Uriel, Uriel. Go outside, Uriel. Why won't you spend time with all the angels? Fly with them, sing with them. Be joyous, like everyone else.'

"I saw a star burst in Pleiades." Uriel's voice filtered out from where he was, not too far, just a little off being at His side, because anything more would be deeply overwhelming, even in this form.

This form — the only one such an elderly angel could feel himself in, not like he was phantom limbs trailing from a heavy corporeal body, dragging against the golden roads and disagreeable always, feeling consistently coated in wet earth that just wouldn't come off. When relief came, it turned his flesh inside out and turned into great clusters of twisting wings, silvery, stretched from the cuts of the fire that made him up, and there were eyes — infinite lively tourmaline all fighting for space on interlocking, spiraling flaxen wheels. Fathomable to Father alone — faceless was the easiest way to breathe. Uriel hovered; there was no need to flap to keep himself afloat, in such a twisted place.

There was color, all of it in patterned spins, consuming but falling into the Lord, who was more than existence, more than the fabric of firmament He knitted and smoked out from His Throne. Without a word, the Father answered: "He will become more stars."

"Yes, I know." Uriel flushed as much as a gargantuan abomination could. "I was only curious about it. How many stars will there be, or... will it continue forever?" A part of him worried; 'Father, you can hear me, you know what I wish to ask permission about.'

"Uriel."

"Yes?" Uriel enjoyed the sound of his name; unlike his body, he had some semblance of, delicate, identity in it, despite everything.

"You will remain in Heaven." 'I see.' "There are many things there, and because Michael is so distracted, you ought to continue ensuring order." 'All I want to do is visit my siblings — all they wanted was to be whole, but they're ripping to pieces again — why?' "Not long ago, I returned Lucifer's voice, and I want no more brazen actions from him. Even after all that I have told him, even after punishment, he is refusing to learn." 'Then, why is he your favorite?' "Disobedience did not exist before Lucifer; when we see the weeds of it sprout once again from him, we must crush the shoots. Do not get so distracted." 'Yes, yes, Father.'

Lucifer, far away in Heaven, hummed slow, tapping one of the limp petals of a pale pink-orange orchid. It composed a bed of many, all tilting downward from a box, which itself was one of a handful that were scattered all along Michael's flat ceiling. That archangel loved gathering flowers, and herbs, and small trees, abundant with plump fruits, to bring them all into his home, this garden, thinking not enough about how he might take care of so many.

'It doesn't help that Father keeps sending Michael off, to do all sorts of things.' "Good day," Lucifer told the orchid, who drew a little away. "I've come with a bucket of water. Please try to hold on longer." His voice was sweet and musical — that was how it'd returned just a week ago, a sudden moment of God's grace in Eden. 'Let me raise this heavy pail, let me sing kindly to you all.' "I'll take good care of you, beautiful things."

Uriel said, "I just do not understand, Father. If Lucifer is not well, why not punish him further? I see no change in his behavior. Nor in Michael's. They're after one another like animals, meeting where they think no one sees them."

"I have spoken to Michael, but your age blinds you, Uriel. You remember the time before paradise — other angels do not. They do not know what they have. Angels have not worshiped since the first days of Heaven. You see them, chasing self-indulgence, stuck in stupor because of their pleasure-seeking, wanting everything and needing nothing. All their prayers are empty; they have never known to be grateful." 'They do not know. They do not know. They do not know what the opposite of this was — what it was all like before the covenant with you.'

Lucifer spent a while speaking kindly with each plant, who gossiped to him about how Michael had been wrong to put together a charming hidden garden he couldn't take proper care of. Waving a hand in tittering amusement, he couldn't find it in himself to argue, moving along between them, watering every flower — and the dead garden began to climb its way back to life, tended to by the angel of worship with little, tumid hearts in his eyes. He finished with a brilliant smile, before setting the silver bucket down and adjusting the heaps of vermilion robes he wore that were too large. Robes that belonged to Michael, smelled brisk like him, that Lucifer had taken because he knew the other wouldn't mind, quite the opposite.

"Lucifer!" Baal appeared, landing right before him in the garden with a great gust of wind that rippled the tender nature and Lucifer's hair. Sucking in a breath, then laughing — "There you are, sweet brother. Rosier is looking for you again."

Brushing off a tease of irritation, now that the orchids were yapping with complaints again, Lucifer thought to himself, 'Was it Rosier, or are you just desperate to see the most perfect angel in Heaven? I can't blame you, Baal. Poor thing, you're obsessed with me, have been for a million years now. More.' Like everyone, Baal had done nothing, had simply watched Lucifer suffer in silence.

Uriel could still see the beginning of the universe, if he so tried. It remained all crystalline to him — the memories — the heated flares, from which the first emotions and thoughts were born, between the great combustion that became everything all at once, vicious and violent as it beat creation into form. Uriel was one such creation, disembodied, opening his mouth to shriek, but sound didn't exist quite yet, nor did he have a mouth, feeling instead strings strum painfully wordless between entrails he didn't have.

During the settling, 'you, Lord, gave me thousands of eyes,' sweltering marigolds in between the coils of feathers, which were so clumped that they resembled just one, initially. All Uriel saw, the first ever sight, was his own sharp tearing as he was pulled across a void canvas that expanded fast, stretching him until the sensation that he was ripping was all there was. Shrieking, all the angels in their nativity tried to cry, but they couldn't — the angels didn't know yet 'that we were angels, that there was a Creator. All we knew was that we were ruptured.'

Knowingly, Lucifer giggled. "Ah, brother, there's no need to walk me home."

"But I've missed you! Tell me how your days have been." Baal put his arm over Lucifer, the way Michael always did; 'I can see why he's constantly got his hands on your body; something feels pleasant about it, about just having you. I want to tell you that, but maybe Michael has already said it.' Baal felt his jaw tense at the thought of that archangel, who ate away at Lucifer's time, took and gathered it all in his fists like it belonged to him.

Hiding a smirk — "I've been very well." 'Try as you might to hide it, Baal, I can feel your gaze combing its teeth up my sides, swiping its tongue, trying to taste my saffron perfumes.'

'I wasn't flesh,' Uriel reminisced, 'but from the hefty void that composed me, I forced a wing out, out through a ripple in the abyss I laid upon. I threw it before me, dragging myself into corporeal torture, as if lugging from ocean to mud — and I was dirty, I was dripping. I wanted to sob, because I couldn't scream even if pain was all I was, but I couldn't cry either, because you gave me eyes but no tears. Ripping — I could feel the linens that folded into my body being scratched with holes. The sphere of existence dented into itself, and it placed me everywhere, and if I was everywhere, I was nowhere. The body I didn't have being ravaged, I had eyes, but there was nothing to see. Millions of years in darkness, silence, the sizzling of a baking vacuum.'

'"Make it stop, make it stop, make it stop," — a wail, consistent. I heard it before I saw him, this heavy mass of ensnarled metals that wandered the empty space like me, up ahead. He was blinder than I was, but he had a mouth, something I couldn't find on me no matter how hard I looked, and so I crawled along behind, in a chase that continued for ten thousand years. Time spent hearing over and over that pleading phrase directed at no one. When I reached the quivering creature, put myself up against him, and he stopped, we both wept dry — and that was joy, that was the first joy — the tenderness of no longer being alone.'

'You said the first new word I'd heard from you in all that time I followed — "Uri."'

'Climbing up as incomplete things, uneven and melted, we continued, and together, we fashioned something of a body. Together, because I couldn't find a pair of lips in my flimsy heaps of piled permanence. I desired to borrow one of the hundred supple mouths that lined down your necks, over your willowy chest and hands, too, and I lent you my eyes, and we became one. You kept calling me Uri, I don't know why; I looked forward and, in between the horizon, darker than onyx, I saw another thrashing — red, red like clay, weighted — creation. It took another million years to reach him. In that time, as I guided you onward, you said to me, "I am Kimah. And you are Uri, and we are an angel." Do not leave me then, I wanted to say, because now at least I am something.'

'Kimah. It was the only word in my mind for a while — not angel, not pain, just you, this only light in the dark ocean we both floated along, facing downward, drowning as we swam, but I stared at you. In the shutters I caught of your face, there was the wish to describe you, even if I couldn't. Your hair was made of feather soft tongues — one for each grain of sand that would ever exist — white as the teeth of the grinning mouths that covered you to the ends of your fingers. I wanted to say to you: I have eyes between the rings of my hair, and even if your eyes are shut, your lashes are longer than mine when they appear on you, though usually they don't. A lopsided bundle of strangeness you were, but you were like me.'

'"You are beautiful," I wished to say.'

'Legs were helpful, but not too much. We scrapped them together, at some limb of time, and true wings, but there wasn't much to do or places to go. Kimah, you and I were a good match; many of the others, as we found them, were much worse off. Those who could shriek, did so, crying and begging to be settled, but none of us could help. All the angels had no choice but to scurry naked, grabbing at each other's soaked clumps and inventing abuse, defiling the spirits we still couldn't command. But not you — Kimah. You gathered the universe into seven fists and quilted it to wrap around, to keep us warm, and I leaned in so your mouths might press to any part of me that was solid enough not to crumble at your touch.'

'The angels butchered each other; because they lacked so many parts, they tried to suture one being from what they stole from one another. I worried they would hurt us next, but then you took me, said, even never having seen me, "I take you, Uri, I take you, to have and hold. From here, forward, for the better and worse, for bountiful, for empty, incomplete, and together. Never will we part." And we were one.'

'I was so swollen with affection. We tumbled over one another, and you were laughing — was that the first laugh? If only I could speak too; I was desperate to cry out your name, loud enough to hurt me, to end me. I rolled onto you instead, and between us, there were fumbles to invent pleasure, to consummate, and I tried, and I tried — you swung your heads and screeched — but these bodies were heavy with suffering. When the other angels saw us, forever intertwined, so we were larger than they and greater, they called us, "Uri-Kimah. Uri-Kimah, the angel in nuptial bliss."'

'I was the one who made fire. Lost in all-encompassing, cold darkness, for two hundred million years in this cut of existence we flared in and out of, I had long forgotten about the hot burst of creation. I didn't mean to create anything; I merely plucked two stems from the ceiling of the empty universe's sprawl — I was sitting in a calm pool with you, only slightly too tired to be devoured by your kisses — and fed them my ichor, my nebula. Then, light.'

'I dropped it, then fell into a crouch to stare closely, overcome with heaves. "Kimah," I wished to say when your embrace found me, "what have I done?" As if I had just started the universe again — because suddenly I was aflame, and everything was, and you screamed in torment, the sound violating me, making me thrash, because I couldn't, I couldn't hear that, Kimah, I'm sorry, Kimah. The others, shrieking at being burned, going at each other again fearfully — we invented terror, we invented it from not knowing, not understanding. I tried to help, but my hands were hot, and they weren't hands, and you screamed, "Make it stop, make it stop!" like when I met you, but I was like all the angels — powerless. I couldn't even comfort you. Torture, battering, searing; please, please, I begged to no one, let me *scream*.'

'It was your hopeless beseeching that made our Creator finally reveal Himself. He took us all. That quilt you draped on us for warmth, Kimah, that was Him, that pool we used to sit on, that horizon we always walked towards — the edge of the universe is from where the Father appeared, like a sinkhole.'

The Lord said, "Uriel," and His hand tapped the armrest of the Throne. "Why are you in that form?"

Uriel hesitated; he had no answer. "I prefer it."

"I incarnated you, embodied you."

"You did, Father."

"Show it to me."

Uriel, again, couldn't act immediately; all he desired was to remain this hovering mass, of something that bent the material world, the source of all his ills once, and quenched it. It was like the body he had for millions of years; it was like the true body, the half of Uri-Kimah. But he knew better than sacrilege. Shutting all his eyes, then, Uriel slipped down onto the ground before the Father, in the weight of flesh he didn't like, he didn't like, he wished to rip off, as he fell into a low bow, so that his gaze would go nowhere near the Creator. 'You heard all my thoughts, just now, so why, Lord? Why are you making me do this? I'm shaking here, in this vulnerable tunic. Won't you have mercy?'

"You," Lucifer laughed as he arrived outside his home, "are too much, Baal. Of course I'll go out and wrestle with you, but today, I am too busy. How about tomorrow?"

"Look at me."

Uriel made a noise, shifting on these feet he couldn't manage well, that kept tempting to trip him. 'Who is that? Who is in control of them? Is it you, Kimah? Have you come reclaim me?'

"There is no Kimah here." A sharp intake of breath from the angel, terrified. "Set your eyes on your Creator, Uriel." 'But that will hurt. Flesh isn't divine enough to withstand the Lord, not enshrouded. It will hurt me. Why would you want to hurt me?' "Will you make me say it a third time?"

'Father, you appeared and told us who you were, and we were scared, and we were angry — the first anger, from lack of mercy, because you watched us suffer for millions of years in silence. I wished to yell at you, and Kimah said the words I thought up, because he could hear them, because we were each other. He flung them at you — every phrase of indignation in my heart — but you said to my beloved, "You wanted it all to end. I will make it end." I watched you slaughter them, Father. I watched you beat my siblings against the void, we begged you to stop, you wouldn't, you called us ungrateful children, we said, "Who are you?" and you punished us.'

Uriel had begun to tremble. "Father," he said, "it will hurt."

"I said look at me, Uri-el."

'Kimah, with your voice, you pleaded with Him, you said, "Creator, we will be good for you, let us be good for you. Look at how Uri and I have made joy, through you and for you." I was furious, but you continued, "We will worship you. All we ask is you make it end — all the suffering. Please, for your angels." And Father made a covenant with us, but His eyes were on the little flames I had created.'

In obedience, Uriel raised his sight to the Lord's face, but he saw for only a second, before his world was red, flooding hot — his eyeballs tore to streams that spilled down his face, screams bursting from his mouth — but he was told not to look away, to remember the wrath of God.

"'On one condition will angels have salvation: I will put you to sleep, set you aflame, and adorn the sky with your bodies — all you here, except for one." Did you anticipate the consensus, Father? In a matter of seconds, the creations all shouted out, "Uri-Kimah, Uri-Kimah! The angel who made the agreement with you and never partook in our violence." You said you agreed, Father. I watched, as one by one, you caressed the faces of those you had tortured so fully moments before, calling yourself loving, wishing them sweet dreams, as they fell onto the bed of the universe. You gently molded them into spheres, and you settled them — they were beautiful — as stars that began to brighten all the emptiness. I was with Kimah, watching, and I felt brilliant relief, until my angel began to go limp in my hold. Kimah? Kimah? He smiled at me with all his mouths, and he tried to kiss me as he drifted.'

'No, Kimah, I thought then. No, Kimah. Come back to me, Kimah. Kimah. What is happening to you?'

Uriel fell, retching dry, all the frail entrails beneath his skin knocking on his throat and asking to spill out. He couldn't look away; he wasn't allowed to.

'You picked him up, God. You didn't let him say farewell to me, hoisting him to the sky to decorate the house you built. You said to me, you are the angel that will be eternal and complete. I cried to you, I was complete. You said to me, your name will now be Uriel. I said, no, my name is Uri-Kimah. You said, you are Uriel. I cried, and I thrashed — but you grabbed me, and walked me to the Throne you had made, and fashioned me drapery of flesh and stitched it onto me. You gave me tears, finally, and a voice, and I sobbed with violence: "Kimah, Kimah, Kimah!"'

'Kimah.'

'I've filled libraries with all the things I wanted to say to you.'

'I just want to go visit you. I haven't in a while.'

'I want to see if you sleepwalk, and if you might speak to me, tell me what you are dreaming about.'

"What is the point," the Father seemed to muse, staring at the writhing, tortured angel at His feet, "of such a body, if you are going to treat it so delicately?"

CHAPTER 29

Rosier was pacing all about the carpet, nibbling on the tip of his thumb, eyebrows pulled together. He'd attempted to tend to an orange tree in the patio, but the branches had blinked down at him and sighed, "Angel, your hands are clammy." All he'd been able to do was startle, apologize, frown. He'd decided it was better to wait in the house, rather than disturb the fruits he was usually so tender in handling. Fruits — that was what he was for, had known it since even before he'd first awoke in Raphael's arms, before the first time glistening apples reflected off both his perfectly amber eyes, wide and wondering.

"Hah," he breathed and turned his head to the way in, where footsteps flowed out from. "Lucifer." 'Those are not your robes. I would have seen you wear them before.'

Lucifer just about skipped over, kicking off his sandals with ease then flopping onto one of the couches with a wide smile that ate away his face. "That is my name! And yours is Rosier, friend."

"You're in a good mood." Rosier moved a little closer. "Did something happen?"

"Nothing did! But Baal was very silly on the way here. Oh, you sent him after me, right? He said so." The angel sat up and scooted to one side, so his housemate could sit with him, and Lucifer raised and bent both legs, hugging them snug. 'I see worry on your face, Rosier. Are you going to scold me over my relationship with Michael?' He stared, then imagined telling Rosier, 'I've been kissing Michael. I've been kissing him on the lips. I don't believe God is happy about that.'

"Now that you're speaking again, I thought," Rosier stopped, swallowed, then shifted to plop onto the couch beside the other, surrendering.

Lucifer's thoughts continued running: 'Or, is this about Asmodeus? You want him to take his room back. I haven't yet asked Michael if he'll let me move in, but he would never deny me, even if he only has one bed. I'll tell him we don't need another.'

"There's something," Rosier mumbled, "I need to confess to you, something I kept to myself all this time— Please forgive me. I was frightened. I only did it because of that."

Slow — "What are you referring to, Rosier?"

"I saw what happened in the cathedral, between you and Father." 'I saw the way He took advantage of you, singing so adoringly to Him. It doesn't make sense, why would He hurt you? Aren't you His favorite? Where was His mercy? I'm not wise, I never have been, but I'm fearful.' "I was the one who dragged you out."

"Why did you never tell me this?"

"I was terrified, brother!"

Lucifer felt his muscles tense. "Then why are you saying it now?" At some point, he'd begun to grip his knees. "All that time I was silent, I thought I was alone. I had no way of telling anyone what happened." A little laugh burst from between his lips, and he saw Rosier grimace, as if he expected to be struck. "Should I tell you what that was like? Do words exist for that kind of suffering?" Another giggle. "What type of paradise is this? Our Father took my voice. He said to help me, but that was a *lie*!" The hiss may as well have pierced the other. "It was a *lie*!" That word — 'do you like it, Rosier? I invented it.' "Father *lied* to me. He wanted to stifle my screams. He wanted me to cry silently while I worshiped Him like an animal in the Garden without a thought in his head! But no, this God didn't take my thoughts. He didn't have the *mercy*—!"

The slap twisted Lucifer's face sideways, bringing with it a shock of silence. His feet, gradually, lowered onto the carpet floor; he didn't stand, he stayed for a moment frozen, his chest just barely rising with sinking breaths. Rosier's face had climbed up into horror seconds before, and he was just as petrified as the other, maybe more so. "What," Rosier said, though he had meant to think it. "What is happening to you, Lucifer?" He was quite tender inside, he realized; all his fear was itching the ends of his eyes, trying to tease out tears, and making his bottom lip wobble. "Please— I know you were in pain, I'm so sorry, I'm so, so, sorry. I wanted to help you, but I didn't know how, and Father is never wrong. He is good, He will always be good."

"Is Father good because He is good, or because He says He is good?"

Inside his body, Rosier felt something rattle and crack. "What... are you saying? It's like you're speaking with an animal tongue." He shook his head because tears were really beginning to leak out from him, dotting the skin of his feet as they fell. "I can't understand a word you're saying— No, Lucifer, shut your mouth. You need to ask for forgiveness—"

"Of course you can't understand me." Lucifer stood, finally, and felt like a mountain, towering over the other. 'All you angels — you covered your ears, shut your eyes, ignored my sadness to admire my body like an adornment, because all your lives you've spent only under-standing what's right by His word.' "I'm perfect, I'm God's most favorite creation, and you are no more than a meek angel of fruit. He does not even *look* at you—" He shoved Rosier, but the angel of fruit staggered back, running into a table, topped with a glass of water which fell, fell.

The shatter was reminiscent. Lucifer couldn't place the sound, not initially, but it was familiar. There was, soon, a memory before his eyes — Azazel tipping over Lucifer's drink the first time the youngest had wine, so long ago now, thousands, millions of years. Had Lucifer grown furious? He couldn't quite remember.

Rosier rushed, dropping to his knees and hastily reaching for the shards, but he met Lucifer's hands instead.

'No,' Lucifer was thinking as he fell to the floor too, trying to gather the fragments quickly, as if they'd come together easier the faster he did it. 'I'm sorry.' He felt as if his heart had fallen too, out of him. 'I don't like to see your sweet face all shattered like that, eyes swelling pink with hurt. There's something powerful about it, something that makes me hunger, but still, still, you are my housemate, my friend.' "I'm sorry." It was soft, because Lucifer felt a loud silence had come between them. "Forgive me, brother." All the pieces were collected in his palms, soon enough.

'I'm more worried than I'm hurt.' Rosier shook his head, slowly, reaching to wipe his eyes with the sleeve of his tunic, which he'd embroidered with sky blues, trailing into little love birds that he'd spent weeks stitching with great attention to detail. 'They seem so silly to me now.' Suddenly, all he wished was to scratch them off, along with the other decorations on his clothes until even the dye came off, and he wore nothing but a white sheet, and maybe he'd remove his jewelry too. 'So that I'm like when I was created.' He pulled in a cool breath — "All I ask is one thing, younger brother."

"Mm?"

"Because I love you, I won't tell anyone about the things you've said, or that terror I saw in the cathedral, and I won't even tell of how you tackled me and nearly snapped my neck." 'Just remembering it,' Lucifer contemplated, 'I am battered with contradictions — arousal and frightened suppression.' "All I ask, the only thing, is that you do not speak of these events to anyone beside me." 'You're silencing me. You saw clear as glass what He did to me, and you are emulating Him?' Rosier stood, just as Lucifer did, took a step closer, and looked at him with tolerant eyes, desperate, pleading, all held together by the webs of fear. "Do you agree?"

'Please, Lucifer, I just want to help you.' "I agree." Lucifer smiled as amicably as he could muster, but it was as if he'd forgotten what that meant, what that was supposed to look like, and Rosier remained with the ends of his lips curved downward, unsure. "But I have to leave to Eden soon. I'll bring you back some blackberries; how does that sound?" 'I just want to return to how things were, before you met Michael.'

"That sounds... wonderful. Bring enough for us to share."

They embraced, and Lucifer eased, but not by much. All there was to do was leave the broken glass in the kitchen, then climb up to his room to change into a modest white tunic and a loose robe the same color. He could, and did, spend hours before the mirror, admiring every delicate detail, sometimes touching, fondling. Hands with a lingering tremble, he ran a brush through the tussles of his hair, sang a little tune to himself, and stared into the stars placed onto his face as eyes, and he thought of Michael. He could spend hours doing that too. They'd promised to see each other immediately after the archangel returned from yet another purposeless mission to God's favorite planet, and Lucifer was craving hosting another feast.

He wished everything would simply go back to how it was.

Lucifer swallowed and wondered if he should do something special with his appearance today, but there would be no purpose. The angel of beauty was so naturally perfect he didn't need to paint his face or adorn his hair or dress in certain gems and robes. He could wear nothing, he could be exhausted or dirty or spoiled; in any state, he was so terrifyingly pleasant to gaze upon that no matter what any other angel might try to do, they would never even come near to matching him.

Lucifer stood up, then left through the balcony.

The first sign of strangeness in Eden was silence, even the crunch of grass, beneath his toes as he landed, came muffled, like someone had placed a cloth over the mouth of all the green blades. Head raising, turning every which way — there were a few animals, but they didn't move to Lucifer, like they always did. He saw a spotted frog on a tree, but it turned away, hopping up onto a higher branch, letting itself be shielded from sight by motionless leaves. A ladybug buzzed by, quickly, as if rushing to escape the angel, and Lucifer breathed, confused, a screw unsettling inside him as the routine he had become so accustomed to — arriving, greeting each creature, walking towards the Father, worshiping, staying a while — faltered.

'Where are the others?' Lucifer walked, his wings pulling into him, and he walked, slowly, he walked, through the garden, in the direction of the pond he remembered his Father told him to clean his face with once. He breathed, walking, stepping close to a tree — it was the one of Knowledge — and placing both hands on the bark. Peeking around the corner, it came to him he could hear a voice — humming.

The Lord sat upon a simple chair, reclined, staring into the water so that His back was to the angel. From by His head, a swirl of smoke filtered out in a brilliant stream, flowing upwards, becoming clouds, perhaps, but Lucifer's gaze didn't leave Him, not any amount. Lucifer remained half-concealed behind the tree, hiding, and another exhale, softer, slipped from between his parted lips. He considered calling out to his Father or continuing to quietly watch Him. God spoke first, short, simple, emotionless: "Angel of beauty."

It was no surprise the Lord knew he was there, but a flush came to his cheeks anyways — a minor fluster. "Yes, Father?" Lucifer revealed himself to the meadow before the silvery pool, before stepping closer, falling into a bow at the waist beside His lounging chair. "I am very sorry — have I come late? Did I misremember the time you ordered for me to come lead your choir?"

"You are here at the proper time. No one was invited to Eden today except for you." The Father waved a hand. "Come. Sit at my side." From this direction, it was properly discernible — Lucifer's eyes flicked upwards for just a second — there was a long oak pipe in His mouth, held delicate there by His hand. It smoked a wild array of hues — every color, even colors Lucifer hadn't thought existed — and illusions, scattering. Lucifer didn't hesitate to do as told, but 'I wonder what might happen if I, just once, didn't do what you said. Is that possible? Has anyone ever done it? What if I simply don't bow? What if I look you in the eyes, God? What would you do?'

Settling down beside Him, Lucifer smoothed his robe, thinking, licking his lips. He felt an emerald clover nuzzle one of his ankles, where an anklet, golden with lapis lazuli, hung loose — it jingled, quietly.

"Tell me how you have been."

"I have been well. Your mercy is great, Father." Lucifer watched the still surface of the water. "Shall I sing for you?"

"It was not the same — when the choir sang but your voice was missing among them. It was good, but it was not perfectly pleasant." 'It was distasteful without me. You realized that yourself, didn't you? That is why, as all the angels sang, you, God, ordered so suddenly — "Lucifer, open your mouth and sing." And I did so, for you. I was so elated, I fell to my knees, and I cried, thanking you, without thinking, praising you and singing louder than all the other host.' "I'm pleased to hear your songs again."

"All I wish is to please you, Father." 'But maybe I was wrong to immediately crumble into gratitude and kiss your feet. You hurt me. Remember? Remember?' "Shall I serve you wine?" 'You did not cast the Beast from me, though you tried.' His Father had not removed the fire or the wings, only torn him. 'There are some things, then, that God cannot do.'

"Here." The Lord took a long drag from His pipe, then blew out a great gust of rocky celestial bodies up to drift between the clouds, then He extended His arm to the angel seated at His side. "Try smoking." The tip was right before Lucifer's mouth; though he lifted his hands initially, to take it, his Father held the pipe tight between two fingers, so instead, Lucifer leaned forward. He wrapped his lips around the end and attempted to mimic God, trying to pull in air then blow it out, and a burst of energy burned through his nostrils and mouth and throat, all the way to the back of his eyes, before it tangled. The smokes entering his body became clumped, then heavy; he lurched forward into a hack that rattled him. A boiling steam spewing out from his body, being rejected — coughing, rasping. "I see."

"Forgive me—" Lucifer put a hand to his chest, steadying himself, seeing the Father return the pipe to His own mouth. "M-May I try again?" Before he could stop himself — "I want to create from the smoke like you do. How do you do it?"

A hint of amusement in the Lord's voice. "I pluck the roots from the air, these that hold the matters of everything together, and I grind them, I smoke them, and then I simply will. My womb is built from will." 'I want to create.' "But you are just an angel, Lucifer, and angels cannot create from nothing." Emphasizing, He drew some air through His pipe, then expelled the smoke through His nostrils. The swirls of gray became shadows, peppered with little, blinking, thousand eyeballs that peered down before they dissipated and scattered among the sky above. "They are unlucky. Had I been in the right mood for it, I would have gathered them up and made an angel."

"It is," Lucifer paused, "that easy for you to create us?"

"I could make a thousand angels with a wave of a hand, but taking good time with each of you is enjoyable."

The angel of worship's lips curled into a self-righteous little smirk. "Was I difficult to make?" 'Because I am so beautiful and perfect?'

"Difficult is not the right word." The Father kept smoking, calm and relaxed, and His hand reached over, found Lucifer's head. He twirled a strand of his hair. "For me, it was time-consuming, because I had to decide what perfect would mean, because perfection is what I define it. You are beautiful because I created you and said, 'This is beauty.'" He kept wrapping the flaxen thread around his fingers, and Lucifer began to feel a little compelled to draw away. "This is why angels have their roles, their purposes."

"You are truly great, Father." 'Ugh.'

"I had the idea of you very early, not long after I had set the first stars alight. I thought I should make the most perfect angel, who would be at my side, as the most beautiful among them all, but of course, that took plenty of time, of pondering. I was never satisfied with my attempts; I destroyed a million earlier iterations of you. You were not difficult, but you were different to make. I have told you that you are different." 'I have learned that very well now. And that is why you stole my voice, so that I could learn to be quiet about it.' "Gabriel told you the work I put into your form. And because you were made to be wise: you should know better than to degrade the creations of others." 'Have I really been called here just to be scolded? I want to go to Heaven. I want to see Michael.' "Lucifer, you are displaying great insolence before your Father."

It made him startle, even with the thoughts he had, the power of the Lord's voice, when it struck like that, when it said his name, it made everything seize up. "No— I am sorry. I did not mean to—"

"Your splendor and your wisdom — you are corrupting it all with your beauty. I molded you, dressed you, adorned you — everything that you have is my creation." His hand left the angel's head, went to an armrest; He kept smoking, even as His voice raised, raised higher, rattling the trees and ground, battering Lucifer's ears and nearly making him cry out. "I named you the anointed cherub."

'No.' Shivering began to overwhelm him, overheat until his skin was charring — breaths coming quicker, thinner. 'Stop. Please don't raise your voice at me.'

"And you have been ungrateful. You have disgraced every pinch of your body, soiled, degraded it — poured out disobedience and exposed yourself. Because of your detestable pride," He spat it out, and set the pipe down. "All I wish is to bring on you blood vengeance of my wrath and anger. Shall I deliver you to the hands of the angels, so that they strip you of your clothes, jewelry, and leave you without flesh? Shall I command a mob against you, who will stone you and hack you to pieces with swords?"

'Stop! Stop it, please!' Lucifer's head was so heavy it kept threatening to roll off him, so he stood, he stumbled, he staggered back and away — chest heaving, vision blurring. He felt the soreness of a throat within his own skull. 'Stop please, please, please stop.' There was wetness on his face, tears perhaps, but then softness — flowers were blooming from his misery. 'No, Father.' The petals tumbled down his cheeks to where his feet trembled above the grass. 'Don't hurt me. Please don't hurt me—'

"Because you do not remember the days of your youth, as an obedient flame in my palm — you have enraged me." The Lord stood now, and all the skies were veiling dark, and Lucifer hugged his clothes, but they felt different, all of a sudden, like they weren't his, like they didn't belong to him, like these white linens were God's and this body was God's. He was crying, but it was beautiful: 'No, no, stop being beautiful, I do not want to be. Let me cry— Real tears— These budding freesias in the folds of my eyes, blooming open and cascading — you're obscuring my fear, you're making it pleasant, stop, stop, please stop.' "Let me bring down on your head what you have done, let pains of anguish grip you."

"No." Lucifer's innards had torn, spilled so he was being filled with something he didn't know, couldn't understand. Unable to breathe, only choke, Lucifer gripped his neck, then turned, began running, remembering that day in the cathedral. And he screamed: "No, leave me alone! Leave me alone!"

"You will ask yourself," the voice of the Lord followed him, "why this is happening to you. It is because of your disobedience. I will scatter you like chaff that is blown astray by winds."

The hysterical angel pushed through branches, that were all suddenly reaching out to him, striking him, attempting to grab him and slashing his robe. 'No, no! Not you! Save me, someone, anyone please!'

"You have forgotten me, putting your trust in yourself, instead." There were animals, up ahead, but they stared with glossy eyes, empty, and then the Lord, the Lord up ahead, even though he had left Him behind. And beneath His foot, a rabbit. 'No—' Stepping, crushing until the bones fractured out through the skin, and the strings of red followed, flattening along the grass, the pop of eyes, and the meat of life.

Horror strangling him, Lucifer unfurled his wings, beat them strong into the air to try and reach the spiraling stretch of the universe. 'But not too high, or I'll come crawling out from the ground by your feet, no matter what direction I run, I will keep returning to you, it all funnels into you.' "You know you cannot run from me." The stars began to reveal themselves to him, in the seas of darkness, beacons of light.

"Brothers!" Lucifer pleaded to them, rushing as fast as he could, but a stray comet shot past, struck a wing, and flung him to the side. He cried out, falling over the wet ground of the abyss and tumbling down mountains of nebulae, before he settled, fast, stood — like when Michael taught him to roll back onto his feet, like when Michael taught him to wrestle, like when Michael showed him strength, Michael smiling, Michael, Michael holding his arms, squeezing them, taking his hands, Michael. "Please," Lucifer wailed helplessly to the stars, sprinting toward them as one wing splurged blood — 'but I can't feel it, I can't feel it, just the rush rattling my heart' — reaching out, screaming, "Help me, brothers, save me!" They didn't wake for him.

Something grappled Lucifer's hair, wretched him back, made him fall. In an instant, the world before him began to crunch together as paper, cracking Lucifer and making him shriek. He saw, above the stars he'd tried to reach, an eye, and it was His eye, composed of everything, all at once, layered over one another, so it punctured a hole in the fabric of space.

The angel was no more than an embroidery, scurrying along a cloth tunic, trying to escape the wearer. A prized possession, bundled in naivety, to be kept unspoiled until he might be torn from paradise. Paradise? He cried one final time for help, for his brothers to wake up, to take his hands and pull him away from this God, from paradise, to hold him to their chests and pepper sunny kisses onto his cheeks, to protect him. From paradise. Paradise, what is paradise, whose paradise, paradise for who, paradise for the angels? Paradise for who?

And then slowly, he began to apologize. Lucifer cried, "I'm sorry, Father," so many times the words tripped over themselves, slurring, as he was dragged backward by the grip on his sea of hair, legs kicking weak just for a while before surrendering too. He saw the abyss with all its shining lights, stretch further and further away; the stars becoming specs of sand on the canvas of his vision. He began to feel grass, crunching beneath him, like when he had arrived, dirt slogging against his side, but not staining his tunic by some immaculate power. His fingers, desperate, reaching for the flowers he'd come to know so intimately, that had always tended to him. They fell to nothing; a white lily wilted in his hand.

The angel begged for mercy, crying soft, as he was undressed. The Lord stepped onto the bed of flowers. And, wrathfully, He took him.

Paradise, paradise, garden of Eden, garden of paradise.

CHAPTER 30

Asmodeus chuckled, grinning, when Rosier startled at his presence. "Hello there." He was sprawled over the couch, eyes shut, not quite napping but not quite awake either. "I let myself in. I hope that's alright. Where have you been? You always return home early."

Despite the instinct to grumble, Rosier's gaze softened, and he smiled. "I was with Azazel. He's been teaching me to paint." He walked past him to the kitchen, calling out, "Do you want anything? I have some lemonade," then served himself a cup, nodding to himself when his friend refused, before he sipped. "Hm." He spooned some sugar into his drink, swirled it, then peeked his head back into the living room. "Are you sure about not wanting any?"

"Certain," Asmodeus yawned and waved a hand, "but if you're feeling generous, I might enjoy a spongy cake with chocolate frosting and strawberry filling. Oh, and I could definitely use a massage. I went out and chariot raced for hours today." Rosier chuckled as he returned to the couch and sat by his friend's head. "Remember when you would drag my body out from the arena? I used to lose so pitifully, I thought they should leave my mangled body there, but you said, 'No, no, that's my friend, let me take him to Raphael.' You weren't embarrassed to be with me, even though I lost."

Rosier scoffed. "What has you bringing this up?" He sipped from a cool metal cup, tapping nails against the sharp designs engraved into its body. "Feeling sentimental, brother?"

Lazily, Asmodeus grinned. "Just thinking about the past: it's what being in this house does to me." He remembered asking Rosier, one day, if he'd like to move in, and then secretly building a new room by the kitchen, that he would pretend had always been there, and attaching a patio, so that the younger angel would never be away from his fruit trees. "Don't you ever look back, darling Rosier?"

Huffing — "Yes, sometimes I think about all the times you've dragged dirt onto the carpets."

"Gah," the older one laughed, "I haven't done that since before you started calling me the angel of friendship."

"You still don't believe me?" Rosier reached over, jabbed a finger against Asmodeus' cheek, right by his smile. "I would bet all of Heaven that it's true. If you weren't such a good friend, I would've stopped putting up with you sooner."

"Hm." Angel of friendship — like Asmodeus' only purpose was to be at a friend's side, as if an angel's purpose could be another angel. "You said Azazel is teaching you to paint? I thought you were learning to embroider. Aren't I supposed to be the restless one?"

A little hesitation, then Rosier's voice came quieter: "I've been trying to get my mind off things." Worries nonetheless resurfaced as he brought both hands to his drink once more, cool lemonade feeling foreign in his mouth; his expression began to fall. "I know you want to move back in, Asmodeus. That's what you're here about, isn't it?" 'You built this house yourself, after all — in that time before the Earth and even the sun, when Heaven was still newborn.' "I haven't spoken with Lucifer about it." 'Even if I miss you living here. Even if I miss you. Before Lucifer, it was always just you and me, us.'

"Don't worry. I should probably be the one to ask him." 'It seems to me that he wants to live with Michael anyway,' Asmodeus thought, sitting up and rubbing an eye. "Lucifer, though — he's been acting a little strange, hasn't he?" Rosier sighed, shaking. "Hm?" He turned his head and saw the other angel nervously shredding his bottom lip. "Is something wrong?"

"It's gotten much worse." Rosier swallowed. "A few days ago, he returned from Eden. He was gone so long that I started to worry, and when he finally returned, his clothes were torn, and he limped as he walked, though both his legs looked perfectly fine. He wouldn't look at me, he wouldn't speak — I thought maybe Father had taken his voice again." 'And you don't even know the details; you don't know the words Lucifer said in the cathedral, the fright in his eyes before the Lord struck him down.' "I tried to speak to him, but he pushed me away, then locked himself in his room. All I heard was crying, and it went on for hours and hours. I was scared, but he wouldn't let me in, no matter what I did."

Asmodeus swallowed, heart stepping off the skeletal carriage in his chest. "Something must have happened in Eden."

"I don't want to imagine what."

"I adore Lucifer—"

"I do too—"

"But we can't deny he upset Father somehow." With all his earlier drowsiness faded away, Asmodeus stood. "Let's talk with him." 'Any angel might have simply begged for Lucifer to stop, without looking to understand him — knowing you, Rosier, I'm sure that's what you did — but something like this has never happened before. Not in a million years, not in a billion. The Lord is always pleased, we're always His perfect servants, that's what we're good at. How can Lucifer be failing?'

Rosier shook his head, held his lemonade tight with both hands. "No, Asmodeus. He locked the door, and it's better we give him time to recover. I'm sure that it was just scolding. He wants to be alone— Brother!"

Asmodeus was already making his way toward the stairs. He would have no trouble getting through that door; 'the lower hinge is weak, a strong kick and it will snap.' He only stopped when Rosier, after hastily setting his drink on the floor, flew to him, nearly tackled him. "No, Rosier— We need to know what's happening. Gather some strength." He could see in the other's flinch that he was fearful, not only of what might lie in that bedroom, but of Asmodeus' demeanor, a serious one neither of them knew well. "I left this house in your care. I trust you. You are my closest friend. Please. And if you really care for

Lucifer, then we need to put an end to this." At this, Rosier frowned and slowly released him. Together, then, they made their way to the bedroom, calling Lucifer's name, and knocking but there was no response. "Brother, it's Asmodeus, come out."

"He won't even leave for food or water."

Asmodeus tried a few more times, but he was impatient. He took the knob, turned it, and upon realizing it was indeed locked, didn't hesitate to take a step back. He slammed his bare foot into the lower hinge; as expected, it came loose enough that he had no problem forcing the door open.

The upper hinge cracked and gave; inside, Asmodeus met a room that had originally been his, entirely different in decor and layout. He saw it messy now too, scattered with toppled furniture and fallen portraits and bedsheets and pillows pulled down onto the carpets. The common greenery of the room, which 'invaded this place when I finished constructing it' had grown unruly. Vines usually on the walls had climbed onto the ceiling and crawled along the floor, where wild flowers and varying shrubs, weeds, were consuming every inch of space they could.

Among them all was Lucifer, sitting on the floor before his mirror, facing away from the front door. He wore no more than a long robe, soft peach, silk, devastatingly thin, threatening to slip off both shoulders, clinging to his body very barely, shielding nearly nothing. His hair was cascaded over his face like a veil, in stormy waves — head hanging forward; all the jewelry that always adorned his body, strewn about everywhere on the ground. The bottoms of his bare feet were smudged with pitiless dirt, enough to make them charred. He didn't move.

"Lucifer?" Asmodeus didn't recognize his own voice. "What's wrong? What—?" Something wet — he heard it squelch, and Lucifer twitched; Asmodeus saw into the mirror.

Redness on Lucifer's fingers, dripping onto wrists, droplets spotting his lap — blood, streaming. A knife gorged into the angel's lower abdomen, but it was resting there, after having traveled down, sloppily, from the middle of the sternum. Having formed a ravine in himself, the angel's body, like an earth, cried molten rock.

"No—" His voice ran away from him, and Asmodeus rushed

forward, shouting without thinking for Rosier to find water and gauze for bandaging. He took Lucifer, grabbed him, shook him, until the curtain over Lucifer's face parted and revealed one eye then both, where brilliant golds had diluted in color, life, shine. "Lucifer!"

"No," Lucifer whispered, and he gripped the handle of the knife, pulled it out with a slick sound that rebounded in his ears — and metal, 'the smell of copper, it's put itself in me, my head, this head, why is it spinning?' He thrust the knife back into himself, and Lucifer's mouth shot open in a sharp, anguished cry before Asmodeus screamed at him a second time, took his 'wet, hot,' hands.

He forced the blade out again, ignoring the tight grip around it, the violated flesh latching on. "Lucifer, stop this!"

The angel of beauty cried, spewing out blood from 'my lips, color-less for once,' and he laughed, being shoved onto his back. 'I don't like this, Asmodeus, what are you doing? Shouting at Rosier to hurry?' "I was," Lucifer explained, little giggles bursting out, "I was just curious. I wanted to see what was, was inside, in this body, I was looking for eyes." 'Like the ones that I see now in the stigma of each flower, in the walls, in paradise, this giant mouth that is shredding me.' "And poppies, I thought I might have them there, between these organs, I'm almost there." 'I can see their black centers, in between my thick blood, pulsating.' "Asmodeus. Stop. Stop." He was forced down some more, and Lucifer hissed, as his wounds were dabbed clean, his viscera returned.

"Lucifer, brother," Rosier cried — he had reappeared — "what have you done?"

'My heart— Oh, my heart, it's there, I'm starting to feel again.' Lucifer shuddered, organized his thoughts, and watched as his friend worked quick to bandage him, pouring water over him too, and that did most of the work. 'What has cured me, too, are your tears, Rosier. Your sadness, seeing it, it's like I'm being stirred from a dream. And now I am aware of this disordered pain, this confusion. Why did I do this?'

'Why did you do this?'

'Why did you do this?'

"Ah." Lucifer hacked, tried to scavenge some breath. "I'm sorry.

I'm not making any sense." He sat up, as best he could, cringing at the sharp stings on his entire front, but they would heal; water healed him when it wanted. "I was— I didn't—" Licking his lips, he said, "I was in pain," and that was true, "very much. Father was disappointed with me. I thought, that if all this pain inside was so great, I needed to find a way to take it out. I'm very sorry, very."

"You're not well." Asmodeus shook his head, because he had no clue what that might mean. "Let's take you to Raphael, to Father—"

"No." Rosier was not so simple-minded, not anymore. 'First, Father strips him of his voice, and now it appears he's cursed him with speaking nonsensically. What will a third time bring? No.' "Asmodeus, please leave. I'll speak with Lucifer. If you must, inquire about knife wounds with Raphael." He reached up to wipe the tears of fright that had stumbled from his eyes.

"Don't be ridiculous!"

"You... have been very kind," Lucifer cut in, shifting back and away, reaching for the bedsheets so that he could use them to wipe his hands of blood. "Thank you, Asmodeus, and you, Rosier. I'll make my way out now."

"Absolutely not," Rosier cried. "You're not making sense, Lucifer! Go to bed, I'll do everything—"

"Please." Lucifer wanted nothing more than to tackle the other and strike his face for acting as his keeper. "I'll be going to Michael."

"What? Michael?" Asmodeus laughed. "You're joking."

"I'm serious." Lucifer put his newly cleaned hands together, held them, and then he stood up. All the lacerations stung, but they were already nearly healed — as if it had never happened. "I'll change, and then I'll go. Michael will know what to do." He looked to them, these two angels, who'd been close friends since before Lucifer's creation. 'No, that can't be right. Them, before me? No. There was no time before me.' He said, "And if either of you get in the way, I'll make my way to Eden instead, and I'll tell Father that you two are harming His most favorite angel."

'What is wrong with you?' Rosier took half a step back, confusion becoming bewilderment becoming terror, not only for his younger sibling but the Lord. 'If Father is good, then why would He hurt

Lucifer? Why?' At his side, Asmodeus continued begging Lucifer to relax, to sleep, to really consider what he had done.

Lucifer, instead, cleaned himself up, pulled on his jewelry, combed back his hair, humming and trying in desperation to fall back into the motions of what was usual, normal. He had shattered it, shattered all the illusions — Lucifer knew that — but what was there to do? In his agony, he saw no escape, except for his beloved archangel, who was most likely back by now from his trip to Earth. Yes, yes, he was definitely back; Lucifer smiled softly and smoothed down the heavy robes he pulled over the peach tunic. He felt the two other angels begin to surrender, the smaller one still sniffling. Everything remained a disaster in the room; Lucifer's feet were still dirty, and he only obscured them with sandals.

"Michael will help me. I promise." He leaned in to kiss Rosier's cheek, then Asmodeus'. He removed the bandaging; already, the water had healed him. "And I will stop by Raphael. I will take in the light, and you two will see that all is well. Trust me."

"We love you, Lucifer," Asmodeus said simply. 'And we can see you won't change your mind.' Rosier's hand grazed him, and it seemed their thoughts had aligned. 'Maybe Michael should really see you, and he'll finally learn that whatever part he has in this — he has a duty to put an end to it.'

"I love you both as well." Lucifer left with some worry bristling his nerves. He breathed, felt all the air in his lungs cold. "Thank you. I'm sorry. Thank you."

'Michael will help me. Michael will protect me. Michael is the only angel who understands me and will always be at my side, even if all the skies collapse. He's my beloved, I adore him, and I want him to hold me, so that I forget everything. Everything but him. The angel of strength. I want to make you feel good, Michael. I want you to help me forget.' With a serene smile, Lucifer headed out, not uttering another word to the worried angels.

Rosier collapsed into cries for maybe the millionth time as soon as the door shut.

CHAPTER 31

E mpty, it was empty. There was the distant sound of the ocean, walking through the door, stretching her arms and yawning as she met Lucifer there, a sultry grin on her thin lips, the edges of which extended a bit too far, and then the tide receded, and Lucifer was alone in the house again.

He wandered, aimlessly, wondering if he might clean a dish Michael had left spotted with some crumbs in the kitchen, or perhaps he should wash and hang some tunics out to dry on the balcony. Maybe he should nap; he hadn't slept, never wanted to again. 'I closed my eyes as you dragged me to the Garden, but my eyelids were not opaque. I noticed the light of your face leak in. You said there is nowhere to run, I will be there.' Lucifer watched the sea, knowing that was God too, and said to her, 'You were the Beast. It was you.'

Then, there was the sound of someone's steps by the entrance, and with a sigh in relief, the angel turned, holding himself, to face the archangel he loved, but it wasn't. He came upon a tall angel, with a crown of braids, whose demeanor was brittle and impenetrable at once. When their gazes met, the two of them stopped, and the air of the room grew dense, so much it was difficult to break through it enough to speak. "Uriel."

"What are you doing in Michael's home?"

'How unlucky, sweet brother. You don't know the state I'm in right now. Come any closer, and I'll rush at you the way the beasts on Earth do, claw until you become unrecognizable. Oh, the beasts, if only I was among them now, so that no one might care if I take out this pain on them, make them scream as I wish to, wail until their jaws snap from the agony, and they die. How beautiful — to die. How merciful. To exist and then to not, to have your time be spent, to have everything only once.' "I should ask you that." Lucifer smiled, turning, and walking toward a window. "This is my own home now, so you're intruding. Please tell me why you've come."

"I came to speak to the real owner of this house."

"What makes him the owner? Because he says, or because he built it, or did Father say so?"

Uriel's eyebrows furrowed; the angel of beauty sensed his frustration through his tone. "I don't have the patience for you now, Lucifer. Tell me where Michael is."

"Why should I?" He hummed as he concerned himself with a potted plant of herbs nearby, whose stems he stroked in a familial fashion. "Because you're an archangel?" 'I'm greater than an archangel.'

"I said I don't have the patience for you," Uriel's voice snapped like a whip. "If you don't tell me where he is—"

"You'll what? Shout at me? Oh, I'm so scared, so very scared. I'm trembling, can you see?" Uriel visibly stiffened, his jaw tightening; Lucifer noticed as he turned his head so that he could watch him over his shoulder. "Go ahead, whine to Father. I'll wait here obediently for my punishment to arrive." Wink. "Don't delay now. Get out."

Uriel was the one who trembled. "Where is your respect?"

"Why should I respect you?"

"I told Michael, I told all the other archangels that you're ruining everything, running your stained hands over paradise and soiling all we have." 'Stained? Am I really ruined now?' "You don't know— You don't know anything, you're young and thoughtless of consequences, concerned with only yourself; you can't imagine what it's like not to have everything. You're nothing but spoiled, blinded by how rotten you've become." 'Impure.' "How dare you think you can stand before an archangel as an equal. You are only an angel, Lucifer, just a mere

angel. You are not even Father's favorite, no matter how much you
adore to think so. Maybe once, it was true, but now you embarrass
Him, you bring Him shame!" 'How stupid your voice becomes, how
grating, when you start to yell, worthless archangel.'

"Tell me, dear brother." Lucifer moved toward Uriel until their
faces were close together, breaths intermingling — either could easily
reach out and grab the other by the throat. "What have I ever done to
you?" A wicked smirk pulled at one end of his lips. "Surely, I did something. Is this really about Father? Ever since you first set your eyes on
me, you've looked at me with *disdain*." It was a new word. "What is it?
Have I hurt you? Are you jealous of me?"

The prince scoffed. "What do you have that I could ever want?"

Lucifer snickered, icy. "Everyone's affections. They all love me, all
the angels of Father, Gabriel, and Michael. Everyone adores me — but
what about you, Uriel? You're not pleasant to be around. The only
reason anyone will even look at you is that silly little title you're
obsessed with. You live alone, don't you? You don't talk with anybody,
and I certainly don't see anyone ever making an effort to speak to you.
All this love in Heaven, and you get none of it, because you're so deeply
unlikable that no one will even bother to be your friend." His voice had
taken on a musically taunting ring. "Poor little brother — all alone,
with not any angel who loves him."

The knife struck the heart; Uriel's entire demeanor crumbled,
violently, until his whole face was twitching. One foot dragged back,
and he shifted away. The first noise that came out of his mouth was
choked, and Lucifer's amusement morphed into thrill. "You—" All of
him was curling up — his hands into fists. "You will face Father's wrath
for your words, Lucifer." 'I've faced it already, and I am still here, and I
am *angry*.' "I hope He brings His fist down not only upon you, but on
Michael." 'You rancid, putrid filth. Rotten, squirming maggot.' "I
hope He beats him so that he becomes unrecognizable. You, who are so
self-absorbed — if Michael became weak, you would lose interest,
wouldn't you?"

It took everything not to break — shriek and lunge at the other,
tear off his head with his own two hands. Lucifer heaved instead,

shaking so much it appeared the house was overtaken by tremors with him. "Damn you."

"What? What did you say?"

"I said *damn you!*"

The door opened; they both turned, Lucifer freezing, because he had been about to lose sight of himself. He had been about to tackle and find out what was inside Uriel, as he had been discovering about his own body earlier.

"Michael," Uriel grunted, "have you been listening to all this?"

Michael raised an eyebrow. He held large golden chains wrapped around one hand; against the cusp between neck and shoulder, he rested his, almost absurdly, massive sword, the one Lucifer had not seen in so long but was now eyeing hungrily. He was in the same frayed cloak he always wore when he traveled, and as per his usual returns from Earth, his face was streaked with dirt of all kinds.

There were a few new rips to his clothing; Lucifer couldn't help but wonder if Michael had stumbled into any great fights against beasts during the trip. He imagined it. Michael, launching himself at the creatures, wrestling them with his bare hands, strong wings carrying him upward; he'd grip his enemies with the chains he carried, bring his heavy sword down onto their necks. With just one cut, he'd slice through them — like water splitting at his word. He'd be panting, red-faced, sweating, exhilarated from battle, grinning in his victory.

Lucifer saw it so well in his head he nearly flushed.

"No," said Michael, "have I missed something?"

"Nothing," Lucifer replied before smiling sweetly. "Welcome back."

"Thank you." Michael laughed as he walked towards, then past, them. Setting all his things down onto the couch, he groaned with exertion. "I can't believe Father sent me away again. I don't know why He would. There isn't much to do except guide the beasts in the directions of food and fight to preserve our limbs."

Lucifer went to stand by his friend, tittering jovially. "Well, I'm very happy you've returned unharmed. You should sleep. Have you eaten? Should I prepare you something?" He ignored Uriel, whose violently bewildered gaze was burning holes into his hair. "If not, I can get you some water." He tilted his head at Michael, who looked back, grinning fondly.

"You're too much."

"Indeed, he is," Uriel cut in bitterly, turning the others' attention. "Michael, I hate to return here over the same topic I've been arguing with you about for so long now," and Michael groaned, "but I spoke with Father, and He made it clear that you're still not doing as told. And Lucifer is the same — looking at himself so much he's forgotten God."

"Don't do this now," Michael sighed, shaking his head, not looking at the other prince, "I'm exhausted. Come back another time." Pleased, Lucifer smiled. "I won't waste my last moments of energy shouting with you."

"Let me make this quick then," Uriel replied, annoyance firm. "Michael, do you support Lucifer's disobedient, spoiled behavior?"

"Uriel, I said I do not want to deal with this."

"Answer the question."

"No."

Lucifer liked hearing that; he liked it a lot.

Uriel laughed but its resentment was poisonous. "And why not? It's a simple question. There has never been a simpler answer."

"If you think," voice tight and slow, "I'm going to say Lucifer is distasteful, or that I'm cutting my friendship with him, then you're wasting the time of us both."

Scathingly, Uriel said, "The Lord will punish you, Michael." He'd caught the chief prince in Eden, and before the Throne, speaking to God, arguing. "He's running out of mercy." Meeting him at the edge of the garden, Uriel had glared as Michael insisted God would begin to understand soon enough, that He was only looking out for them, but His parental worry would dispel, to be replaced with the love and empathy that composed Him. "And you're being led astray by a beast."

"*Beast*?" Michael's voice may as well have been a whip, his face crushing in an anger Lucifer had never seen on him. "Doesn't Lucifer lead us all in songs of worship, the likes of which no one can match? Doesn't he brighten the day of every angel he speaks to? The only

Lucifer there is this one — the kindest, sweetest creature in Heaven."
Lucifer rested a knee on the couch. "I know him, and I believe him."

Uriel had told Michael that God's love was conditional, but
Michael hadn't listened. "You're wrong—" 'Angel of strength, who
knows no peril.'

"No, it's you who's wrong. You misread the Lord's intentions and
take your loneliness out on us. Maybe you should be the one to apologize to Father, Uriel. I want nothing more on this subject. Leave us be."

"Michael—"

"Hurry and leave, before I grab you and throw you out myself."
Michael moved to where Lucifer was, plopping down tiredly on the
couch before falling to rest his head against the younger one's chest.
His eyes were half-lidded, his body was heavy; exhaustion became very
visible, all of a sudden, pulling down on his features so that he became
a drooping, needy plant. Wrapping his arms around him, Lucifer
tugged his friend a little closer, and he glanced upwards at Uriel, whose
face twitched in uncertainty and fury. A smirk, savage and curled,
stretched Lucifer's lips as he watched the oldest angel glare, scoff, leave,
then slamming the door. 'And I've won, he knows it. Let him cry to
Father all he wants, but Michael adores me, no matter how much
anyone hates it.' He rubbed Michael's back, hearing him breathe slow.

"Thank you," Lucifer decided to say, "I can't say it enough, but
you shouldn't have said all that. You're so tired. Let me take you to
bed."

"I'm not tired anymore. All that made me quite alert again." A
smooth chuckle, but the prince remained where he was, nuzzling his
face against Lucifer's chest in innocent affection. "Did he bother you
while I was away?"

"No, but I was injured recently, so I spent time resting, all by
myself."

"Injured?" Michael drew away, then glanced downward, without
explanation sensing where Lucifer had stabbed himself. "How?" 'Did
you feel it too, Michael? I'm sorry. If I'd known my body was also
yours, I wouldn't have hurt myself.'

A lie, the first time Lucifer said one so easily: "I tried chariot racing.
Didn't go very well, as you can imagine."

A full, rumbling laugh, then Michael shifted away, gesturing for his beloved friend to sit with him. "At least I'm back now, so that I can teach you again. Though, once I calm down, I should rest. Or else I'll collapse."

"If you'd like, I can massage you." Lucifer sat close enough their thighs touched, and he felt a little sadness drawn out from within again. Soon, he'd ask Michael if he could lay with him in bed a while, just to try and disappear into the soft duvet and the warm body of the prince. And beautiful Lucifer would be no more. No more, no more.

"Let's wrestle," Michael suggested instead. "It's been a while since we did it."

Lucifer blinked in surprise, realizing that was true. "But you're tired."

"I told you, I'm very much not now." Michael grinned, a bit sluggishly, up at him. "Or are you scared of losing?"

"I've practiced extensively, you know. Even when you're not here." Lucifer pursed his lips, then snickered. "But you'll have to go easy on me because of this injury." The other nodded and agreed. "Should we go to that garden we used to always meet in?" 'I remember the day we first spoke, really spoke, you had looked a bit like this, all disheveled. I was very different then. So were you. It hurts to remember, but not with regret, not really. Whatever happens, I'm happy you're here with me. Things are so difficult now — incomprehensible; within it all, you're the only thing I see.'

"Ah, don't you know?" A little sadness in his mouth. "They decided to remove it — the garden. They couldn't get that fountain under control." Michael waved a hand. "But it's no problem. Let's do it in here, we'll just move some things around."

Achingly — "Of course. Let me help." 'One time, you were half-sprawled on top of me, your head on my chest. You were heavy, I let you crush me. You said you'd never slept better. I don't know if I slept — if maybe your smile was no more than a sweet dream.' They made the room to wrestle. 'Do you know? Do you know I obsess over you so much it's starting to burn this chest, with all these stuffy poppies inside, so many I can't breathe? It hurts. You're hurting me, but I want your lips never to leave me. I see ambition in you, Michael. Please, let's harvest it together.'

They got into position to fight.

'When I ran from Father, I thought of you. When he captured me, I thought of you. I waited for your touch to save me.' At first, it seemed Michael was going to win, as he always did. 'Though I am greater than even you now.' Lucifer took Michael into a headlock and squeezed, crushed, in a moment of hesitance within the other. 'I can see everything there, in those eyes. We could have it all if we wanted. Let's take it together, let's gather the seeds in our hands and run away as fast as we can past the gates of Heaven.'

Michael, gasping for air, surrendered; Lucifer had finally beaten him.

CHAPTER 32

The angel chewed, swallowed, and Lucifer pulled back his hand, holding the little green stem of a strawberry. "Good?" Lucifer asked the younger one with amusement, because he already knew the answer from those widening galena-silver eyes, glistening with wonder.

"It's amazing," replied Dina, face invaded by a bright smile. "Can I have another?"

With his other hand, Lucifer held a small porcelain bowl, filled with a colorful assortment of berries that he kept picking from to feed the newborn angel who sat with him, a leg draped innocently over one of Lucifer's, their bodies snug together on the couch. He was beautiful — the brown skin of his face peppered with a few scattered, tiny dark dots, and his onyx hair long enough to sweep by his knees — 'that's why I like you.' Lucifer tossed the strawberry stem into his mouth before answering, smiling, "Of course." Reaching to get another of the same fruit, he turned his head and called out, almost whined, "Seir."

There was a mist of music among the room, the simple strumming of an oud settled in the arms of Seir, one of those angels who was often in Eden and singing alongside Lucifer, one of those angels who adored him. Jostling a little at being addressed — "Oh, yes, brother?"

Seir was partly shrouded by the smoke trickling from a bronze censer — 'Whose house even is this?' — herbal amber. The incense drifted between the many plates of simple food, on the floor with the couple of angels who sat, or on their laps as they relaxed over low couches, or in their hands as they stood about and chattered. It was a gathering of maybe two dozen; 'I can't remember who invited me. I'm always getting invited to things, even since I was a newborn, like this one.' They weren't doing anything, as usual — gossiping, eating, listening to Seir and two others play songs, and watching a few play a strategy game consisting of ivory pieces on a checkered board.

Lucifer had tried his hand at it, beaten everyone, even Phanuel, who claimed to be an expert, then fallen into boredom with the whole thing. He'd decided to sit with Dina, whom he found to be easily startled, and took great pleasure in flustering him over and over. It was fun, also, to teach young angels the little pleasures they were all quite used to. 'I remember Michael had said something similar to me once; that was why he took me to Earth.' He told Seir: "Can you play something else?" 'I want to go to Earth again.'

"Of course, of course!"

Lucifer smiled, delighted, as he finally took another strawberry and pressed it to Dina's lips, parted already, eager, compliant. 'You didn't even hesitate, Seir. I know that's your favorite song, but just because I asked you to, you're playing something else now.' A little shift, and the angel of worship nearly laughed at his realized power.

What followed was a stream of curious thoughts: what would Seir do, if Lucifer told him to do this, or that, what would this young angel Dina do, if Lucifer ordered him to smash his head against the wall; where might the line be in all the angels' sweet obedience to him? 'This is what Father wonders, isn't it?' He kept feeding Dina, noticing his bare neck; there was not a lot of jewelry on him, only emerald earrings with silver wheels that jangled like bells. It was a shame.

"Crown Him the Lord of love," sang Seir, with an angel at his side, beating a small tambourine, not nearly as adorned as Lucifer's, "behold His hands and might, in beauty glorified."

'I waited for your touch to save me.'

"No angels in the sky can fully bear that sight, but downward bends a burning eye, at mysteries so bright."

He thought, he thought, saw in his mind certain angels in the room, their eyes overtaken by the holes of a wasp nest he saw in Eden once, and they would be watching him, tongues black. 'Instead of a raspberry, I keep bringing the squirming liver of a raptor to your mouth. Can you feel the way it struggles against your throat, trying to keep from falling in? I'm having visions, of featherless wings and furred legs, hands beaten with a stone until they harden into hooves. A halo dripping punctured flesh, a face with holes, a butterfly settling over your face and replacing your eyes, holes,

Remembering your broken reflection in a shimmering river abundant with pulpy fish, the sound of Raphael splitting the waters with his feet, approaching, your mirror looking fixedly at you and those hands peeling apart the layers of your skin like they're robes, remembering nails scratching against the soft plains of flowers between golden organs, the surface of the pond you bathed in on Earth, remembering you, you will live a hundred million years, you will watch the sun set again. Remembering the moon. Winged as it comes to you, abyss of memories, it all falls in, remembering

the ceiling of naivety, nothing but grass on your naked back.'

Dina thought, all in affection, 'This angel is so kind.' He lapped at the juice of a new fruit, then heard the rumble of his own quiet, pleasured noise. Smacking, licking, his lips, he stretched and told his older brother, "Thank you, but I think you should have some too." He didn't look directly at Lucifer, content with relaxing against the other angel's curiously comforting body. Dina smiled, gentle, when the angel of beauty — 'who is that so strongly that I can't even glance at him' — put his arm around his shoulders. By now, he'd heard something about roles, the purpose of an angel's life, and he prayed to the great Father his identity would become known to him soon. He rested his head against Lucifer's shoulder, sighing, at ease.

Dina's gaze staggered onto Phanuel, an angel he didn't know well, who wore an excess of rings. He was fascinated with the way the gems glistened when the lights of candles, scattered about the room, struck them when Phanuel waved his hands as he spoke. Dina watched, not realizing he might look strange. He wished the Creator had dressed him nicer, then he suppressed those thoughts. He told himself to be grateful.

Lucifer breathed, slow, and picked through his bowl of fruits. His free hand went to Dina's hair, tussling it. There was a pounding in his head; he settled into his surroundings like a drifting piece of paper. The music: "Crown him the Lord of years, the potentate of time, creator of the rolling sphere, ineffably sublime." The smells of the room assaulted him, the tiny noises of angels moving — thumps and rattles — their laughter as they spoke about various things that didn't matter because nothing did in Heaven, nothing except worshiping Father, of which everything was derived. He thought he saw, for a moment, eyes on every tile of the floor, between the designs on the carpet. Then, he returned to the threads of hair his fingers played with, that belonged to this angel here, innocent and pure.

That period Lucifer spent curled up over the carpet with the door locked, there had been bulging, dilated eyes composing the walls of his bedroom, never blinking. Rosier's fearful calls filtering in, every now and then. Lucifer, being observed, inspected — all he'd been able to do was hug himself in terror, but there was no warmth, no shielding from His sight.

Lucifer cleared his throat, then sang, to the delight of every angel in the room, "All hail, redeemer, hail, for we have eternity for you, may our praise never, never fail, throughout eternity." One angel gestured, urging for the angel of worship to stand up and lead them. At Dina's curious blinks, Lucifer smirked, took the young angel's hand, and tugged him to his feet before setting the bowl on the couch, leaving it there. Lucifer hadn't brought his instruments, too lazy these days to lug them around. That was fine — the angels of music could get a decent enough rhythm going on their own. And Lucifer's feet struck beats against the table he pulled Dina onto — *ta, ta, ta, ta*. He sang, "How Heaven's anthem drowns all music but its own, awake, and sing of Him, who will never leave us alone."

The angels cheered 'for me.' They praised him for singing to them; someone as great as Lucifer, taking pity on them. 'Mercy, mercy, you will find mercy is useless.' And he danced, holding Dina's wrist as the young angel stumbled. Look at Lucifer, kind enough to teach the newborn how to dance. Praise the Lord. Praise the Lord. 'Saying that, but it's me you're raving over. Lucifer, my name is Lucifer. Say: Praise Lucifer.'

"Hail Him as our matchless king, through all eternity," the angels sang with him — with, for, against, 'it all melts into the same.' He laughed, brightly, not sure at what, and spun around with Dina, who was laughing too, whose face heated extravagantly when Lucifer brushed it with his palm for just a moment.

Two great realizations came to him at once. The first was that he hadn't seen Michael in hours, and that it was having a terrible effect on the state of his mind — it kept tripping, then tumbling down an endless staircase — and the second was that he wanted to hurt Dina. The urge was overwhelming — to stab him, to see if he would cry. Phanuel was there too; he might scream if Lucifer grabbed him and tore his tongue out. What would Seir, at the other end of the room, singing joyfully, do if Lucifer took his time sawing off each finger? Would he squirm?

'Lucifer is so great.'

'Lucifer is so beautiful.'

Like a symphony — the thoughts.

'Lucifer is so perfect.'

'I sing louder, hoping to catch his attention. In Eden, he's always distracted, but here, he might notice my devotion to him.'

'Michael calls him the most wonderful angel in Heaven. Suddenly, I see what he means.'

'Leave that young one, come dance with us instead.'

'Brush against me again, Lucifer.'

'Look at me. No, over at me.'

'Won't you dance with me? Am I worthy?'

Dina stumbled, but Lucifer caught him, twirled him around, and everything inside Dina felt like it had burst. All he could do was grin adoringly up at the angel who was very quickly guiding him through all the delights of paradise. It made his heart swell, all of him surge with such love he thought, 'I would do anything for him, I would do anything he asked, this beautifully kind angel.'

'You could be greater, you realize. He said, you are not God, you are an angel, but what makes you God? You could be God, take His pipe and His clothes. If you stand on His lap to reach the abyss of His face and peel it off with your teeth. You could be

his angel. the stars. not an adjunct of the heavens but the heavens themselves. agony of digging a knife into the soil of your body. *ta, ta, ta, ta.* the regret and the scarves and weight of your shame disguised as jewelry. let this flesh become the cosmos. you could be him. what if. And it all comes together, that maybe there can be more, if there was someone who was more than God. you could be. you could be god. even you, the beast, would be less cruel than he.'

The song ended, and everyone pleaded Lucifer to lead them in another few, but he waved a hand to tell them to cease their nuisance. In his fatigue — he made his way over to take a glass of wine and down it, eyes half-closed. He thought maybe his wild thoughts would scramble away from him, but they didn't. They lingered, they hung on his eyelids, so that if he closed his eyes, the weight of this blooming decision continued to glare at him. It was no use; not after the stabbing, not after Michael, not after what God had done to him, would Lucifer be able to return to what it had all been like before. There was no paradise anymore, no angel of worship, no angel.

Dina was beside him, staring at Phanuel's hands again. Lucifer had noticed it earlier, and he saw it again with a knowing glee. He could recognize jealousy anywhere now, and so he put a hand on the naive angel's shoulder. He leaned in, whispering. "Dina, if you admire his rings so much, you should take them."

"What?" Identically hushed voice, and a quiver landing on his bottom lip. "They're his."

"They could be yours."

"He likes them."

"But you like them too. And if you swipe them, while he's asleep, you could keep them. If he saw you another day, he would think you own a pair of similar rings to the ones he lost. He would never suspect it, never even consider." Lucifer's lips brushed Dina's earlobe, and he cheerily saw the other shiver. He left the decision to him but knew what the angel would do, because he was so lost in Heaven, so young and open to do anything because he didn't know God, hadn't dedicated his life to Him, not yet. Bidding farewell, then, Lucifer stepped back, then headed for the door.

The eternal gleam of Heaven came down on him like rain, but it didn't wash his thoughts — plans, now — away, and it didn't restore the once pristine purity of that body.

'All I ever wanted was to be loved, and now you've shown me that to be loved is to be broken. What is inside me?' Someone had once said there were flowers, within him, but his fingers had only found the smooth, wet tissue of organs beneath flesh. Could it be he was made up of both beautiful and horrible things? Maybe it was something that couldn't be explained, something unknown, something like God. 'Maybe there is a little bit of God, inside me.'

He felt his wings, and three other faces, tucked into his blood, promising salvation.

CHAPTER 33

Today.

He returned, thinking it, with his hands cupped together to hold a sparrow nuzzling his fingers with her beak, round body occasionally inflating with tiny breaths of sleep. Lucifer held her to his chest, draped by the soothing, soft linen of his long white robe, pure enough that he could have simply been a spirit, having escaped its flesh bindings. There was a harp strumming above — someone sitting out on their balcony, practicing; the notes traveled down to Lucifer and circled his head. Looking down at the shivering animal, the notes asked themselves why a creature of Eden was in Heaven and where the beautiful angel was taking her. They trailed behind, but Lucifer didn't pay them any attention. Instead, he turned a corner and found himself at the bazaar.

The sounds of the harp looked on, climbing up the pool of light, worrying as they died.

"Hm." Gabriel, far off in the north, drifted his fingers across the binds of some books on the upmost row of a towering bookshelf in Uriel's living room. He flapped his wings behind himself, so that he could hover and pick one out, before Raphael called him down. The angel of healing was far below, leaning against his walking stick, all his hair gathered in a braid, as seemed to be his preferred way to wear in the past ten thousand years. At his side was Uriel, wrapped in a shawl, as if he were terribly cold; and there was Michael, who was further away, stretched over a chair and finishing chewing a coca leaf. "Oh, are we done here?"

"Maybe you shouldn't have been so distracted," Uriel grumbled as Gabriel landed beside him, but Raphael waved a hand, coming to his defense as he always did.

"Come, brother, I'll explain everything on our way out." Raphael moved to Gabriel, settling his free palm on his shoulder, but the latter looked at Michael, who was gathering himself to leave too.

A tug on his cotton tunic — Raphael just about dragged him towards the entrance to Uriel's immense, lonely house, and Gabriel walked, did as told with his eyebrows confusedly scrunched together. He raised a hand so that he could wave to the two archangels left behind, but it appeared Michael was leaving out through an open window and Uriel was looking away. Raphael shut the door behind them, and a sigh, heavy, dropped out of his mouth. He released Gabriel and walked down the pathway, his walking stick thump-ing in step with him.

Lucifer gathered himself some admirers, ushering them over with no more than a few pleading words. They dropped everything. They thought, 'The greatest angel needs me,' and over two dozen crowded around him, following. They were led to a gallery, the same one where Lucifer had met Michael — after the prince swooped into the party, grabbed the beautiful angel, took him out to the garden, and threw him over the daisies, then ravaged his mouth — but that garden had been removed by now. An angel sculptor, at Lucifer's side, detailed the great statues that lined the now well-maintained grass, stripped of the restless flowers, myrtle trees, and nervous, bustling fountain. With a forced smile, Lucifer continued hiding the bird in his hands, nodding at them, asking if anyone would like to come into the building with him. All of them, yes — none faltered in obedience.

Once the two archangels had moved out of the mountainous, sandy corner of Heaven toward grasslands, Raphael grumbled, "It's so difficult to be in the same room as those two." He smiled and nodded at those who bowed respectfully to him but kept returning to annoyance when he spoke with Gabriel. "They won't talk, won't even look at each other. One of them should apologize, but Michael is too proud, and Uriel won't admit he's wrong." Especially because he wasn't. 'I don't understand — what happened to the sweet, timid angel who I nursed to life for months? The sleeping beauty who sometimes tossed and turned but often remained still, like a portrait of an angel?'

Gabriel frowned. "They must have argued again. But Michael has been acting so strange. I heard him, in Eden, arguing with Father too." 'I know what you think, Raphael. You think this is Lucifer's fault, but how could that be? You cared for him that long, and I told you the marvelous stones Father shaped him from — don't you trust my perception?'

"Uriel told me he confronted Lucifer and Michael recently."

"And what did he say?"

Raphael stopped, by the gated entrance to a cornfield, a tall, feathery sea, but he stared straight forward, looking at nothing. He blinked, instead, seeing his thoughts: 'Gabriel, you'll think I misheard.'

"Raphael? What's wrong?"

Lucifer, sitting on the upmost step of the grand staircase, revealed the sparrow from his hands and the folds of his robe. The breaths of the angels who'd followed him, like ducklings, hitched; some had never gone to Eden, some had never seen anything remotely like a bird, except, perhaps, each other. Arranged on the steps, the crowd cascaded down from where Lucifer was — a great circular window on the wall behind him, showering light onto his body, brilliant. "It's a sparrow," he told those who didn't know, and little chirps danced along the air. 'Father saw me take the bird. He didn't stop me. His hands itch for me, crave to punish me again. Something amusing to do, in paradise.'

As expected — "No," Gabriel whispered. "Brother, that can't be true. Lucifer would never say all those things." They were impossible things to say. "I know him. He can't— Father would never allow it!"

"That's why He punishes even His favorite angel." Raphael's expression turned tired, or returned to it; 'You always look so exhausted, poor Raphael.' "Who I'm more concerned about is Michael. I don't doubt our Father will put an end to Lucifer's bizarre behavior, but what of our chief prince? At this rate, I wouldn't be surprised if his title were stripped from him. I don't know what to do."

"I believe in Uriel, and I believe in Michael." Gabriel took Raphael's free hand and squeezed it, reassuring. "And in Lucifer too." To him, he handed a kind-hearted smile, as if gift-wrapped. "You'll see your fears are unfounded, and everything will return to how it was. You should rest." No, Raphael had so much work to get done, so many angels to tend to. "Come on then. I'll go with you, to put weights on your body so you can't escape. What kind of angel of healing is always on the verge of collapse?"

"Don't say that." Raphael laughed fondly as he scolded the younger one. "You'll hurt my feelings, and now I'll be an angel of healing in pain, too."

"But will you do as I say?" 'Gabriel, the eternally youthful angel. You spend all your time laying over the clouds with the wonder of someone who just met the sky.' Raphael remembered all those million times he'd awoken over his desk, having fainted from exhaustion, with a blanket curiously draped over his shoulders. Gabriel had never admitted it was him, but Raphael caught him once, slipping out of the room after tucking a pillow beneath Raphael's head. "Hm?" 'He's the kindest angel, and one can't be too kind, right? Perhaps he's correct. All will be well again. There's nothing to worry about.'

After the fact, Lucifer remembered his words rather unwell, something of, "Look at the way it bounces, and tilts its head around, how it doesn't fear us," as his army watched on with devotion speckled onto their gazes and voices. They said his name, kept uttering it and tasting cinnamon. Their hands had moved forward and attempted to stroke the little bird Lucifer handed over, so that they could each cradle her a while.

Lucifer moved through the streets with heaviness, hands held behind his back; that which had occurred in the gallery, with the sparrow, was maybe hours ago now. He didn't know why he was remembering. The way up this road was steep — usually he flew, but his breaths were coming unsteady, and he knew his flying would be lopsided enough to make him crash. How was he supposed to concentrate when his heart was bashing against his chest, trying to break it down, kissing colorful bruises within? He was too conscious of his movements, walked unnaturally stiff.

The precious stones and chains of jewelry were all exceptionally cold on his heated skin, but he'd been very careful about his choices, today. He'd racked his brain for memories of Michael's compliments, all the times he had remarked about a certain gem or mentioned Lucifer looked especially pleasant. As well, he'd rummaged through drawers for those adornments that the chief prince, the greatest wrestler, had won for him once. It was soothing to remember, warming away all the shivering that'd begun assaulting his muscles. A swallow, saliva turning into crystal, sliding down his throat and slicing it open — his nerves made him clammy enough to twist his stomach.

Before Eden, Lucifer spent three hours before the mirror, preening and preening, staring at himself until something was out of place. He couldn't stop touching his hair, rearranging the strands, pouting in frustration. Of course, he was perfect in appearance no matter the state of any part of him, but anxiety continued to eat away at his soul, wondering what it meant to be perfect not in beauty but *for* someone. He thought of Michael as he dyed red-brown, winding spirals onto certain patches of skin — Azazel taught him how to once — and he sang softly, only to himself. He noticed Rosier at the door, eyeing him sadly, but he ignored him. Lucifer, in his catastrophe of a room, stood, then headed for the balcony and took off to Eden.

Eden. It came and it went. Lucifer brought the bird. He'd walked through the streets, hearing music, gathering followers as planned, then entered the gallery with them — surely, that had happened. Even if, now, he was treading up the hill towards Michael's home. He didn't think about the sparrow anymore, couldn't even remember her colors anymore; he looked ahead. Surely, that had all happened.

'i waited for your touch to save me'

Lucifer let himself in, traveled up the stairs, and put one hand against the open door so that he could peer inside. Delightfully, he noted Michael was there, sitting on a large chair that faced the great windows revealing the waters beating the shores. In one hand, he had a book; in the other, he had a slice of sourdough bread, buttered. Chewing, the archangel turned his head at the sound of footsteps — always perceptive of his surroundings, the trait of a fighter — and, beaming, saw Lucifer. "I was wondering where you've been. Did you just return from Eden?"

Lucifer walked toward him, watching as Michael removed an elbow from the armrest, so that the other could sit there, as he sometimes did. Today, he did it; he plopped down onto it, smiling, softly. "I did."

"Did Father tell you a story today? Will you share it with me?"

"To tell you the truth," Lucifer confessed, "I wasn't paying much attention." Today; it had to be today; no more waiting. "I don't remember."

Michael sighed but didn't fully frown, as Lucifer had predicted. He replied like he had mulled over a response for months, and perhaps he had: "When I speak to our Lord these days, I feel like I've fallen from His favor. It frustrates me. I'm supposed to be the angel of strength, of God, but I'm recognizing myself less and less. All of us archangels met earlier today, but Uriel was angry, Raphael was disappointed, Gabriel was Gabriel. I used to lead the meetings, I used to be a leader."

Lucifer laid a hand on Michael's back, rubbing coaxing circles. "Everything feels different now."

"I'm happy you feel similar." A quiet sound of relief, and ease made him untangle beneath Lucifer's fingers.

"Do you want everything to return to how it was?"

"To how it was before you?" Michael laughed a bit. "No. Never in a million years."

"Why not?"

"Don't make me say such embarrassing, affectionate things, beloved Lucifer." Michael's tittering, sweet smile had Lucifer's chest ache wonderfully. "But, let me say that — before I saw you on the street, dancing and singing, I was never very joyous. I was content with serving Father, I felt I had no room to complain, but then you arrived. And being around you, I had so much joy I became irrational, and now — now, it's all spilling out. You make my heart swell and rise, like smoke."

A pause, as Michael finished his bread, set the book down.

"I thought earlier that if Father scolds me over being your friend again, I'd have to argue, that if He punishes me, I'd have to resist. You don't know this, but since your muteness, I've fought with Him; I've said I don't understand how He can be furious with us, hurting you, when He knows everything, when He can see eternity, when He should have seen this when He made you, when He made *me*. And, suddenly, I'm questioning everything, asking myself if this is really paradise or if *you* are paradise." Falter. "I— I don't know what I'm saying."

'You're paradise to me, Michael. And you're not like the others.' Lucifer moved his hand to his friend's curls and scratched lightly at his scalp. 'Ambition in your eyes — strength and desire for more. You could be a king. When I take the Throne, you would love to sit on it with me, right? Or would you want to build an even larger one, so that we can settle it above the Most High's? You're starting to wonder it too, aren't you? What if there was no God, no Father? Only you and me, who are like Him, who together are greater than Him? We could be kings, gods.'

"E-Enough of me — what about you? You've done a commendable job trying to hide it, but I know you well. I hope you can trust me to hear what's been bothering you. You know I— I really enjoy hearing you talk."

'Let's forget everything about before today. Let's cast God down to dwell with the beasts, where He belongs. And let's wash ourselves of guilt like dirty clothes in a river.'

Instead of answering, Lucifer moved off the chair, took Michael's hand, pulled him to his feet. "Michael."

"Hm?" His expression became curious, one eyebrow quirking up. "What's wrong?"

"Everything is, all around us." Lucifer took Michael's other hand, and now he held them both, and there was a thrill in his bloodstream. Gazes met one another — one pair worried and the other joyous. All the uncertainty within his body streaming down. "Paradise is coming apart at the seams, stop covering your eyes and face it."

"Lucifer—" Confusion.

"I've been punished for disobedience twice now. And you, feuding with Father, seeing His irrationality — open your eyes." And he took

Michael's face, held his cheeks, tugged him closer so that their foreheads pressed together. He urged, urged how he used to beg fruits to ripen as a newborn so that he could collect them, urged, "What if there was no God? What if there were just the angels, and you and me, and the Throne left behind? We could sit on it together, we'd both fit. We could rule together, couldn't we? Everyone admires us, adores us, does everything we say."

Michael's face twisted, thoughts Lucifer was sure he couldn't comprehend battering his brain all at once, physically recoiling. "Wait." He shook his head. "Wait, Lucifer— What are you talking about?"

"Michael, open your eyes. See for yourself how He has caused us only pain. All those years I was silent, did your heart not ache for me? You saw me cry, you held me, you heard all the angels say Father was good even as He hurt me, *hurt* me—" Breaths were spluttering out of his mouth as bile. "I can't do it anymore, not again—" His hands fell, onto Michael's shoulders, gripping tight to keep steady, to keep the other captive. "I want Him gone."

"Stop. Stop, don't say those words." Yet Michael's resolve was weak, after all. His head shook some more, negating, but trembles racked his body. His mouth moved, saying nothing coherent, only Lucifer's name, chanted, over and over.

"I want us to be God, to be more than that. I want us to create like Him." Lucifer, exhilarated, feeling all of himself flush as scorching hot as a sun, dragged his hands down, down Michael's front, settling palms over his strong chest. "We could do it, everything could be ours — the most perfect of the host. I want to make new things with you, build something better than this mirage of eternal pleasure. Haven't you ever wondered why Father is so strict about our subservience? It's because disobedience is creation," a shivering breath, "create with me, Michael, and let's call it *sin*."

Flames of conflict within the other, killing the forestry in his eyes. He whispered, "We can't—"

"We can."

"It isn't— It's not good—"

"It will be good. It will feel good." Lucifer paused, let out a breath he hadn't realized he clutched tight. "I want to make you feel good,

Michael." 'I'm having so much fun creating and inventing. Just yesterday, I thought up a few new words: cock and cunt and fucking.' He smiled, then laughed again, blithely. The air between them was scorching, as molten rock, becoming dense and damp; and memories rushed of when the two practiced fighting — all those first times that Lucifer just couldn't position himself right, his hands weak fists, hair all over his face. The slides of their bodies against one another, muscles clashing, and the younger one getting pinned over, and over, and over, falling. Laughter falling from their smiles. "I want to please you."

Michael whispered, "But you already please me. You're my... friend."

"Friend?"

"Lucifer..." His voice trailed — already knowing.

"I want to taste you, Michael." He gripped the vermillion robes the other wore, that fit him snug. "I want you in my mouth." There it was — he'd finally said it, and with those words, the dam crumbled and oceans of secret cravings poured so fierce they both got ravaged by the tide. Drowning, Lucifer continued, desperate — all the color of life was draining from Michael — "I want your cock so heavy on my tongue that it breaks my jaw." He began to laugh, little giggles, in his frenzy; he had never imagined, never even thought, that this would feel as nice as it did. His head was pounding, his heart was thundering; he trembled with delicious, saccharine desire.

Michael tried to step back, but Lucifer's hold on his robe was violent. "What are you saying? I don't understand. Lucifer, you're not acting like yourself— Are you okay? You're scaring me—" 'Why? I said I'm going to make you feel good. How can it be wrong if it feels good? Why would Father make something that feels good wrong?' Michael's hands went over Lucifer's, but the jolt of fire between their skin made him tense, then quickly push the younger one away. "Please. Just wait — I don't—" Michael staggered back so fast that he tumbled over a cushion on the floor and fell backwards onto a carpet. But he shot up to sit, shoulders rising and falling, rapid.

Lucifer looked down at him, took in the archangel's expression, and felt something warm swirl his belly like a hand in water; his body felt lonesome, quite suddenly, empty, needing company. He lowered himself, onto his knees, and then onto all fours, and he crawled. Figure moving slow, swaying, his eyelids fell halfway, so all his world blurred except for the chief prince. And the other's gaze flared, taking him in, maybe noticing Lucifer had worn all his favorite jewelry, plenty that he had won, and layered on a pure white robe, 'for you to rip to pieces as you spoil me some more and let me rot.' Purring — "*Michael.*" 'Bend me over the Throne and desecrate it with me.'

Michael swallowed, loud, painful, and the fear in his eyes was nearly enough to make Lucifer stop — nearly, nearly.

Heaving, cheeks ravishingly hot; all of him, a furnace. Desperately — "Haven't you imagined it? I know you have. Me beneath you, crying out your name." 'Pleading for you to be gentler but not meaning it.' "In front of everyone, right? So they all know who I belong to." 'My hands clawing at your back, pulling at your wings, legs raw and sore.' "You, violating this body," 'eviscerate me,' "and even He would be jealous of the way I'd sing for you." The noises of their pleasure, rising, the rattles of jewelry, cool sweat rolling over burning stones. "I need it." He reached Michael and took his clothes again. "I need you—"

Lucifer kissed him, wildly, hysterically, sick with longing.

"Lucifer—"

But despite all the hesitance, there were a hundred million years of want between them — Michael splintered. Came undone. He surged forward, stole Lucifer's plump, rosy lips for himself, reached for the angel of beauty, grabbing him tight and tugging him close — all that strength greater than mountains, greater than God. And, '*oh*,' the kiss was ravenous, desperate and thirsty, devouring like they'd find the juice of fruit if only they pressed deep enough into each other's mouths. The tiny taste of honey, of lavender — the sweet richness of an angel.

Euphoria flooded him in tremors; it was so much Lucifer could only part his lips to try breathe before Michael's tongue slithered inside. He invaded him, possessed him, plunged into him wet and burning. Soon thereafter, Michael's hands gripped Lucifer's waist and hip tight; when he picked him up, it was with ease. And legs hugged Michael, urging him closer, trying to invite him in. Little hums of delight between them both, slipping from between the needy slide of their bodies just as Lucifer reached to drag his nails right along

Michael's shoulder blades, skin pinking in the wake, and from Lucifer's own back, wings unfurling, twitching, flapping in pretty flutters. Beneath this light, their royal violet coloring had drawn away, revealed some hue of gore.

Hands landing on Michael's heated cheeks, thighs stuck quivering and pressed up to the prince's hips. "Take my body, my blood—" The lovely shape of each other, fitting almost snug, like they were fit, even inside, for each other. But they were not, they were not.

When Lucifer tried to yank, harsh, at the loose robe of Michael, hoping to expose every inch of skin overdue to be grazed with teeth, the angel of strength began to wilt. He said: "N-No— Not like this." He inched backwards, pulling away, and soon they had both crashed to the floor again, brought something that shattered with them, and Michael was trying to crawl backward, though Lucifer reached for him. "Stop— The Lord—"

Cold, so violently, Lucifer cried, "Please, don't deny me—"

Michael shook his head, clenching his eyes shut. "Father—"

"Don't say that name."

"This is too much. He'll be angry, Lucifer," Michael was saying, fumbling, as if searching for something, his strength. "Let's stop. Let's pray—"

"No," left Lucifer's mouth, devoid of life. "You can't make me—"

"I can't. No, I can't, I'm sorry—" Michael, shivering, drew away at Lucifer's touch, as if it were burning him. "I don't want to. I'm sorry. Father—" Lucifer told him not to say that word again. "I'm sorry—" Those apologies were not for Lucifer. "I'm sorry."

"Let me." 'Pray to this body, mold you into holy communion, cry your name like psalm.' "Let me worship you."

Michael was quiet — the sounds of water, moving — before he said, "Get out, Lucifer." Lucifer didn't move. "You're not acting yourself. I don't want to do anything with you like this. Please. Come back when you feel better." He didn't want to. "Let's talk then."

"About what?"

"Everything."

"You're going to stand by my side and face Father, right?"

Michael wouldn't give him an answer, even with the seeds of rebellion gracefully planted into the cusp of his viscera, doubt remained; and, his eyes were sad. He told Lucifer to leave him again — he begged miserably for his purity, the love of his Father. And Michael blinked, over and over, through the red invading the whites of his eyes, trying to turn away, gesturing for Lucifer to retreat so that the younger one wouldn't see him cry. Grief — caving into itself so deep neither could escape plunging down together.

When Michael said it, once again, Lucifer did as told. He stood gracefully. He walked towards the door without another word.

Stepping into the garden by the gate, he remembered earlier that day, after returning from Eden. He thought of the gallery, and all the adoring angels who watched him from the steps, holding the bird. As if an angel was coloring in the gaps of a painting, Lucifer began to re-experience the event, spottily.

His voice, caressing, ordering for the angels to kill that little sparrow, to squash it between their hands. They said, "Lucifer, no, we can't." He told them it would make them feel powerful, they said that she was just a poor, defenseless creature, but he told them again, and again. It will make you feel almighty, like God, he promised, and they trusted Lucifer, adored him to pieces. Thus, each angel, in turns, took to crushing the bird. It wasn't difficult, felt her flatten beneath their feet, heard the sharp cries of death grow dim, slow, like the bird was really flying away, away from here. Then, they all turned up to the angel of beauty, searching for his validation and his comfort.

When he, smiling, cooing, replied with sweet compliments, his angels wept in joy.

CHAPTER 34

He'd dreamt that all his innards had fallen, out from between his legs, and when he awoke, he'd felt empty.

Asmodeus said, "Brother, let's go out on a walk."

Now, Lucifer sat before his mirror. "No." In the nightmare, all the angels had cheered as he danced in the midst of them. They spoke in each other's voices, the wrong ones, and all the scenery had begun to eclipse, after a while — darkness, like a return to infancy. 'I never asked to be born.' Had never needed, never wanted, found that if he reached there was still an umbilical cord, wrapped around his neck, and it was chaining him to his Father.

"Don't you want to spend time with me?"

"No." 'I think I remember it now — my birth and crawling out from your floral gore.'

Pause, then a confession: "I fear that if I leave you alone, you will start to hurt yourself again." Asmodeus stepped inside, past the doorway, to stand by Lucifer as the younger angel looked between his reflection— he sat before it, on a cushioned chair this time — and a map of Heaven he had sketched out on bark paper.

"It's not myself I will be hurting if you don't leave my room." Lucifer's gaze flickered up, met Asmodeus' eyes in the mirror. "Don't stand so close."

"Might I remind you — this is my room, and if you ask me—"

"I didn't ask you—"

"You're being incredibly disrespectful."

It would be easy to snap poisonously back, but that wouldn't be beneficial. The last thing Lucifer needed was for anyone to become a nuisance right as his scheming was coming to its fruition; he didn't want enemies this early, he couldn't afford them. Asmodeus was not like the others — he knew the true character of Lucifer, had known him since his very first moments — he would see right through anything the angel of beauty said, and he wasn't too moronic either. It wouldn't be the worst idea to have him as a supporter, a true one, not like all the gullible, dazed angels who were simply smitten with Lucifer because he looked sugar sweet and sang charmingly enough to drunken them.

But what was there to say to convince Asmodeus, so that he support him sincerely, fight for him no matter the punishment? "Forgive me," Lucifer decided but noticed a glimmer of excitement in Asmodeus' eyes, "I was disrespectful." This was probably the first time in Asmodeus' long life that he'd berated someone for true insolence — because all angels were polite, well-meaning, gracious little worms.

"You're forgiven, but you've given Rosier a fever from worry. Can I convince you to have something to eat?"

Lucifer turned his head so that he stared upward at the real angel, feeling Asmodeus' shadow cast down upon him, as he replied, "I'm just curious of one thing, brother. And then I will be as obedient as you like."

Asmodeus raised an eyebrow. "You want to ask me something." Not a question, and it became transparent, in an instant, to Lucifer that he really had no need to lie to the other. He knew what he desired, what he was restless for.

"You're very bored, aren't you, Asmodeus?" Initially, the older one showed no sign of reaction; that was good, 'I don't want a weakling on my side.' "So many millions of years, the same things every day, building new towers because there is nothing else to do, playing ball games, inventing new ones, drinking wine, eating bread, waiting for the sun to set, but it never does, and all you do is stare off into the walls, praying, but not to God, because you know He wouldn't like that — hoping that perhaps one day, something, anything, will happen that will give your existence some kind of true purpose to exist." A crack of composure — a twitch at the end of his lips. "I am what you've been waiting for, Asmodeus."

"No, you aren't."

"Ah!" Lucifer laughed, musically. "You admit that my perception of you is right?" Grimace, grumble, looking away, and Lucifer stood to take a good look at himself. He once again donned a terribly thin white tunic, and robe, today, as he'd planned — today, today. But his jewelry was much more extensive, clinging to his neck, his waist, hips, thighs, ankles, wrists — venomously tight bondage. If Michael saw him now; if Michael saw him now; if Michael saw him. Michael. 'Stop. Not now. Don't think of him after what happened. Coward.' 'No, Michael is not a coward,' said one of Lucifer's faces. 'He's a rotten fearful animal.' 'Don't ever say that.' 'Doesn't he want to be with me? To have fun together? To pleasure one another? He never liked me, he never loved me.' Breath, sharp, and then Lucifer forced a grin, a giggle. "Go ahead, pick me up, take me to Father. Tell him to punish me and hang my body in an eternal sleep over the Fountain of Life, as a lesson to everyone in what disobedience brings."

Asmodeus breathed through his nose; Lucifer heard it.

"And after my defeat, you'll return to how things were, to the dull drone of every second of eternity, pleasuring yourself but never too much, for nothing. The Messiah of your boredom, that you so prayed for, that you ignored, that you turned away from — defeated. You can spend the rest of forever wondering what could have been, if you had only joined me." They stared at each other, and with a little smirk, Lucifer saw the failing resolve in Asmodeus' eyes and grinding teeth. "How about we go on a walk?"

"I could continue without you."

"No. You couldn't. And it would be pathetic." Lucifer reached for some flasks of oils intricately arranged on a table — Rosier had cleaned everything earlier— and picked out rosewood. It was sweet, floral, and he mixed it with some light, leafy geranium. "But that's not my problem, I suppose. At least I'll be punished with dignity. I'll have a purpose and a will, and all you angels, you will all remember. You might no longer love me, but you won't be able to forget me." A sultry smile, before he reached for his sandals, then decided he didn't feel like wearing them. He wasn't planning to go to Eden today; he had been told to go, he would not go.

Asmodeus followed him. As Lucifer made his way out of the room, the other walked close behind, down the stairs, out the front door.

'you will inherit heaven. the golden streets curling into themselves, frightened as your feet step upon them, so they become flaxen spirals each, whirlpools that twist you until your bones smooth into tides. and the houses tumble, and cuddled angels slip off clouds, trip, fall. collapse. when you rebuild there will be needs. make. needs instead of wants. you let him feed you the painted tiles. all rolled up so you can blow into one end blow suck blow retching lungs squeezing then bursting as you try to will smoke to brew and from the gray, a set of eyes and mouths and hands an angel like you and maybe fashioning yourself a pretty little creature in your palm to keep you company. beady eyes fluttering up as it gets on the tips of its toes to try and slip a ring into one of your fingers and then in a fist, you crush the tender creature crying begging for mercy. inheriting the dazzling sparkling swirls of the abyss. inheriting with the death of the king all his body. all he is will become yours. creating a corpse inheriting inheriting every-thing inheriting nothing.'

Baal smiled, warm as he saw his two friends coming up. "Oh, hello, Asmodeus." He crossed his arms, straightened his back. 'Though I had been hoping it was just going to be Lucifer and I.'

"I thought it'd be fun for him to come along," Lucifer said before the other could respond. "Ah, speaking of — Baal, do you mind if we go to this observatory I like instead of your home? I want to show everyone something." He had invited more angels — very early that day, he sent out an obedient messenger he picked out on the street — though he hadn't told Baal. "Please? I promise we can wrestle tomor-row. Just you and me."

Baal blinked, then nodded profusely. "Yes, yes, of course, brother. Where is the observatory?"

It was where Lucifer had first met Uriel, where he had met Azazel, who fed him needles, where he'd been told angels were shepherding the universe; it was odd, that angels did all the work. They tended the gardens and painted the flowers and tied the threads of the planets around their suns, and they were the suns, and they laid all day, too, just running their hands through their hair, kissing. Paradise. And all they had to do in return was worship. Worship. 'I want to be worshiped.' Why would God create then ask the creations to bow? 'I want to create.' They came upon the great dome of the observatory as they waded through fields of wheat that waved to them cordially, parting before the three, moving out of their way. Ahead, Lucifer saw many angels, most of which were waiting outside, chattering, before they saw the most popular among them, coming nearer. Lucifer heard, behind, Baal ask Asmodeus what was happening, but Asmodeus replied he didn't know.

Lucifer greeted the gathered with a bow. "Thank you all for coming. I'm really grateful. I never thought so many of you would come." It could have been fifty, maybe a tad more. Regardless, they showered him with great smiles, honest compliments. "I do hope you all received my message."

"Message?" Baal put a hand on Lucifer's arm, right above his elbow. Quietly, he mumbled to him, "What are you talking about?"

"Let's go inside," Lucifer told them all, then faced Baal and Asmodeus and giggled at their confusion. "There's something I wanted to show everyone. Will you two help me?" Instead of answering, Asmodeus took a cautious step back, but the other nodded. "Thank you, Baal. You're always so kind." He leaned in to kiss his cheek, felt the blush there, before brushing past him. Lucifer tried to hide a smirk. It was going to be very easy, of course it was, Baal adored him, all the angels did — having left to meet up with Lucifer without any explanation, simply going because he requested it. They would do anything to make Lucifer happy.

This wasn't coming out of a place of harm, really. The angels would surely enjoy themselves and in doing so, find out there was a way to be joyous that didn't involve Father, pleasure that didn't derive from lowly worship. Lucifer would be a good king; he knew angels, knew what they liked, their little frustrations, knew that ultimately all they ever wanted was to feel good and keep feeling good. He would show them a glimpse of what it could all be like if they followed him. 'And Michael.' There was still hope for him. 'Michael would look so pleasant sitting with me. He would be a good king too. We could cast judgment on the unruly ones, and I could spend all my days touching his hair and breathing against the warm skin of his neck.'

Lucifer arranged for all his army to sit in a wide circle in the center of the building. There was a carpet, a massive crimson carpet — that was helpful, if blood spilled onto it, which it would, it would be difficult to notice — beneath their feet with some intricate golden starry designs. At the center of them all, he stood feeling pride bristle in his chest, eyeing the pretty angels who looked back with eagerness. It made him flush, in exhilaration, swallow — made his pulse quicken. "Hello. You all."

The angels laughed, and they greeted him back. One called out, "Why have you called so many of us here? I'm devastated, I thought Father's favorite—" Lucifer nearly gagged, "—had taken pity on a regular angel as myself, to invite him out so suddenly."

"Don't feel so sad just yet," Lucifer replied, coy. "I'll make it up to you. I promise."

"How?" one called out, and there was laughter yet again, curious, excited. Lucifer had never disappointed; that Heaven-wide celebration all that time ago for Michael's return had been such a great success it was still discussed regularly. Everything Lucifer promised, he fulfilled. They trusted him; Lucifer realized it fully, dizzy with the power it gave him. They trusted him; they would do anything he said. They wouldn't hesitate. They killed that bird — many of the murderers were here, still behind him, still adoring him. Hearty affection in their eyes — Lucifer matching it with a smirk.

"Baal," he cooed, "come here."

'A long time ago, I collected the flower petals stained with my first blood; I thought there was something significant about that, there was importance in all the little moments of experience, because when you live forever, the first times matter. The first time you bleed, first time you cry — I don't remember that — first time you see your wings, because new things defile you, purity chips away. your purity. nestled flowers in your belly, waiting to be picked. do you want innocence back? small and young smiles that make your eyes squint and cheeks flare the feeling of your face dripping down onto the grass'

Baal did as told but startled when Lucifer gracefully lowered onto his knees. "What?" His breath caught in his throat when the angel of beauty draped a hand over one of his thighs, gazed up at him through long, curled eyelashes. "Wait, what are you doing—?" Everyone was watching now, puzzled, but not frightened, not yet. 'I need to push Lucifer away. I want to push him away.' No, he didn't. Lucifer's hand skimmed upwards, began to slither between the folds of his jasper robe to find a simple tunic, fingers twiddling with the embroidery at the hem. Tiny, lukewarm brushes of his skin against Baal's inner thigh — a single shudder — and his mouth opened; he wanted to say stop. He looked up, then back down, because everyone was staring, and he wanted to say stop, what are you doing, but no he didn't. 'But I want to.' But he didn't.

Lucifer reached for the stem, held and caressed it, then brought full lips to the Rose of Sharon.

'there:

a sleeping angel

curled upon the grass with his hair sprawled. pale flowers over an unknowing body, bedsheets that you pull. and there: an orchard of pomegranates near you both. henna and nard, nard and saffron, calamus and cinnamon, every kind of incense tree, with myrrh, and spices. paprika. the sleeping angel with a rosy, full mouth, inviting, as air skitters in and out. there: his eyes flutter and the angel stretches all his limbs. you tell him say your name. lucifer. no. that can't be, because i am lucifer. eyes of gold meeting eyes of gold.'

Baal's two hands found Lucifer's hair and curled into fists, but his cry wasn't in pain. 'Right?' What was happening? 'Heat, wetness, tightness.' Sensations coming together into something that was only inexplicably right. And there, there, this sliding, scorching tongue, right there, pressed to the underbelly that beckoned hips forward. 'His throat, embracing me, choking me.' Desperate reels of breath and an utter of that name.

'you take lucifer, this little angel who doesn't know he's naked, to eden. you ask do you know of paradise and he says no. you tell him there is a place where you will never have to suffer. where all is well and happy. you want to be happy, you think.' Lucifer gagged on honey, dribbling down to his neck. 'novice little angel, with nothing in his mind, except the wish to worship, to belong to a god. for a hundred million years'

'He's so pretty, suckling like that on me. It's not worth it. To escape.' Baal crumbled. 'The cute noises of struggle and want, the dulcet notes of Lucifer's voice, even muffled, they pour burning oil into me.' Behind Baal's eyes, rust fogged into a sea, and he bristled until he became ember. If the coiled warmth gutted him, he wondered, seeing nothing, if he grew devoured — it didn't matter, anymore. Nothing did, except this mouth, this mouth on his cock, this mouth. Tilting forward, ravishing until it was all his, every drop, every shiver of the kneeling angel.

'lucifer in his youth asks timid who are you. you say i am you. you are looking into a mirror. it reflects existence back to you. taking you and reversing it so instead of flying you fall. fall into my arms float along the water where flowers bloom from ripples warmed by the shimmering sun sit down angel lucifer lay back what are you scared of stare up at the eternal day of heaven the flowers are watching an eye in each stigma budding angel you feel so pleasant because youre untouched innocent pure your thighs taste like spiced wine'

Baal withered and spilled 'blood.'

'lucifer looks at me, and he says, no, you can't be me, even if we look alike. We sit together in this garden of paradise. No, no, I don't know who you are, cries young lucifer, Please do not throw your gaze on me, see that I'm not wearing any clothes. Who told you, I'm grabbing, I'm screaming, kicking, begging Him, that you were naked?'

Poison rinsing his mouth, Lucifer listened to the beats of his heart, booming louder than all the noise of the room. From where he was, still on his knees, he turned, shifted forward onto his elbows so that his back curved flavorfully. His forehead pressed to the carpet, and he became vividly aware of his wet mouth, open as he shuffled air in, out. In, out. Baal came at him, tugged fine linen up to expose a roused body.

His hands explored and felt, teased the flower until it unfurled, and unable to resist temptation, he tasted.

"Mmm. That feels nice, Baal... I want you deeper, inside me, come, come inside... Baal... Baal..."

Baal considered the juice of a fruit, sweet and ripe, succulent and rich, as he kissed, tongued, Lucifer's yielding entrance.

'young lucifer cries to me, What are you doing, lucifer? What are you doing? I wrestle him until we're on the bedding, and he begins to throw his head in every direction, kick, flinging out weak fists. He says, Stop. Please. You're scaring me. and he's whimpering, his eyes becoming pink. little roses. he's so beautiful you want to kill him'

Baal — drunk off Lucifer's soft, giggling moans and deliriously hungry — found a way to get the other beneath him. 'Before he escapes. Before Lucifer laughs and sprints out to latch onto Michael. Michael. Are you seeing this? Your prized possession, whispering for me, pleading for me, not you. My body. Me.' Baal realized he didn't have long before the density of the room collapsed upon them all. He was hasty, holding a perfectly nimble waist and eyeing hips, legs, all adorned to jangle with jewelry. Perfumes making the airs muddled — Baal, 'taking a blade and piercing the most beautiful angel.'

Sloppy rutting. Baal's fucking was merciless. Each ram forward — hard and accompanied with a vulgar slap of their dampening flesh. Lucifer barely felt it still; he was turned away, singing for the audience. Cooing, calling them closer, telling them that this could all be theirs, all of him.

'The little lucifer crying on the bedsheets of a garden. he puts his hands on my shoulders and tells me he doesn't understand. but you don't need to. you will thank me. you will kiss me with love our chests pressed flush together and say pretty little words of gratitude. youll be happy it was me who did it. it's better if it's you. tending this garden and sniping the weeds and deflowering it. it is better like this. you will thank me. it is better like this than how it was. you'll say you love me. wilted, you'll say thank you'

All at once, a hundred hands took Lucifer — the grip of a hundred beasts, turning him into an altar. A perfect body revealed to mouths keen on having every inch of skin — each kiss like a bite that, in its devotion, devoured. When the angels took him, they wanted him with their fingers and every firm, beating, cut of flesh. He felt their tongues at his throat, his heaving chest, his belly, lower.

Baal was shoved and held back, kicking, crazed, fighting, as Lucifer moved on top of a stranger. Glancing, for half a second — he caught an angel kissing another, and an eager angel moving to lay beneath a friend — their little gasps and loving twists of their bodies betraying their inexperience. Lucifer heard the lovely cry in pleasure of an angel, then returned his gaze to this unfamiliar one he was perched on and saw the fair, smiling reflection of beauty in his eyes. That was all he saw. Sinking down, up, down, in, out, rhythmic — the threads of his hair tossing. Like the stabs of daggers, finding flowers, finding poppies; the angels took turns with him, they took him all at once. The windows darkened.

And moans fell, from Heaven. 'the little Lucifer defiled beneath me. all the life fading from his eyes. ichor warm on his legs. free at last. you will thank me. you, will feel your breastbone molded by my kisses. i say there is just me now in my heaven just

this singing lucifer walking toward the morning

a tiny star, lovelier

than his father.'

Asmodeus made his way out of the devolving orgy quickly, heart a fierce chariot, shaking so much he couldn't see. He hurried to his old house by mere muscle memory; it didn't register that the streets were dark; they had never been dark. All he could think of were the oceans of bodies, melting, as he stumbled into Rosier's room. He saw his friend, seated, slicing an orange, and the kind angel smiled, then raised a brow. Rosier said his name; Asmodeus stepped forward. He thought that he had just seen the end of time, the collapse of curtains they'd painted the planets and moons onto. "Rosier," left his dry mouth.

"What's wrong? You're so pale, Asmodeus." Worry growing fast, setting aside what he'd been doing. "Tell me what's wrong. Please."

Asmodeus saw paradise lost, and he took another step, towards Rosier and his wide, frightened eyes. 'To help him, to pull him away from the sinkhole that's coming towards our feet.'

'i waited for your touch to save me'

CHAPTER 35

'**G**ross.' Lucifer gagged as he escaped the clutches of the angels and slipped out of the observatory, feeling blind, feeling like there was something caked onto his face to obscure his vision, and so he reached to try and scratch it off. There was nothing there, maybe a mangled, squashed bird, splatted on the floor of a gallery somewhere, but probably not. Breathing in hollow, he stalked down the steps, each tap of his bare feet on the stone making him shudder as he contemplated to clean himself somewhere. With someone's robe, he'd attempted to wipe off earlier, but it hadn't felt like enough.

He rubbed his face with a sleeve, barely clinging to the pristine white tunic, ripped in various places due to the beasts in the observatory, who were probably still fucking each other and would be for a while. There was no time; Baal would probably come after him soon, and where was Asmodeus? Lucifer nearly groaned. Where was Asmodeus? He would have remembered seeing him, even in all the chaos. How could things be going awry this quickly?

He cursed luck, told it to stop sucking his Father's cock like a whore. Whore. 'That's a good word, has a nice, solid rhythm to it.'

Lucifer stopped, eyes on his feet — curtained by shadows. His breath caught; he turned his head upward and saw it: the brilliant firmament that always hung over the city had rot into a dark overcast, with just a small peppering of stars, only enough light not to be blind. They hung up there — Lucifer's oldest siblings, threatening him, saying, "Don't do this. Look at what Father will do to you." But Lucifer had no interest in speaking to sleeping things, and what was there to do now? Ask for forgiveness? Even if he wanted to — a hole had been punctured into this body and all his soul was spilling out, and there was nothing to return to anymore. The singing, the pleasant indulgences, no troubles, and innocent affections — it would all be memories, because that paradise had shattered itself, and he thought, 'I overthrow God, or I immolate myself until I become as close to death as death. Creation at last — the death of an angel.'

"Lucifer!"

The angel sighed. He'd spent too much time internally monologuing, and now he was turning his head to see Baal, panting for breath, at the door into the building. He was just in his robe, hastily thrown on, and his face was flushed, more violet than red. "Hello, Baal," Lucifer said. "Very good work in there." He saw the other splutter. "Tell me, did you see when Asmodeus left? I fear he's ran off and told the archangels about our fun."

"No— No, I—" There was fatal disappointment in Baal's voice, as if he'd been hoping for Lucifer to say something else, some sort of confession; Lucifer pretended not to notice. "I don't know when he left." Three, four, angels emerged behind the angel of flight, just as disheveled and tired, looking confused, looking for the one who had corrupted them. "Why is everything dark? What's happening? What did you do?"

"Hardly anything yet." Lucifer shifted so that he faced the angels directly. "This is just the beginning. We need everyone out of their houses." There were a few already, lost in the streets, staring up in terror, asking among themselves where Father had gone, if He had left on a walk, but most of everyone had frightfully run into their homes. 'They think they've done something, that maybe they didn't pray to him well enough today. Poor, helpless, little creatures.' Straightening up. 'You see? I will show you all what it means to have some self-respect.' "I want every angel gathered in the center, by the Fountain of

Life." One of the angels tried to speak — glancing at him, Lucifer realized it was Moloch — but he interrupted, "It's what I want, and if you trust me, you'll do it. All will become clear soon, I promise." A smile. "Have I ever let you down?"

Lucifer went on his way, hearing the others scatter to follow orders, except for Baal, who hurried after him. "Where are you going?"

"I'm going to find Asmodeus and rip out his liver."

"Liver? Why?"

"First thing I thought of." Lucifer laughed, jovially. "Why, would you rather I take something else?"

Baal startled, then rolled his shoulders as if to dislodge the gnaw of a beast on him and mumbled, "Asmodeus is my friend—"

"I'm your friend, Baal." Lucifer pouted, looking over at him momentarily, huffing. "And if you don't help me teach Asmodeus a lesson then you can say farewell to all the good times we've had. No more flying together, no more wrestling, no more of what we got up to in the observatory."

"What was that? What we were doing?"

"Sin."

"What's sin?"

"I created it. Do you like it?"

An unsavory swallow, then Baal looked ahead — 'He created it, like how Father creates. I don't have the words, like there aren't any for the heights of pleasure he gifted me.' "I love it." 'I love you. It's hysteria; I'm obsessed with your voice and the taste of your neck. Obsessed with you, in terrible love with you, your face, your hands, your fingers — I want to be like a ring on them. Like the rings of planets, like I've been searching for you all of my life. And it's destroying me, you're destroying me.' A flaring urge, to feel the inside of the other again, whipped him. "You're becoming like God."

"Oh, you really think so?" Lucifer kissed Baal's jaw. "Thank you."

It was far for a walk; countless faces peeked out from behind window curtains as terror overtook the streets, spreading as an ink blot, ushered in along with the first night in Heaven. A few angels called out to him, thinking maybe Father's favorite knew what was happening, but Lucifer replied with a dismissive wave. Even still, some went to walk behind him — admirers and the feeble-minded and the bird-killers. It was overwhelming; this trait of leadership Lucifer hadn't realized he held — so obvious on him that all the angels flocked to him for guidance, the mark of a king, the first spectacle of a deity. There was bile in his mouth, but it was good, it was metallic, but it was good, he would make it good.

Soon yet: an angel flew to Lucifer, stammering with news of something, confusion wobbling over his words so that he was incomprehensible until Lucifer snapped at him to speak clearly. Lucifer recognized it was one of his neighbors. Orcus.

In the southernmost house in Heaven, Phanuel shook Michael awake with a kind laugh. "Are you okay, brother? Should I get us some water?"

Michael groaned but made no move to sit up on the bed. "What time is it?"

"Mm, not sure," said Phanuel, as there was no clock in the room and all the curtains were drawn to drown them in darkness. "Are you feeling any better?"

The grunt from him, tired and rolling, was enough of an answer, but Michael still replied, "Not particularly."

"Then I'll stay with you here." Phanuel patted his friend's shoulder. "But I can get more wine if you like."

"We've already had too much."

"That's true." Phanuel shifted where he was, then flopped to lie beside the archangel again. This was the position in which he had slept, slept after having spent so long comforting the chief prince of Heaven, who was allegedly the same Michael as his friend here. Mundanely, Phanuel had arrived much earlier, whistling, only to return a jug he'd borrowed some time ago, only to discover Michael on the floor, sobbing into his hands like he'd been born minutes ago. "Are you planning to sleep some more or just lie here in the dark?" Michael had never cried before him; Phanuel was sure Michael had never cried at all.

"My eyes are closed, but I'm awake. I might fall back asleep soon."

"Are you ready now," Phanuel asked carefully, weighing each word, "to tell me what happened?" He drummed his hands on his belly, something he did occasionally, but it was wrong; he wasn't wearing his rings. They had disappeared, a few days ago, all by themselves, because every angel he'd asked said they hadn't seen them.

"If I could explain it to you, I would." Michael took a deep, shallow breath, then turned onto his side, away from the other.

"It really worried me." Phanuel set his hand against the space between Michael's wings, and he patted him there, humming softly. "To be honest, I don't think I've ever seen any angel cry like that before. There's not a lot to be weeping over in paradise, I suppose." When the other didn't reply, he rambled, "Once, on Earth, I saw a family of beasts leave behind a little one, and I heard it shriek before it was crushed by a stampede. I always thought they were threatening us, cursing us, when they make all those noises but now," 'that infant creature, all our stars reflected in its eyes, before its skull sunk into itself like a raisin,' "they're crying, aren't they? That's what they do all the time — cry and eat one another. I can't stop thinking about how it must feel to know nothing except that you can die." He knew that Michael didn't think the beasts felt; he didn't know why he was saying this. He had been meaning to connect it somehow, something about crying and misery, something there was none of in Heaven.

"I fought with Lucifer."

Phanuel chuckled before he could stop himself. He'd wondered if this was about Lucifer somehow, it always was. A part of him wanted to lightly slap his friend on the head and scold him. 'Where is the proud, strong angel I've always known? What has Lucifer done to him?' "Who was at fault, you or that angel?"

Michael mumbled, "I think it was me."

At the center of Heaven — Orcus explained to Lucifer that, maybe an hour ago, two, he'd been alerted by the sounds of struggle and shouting from inside Rosier's house. He wouldn't have cared so much if the noises weren't so rare from this home in particular. He knew Rosier and Lucifer decently, knew they weren't the kind to break out into arguments, nor the type to wrestle recklessly. When there was a particularly loud crash, he finally rose from his seat, concern trickling from his brow. He went outside but didn't see anything except the sky being consumed by a sprawling darkness. Fearfully, he stopped, then heard yet another clang from the house, and his heart pounded once, twice. Something was wrong, he felt, incredibly wrong. He hurried to the door, noting it was open wide.

And though Orcus wouldn't know this, Rosier thought of the silence that struck him like a slash and settled coolness over the air. He shifted on the mattress, hearing the squelch of blood as it trickled from his skin and the crunch of his soaked clothing. His fingers began to run through Asmodeus' hair, comfortingly, just because he didn't know what else to do.

Asmodeus was deliriousness, the desire to move but inability to. His mouth moved, but no sounds spilled out from his lips, and he would think, would think, would glance, question where his voice had always come from.

Rosier felt the weight of a head against his chest.

Orcus made it to the doorway beside the kitchen, stopping there. A pool of redness on the bed was first to catch his eye — Rosier sitting amid, like a water lily in a pond, all his drapery clawed open. Calling his name, Orcus moved toward the angel in the shadows, but soon saw that Rosier held a person, a limp body whose head rested on the angel of fruit's chest, almost affectionately. And Orcus noticed Rosier's eyes, all the light in them burnt out, fierce flames all dwindled to reveal rocky coals beneath, gray and jagged. All the expression had fallen from his face and into the blood. He stared forward.

Rosier stared at a wall, remembering having tried to paint a meadow on it once before becoming frustrated and giving up with a little huff.

Orcus lost his balance and tumbled against the door, reeling in a breath. It was Asmodeus' body in Rosier's hold — mangled and with the head nearly detached. Rosier's own head was clouded in tangles of hair clumped with blood — Orcus thought, 'Six wings,' — the remnants of feathers still littered around, many darkened by crimson. They must've sprung out from Rosier's temples, spine, and his feet — the signs of an unstable seraph, obscuring power beneath a blanket of flesh.

Asmodeus was stuck in the past; he'd never gotten used to time, he once said. Him, climbing onto the mattress, putting his hands on Rosier, who kicked, asked what he was doing. Asmodeus whispering for Rosier to not be afraid. Rosier — leaning back and feeling himself be touched, then shaking his head, saying he didn't want this. Asmodeus — listening to the drag of clothes pushed apart beneath his hands. Too hasty, too desperate — the trance on him like those Lucifer cast to make the angels on the street cheer for God. When Rosier, in terror, tore through his own body and attacked Asmodeus with all his wings and flames and eyes — thousands of them — it must have been divine retribution.

Rosier had found his flesh soon thereafter, tugged it back on, and sat, pulling closer his friend ripped into something anew. But, because he was still no more than an angel, whose hearts were plum soft, there was instant regret: 'You took my legs and spread them.' Wearily, he looked at Orcus, who was running back out, sprinting like he'd seen a beast. 'You wouldn't speak to me. I didn't recognize you.' Maybe all the angels were really beasts. 'I'm sorry. Forgive me. I forgive you. I'll put you back together again.'

Lucifer didn't understand; he stared at Orcus, waiting for this story to be explained, but the angel said nothing else, overtaken by his trembling. All the beautiful angel could do, then, was move, feet sizzling on the gilded street, turn around, wander away in silence. His pulse bled from his ears. Angels called after him, hurried to reach him, but the knocking of Lucifer's knees was too much. Wings sprouted from his back instead, and he launched himself into the sky.

It all looked different, when it was dark, when Father was gone. It had become the black abyss, freckled and scratched by all the stars and their adornments — some with 20 planets, half precious stones and half turbulent perfumes, and 300 moons, and singing comets dancing along the suns' crowns.

'siblings, are you still there, i want to talk to you now.'

One of Lucifer's other three faces thought, 'nostalgia will tempt you,' and another, 'you will live a hundred million years,' the third, 'and spend the rest looking back.' 'before god, when you thought you were alone, you were happy, weren't you?' 'the painted walls you tore down, the roads you chipped away, they'll eat away at you, the lingering feelings of a warm hand on your waist, the taps of your feet as you dance, the beats of your timbrel.' 'and now you are like Gods, sparkling brilliant with jewelry that worships you, and you're splitting in order to create.' 'The tosses of your wet hair, the rushes of chariots speeding past, the holy, holy, holy lord god of hosts, the sweetness of a strawberry, knocks against the window by your head, the little tunes of your pipes, the cuts sliced into your fingers by uptight cacti, the brisk scent of a sea crashing into the rocks, the sweat of wrestling, onions, cumin, parsley in a metal jug, mud clinging to your skin, a friendly mouth on your cheeks then forehead, chimes, chirps of chatter in the bazaar, amen, amen, the plump fish rushing to take the bread you toss, scraping of a carpenter, the hiss of chalk, the wisps of clouds cradling you as you nap, the splashes of water in a hot pool, the picnic in a meadow, the pounding of feet that are chasing you, the velvet of petals rustling you awake, a giant water lily beneath you, the innocent kiss, the sprawl of the universe reflected in your eyes for the first time, the bloody wings that shred out of your back, the apples in orchards, a basket of stained flowers, excited chants of a stadium audience, the heat of spinning and bouncing to drums and claps, the love braided into your hair, the trickles of a piano, smell of myrrh, the scratches of a spoon in a cup, the coarseness of a carpet, the stringed instruments and trumpets, the serene smile of not knowing, the sleeping angel, the delight of a creator, the amusement of gossip, the rumbling laughter between shy singing, the tangling of legs, squash, celery, carrot, and chayote, the swirled face paint, the warmth of honey in your tea, the timid face in the mirror, mahogany beams, the embrace of a bed of flowers, the taste of a grape as its fed to you, the lip smacks of an angel as you feed him a raspberry, the first dizziness of alcohol, the cool water and scent of natron and the scratch of the rock you beat your dirty clothes against, the strain of your arms, the columns of an entrance, the high ceilings of a dark cathedral, the boiling surface of bubbling stew, the burn of stained-glass, the little joyous jump you do seeing bread rise, the silky taste of olive oil, the lap of an angel humming as he embroiders a little fox into his tunic, the softness of browned feathers lulling you to sleep, the weight of a dozen blankets and pillows on your small bed, the proud smile on the other side of a window in a newly-finished building, the myrtle trees only you two know about, the palm of god as he fashions you from threads of copper, his praises, his love, his kiss to your hair, your father'

Lucifer settled on the very top of the Fountain of Life, then nearly withered over it, feeling a drought inside, empty inside. He remembered Rosier, the angel who'd laid in bed with him and wiped his tears and held his hand in his youth, an unimportant angel, an angel whom God had never the mercy to even meet. His friend. He had friends. A hand raised to Lucifer's sternum, the same chest Rosier had once patted idly, now feeling like it was sinking into itself. The crush of pain was so much it softened into the sensation of blood dragging out of his body, into the air, smoking away, and he forced himself to see eyes among it, as if he were creating more angels, as if he were God.

What tumbled out of his mouth first was a laugh, throaty and guttural, rasping up into delightful mania — and it made no sense for him, why all the horror twisted into exultant humor. He threw his head back and did it, and it was loud enough that some angels began to step out of their houses, joining Baal and all those who had followed Lucifer. They watched him, but Lucifer didn't bother to see what might be in their eyes; he pulled in a sharp breath, shuddered, felt something inside rip, like when Father had torn out his voice. Like Father and him, on the bed of flowers.

He screamed in agony, wailing, choking on it, sobbing more than he ever had, more than he ever would again.

'you birthed lies shrieking and convulsing'

'nostalgia will lie to you'

CHAPTER 36

Third, he sang. It was the most natural thing he could do, so he did it, finding an angry ballad budding, then blooming from his mouth. Even without instruments, using only those within his body, without words, he explained everything to all the angels who had gathered around the center for him. Thinking of all those years he wasn't allowed to communicate, of how he expressed himself with noises that had no coherence but were bloated with meaning — it was this song that drew nearly every angel from their home. They whispered his name, rushed to the fountain, and many appeared to crave ministering to him already, wanting to coo and kiss God's most beloved angel. One third of those who'd gathered began to sing too, and their conjoined cantina smoldered with fury, wrath.

Lucifer breathed; he raised his voice to all the faces that looked up to him, "Look at how our Father has abandoned us." His pulse throbbing in his head — he tried to pull more air into his mouth as he straightened his back, raised his chin. "Take a look at how such a great and almighty God reacts when an angel dares to question His right to be King." His spit became venomous. "This is the being that calls Himself our God? Our Father? Look," and he flung an arm across, "at how He runs away like an animal, rather than face me when I demand from Him, 'Give me one reason to worship you!'"

Gabriel, among the crowd, crushed between two taller angels, stared upward, and his face became paler than lilies. He wobbled, nearly collapsed, but one of the strangers at his side tried to argue, "He created us!"

"Do we ask the fruits or the flowers, that we," Lucifer spat it, and some angels startled, "have planted and grown, to worship us? Do we demand the towers and bridges we've built to sing our praises forever? Do we say to our wine, 'Kneel and beg for mercy?'" Gratification butterflied on Lucifer's tongue, made him grin, as the crowd replied to him, saying they didn't. "Because we're so above these things that we do not need, do not even desire, to be venerated by them. If God is so all-powerful, then what does He gain from our servitude? What does one derive from subjugating meek, tiny creatures? Do any of you see dignity in punishing a rose that cannot defend itself from you?"

Swallow, as he saw some, plenty, of his listeners begin to shift, to glance at one another, ask themselves why they had never considered this.

"Oh," Lucifer laughed, taunting the sky, "our *great* and *powerful* Father cannot serve Himself a drink. He cannot feed Himself. He cannot sing for Himself or even wash His own feet." Small amusement chuckling about, quiet and ashamed. "That must be it, right, brothers? Or else why hold us captive, all to Himself, and just for Him, because it's forbidden to love one another more than we do Him. *Why*? All that I have ever wanted to know is why."

He turned, looking at each face staring up at him, and he stopped, when he thought he saw a familiar angel in the crowd, one who had accompanied Lucifer the first time he went to visit the Lord.

Lucifer spoke, slowly, "What is our purpose? To carry out Father's will? If He cannot carry out His own, then is He really so almighty? If Father claims to own us because He made us, then do we not own Heaven? Look around. See everything that *we* have done, and look above at the stars, and think to yourselves: 'Why do I worship this God?'"

Someone called out, again: "But He is good."

"Are we not also good?" Lucifer countered, and the angels kept looking among themselves, and the signs of rebellion brewed, restless.

"What are you suggesting we do?" It was Baal.

"I want paradise," Lucifer said, and it was a confession, really. He could imagine it perfectly: all the leisure of before, with the added pleasures that escaped the boundaries the Lord had set, rebuilding the city, perhaps turning it so the south became the north, perhaps founding another Heaven on Earth and on every planet there was. They would find a way to make more angels, and if there began to be so many the universe grew heavy, then they would just create another.

It would all be possible, once God was dead, once Lucifer sat on the Throne, once he harnessed his capabilities and Michael's. Michael. He nearly screamed: 'Where is Michael?'

"We," he almost stuttered, trying to continue, "deserve a paradise that's for us, by us, not Father's, not created on His terms. If the princes are angels, then why can we not have a king? An angel-God would know us, understand us." The murmurs of the crowd encouraged him. "Our Creator gives us love and paradise in return for our captivity, but we do not need Him. We never have." Then, he said, loud, almost shouting: "And so I ask you, brothers, why do we take it? Why do we bow our heads? Why do we worship this God?" There was nodding now, agreeing, and Lucifer giggled a bit, this time. "Look at how He has run, just from me — if all of us stood together, stood up against Him—"

And a cheer erupted from growing portions of the listeners, as they began to swell with pride and confidence at the angel of worship's words.

"Imagine no God!" This time, louder, and Gabriel began to tremble, taking a half-step back, wondering what was happening, how this was all happening. He had to leave; he had to find Raphael, Uriel, Michael. Where was God? Had He really abandoned them? Why was it dark? 'These angels are standing too close, it's getting harder to breathe. I have to escape. I have to run away and find the others.' "Imagine a King that is one of us! Imagine everything. Imagine it as ours!" Gabriel shook his head, wanting to shout denials; 'Lucifer, what has happened to you? This can't be true. I don't want it to be — you're supposed to be perfect, you're His favorite. The Lord told me, as He made you.' "We can have it all. We only have to seize it!" A shock of ovation burst out from all the angels now, and Lucifer's delighted laughter danced upon the fists raised into the air.

And a chuckling, knowing admirer called out, "But which of us will be the new king?"

A curled smile before Lucifer shrugged; angels were intelligent, maybe not as much as him, but they were. "Well, what do all the angels say?"

"Be our king, Lucifer!"

"The most perfect!"

"The most beautiful!"

"Our beloved Lucifer!"

"King, king, king!"

'They adore me. I didn't even have to suggest it; it came from their mouths so naturally that it becomes obvious that the Throne belongs to me, that Father's time on that Throne was not so eternal, after all. And I think of Rosier — I will make it up to you, I will give you everything. I will punish Asmodeus. I will cast Father down to live among beasts, and Michael will travel to Earth with me again, and we will slice off His head. And we will be free. I will rule, and all will be well.' 'Nostalgia.' 'It will all be better than before.' 'I can do it. Only I can do it. I am the greatest angel.' An elated smile. "Would you all really have me?"

King Lucifer. God Lucifer. It sounded right, like Lucifer had become complete, finally.

Among the cheers, he said, "Then go out and scorch Heaven to its roots," exhilaration making him spin to try and see everyone before him, "so that we can build it anew. Go out and tear down the walls, so that we aren't bound." A blur of movement, and he glanced down, and he saw who he'd thought it was, and simmering infuriation grew hot, wild, in an instant. "Look there, it's one of the princes." All eyes landed on Gabriel, who was pushing through, trying to escape the tide of the crowd. "Running away like his King." Laughter, boisterous and taunting — a kind of which angels had never really done, not before today — before Gabriel attempted to unfurl his wings, but hands reached out and took him.

"Lucifer!" Gabriel couldn't delay this confrontation anymore, whipping around to try and escape the grips on his arms, clothes, wings. "End this charade now!"

"There is no charade." Lucifer finally stepped off the fountain, tilting his wings so that he could glide down gracefully to land upon the water, where all the flowers that normally bloomed out from the ripples had all dried, deprived of light as they were. He put one bare foot on the edge of the fountain, hopped off, and the angels moved, parting, creating a circle so that Lucifer could speak directly to Gabriel, who was held in place for him. "There is just me, now, your new king."

"You're no king. You're an angel!" Gabriel shook his head, hair tousling, and he trembled, so much and so consistent he might have been shivering from cold. "Repent, I'm begging you. Ask Father for forgiveness. You don't know what you're doing." Lucifer crept toward him, thinking, 'I thought you loved me, Gabriel, I thought you would understand me. You told me you foresaw great things for me. Is this not great to you?' "Please, Lucifer, please."

He punched Gabriel, hard, across the face.

Lucifer heard the gasps, before the tingling sensation in his knuckles came to him, before the strike registered in his mind, before the archangel's face did — eyes wide, pleading, red-pinkness spreading on all the pale parts of him, terror flooding in. It was deeply, gutturally, unsettling to see it, for even the angel of worship; one of the angels that had been holding Gabriel jumped away, but the other two remained. Of them, one had killed the sparrow, and the other was a part of the choir in Eden. Breathing, very violently aware that he was breathing, Lucifer said back, "Please what, Gabriel?" It came to him, as his fist stayed curled tight, that Michael had taught him how to punch, he had taught him how to fight. Where was Michael? "You want me to fly up into the universe, find God, beg and whine for His mercy and love?"

Baal grimaced as he watched Lucifer level another hit against Gabriel's face. But he couldn't deny it to himself — something about seeing this made him feel right, made him feel like Lucifer was on the winning side of the battle, like Lucifer was powerful and so his angels were powerful. King Lucifer — 'it really does sound nice.'

"You want me to forget all of this, to pretend everything is beautiful and pure and perfect?" Lucifer was getting warmer, his entire blood rising and steaming out from his tear ducts. "He is the one who should be asking for forgiveness, for what He did to our oldest, for what He has done to us — treated us like submissive animals!" A third punch, so hard against Gabriel that it nearly sent him to the floor — instead, blood shot out of his mouth, spewed out onto the golden street — now dark gold, the radiance of Heaven gone, everything dark. There was some fright again, but noises of awe too — the city beginning to split. "Fine then. You, who adore and trust our Father so much — just sit there and take it, like you told me to do! And trust that this is part of His *loving, almighty* plan!" Stepping back, he turned to those around. "Make him suffer."

"Lucifer," Gabriel cried, "stop, stop, please."

'I waited for you your touch to save me you'

"Think of all those times he's annoyed you with inane orders from God," Lucifer said, moving away, so that his angels could take over, and they did, stepping toward the quivering prince, "and show him there are much worse things than death."

Because God had left, because the angels had only known goodness to be obedience, they did as told.

Lucifer didn't look back as he heard the thumps of someone following his lead, rushing forward to hit Gabriel, and neither did he look as Gabriel began to cry out in pain, still trying to reason with Lucifer, telling him to look at him, to stop, to ask for forgiveness. Lucifer didn't. He walked towards one of the angels he recognized from Eden, one from his choir, Ishtar, someone who loved him. He leaned close and noted the blush crawl along the angel's face. "Have you brought your timbrel? May I borrow it?"

Lucifer smiled as the instrument was nervously, but promptly, pressed into his hands; the weight was off, and the material was different, and it jangled a bit differently than his own, but it would do. "Are — Are you going to sing again?"

"You'll do it with me, won't you?"

"Yes." So quick it seemed to surprise Ishtar himself.

Lucifer beat the timbrel with a little huff. "This is a glorious moment, after all." Once again, he looked at some of those around, though avoided Gabriel's on-going torment. "We've already won this war, brothers. Let's celebrate as we rebuild, shall we?" A few cheered, a few laughed, one calling out for Lucifer to dance too. "Of course, and let's collect all the precious stones, from the walls and from all the jewelry, and hoard them. Gather all the liquor in Heaven so we can drunken." Chuckling, cheering, and someone had begun to beat a drum along with him. "Torture all those who resist the new kingdom of Heaven. And let's sin and let's sing, for ourselves this time, as we destroy this worthless, God-damned city."

'Yes, Lucifer.' 'Whatever you say, Lucifer.' 'Lucifer, stop, please stop, stop, stop.' Half of his army had already begun to scatter, laughing, finding oils and tearing down trees so they would have bark to create bonfires with. Flinging angels out of their homes, they told them about sin, forced wickedness onto their hands, tempted their mouths to skin curiously. And then the twist — they began to wonder where kindness was, where it was inside them — looked for it, fucked for it, with knives, with nails. They mutilated, to the brink of not-death, something worse, inescapable. They ripped each other's teeth out and plucked eyeballs free to squash, discovered agony. Chewing at flesh, they searched for the bodies beneath, where there were supposed to be more wings, and they stared at blood, colored and heated as flames. Fire, coming from flesh.

They stole, tore every painting off the walls, they pillaged, they sacked each home until it was stripped and the walls watered to pebbles. They ate, they lied, they laughed and laughed — in between it, they cried. God was missing. It was the most free many of them had ever been, the most joyous ever in paradise, after paradise. Some, still, murmured to be forgiven, said that they knew not what they did. 'Anything you want.' 'We love you, Lucifer, we would do anything for that smile.' 'You make me feel powerful.' 'He gives me purpose, finally, I have one.' 'King.'

And at the center of Heaven, at the Fountain of Life that was being triturated to waste, too, Lucifer sang delightfully with the other half of his army, who tortured Gabriel and all who resisted and were thrown at them to be devoured. He danced, they all danced — feet drumming on the ground — among the flames climbing high around them, spreading to throw themselves onto their world. Passing chalices, cups, bowls of alcohol, around, breaking their adornments, stomping on them — the screams became music too. All the angels fought over Lucifer, who had found dancing up against their bodies was fun and also tremendously hilarious. He couldn't stop *laughing*, couldn't stop grinning — the arousing pleasure of power, rippling into arrogance — until he broke away from them with a stumble.

The first war — unlike any of those that will follow, but with that recognizable plunge, the pit of ash. The return to ash.

Lucifer ordered, "Find all the archangels, bring them here so that we can torture them." And then, he amended that, "But leave Michael to me. I'll go get him myself."

An admirer, named Mammon, asked him if they should keep torturing Gabriel, and all the other rebels among them, including a young, terrified one named Dina, and Lucifer said yes.

"Don't let me down," Lucifer began, "and if you're a good, sweet beast for me, I'll reward you well." He could do nothing but snicker as the other straightened up in excitement, anticipation. Lucifer tugged on a number of arms, including Baal's, and commanded them to follow. And as they moved out from the chaos of the center into the disorder of the roads, he thought, 'See? I'm a good king, this is goodness.'

Lucifer had no idea who he was trying to defend himself to.

CHAPTER 37

Michael had fallen — back asleep — but a heavy sleeper he'd never been. When Phanuel heard the first hints of laden wrongness in the air, the prince and him both started. The archangel seemed to break through his misery in an instant and scampered toward one of the windows, his muscles, shoulders, visibly tensed. He latched onto the curtains and split them so that they could meet the light of Heaven. On the contrary, night faced them — brought none of the brilliance they had earlier concealed to sleep. "What?" left Phanuel's mouth. "Where—?"

Michael was completely frozen, a statue, not unlike those in the garden Phanuel had seen outside a gallery somewhere.

"Where is the light?" Phanuel finished; he didn't know why. What he really meant to ask — 'Where is Father?' — he couldn't do. Instead, he went to every curtain, one by one, and they all came down to pool the floor, revealing that the cosmos were low, dribbling down like thick paint. The ochre firmament that cradled Heaven safely had disappeared, as if misplaced, so only the stars sparkled some light, but it was barely enough to shimmer the sea. "Something happened."

What else could he say? Phanuel had no choice but to say it again, turning around, in every direction, feeling his heart pick up its pace in his chest, knocking him as if on the back of the head, telling him to go off and do something, 'but what, what?'

"Michael," he blurted, except the other was stuck petrified. "Michael." The neighbors, their houses — Phanuel's breath hitching as he saw flames cast upon them, rapacious.

"Outside," Michael ordered and immediately moved away from Phanuel's side, took a robe draped over a chair, tugged it on. In the living room, he saw the archangel take his sword.

Lucifer saw eyes in the debris. The piles, lining the streets, spilling onto it, were composed of the slabs of walls knocked to the ground, various ingredients and spices, torn blankets and carpets, the tiles of floors, the columns of buildings, the mosaics, the paintings and all the statues, pots of every kind, of shrub or tree or flower, the sorts angels excessively decorated their homes with. They swirled all together, so nothing could ever be separated anymore, and the debris became one body of a misshapen abomination, a stew. The eyes sprinkled upon them blinked at Lucifer, but they said nothing, because all put together, these million trinkets became alive enough to see, but not to speak. It reminded Lucifer of something, and then it didn't.

He turned his face forward; he saw destruction as he moved between it, as if he were splitting a sea. His army allowed him through: they grinned at him when he passed, they cheered, they, maybe in the midst of strangling a fellow angel, would see their king, and they would sigh his name in the first amore.

'But I'm sick of the name that God gave me.' Lucifer thought he might have to come up with a new one, sometime soon, after every last remnant of Heaven was destroyed, and they could begin rebuilding. It wouldn't be long now. He would find Michael, reassure him, and they together would go to the Throne. If Father was there, they would face Him, and if He wasn't, they would sit. It wouldn't be long now, all the archangels were weak — Gabriel was weak, Raphael was weak, Uriel was weak — the only one who could hold his own against an army was Michael, but Michael was on Lucifer's side. Of course he was. Lucifer swallowed. The rocky cliffs of the southernmost point of Heaven began to rise on the horizon, among the falling celestial spheres, the jewels and perfumes of the stars.

"If anyone is with Michael," Lucifer said lowly, "seize and take them to the Fountain of Life."

Of the six angels who followed him, the one who'd joined his side of the battle a mere few minutes ago, searching purpose, finding it in the charming angel who called himself king, said, "Yes, Lucifer."

Baal asked, "Will we bring Michael to be tortured along with the other archangels?"

"Michael will decide that for himself." Lucifer hopped over a stray pillar that had fallen onto the street, and he watched the fires consume indiscriminately, tumbling on both the rebels and his army alike, who shouted and scrambled to escape. "He has always stood by me, and if he chooses to continue that trend, then I will have," and a pause — Lucifer wasn't sure yet if the others would accept Michael as a fellow king, "the strongest angel there is on our side. If there's any confrontation between us and Father, then the winner is decided."

Baal, once more: "But what if Michael doesn't surrender to you?"

"Michael will surrender to me."

"Are you sure?" The angel of flight stepped a bit closer. "He's proud."

"I'm prouder." Lucifer heard them laugh. "And Michael adores me." 'He knows me, he trusts me.' "He wouldn't hesitate to place me before God." 'He already has.' "But," Lucifer was not an idiot, as much as he would love to be, as much as it would have saved him to be, "in case he betrays me and you must seize him, I'll offer you a sign."

"What will the sign be?"

Michael shouted at the chaos, and all the angels, rushing out from the homes and scattering everywhere like insects, stopped. Those who were the perpetrators of the violence did too, but they didn't dare confront Michael. Looking at one another, they turned and flew away quickly, as most didn't have swords with them, and even if they did, a brawl with Michael was frightening enough they didn't consider cooperating in an attack. Watching the maybe twenty arsonists, defacers, bolt away, Phanuel noticed twelve angels who remained, loyal to the hidden Father still. They made their way to Michael quickly, yelling all at once, saying a hundred things about not understanding, about how many of their own brothers, their own housemates, had joined in the disorder after being told of God's abandonment.

And they spoke of something called sin.

Phanuel had never heard of such a word and turned his head to ask the archangel, but 'a hitched breath, a bolt of terror on your face.' "What's wrong, Michael? What is that?"

Lucifer saw the commotion as he neared the initial slope up to Michael's home, against the rocky shore overlooking water. He remembered seeing his reflection in it, and then Michael's, as the older angel stood closer to peer at the sea too. 'Rosier said once that we completed each other, I don't remember when.' Michael had met his eyes in the sinuous mirror, and he had smiled, and Lucifer had smiled back, softly. Their faces, beside one another, then sharing a peck of a kiss; the two of them perfect, more perfect than God.

'Jealous God,' the angel mocked. 'Jealous God. Jealous God! All-knowing creature who can never know devotion.' Never a fond kiss, nor a desiring touch. 'Does the Lord envy us this? Is it sin to love? Can it be death?' This would be His death, the proud angel decided; Lucifer would bring out the envy of God, burn Him in it.

Now — he saw Michael among a mob of hysterical angels, one of which had crumbled to the floor. At his side, Phanuel stood. Lucifer didn't react, not initially, but then his gut felt gripped, pulled out. His eyes widened, before squinting, a scalding taking a mouth twitching to shriek in fury. 'Why are you with that angel, Michael? Why not me? Why were you with him, not me? You should have been with me at the center.'

The two finally met each other, and Lucifer wondered what he looked like — perhaps disheveled, likely exhilarated, like a king with the world falling apart in flares behind his head, so he appeared to have a halo. "Michael." Lucifer moved until he was close enough to reach out, to be struck by Michael's sword. His breath spilled out of his mouth and shattered in between them; Michael was watching him with muddled eyes, a twitching brow, sorrow. "He abandoned us."

"What did you do?" Phanuel said.

Lucifer didn't have the patience for this; he waved a hand, as if sweeping the air. "Baal, take Phanuel. You know where."

"Yes, Lucifer." Baal went to grab Phanuel's upper arm tight, tugged on him violently, then took him with both hands. When the angel struggled, Baal matched it.

Michael stepped forward, but Lucifer did as well, touching his friend's wrist and smiling, saying, "It's alright, Michael. He'll be safe." He knew the other didn't know what a lie was and felt the archangel lose his tension.

Looking to Phanuel, Michael nodded at him, and Phanuel hesitated but stopped resisting soon after. He grunted and rolled his shoulders, snapping at Baal to tell him where to go. Baal responded to follow him, and his massive, dusk-dark wings shot out from his back. He leapt upwards and Michael's friend, anxiously, also took to the sky. Watching them, Lucifer felt that he should giggle to himself, but it wasn't fun to lie to Michael. 'You're not like the others to me. You know that. I've told you that.'

They looked at each other again, Michael's eyebrows furrowed in concern and uncertainty, and Lucifer spoke, "Where have you been?"

Michael snorted, seemingly before he could stop himself. "Sleeping." He stood his sword down by a foot, holding the handle tight.

"Well, you've always been a deep sleeper."

A little titter of amusement. "You're mistaken."

"It must just be with me then," Lucifer teased, naturally, as they always did, and let his touch drift away from the other. "You missed the end of the world."

Seriousness crawled, slow, back onto Michael's face, as if he didn't want it to. "Where is Father?"

"I told you. He's left."

"Where has He gone? Why would He leave us? Have you checked in Eden? Have you checked His Throne? And—" He gestured. "What about all this destruction? And what of—" A roof, nearby, creaked and crumbled to its floor. "The angels, Lucifer. They told us the perpetrators were speaking of something called sin."

Lucifer swallowed; an elaborate lie formed in his mind. He could say, 'No, they're wrong! Michael, come with me, let's find the Throne! Let's look for God. Oh no, He's attacking me, please save me! Ah, and now He's dead! We could replace Him. We will have to.' But it was impossible — 'not you, Michael, I can't do it, Michael, Michael, I want to be honest with you, only you, look me in the eyes. I can see ambition, I know I can, I know it's there.' "I told you," his uneven voice replied, "about sin."

"Tell me what it is. Be clear with me." His tone had become sharp, like a whip, his gaze shooting between the angels that stood behind the new king. "Look at the sky, Lucifer." 'There is no sky anymore. It's our brothers, coming down, asking us to wake them, because God is gone now.' "This sin, whatever you call it, it's destroying everything—"

"As of now," Lucifer replied slowly, "we cannot create from nothing. If we plan to remake the fabric of the universe, we'll need to melt it all down, and then put it into molds. Everything will become unrecognizable soon, but it's okay, Michael." A smile. "When everything is rebuilt, it will all be more beautiful than before. Trust me."

Grimace. "I asked you what sin is."

Lucifer hesitated, felt the gaze of angels on his back, those who followed him and those who followed Michael, judging, listening. "Let's step inside for a moment, Michael. I need to speak to you. Alone."

The archangel opened his mouth, but whatever he wished to say must've died on his tongue. He moved his jaw, glanced away, and said, in a rapid, tight voice, "Make this quick." He turned, lifted his sword again, and moved past the gate to his house, not turning to check if Lucifer followed.

The angel of beauty shivered, feeling so incredibly cold without warning, feeling like all his soul had left him, and now he was only flesh, seeking embrace, seeking warmth. Lucifer waved for his army to hold off, for just a minute or two, before stepping forward, making his way up the staircase. And he remembered, long ago, welcoming guests into Michael's home from there, for a little party Lucifer had spent so much time planning. A quivering smile on his lips; 'When this is over, I'll host another celebration. It'll be fun. We'll all be really happy.'

"Talk to me," Michael said, by the structure of the sun in the living area, his sword once again stood by his feet. He stared back at him, everything and nothing in his eyes. "Explain yourself. This sin."

Lucifer took a moment to settle, to recover, before laughing soft and admitting, "It doesn't have a good definition, but you know that disobeying Father used to be unthinkable — so I made a word for it. That's all it is. The simple act of disobeying. God says be kind, but we choose sin instead. He says be pure, but we choose sin instead. Everything He demands, its opposite is sin." A shaky breath tumbled out. "It couldn't be simpler."

"But to disobey like this? This is too much, too far." Michael shook his head, slow, as if it pained him. "Let's look for God and speak to Him. I don't want any of this destruction. I need every angel safe. All I see this *sin* doing is spreading pain and misery."

'No, no, no, no—' Lucifer rushed to him, took Michael's face quickly and nearly burst into tears right then. "That isn't true, Michael. It doesn't have to be. It's only independence, rebellion, freedom from Father — sin can be anything we want it to be." He hesitated, seeing that Michael's gaze was still not on him — attached to the floor. "Please, why won't you join me?" As if he'd been sliced, all of him was pouring out, blackened and burning like the debris. "You said I was yours, your beloved Lucifer." And now the entirety of Michael's face was cringing, crumpling up as if he were a frightened shrub; he clenched his jaw.

"I can't."

"Can't what?" Lucifer's thumb swiped across Michael's cheekbone to catch a tear. "You remember what I told you, right?" And slowly, he began to uncoil for him. "The angels trust me. They won't hurt me, they say Lucifer the light-bringer, who will guide us now that Father has turned away and left us in darkness." His voice had fallen soft, caressing the trembling angel of strength. "We could rule together. We could be happy, together."

Slowly, Michael's free arm snaked around Lucifer's waist, hugged him tight, and he lowered his head, away from the younger one's touch. He brought his face to Lucifer's neck, nuzzled him there, and he breathed, loud. The gentle scent of oak — wrapping itself around Lucifer; it had him wish to melt, right there, into nothing in his beloved angel's hold. "*Lucifer.*" The word rumbled.

Smiling, wrapping lithe arms around Michael, whispering, sweetly, "You make me happy. I want to be happy with you forever." They could kiss for eternity, lay with their legs tangled in the heat of any sun, they could take each other's hands and run until the last star burned out.

"I asked the Lord, once, if you were really an angel. I couldn't convince myself you were. You made me feel like no other angel had. And He told me that you were simply Lucifer, His most loved creation. That you were temptation — beautiful, ripe, prohibited above all else." Michael's voice lingered feverish against the skin of Lucifer's throat. "Forbidden fruit." Then, his teeth, pressing down slow, tender, biting.

The forbidden — the only thing an omnipotent God could covet.

Lucifer, eyes fluttering closed, sighed in love with an untranslatable snugness in his chest. The wet of Michael's mouth — baptismal, like it'd save him, and when Lucifer opened his eyes, it would be in bed, somewhere else, to be helped to walk again, to be met again. Do not be afraid, a faceless angel had said, but now he was afraid. He was scared, feeling too small for the beast of his rage. He wanted to touch the paint of the kitchen tiles, again, to be carried to an orchard to pick fruits.

'youre like god. And im really god. reaching into my mouth, tangling my fingers in intestines, tugging them free to simmer formless, forming. a universe, i have it here. feel it. i could make a meadow. for you. here. to be. this body. this mind. the sun. the moon, this mirror, it all becomes a mirror.

father is love. indeed, he is. this is love:

torture and ruin and possession and the dips by Michael's mouth. this, here, disobedience, such a god who adores you and kisses you and calls you creation, what is love if not parting these ribs like a sea and finding fitting you inside. like a pearl. I think we are like gods, and if he comes back, us together can become more, come closer, I want us to embrace until these bodies curl like vines, turn inseparable as debris, knotted together, our mouths interwoven. your divinity in my mouth, your worship salted on my lips. I want to be so close I can read your mind all I want I think: you think: I:

I would do anything to hear your thoughts'

"You've tainted me," the prince grieved, "worse than if..." If what? 'If you'd feasted on me with lust?' "You've spoiled me dirty, ruined me." 'God will never love me again?' And he inched backwards, lips abandoning Lucifer. 'You don't want His love, my angel.' "Forgive me." Michael's weighted gaze lifted. "You're everything to me, the stars and the moons, the heat and the cold, the earth and the seeds, the waters and the flowers, but you are not God."

There was more to say, to confess, but there was no time left; Lucifer heard shuffling by the entrance. He managed, hushed, "Forgive me too," before the front door opened wide and before the prince could react.

Lucifer's lips landed on the archangel's mouth, molding against his as soft and gentle as a wind of cinders. Inside, the faint flowers, now long wilted, withering away finally, fragmenting into cuts of glass, slicing from within. Lucifer kissed Michael, long and forward, miserable, pressing deep to taste his heart; kissing to death.

Kissing as if it were the last thing angel Lucifer would ever do, and it was.

He took Michael's sword, stepped backwards, and Lucifer breathed soft, expelling everything, everything. His adored angel with shattered eyes, left with betrayal slithering into his mouth. Lucifer's army, who'd been waiting, anxiously, for a signal, moving forward to take advantage of the greatest archangel's weakness and grab him.

Lucifer strained, but he dragged the sword with him, and he didn't face Michael, no matter how loud he screamed his name, shouting for him to stop.

CHAPTER 38

Rosier moved through the street, seeing none of it. As if his eyes were closed, he let another sense guide him — touch: when his foot tapped into something in his way, he raised his leg, stepped over the obstruction. The weight he carried in both arms took up his thoughts, not the state of his surroundings, or the sound of pained shrieks that had been entirely unknown to him until today. It was difficult to register; he had no desire to. It had been enough effort stumbling to put on some clean clothes, to face Asmodeus, and even more to walk, to step outside of the house.

When calls of his name came, Rosier didn't hear them. He thought, 'Heavy in my hands, heavy, heavy,' until fingers went around his arm, making him stop, and then Rosier turned his head. He tried to see, barely could.

"Rosier, stay off the road!" It was Azazel, who tugged him quickly along, rushing to take him toward a house whose fires had already died down, having had its meal, content enough to simmer. "What's wrong with you? Have you missed everything? What—" A blink, then slow, shaken — "Your hair."

"I cut it." Rosier didn't realize it was his own voice for a moment, but then he did, and it frightened him. "There was blood in it, and—" 'there were these scissors, cold in my hands, after I dropped my hairbrush.' "And," 'I cried because the clumps wouldn't come out, no matter how hard I tried to wash and comb,' "And," 'I cried because I would be dirty forever,' "And, I—" 'forced myself to snip at the hair I've always known, that will never grow back, so that it would only come here, here, to my shoulders.'

Azazel swallowed, not understanding in the least, but his eyes flickered down. He saw what his friend held in his arms, and his eyes widened before he jumped, stumbled. "Rosier!" Asmodeus' head, mostly cleaned of crimson and half-wrapped in a cloth to cradle the back and leave his face exposed. He was mostly expressionless, with his gaze cast downward, with colorless lips. "What happened? Who did this to him?"

"I did," said Rosier softly, and Azazel's heart stopped. "He tried to hurt me— I didn't mean to attack him, but— I don't know. It didn't make any sense— Nothing really makes sense now, does it?" A wobbling sigh before he glanced down at his friend's head again in his arms and, without thinking, kissed his cheekbone. "But Asmodeus will be okay, won't he? We'll stitch his head back onto the rest of him, and then we'll pretend like nothing happened, right?"

Azazel bit his lip and used the back of his hand to brush Asmodeus' jaw, nodding. "Yes, everything will be fine. It'll all be like before." Still, with his other hand, he pulled Rosier so that they could scoot behind a portion of a wall that hadn't tumbled. He peered through a chip in it, watching as a group of four angels passed by, one of them whistling a little tune.

The legion stopped any vulnerable angel nearby or caught hiding; they demanded to know whether they vowed to stand with Lucifer as king. If they swore, then they let them on their way. If they didn't, they tortured them until they did, or until they went silent from the pain, or until they posed no threat as just a crippled set of broken limbs on the ground.

"Lucifer? King?" Rosier whispered it.

Azazel furrowed his brows; he had just narrowly escaped a brigade himself but was forced to abandon two of his housemates and had been left scrambling to hide by himself, waiting, knowing he'd be caught at any moment. He was already considering surrender; Lucifer's allies seemed to be having fun, and Father was nowhere to be seen, and he didn't want to be hurt. "You don't know anything?" When Rosier shook his head, Azazel sighed, so long he thought he was expelling his soul.

Elsewhere — Raphael hit the ground and opened his mouth to gasp but a cry shot out instead, as a sandaled foot made contact with his lower abdomen. "Hah," flowed out from between his lips, and again, then a hiss as his muscles stung. Unable to stop himself, he thought of the prognosis for a ruptured stomach, and he nearly laughed in his misery. The rope tying his wrists at his back dug into skin, tighter when Raphael tried to break free, and before he could stop himself, he was imagining the advice he'd give to an angel with both wrists broken. None of those thoughts would be useful now; circled around him were so many angels they could have been an ocean, all with grins or broad laughter spilling out at the humiliating state of one of their princes.

Raphael couldn't stand without his walking stick; it had never been a problem before; all the angels had always accommodated it; Raphael had never troubled or even desired to be different. Wiggling backward, he felt an object bump against him. He wasn't alone, and he peered over — "Gabriel," immediately.

The clothing and hair he'd recognize anywhere, but the fellow archangel's face was not Gabriel. It belonged to someone who'd been invaded by red cherries, blackberries, blueberries, a conglomerate of them bursting from his skin — no, not bruises, they couldn't be bruises. Gabriel could never look like that; 'I must have made a mistake.' It was Gabriel. No. From his mouth, his eyes, his nose — rivers of blood, seeping through his tunic. Raphael said his name again, but the other didn't move and continued laying limply on his side; his eyes were open, but barely, and his irises were dead. Cracking, thinking, Raphael was thinking of screaming, of crying and thrashing as all of his heart seemed to surge forward and crash into a wall.

Laughing again. Raphael had begun to tremble horrifically and could hardly meander his body enough to turn his head, but he did. The nose came from the angels parting so that Uriel could pass through — unlike the other princes, he didn't resist, simply walked with his hands bound behind his back, his face polished stone. Slow, he sat down at Gabriel's other side, muttered lowly, "Excuse my absence, I was reading."

Raphael clenched his jaw and whispered, "A thousand angels rushed my house at once. All of them had wounds that weren't natural."

"Yes, it seems we're in a war."

"War?"

"Lucifer made up the word — one of his followers told me." Uriel paused to glance at Gabriel between them, still catatonic. "This is probably a bad time to remind you that I've never been wrong about anything."

"You're right," Raphael grumbled. "It's a bad time."

Uriel chuckled a little and thought to brace himself for the angel nearby who held an ax, but it wasn't long before yet another struggling angel was shoved into their midst. Immediately, he said, "Michael, look at—" Those feather-y layers of hair didn't belong to Michael. "Phanuel?" The angel in question squirmed, attempting to yell through the cloth that had been tied over his mouth, but it all came out muffled, incomprehensible. "What are you doing here?"

Lucifer told all those angels who made frequent trips to Earth to get their swords, if they hadn't already. Then, he returned to the center, dragging the titan one he'd taken from Michael, thinking of the last time he had held it, on Earth, with Michael guiding his grip, reassuring him, advising him. It was a shame, but it would be fine; Lucifer would simply do everything himself, and Michael would have to stay out of the way for now. Michael would love to be a king. He would like it, he had to. There was no choice for him anymore. So — Lucifer dragged the sword, then grunted, lifted, and rested it over his shoulder. It was heavy but manageable.

As he arrived at the plaza where the Fountain of Life had been, Lucifer smiled wide at the sight of the three archangels and Phanuel already restrained, as he'd ordered. The other rebellious angels who'd denied him had been moved elsewhere to be tortured, as well. Delightfully, he saw his victims take note of him, walking forward, between the crowd that split open, some bowing, some cheering, for their beloved king passing through. "Hello there."

"Lucifer," Raphael said, "what have you done? Where is Michael?"

"Oh, he's tired after pleasuring me for so long. Don't worry — he's safe, very happy too." The laughter from the crowd was boisterous, the angels all taking this to mean Michael had been defeated. "Unlike you, Michael's accepted me as king." Lucifer stepped forward, bending to their level. "But I'm merciful. I'm giving you a second chance. Pledge allegiance to me, and you'll be spared from torment."

"But we'll no longer be princes," Uriel said.

"Try not to cry yourself to sleep about it. Relax. Drink a little wine. Choke on some cock or some cunt. Trust me. You'll have a much better time than before; I can assure you that much." Lucifer lifted the sword, placed it beneath Uriel's chin and raised the tip, forced the archangel to tilt his head upward. "Mm, so what do you say? Answer quickly."

"You know my answer."

"Oh? You think I'm really God then? Because only God can read minds."

"The disrespect you have shown — when the Lord returns, He'll unleash wrath upon you, upon all of us because of *you*." Uriel saw the massive grin in the other, all the teeth; it made him think of another angel.

"I won't bow for you either," Raphael interjected. "You're deluding yourself, brother. Stop this. We can still rebuild everything, we can all move on. Please. Gabriel trusted you. He defended you until his voice ran itself out. If not for Uriel and I, do it for Gabriel." 'Who is Gabriel?' "Do it for Michael."

'I am doing it for him. He'll become so powerful, he'll never know why he ever denied it.' Lucifer snickered a little. "To be honest, I was hoping for this." He stepped back and returned the sword to his shoulder, tilting his head. "I'll take my time with each of you, starting with this pretty angel here."

Phanuel raised his head, squirming, trying to sit; Lucifer threw out a kick, striking the other's skull and sending him to the ground again.

A groan through the binding, before a hitched breath as Lucifer stomped his foot down onto his head, digging Phanuel's face into the ground. "You," stomp, "stupid," stomp, "fucking," stomp, "God-damned," stomp, "beast shit." He heard Raphael scream for him to stop, heard the buffered noises of Phanuel's cries. 'You did this. You're why Michael denied me. It had to be you.' He saw it so perfectly in his mind that it had to be true.

Michael telling Phanuel that he regretted his decision, that he was going to apologize to Lucifer. Phanuel saying it was a bad idea. Michael, who would have left to find Lucifer and stood with him in the center, surrendering. This was all wrong because of Phanuel; it was his fault, it was all his fault. It had to be.

Lucifer, so furious now that he was out of breath, removed his foot from the other, then snarled, "Hold him for me." He heaved the sword up and put his free hand near the tip of the blade. Three angels were grabbing Phanuel, forcing him onto his knees, and one of them, Baal, gripped his hair tight by the scalp. Phanuel's nose had already burst, obscured by the blood spewing out. Eyes almost shut, not quite — but what was worse is that there was no anger in them. Sadness.

A million fires might as well have ignited within Lucifer, a ravenous fury that overtook him, made him blind and unreasonable, completely lost to all sense of self, replaced with the desire to hurt, to create pain larger than the universe, larger than his despicable Father. Than what He had done to him, with each embrace, in the cathedral, on that bed of flowers, in paradise.

He brought the edge of the sword to where Phanuel's jawline met his throat and pressed. The skin opened, unfurled. And Lucifer began to saw.

Elsewhere — after Michael's betrayal, the twelve angels nearby scattered at the sound of the prince being restrained, running before they might be caught too. Independently, each of them cried and fell to their knees, praying for the Father to return and save them from whatever had happened, to please return because they didn't know what they had done wrong. But the absence of God was too much to bear alone, and it wasn't long before the angels scampered between the burning carcasses of their homes, searching for any hints of goodness again.

It was after they'd gathered again, hidden by the tall cliffs at the sea, standing over the water, that they tried to conjure any idea of what to do. They looked between each other, and counted themselves off, and with a hearty sigh, one said they had no choice but to fight for Michael to be released from where he was being held captive, maybe tortured, in his house. There were more of them than there were holding the prince; none of the dozen were combative angels, none of them were even wrestlers, but they had to try.

"It's a bad idea," Azazel told Rosier. "Lucifer has died. That isn't him anymore."

"Died?" Rosier repeated it quietly, because he didn't know what that meant; he had never gone to Earth or eaten a fish or allowed a fruit to rot. He'd only ever known monotony, the reassurance of it. "I don't know what you mean. I don't want to. I want to speak to Lucifer."

"No. He'll hurt you."

"Lucifer is my friend."

"He is no one's friend anymore."

Lucifer found it like peeling a citrus — flaying. 'I thought I might see, beneath all the skin, the hundred trinkets the Lord puts inside us — all the flowers, the golden organs, the hidden wings, the folds of the universe — but there's only red muscle, pouring. Flesh, meat, plump and wet rivulets; with no eyelids, you can't blink, Phanuel. Your face, I'm holding it in one hand, thinking about placing it over my own, so I might pretend to be you, just to know what it's like to not be Lucifer. Maybe it's deeper that I have to go to force out all your wings. How many do you have? I have four, Gabriel has six. Phanuel, can you hear me? Are you sorry yet?' They dropped Phanuel, who fell over in weakness, and there were sobs, among the angels, and screams — the shrieks of angels, like their songs turned inside out, a regurgitated meal.

It was a blessing that our Lucifer was so beautiful, or else he might have lost his army in its entirety, instead of only half.

Blind, Lucifer handed Phanuel's face to someone, probably Baal. He moved away, and some of his angels were still unaware, dancing and singing and drinking, and some were perfectly cognizant, morbidly curious at seeing the pain of another, outside sport, outside fun and its consent. The majority, however, had been reduced to terror, absolute, and then the act of running. The gates of Heaven closed and the cosmos above so carnivorous, they could only reach out of the cage in frenzy, stampeding one another. The spew of panic, and the city staring at her body plundered with a gaze that she brought, soon, back to the favorite angel.

This angel, who breathed in, all the fire in his chest becoming warm enough to suffocate him. It was like being drunk, he thought, deliriousness making him wobble and giggle, even with all these pulsing aches inside him, because of them. His disbelief, confusion driving his mind somewhere that bled raw at the loss of innocence — all these things they could do to one another, all the power God had always had, His dreams.

'Does God dream?' Lucifer had asked his other faces once. They said, 'He does. I think He's dreaming now.' 'What is He dreaming?' 'This nightmare.'

Raising the sword again, dripping, 'dripping roses,' Lucifer stepped forward and swung, hardly catching Raphael's horrified expression. He slashed across his face, hoped it would slice him open and that nothing would spill out. Then, he brought the sword down on Raphael's body, stabbed into his chest, heard a gurgled cry, and he did it again. Squelching with each jab, the sword came back up bloodier each time, heavier.

'Beats of music, Father. Everything defiled now. I'm saying something. I don't know what I'm saying. Can you. Return my innocence, open eyes and little smiles. Return my love. My embrace, like the twigs of a nest. I waited for him his touch to save me.'

Uriel, composure finally broken, rasped, "Lucifer, please. Enough."

"I've never been happier," Lucifer seethed, bursting out high laughs in between the tears forcing their escape from the crevices of his eyes. 'Flowers spurting from tears, do you remember?' "Never in my life." And he lifted the sword, ready to cleave Raphael's head off, then maybe Uriel's, thinking maybe he would hang the four mutilated angels on high strings, so that all the last rebels would come out of their hiding and bow for their god and new age. A new civilization.

Instead, a droplet fell onto the top of Lucifer's head, a single one, its consistency too thick. He froze, turned his face upward, as the shower soon tumbled down onto them all — so sudden that everyone stopped. The music halted, everything did; the gaze of every angel climbing up at the universe that had cast on them a rain of scorching, sizzling blood. Arms raised, all at once, to cover their heads, some of Lucifer's army scrambling away to find shelter, desperate for any roof that might remain standing.

"Father," Lucifer said simply. He felt his tunic dampen then stain, the last of the white cloth becoming corrupted by deep redness. "Welcome back."

CHAPTER 39

L ucifer met with the angels who owned swords, a lot more than he'd anticipated — even better, many had fashioned their own quickly or repurposed any knives they owned, axes and mallets, spears, sickles, scythes. After the announcement of Father's return, Lucifer ordered all his followers to prepare for a confrontation calmly, and with a wave of a hand, gestured for the archangels to be taken away. He commanded they be put in the ruins of the bathhouse, because that was probably humiliating. It was difficult to tell; for now, it was difficult to concern himself with anything other than the thousands of angels that were gathered in the largest amphitheater, which had remained relatively intact, likely because it'd been built to withstand the beats of chariots and grand fights.

The downpour of blood had become a soft drizzle.

They stood over the sandy ground, Lucifer walking among them, answering questions about how they ought to swing their weapons and whether their armor would be of any help. There were a few blacksmiths, hard at work heating the metals of jewelry and cutlery until they became soft enough to shape with their anvils and hammers — the metallic strikes rang high in between the chatter, the excitement, and the terror. They hastily put together helmets and cuirasses, then handing them to the whitesmiths, who applied the finishing touches and engraved designs into them. They built scale armor, cuisses, greaves to cover the shins, and rounded shields they could strap to their arms. Every metalworker went to Lucifer, asking him to take the armor they had made for him, saying he would look beautiful in it and powerful. He raised his hand each time, smiled; "Thank you, but take it for yourself."

"Lucifer," Baal warned, "you shouldn't risk fighting without armor. Father will want to punish you the most." 'For freeing us all, and then He'll make us forget you. He'll do everything to make us forget that we can be happy without Him.'

"I'm perfect, Baal. Nothing is going to happen to me." 'If Father won't wear armor to face us, then I won't either. Besides, I look very good in this red tunic.' He laughed a little at his thoughts; 'What else is there to do but laugh?' Various calls of his name turned his head, and Lucifer sighed, quite prepared to turn down whatever he was going to be offered. Instead, it was Moloch, one of his hands gripping Rosier's soft bicep. The smaller angel looked at Lucifer with weighted, curved eyes; in his arms, he cradled a bundle of cloth to his chest.

"He said he wants to talk to you, my king."

Baal immediately turned away, walking over to speak with some soldiers on the other side of the arena, clearly not wanting to be seen by the angel of fruit who had been a dear friend once.

In contrast, Lucifer wasn't a coward; he faced Rosier directly, lifted his chin, and said, "I'll allow it." He walked, keeping his gaze forward as he moved past him. "Follow me." It would be better to escape everything, all the bustling of movement and preparation, just for however many minutes it would take for him to convince Rosier that their Father was a beast. Not turning back, he stepped past columns into the roofed area of the fourth ring corridor, then into the third. He trekked all the way to the second, staring at a mosaic that had been plastered to the wall beside him and stayed, for the most part, unscathed — it depicted a sea and fish among navy blue waves. Before them, Lucifer could see past the archway into the outside, still dark, still in disarray, but quieter now.

"They took Azazel," Rosier's voice filtered out behind him. "He was with me, but they found us — your angels. They asked us if we would support you. I don't know what Azazel said."

"What did you say?"

"I said I wanted to see you."

"You're seeing me now." Lucifer turned slowly, seeing the other, again, and a breath tumbled out from between his lips. Some of his composure — decaying. "I'm happy—"

"Happy?"

"Happy you're okay." He moved back toward Rosier, unable to stop himself before spreading his arms out, wrapping them around the other in a warm embrace. "I never meant for anything to happen to you. Please believe me." Lucifer would have liked to say more, but the object between him and the other angel made him stop, look, then jump. "Asmodeus."

Asmodeus glared and spat blood onto Lucifer's front.

"Don't mind him," Rosier mumbled, having caught the fury already building in the crazed angel's eyes. "He's in a lot of pain, I imagine." He stepped backwards, pressed up against a pillar, and then he slid down, until he plopped onto the floor, his legs bent before him. "I didn't believe anything anyone said." Lucifer had no choice but to sit at his side. "I thought that my friend Lucifer could never be capable of such horrific things."

"Brother, you're the only angel who should know that I've been capable of this for a long time." The air was heavy, virulent and coarse. "Are you going to deny me? My army will slaughter you."

"I want to know why you're doing this. Does creating pain really give you joy?"

'Why should I explain it to a feeble little angel like you?' 'Who are you, Rosier?' Lucifer shut his eyes, seeing his four faces argue, laughing between themselves, wondering why they would ever come down from their heavens to converse with an unimportant angel. And yet his mouth opened, spilled forth, "It's not about pain, or wickedness, or even the pleasure. Do you think that you must be good to be God? That isn't true — to be God is to be good. I saw it, when He punished me, the second time; I saw everything." 'Don't return to that,' said a face, like an ox, 'don't remember.' His eyes fluttered open, once more.

"Evil is what He chooses, so is good. But we could define it on our terms. I know that we could. We can find our own morality, in each other, in the love and pain of one another."

"Do you really think you'll succeed?"

A second of hesitation, then a confession: "I lost half my army, maybe more." 'Heaven will despise me. No one can ever love me again.' "I've done the unforgivable." Lucifer had become the unforgivable. But he was breathing easier, though he didn't realize it yet; he had unshackled himself from the pity of angels. From the promise of salvation, he had been liberated.

"But you'll still fight Him," Rosier replied; it wasn't a question.

'I had a plan. I wanted to show the angels that we could be happy, without Him, but then pleasure and pain — the words melted into each other. What does it mean to feel good? I don't know, I don't remember.' "I'm His greatest angel, His most beloved angel, His most perfect." 'Father, will you miss me? Will you think your choir is not the same without Lucifer? Will you stare at the flowers of Eden and wonder where the pretty angel who used to lay there has gone?' "If I'm perfect, then I can't lose." 'Will you hold my cheek with one hand and pull me apart with the other?' Smiling, Lucifer leaned his head against Rosier's shoulder. 'You'll say you hate me and lock me for a thousand years, but then you'll set me free. Father loves all His creation, I sang it in a psalm once, and you smiled. In wrath, you will still love me, won't you? You will always love me.'

Rosier rested his cheek against Lucifer's head. "I've lost everything."

"I'm sorry."

"When we restore the city, let's make it nicer than before." Rosier smiled distantly. 'Our house is probably toppled now. All the flowers are wilted, I saw them as I passed by, all the fruits shriveled and dead. My world is over now.' "Let's put pretty orchards everywhere." 'Wherever you go, wherever Baal goes, wherever Asmodeus goes, I want to go too.'

Lucifer leaned to kiss his friend softly by a temple, speaking against his skin, "Nothing will compare to the city we build. You'll see. I promise." 'I'm sorry. It's all going to be made up to you and the others, everyone marred in the horror of rebirth. It wasn't supposed to happen like this. It's all going to be better now.' Pause. "I like your hair, like that."

Rosier laughed, and Asmodeus laughed too, between the blood in his mouth. "It's not so bad. I feel a lot lighter."

Some time passed before Baal saw Lucifer again; he dropped everything, smiled wide, and watched his beloved king rise to stand on an anvil. He wore, still, no armor but carried the great sword used to skin Phanuel and torture the archangels, now polished and cleaned so that the light of the stars twinkled in the reflection of the blade. Some major planets had begun dripping onto the skies too, casting smokes of hydrogen, helium, methane, ammonia. "I don't imagine Father has much of an army put together, but He'll gather one quickly. He could create a thousand angels to defend Him in an instant." Lucifer cleared his throat and admitted, "We might not stand a chance."

Baal's eyebrows rose. 'Why would you say that? You want everyone to abandon you now?'

Lucifer continued speaking, not particularly motivating: "He might put us all to sleep and transfigure us into stars. Perhaps moons, this time around."

"Are you saying we're going to lose?" an angel called out.

"We might not win," Lucifer replied, and there was a disgruntled buzz among the crowd, "but there is no defeat for us anymore. We have left our mark on Heaven, and we have broken free from His will. Now we know the furthest extents of pleasure and pain, that He forbid us from ever exploring, and no matter if He casts eternal nightmares on us, if He destroys us, if He silences us — He cannot take this away."

Lucifer put a hand to his own chest, and his angels listened.

"This truth that we can be more, without Him, that there is euphoria outside of Him too, that we can *hurt* each other, and that we can *love* each other, more than He ever could. So," Lucifer's rising voice was broken by an intake of breath, "I say, let Him annihilate us, let Him mutilate us."

Baal heard the wave of choked up cries around him, and he felt despair build up within himself, too. Itchy flames behind his eyes, like those that had incinerated the city he'd always known.

"No matter how He punishes us, we'll be free!" Lucifer shouted out and the army replied they would be. "He cannot take this away from us, these memories, this pride, this will. Let Him disown us!" Between the tears of sorrow and soft wails, the army fisted the air and cheered for their suicide mission. "None of this can ever be forgotten. He will remember us for all of eternity." Lucifer spread his arms out at his side, gesturing to everything, and he ordered them, "Now, let's face Him once and for all. Expose all your wings," and they did — the sound of a million feathers — "liberate yourselves of flesh, and march with me to the Throne."

The adoring roar for their king came amid the hopes that reality would shatter for them, so that they win, so that they have a chance. Together, they took off into the air. They would pass through all the cosmos.

'i was made with four wings and four faces. i came crawling out of a red-blazed blister cut into the air. you gave me the fruit of eternal life. and that is where you should have ended it. i could have spent forever in eden, with you, and in heaven, with all my siblings. i could have lived hiding behind my fingers meekly, instead of forcing eyes to sprout from the back of my hands, so that I had to see. I could have been left blind, and I never would have called myself king. I never would have seen michael. I never would have chased after michael. you imagine: you never ate that fruit. you, an eternal temptation. you, unknowing, like an animal or like a beast. I cover my body with two of my wings and fly with the other two, I head towards the Throne, seeing God already there with a brigade of angels, maybe double the size of my own army, but I'm not afraid of anything. I'm enticing you, Father, wondering how you'll torture me for the third time, for this heart, swollen and lifted up by my wisdom and beauty, this pride, this delusion.'

The tortured Uriel, Raphael, and Gabriel were already there before God's army, having escaped the bathhouse likely through some sort of miracle. Each was incomprehensible, each their own horror, and the Father was above, even more impossible Himself. All His angels were in armor too, clutching the hilt of their weapons tight, nervous in the face of the first crusade, but Lucifer knew they didn't believe in anything. They revered their God in terror, prayed they would be spared from punishment for loyalty, crying they will accept eternal captivity, so long as it's in a gilded bird cage, in their Father's paradise.

"Lucifer," said the Lord, "how far you have fallen."

Freed of flesh, Lucifer was the most beautiful of all the angels and, by virtue of that beauty, the most grotesque, most eldritch. "We come demanding you hand over the Throne to the angels and to me, their new king." Holding tight Michael's onerous sword, he moved forward, felt his army follow, felt them fall into position to fling themselves at the bloodiest battle that would ever occur. "If you do not meet our demands, we will slaughter your host, and I, your most cherished angel, will cast you to a lake of fire for eternity."

"You will not do this."

The angel knew this was his last chance, but for the first time since he'd awoken in paradise, his mind was completely silent.

"I will ascend to the heavens;" Lucifer answered with four voices, "I will raise my throne above the stars of God; I will sit enthroned on the utmost heights of the sacred mountain; I will ascend above the tops of the clouds; I will make myself like the Most High."

And he raised the sword, pointing it forward, and his army obeyed. They dove into the sea of Father's angels, the clangs of metals steaming out only to be soon broken by the rip of spirits being pierced. Brothers and friends — colliding in a kaleidoscope of attack, with their hundred wings whipping at everyone near. Yet, Lucifer saw that the angels at God's feet were hesitant in their strikes, on the defense entirely. Flying above and remaining still, the greatest angel watched how those at the instruction of Gabriel, Raphael, and Uriel took too long to raise their spears of jade, and they fell backward at every surge forward from Lucifer's aggressive host.

"Weaklings," Lucifer taunted the soldiers of God. "Faithless unbe-lievers!" He saw many turn their hundred heads up to him, and he knew that even here, he could turn the skeptical to his side. "You fight for a God who doesn't love you! You fight for nothing! You fight because you are afraid!"

"Beast!" snarled one of the archangels, many-eyed and made of golden spirals, but two of Lucifer's believers launched at him, trying to splinter him with their swords, trying to scald him with the fire that composed them.

And Lucifer's gaze engulfed the mass below of violence that devolved into the one being, indistinguishable, of a massacre. Even still — he raised his sight once more — Father had not lifted a finger, sitting on the Throne, staring forward, meeting Lucifer's gaze with His own, much stronger, much larger, much more of everything, taunting him because He had a billion gazes in His own. The angel saw every memory there, His own creation there, saw all the tenderness, and he grinned, because that didn't fill him with regret. It would have, if this were yesterday or weeks ago or even minutes in the past — now, there was only strength.

"I will show you all," Lucifer shouted out, "how great your God really is!"

Charging forward, he dodged whatever hands reached out to stop him, then seizing any angel who dared to surge too close and flinging them down into the disorder without remorse. He rose higher, higher, raising his sword, approaching the silent Lord and His Throne as rapid as the light which Lucifer knew he was born from. Nearly above his Father, so close to shadowing Him, Lucifer wondered if he would cut through all of the space and time and distance there ever was to find fire — like there was at the beginning of everything.

But the sword never made contact; a golden chain shot out from somewhere, grappled his entire body, flung him downwards. And Lucifer, frozen, kicking, screaming — he saw Michael suddenly above him, then grabbing him by the throat and crushing with both hands, one with the other end of the chain wrapped around the palm. He had six wings, obscuring his details, but they couldn't hide the droplets that trickled down from between the hoard of feathers. Lucifer felt the tears land upon his own cheeks, as if they were his own.

CHAPTER 40

How can a story like this end? It doesn't, no story ever has, so long as the Lord has remained. The twelve angels, much earlier, had rushed the house, forcing flimsy weapons into the sides or necks of Michael's captors and partaken in a messy struggle that toppled furniture and splattered skin onto the floor. Two had made it to Michael, tied excessively against a wall, his limbs bound, mouth covered, a blindfold strapped tight. There was a splash of bruises beneath his tunic, where he had been struck repeatedly by Lucifer's taunting angels.

One of the twelve tore the cloth from over Michael's eyes, and another sawed at the rope all around the chief archangel until the prince was free, was reeling in a breath. Upon this, Michael subdued those who'd captured him, grabbing one. He demanded to know everything, screamed until the angel he beat spilled the truth. The twelve angels had then found him some armor, and his golden chain, and they fashioned him a helmet as fast as they could; they explained all they'd seen.

"Michael," Lucifer rasped, "Michael, what are you doing?"

"Silence, Lucifer."

'where did you get that golden helmet that obscures your eyes? where have you been? you should have been with me in the center. I think you look pleasant — furious and vengeful and agonized. But you're attacking the wrong god. Crushing the neck you just put your beautiful lips to. im dropping your sword now. why. Michael, your sword has fallen, and its falling to a. Sapphire floor a million miles below; hello Michael, hi, Michael, good day, have you eaten? should I prepare you something? You're tired. give me half your strength. brush my wings. how to respond to your kindness. I'll leave if you're too tired to talk or wrestle. Do you kiss your other friends this much. Keep complaining and I will make you dance with me. Let me tuck you in. Beloved? Your beloved what, exactly?'

"You—" Lucifer panted, hissing when the golden chains burned him. "Why are you doing this?"

Through his teeth, Michael seethed, "You are not God."

'And now you say: it meant nothing to you — none of it.' Lucifer's cling to the heavens snipped; he fell, fell down with Michael, the million hours to the floor of the Throne. Limbs and wings slashing every direction as the two plunged, rolling over one another, Lucifer fiercely struggling against the chains, forcing an arm out — struck Michael's chin, if that was what it was. There was no way to tell — waves of light, that's all anything was. He opened his mouth, to speak, but an outraged, devastating shriek ruptured outward instead. All the fire he'd ever felt, in anger and in shame, all ripping from his body until it composed him.

"Apologize, apologize now!" Michael met Lucifer's subsequent scream of anguish with a punch of his own, but the other evaded him with a flap. "Stop this now!"

"Coward! Stupid angel of weakness!" Lucifer spun and landed a kick directly on Michael's throat, forcing out a hack. "I won't — I will never apologize. Never, never, kill me instead!"

Another kick, but Michael caught his ankle, pulled him, threw his head back, thrust it forward, knocked Lucifer's forehead with his helmet. Pained yell. He shouted, "Look at what you've done! Look at this destruction! Are you happy?! Is this what you wanted, Lucifer?! Is this it?!"

Melted ruby spewing out from the feathers over his faces — "We could have had everything." The words were torment. "I could have made you a king. We could have ruled." Michael begged him to stop, beseeches eaten by broken cries. They threw out vicious punches, and Lucifer's hysteria engulfed him as he kept talking, kept, kept talking, "We could have had eternity, we could have had forever with one another, we could have counted every ripple in the sea." Michael cried, still saying stop, stop. "Together — we could have done it. We— We— It could have been us on that Throne. We could have been happy. We could have rebuilt Heaven. We could have had everything—"

"Apologize, I'm begging you, Lucifer, stop, I can't do this— *I don't want to lose you—*"

"It was for us. It was always for us."

"I can't— I can't—"

Michael reached out, took Lucifer, and the younger one laughed, miserable, as he was flung furiously all the way to the ground; Michael shot down after him with a flap of all his wings. He, must've, sought to crash down onto Lucifer, bring all his weight on him, so that the angel would shatter beneath. But Lucifer evaded him again, rolling out, shifting instantly onto a stance for brawling once more. "Do you like that move, Michael? You taught it to me."

'Where is all the ambition I caught in your eyes? Or was your gaze just another mirror to me, and it was my own that I saw in you?'

Both angels stopped, staring at one another, and then at the sword that clanged to the ground several steps between them. Without a second of hesitance, they sprinted toward it, flung themselves forward, and Michael's hand reached out, but Lucifer threw his foot out instead, kicking the sword away, shooting past, underneath, Michael. Lucifer maneuvered over the archangel, laughing, entertained nearly to tears from his little trick. His own hand went for the sword.

He didn't move fast enough — Michael hadn't stuttered in throwing out his golden chain, catching the sword by the hilt. He pulled it to him, Lucifer stopping as the blade flew back to its proper owner, narrowly missing severing his heads off in the process. Michael caught his sword, with one hand, then held it with both. "Lucifer, don't do this. You won't win."

"Bastard."

"Please—"

Lucifer flew, upwards, evading this encounter and thinking he should simply go and pummel God to death with his wings and fists. With his speed, it wasn't long before he had returned to hover before Him, but the Lord had still not moved, not a sliver. Faltering, the greatest angel faced that his army was drawing back, many falling, tumbling, despite their advantages — all because they didn't have the support of a god, and Lucifer cursed, cursed his own fate. There was no choice now but to attack Him like an animal; if nothing else, the Lord would move a finger. But Michael reached him again, Michael's chain. 'What a Beast you are! How I expected this destiny, Father, and yet still — you made it worse, created something greater than torture. Just to prove your superiority, one last time.'

"I will bring forth the fire from your own actions," said the Lord, as Lucifer thrashed against Michael, who held him captive in gold and held his weapon high. "I will burn you to ashes upon the Earth in the sight of all those who have adored you. All who know you will be appalled at your fate; you will come to a terrible end, I will destroy you forever."

Lucifer shot out his wings, flapped, tried to heave himself closer to God again. Instead, Michael brought down his sword into the kiss between Lucifer's wings and the rest of his body, and there was a shriek in pain that would erupt into the air. "No—" Lucifer's entire form convulsed with agony. "Michael— Stop— What are you doing? Don't do this, don't hurt me—" Michael, reduced to uncontrollable, ravaging cries.

"Because you have corrupted my creation, and turned yourself into a Beast, you will be cast down from Heaven."

'No, Michael, Michael, stop.' Another yell as Michael stabbed into another of the tender points where wings had been stitched onto Lucifer.

"You will be the most cursed creature, and you shall eat dust all the days of your life."

A third cry — Michael sliced at the trinity wing.

"You have broken the covenant with the angels. They will all suffer because of what you have done. And you will no longer be an angel, nor will you have that name."

The final wing was punctured, and they were still attached to Lucifer's marred body, but useless as ornaments. 'There have always been so many things in my head to say, but now, now, at the end of everything, on the Final Judgment for the angels, nothing, silence as I turn my face upwards, and I proclaim,' *"Damn me."* Lucifer spat at the Lord's feet. Hate, absolute, unfurling for the first time in his heart, and it consumed him.

'you will miss flying'

And, finally, the God stood, and He was the one who cast Lucifer down, taking him like when he was created, delicate and pretty in His palm, eyes blinking up, full of wonder, a little smile. He let him slip, through His fingers. Fall.

The force broke through the Throne, through Heaven, and as he fell, Lucifer was ignited with as intense a fire as the beginning of time. Hurling toward Earth, he saw the beasts of the planet the Father had chosen for His garden, eating, some wrestling, some watching the horizon, unaware — in their own version of paradise. None of them would know, as the sphere of flames fell toward them, the immediate moments after impact — the pulverized rock that'd toss up high into the Earth and the tidal wave that'd shatter the crust. Rain, following, of flames striking all the beasts that didn't fall dead in the first seconds, that didn't get swept away by the great oceanic waves that suddenly devoured the forests; and the sun would disappear thereafter. The creatures of Earth left without God, and all the greenery beginning to wither, as now His adversary was among them.

But it was not over — the angels, who watched their leader be banished, screamed out for him, and chaos ensued. The Father settled back into His chair, as all the archangels barked orders for Lucifer's army to be restrained — even Michael who could not breathe, who faltered in flight. But it was not over — from the sea of war, an angel broke through the surface and shouted to Him, "Cast me down too! I will never bow for you! You are not my God! You are not my Father! Cast me down!" It overwhelmed Lucifer's supporters, who raised their fists and cheered for their brave friend. It was not over — another angel shouted to be banished, another said, "Damn me, damn me for eternity!" The angels who loved their Father still shook their heads, tried to latch onto their siblings, imploring for them not to say the words. Covered in each other's blood, that of their souls, they told them to ask for forgiveness instead. "Send me down to worship my true king!"

A dead face, belonging to the chief prince.

The Father would do as they wished, but they sang — the corrupted angels' chorus of joy and melancholy for everything they would lose and the hope they would make their own paradise somewhere else. He moved a hand, gesturing for Michael to saw off their wings, but they continued singing. When the Lord ordered them cast down, they fell in joy — the first shooting stars. And all the angels who'd fought to victory stayed in their place, crumpled. They grieved to one another, terrified, thinking their Father might decide to punish them too, for not doing enough, for weakness.

They watched the last of the city between the Throne and Earth become desolate and ravaged; and it was like watching the sun set on their time, their period of everything, their own tiny eternity — finished.

When He was satisfied, having chosen the elect, the Lord spoke again, ordering His princes to stand before the angels, and He cast judgment: "From the animals on Earth, I will make one in our image, according to our likeness," and the host stared in confusion, "and let them have dominion over the fish of the sea, over the birds of the air, and over the cattle in all the Earth, and over every creeping thing. I will call this being Man. Because you have broken the covenant, you will all have to bow for the new creation. You will worship and minister to him as you do me, and you will love his children and nurture them, knowing they will inherit Heaven from you. You will rebuild the eternal paradise, for Man."

The angels wept at their punishment — Michael, between them all, his tears morphing into crystals, slicing down his cheeks and making him bleed.

CHAPTER 41

Gabriel watched from the clouds. Following the Final Judgment of the angels, those that had been cast from Heaven shattered as they struck the Earth — apart from no longer being able to fly, their bodies could no longer be healed. They would have to rebuild themselves using the carcasses of the beasts, sawing off their limbs and stitching them onto themselves, contorting tough skin and meats so that they might be able to use them to patch their wounds. Baal, the once greatest flier in Heaven, wrenched the wings off a dying beast and attached them to his own back, and he was the only one of the banished that could still take to the sky. In that time, the Earth had become the opposite of paradise.

Nothing tasted good; the damned ones vomited largely any food they could salvage from the wasteland following the mass extinction of the beasts. The ground was difficult — all the greenery they had been accustomed to speaking with would be scattered and rare along the land. Natural vegetation would be next to nonexistent, and agriculture would succumb to failure after failure. Death and pain surrounded them, and the few that whispered privately if Father might take them back would receive no answer.

"Gabriel, what are you doing here?"

He didn't move to face Uriel and continued laying on his belly, peeking out over the edge, but still smiled, gentle. "I was thinking. I'm sorry. I'll return with you soon, if you want." There was a dip of weight by his side. "But I was thinking that there's so many things to be sad about. I don't like to be sad, but sometimes it can't be helped."

"The breeze is nice here."

"I was thinking about Father. He must be lonely."

"Father isn't lonely. He has us, and He will have Man."

When the corrupted angels found Lucifer, he laid quietly in the middle of a crater — a disfigured, grotesque beast. They carried him out, brought him to a cave, and with the last of their knowledge and abilities to heal, they remade Lucifer's appearance as the most beautiful angel of light that ever was and fitted it over him like robes, so he was like before. It was a disguise, but that was enough for them, and for him.

"We are not God, and Man will not be God either, will they?" Gabriel tilted his head down at all the land they passed over. "I thought that might be His own tragedy. He will always want company, after having only known to be alone for eternities before this one, but He is so Great, He will never have it. Father can create and destroy, but not Himself; He is indivisible, He cannot break Himself down. He will never see another and say, 'This person is like me,' because there is only one God."

"You shouldn't pretend to know Father, Gabriel."

For the demons, nothing would feel good, except various sins of the flesh, but that was exceedingly temporary, unless they went on for weeks, which they most often didn't. They found some comfort in dancing and music, with instruments fashioned from the bones of the vast cemetery they wandered as they moved along the Earth. They built every cave system that will ever exist and considered planning cities with excitement, but hesitated out of sloth. When animals began to reappear, they found some amusement in chasing and feeding them until they grew to the size of the earlier beasts.

And there was, of course, Lucifer, who held them and comforted them in between all his untouchable coldness. He was, occasionally, violent, tormented, and vengeful, but other times, he pulled them to his chest and kissed their heads. The demons fashioned him a crown of bones, thorns, and weeds that gave him the illusion of having horns. And they loved him.

ABOUT THE AUTHOR

rafael nicolás is an author of queer fiction. He likes marigolds.

Standing Figure of a Youth,
Giovanni Battista Tiepolo

Printed in Great Britain
by Amazon

38531983R00215